Veronica Westbrook is a psychopathic con artist, who thinks she's hit the jackpot when she discovers that she has a very wealthy identical twin, separated from her at birth. She hatches a diabolical plan to kill her and take over her life. But a brilliant, tough-as-nails detective is on the case.

Identical Misfortune has its action scenes, plenty of them, but it is primarily a duel of wits between two brilliant women—a con artist and a cop. ... The duel of wits at the heart of the book is a lively, energetic, and intelligent one, and readers who enjoy watching a clever cop piece together a plot laid for them by an equally-clever criminal will find this book a pleasant diversion.— *Indie Reader*

A convict takes over her identical twin sister's life in New Orleans, only to arouse the suspicions of a clever, intuitive detective in Zappa's debut thriller ... an energetic tale with wonderfully complex characters; Veronica isn't a one-note villain; she's a sociopath who doesn't experience a normal range of emotion ... Crowder isn't a squeaky clean hero ... A grim and engrossing procedural with a stellar cast. — *Kirkus Reviews*

The role of genetics in antisocial personality disorder is explored in this utterly spellbinding crime drama/thriller... From the compelling plot and the writing to the dialogue to the impressive character development, everything was top notch ... a well-imagined and outstanding work of fiction ... 4 out of 4 stars. — *Online Book Club*

Zappa takes the reader on a winding roller-coaster ride of betrayal and intrigue, and the aching feeling that evil will triumph in the end. Like life, this story raises as many questions as it answers, and will disturb many, but in the end, as harrowing as the journey is, it's worth the effort. — *Charles Ray, Awesome Indies Book Award Assessor*

Identical Misfortune

AIA PUBLISHING

Richard Zappa

Identical Misfortune
Richard Zappa
Copyright © 2020
Published by AIA Publishing, Australia
ABN: 32736122056
http://www.aiapublishing.com

Paperback ISBN: 978-1-922329-03-5
Hardcover ISBN: 978-1-922329-04-2

Cover design by K. Rose Kreative
Author's photograph by Scott Ellis

For June, Katie, Holly, Mallory and Michael

Acknowledgements

Four years ago, I woke up one morning and decided to write for the pure pleasure of it. At first, simple poems; then, a few ballads, essays and short stories, all of which, after years as a trial lawyer, made me reflect on my life going forward. I saw the path clearly—one that led me to the Elysian Fields of writing, and to this first novel.

I owe special thanks to my editors and publisher, in particular Tahlia Newland—author, editor, mentor—and exceptional at each. She and others at AIA Publishing helped me make a wordy, often rambling, manuscript of my story into a readable, entertaining novel. The rewrites, as Stephen King darkly warned, were "a little like murdering children, but it must be done." Those tasks, I've come to learn, are ones all writers should embrace—like the sculptor who relentlessly chisels away at a large block of granite until what appears is the true, finely crafted reflection of what he or she intended to create. Every word written must be scrutinized with an eagle eye. Mark Twain was right to say, "The difference between the almost right word and the right word is the difference between the lightening bug and the lightening."

Added thanks to my transcriptionist and daughter, Katie Zappa, for deciphering my babble and transforming it into the English language, and to my proofreader, Amy Spahn, not only for spotting and correcting technical errors, but also for making editorial suggestions that bring some sparkle to the printed words.

Finally, I want to thank those who read my novels and are entertained by them. P.T. Barnum said it best, "The noblest art is the art of making people happy."

Prologue

February 18, 2018,
Maryland Hospital for the Mentally Ill.
(Formerly Shippensburg Asylum for the Criminally Insane.)

"Inmate forty-two is near death," the physician said to the elderly priest. "Her feeding tube was removed two days ago by court order. The IV lines were also stopped, even the morphine drip. It's amazing she's hung on this long."

"What's her name?" the priest asked.

"Monica Millings."

"How old?"

The physician glanced at the patient's chart. "Turned seventy today."

"Is she Catholic?"

"I don't know."

"Family?"

"No next of kin or relatives that I'm aware of." The physician knew little of the old woman's background and hadn't bothered to check. "She's been in ward eleven, the isolation ward, since I was transferred here two years ago. Never had a visitor, not one, the entire time."

The priest sighed. "Poor soul. I'll anoint her and say a bedside prayer."

The physician and priest followed a portly guard through the corridors of the asylum, the squeaking of the guard's rubber-soled shoes against the linoleum breaking the silence of their pilgrimage. Handcuffs, a billy club, and a canister of pepper spray hung from his belt.

1

It was a sunless Sunday. Outside, the rain poured constantly, punctuated by bone-chilling gusty winds—a contrast to the stale air inside.

They entered ward eleven, where security cameras provided 24/7 observation, through a windowless steel door which clanged shut from behind, locking them in.

The physician was familiar with the administration of last rites. With family members present and a conscious penitent, it could take twenty minutes or more. But neither was the case here.

The physician noticed the priest looking at his watch. It was already past four, and he had a Mass to celebrate at five. "Don't worry," he assured the clergyman. "You should be no longer than ten minutes."

Inmate forty-two lay on a bed in room four. The guard peered through the door's small glass window before opening the door with his key.

They entered, and the guard stood sentry with his back to the door.

The physician walked to the bedside and placed his stethoscope on the old woman's chest. "The heartbeat's faint, but she's still alive," he said in a hushed tone. He nodded at the priest as though to say, "She's ready for you," then stepped away.

The priest took the physician's place. The furrows above his weary eyes deepened. "She's at death's door," he said. "What will be waiting for her on the other side is now in the hands of God."

He placed his Bible on the table, retrieved a small glass bottle of holy water from his pants pocket, and placed some of it on the fingertips of his right hand. When he reached over and placed the blessed liquid on the old woman's wrinkled brow, her heavy-lidded eyes opened wide. The whites were dusty gray, her cornea and lens, once crystal clear, now opaque, and her pupils dilated. Only the irises remained unchanged—piercing, coral-blue marbles that stared fixedly into the priest's eyes.

In the blink of an eye, the old woman's right hand shot up and clutched the priest's throat in a talon-like grip. Blood oozed from the punctures made by her hardened, unclipped fingernails. Instinctively, the priest grabbed hold of the old woman's wrist with both hands, trying to pull free from her stranglehold, but the force of the initial strike had crushed his windpipe. The guard moved quickly, but not fast enough. Unable to breathe, the priest's body convulsed, his eyes bulged, and his tongue drooped from his mouth.

The physician stood frozen, mouth agape, watching in horror as the churchman slumped forward onto the bed. Inmate forty-two's hand remained clenched around his neck until the guard's club crushed her skull.

The old woman and the priest lay dead upon the bed.

There were now two souls journeying to the afterlife.

PART ONE

Earth provides enough to satisfy every man's needs,
but not every man's greed.
Mahatma Gandhi

Chapter 1

May 17, 2016

He winked at the cute, slightly plump, barely-legal waitress while she took an order at another table, and the girl responded with a dimpled smile. After completing the business of the day that brought him to the outdoor café across from Adler's Fine Jewelry on Ocean Drive in South Beach, he'd be drinking and dancing into the wee hours with someone like her … and having some kinky sex afterwards.

So why not her?

He smiled back, and she walked right over to take his order.

"No lunch, sweet thing," he said. "But you can rustle me up a double Knob Creek and a Grey Goose cosmopolitan. I'm curious about something, though. Does the owner require all the waitresses to be knockout beauties, or are you the exception?"

Guy Hamilton—forty, tall, tanned, and handsome—knew he looked dashing in his beige Armani suit, pale-blue silk shirt, and diamond-studded Rolex watch. The sexy-looking waitress aroused him in her size-too-small, white, cotton blouse. More so after she reached over to remove his silverware and dish, and he got an upfront view of her assets.

His flattering made her blush. "Will someone be joining you?" she asked.

"Yes, my sister will be joining me for a drink," he said behind a devilish grin.

He sensed she cared little about who he was meeting for a late-afternoon drink and more about who he'd be taking out on a late-evening date. And it looked to him like she had every intention

7

of throwing a pair of panties in the ring for the chance at being that special someone. She walked away, and he waited until she turned her head and beamed back a smile.

Just then, a taxi pulled up to the curb in front of the café. The driver got out, opened the rear passenger door, and stood at attention as though for a celebrity. Long, tanned legs emerged from the rear seat, one after the other, leaving the men seated outside gawking in anticipation for the rest. She eventually stepped onto the sidewalk in a turquoise mini-skirt and white-satin top with a plunging neckline. A pearl necklace dangled in her cleavage. She looked mysterious and alluring behind her three-hundred-dollar Christian Dior sunglasses.

Enter center stage, Veronica Westbrook—early thirties, a professional woman, and drop-dead gorgeous.

Hamilton watched as she posed on the curb for a moment to allow the staring men to get their close-ups, then she walked over to where he sat at his table, her five-inch stilettos clicking melodically on the pavement. Her gait, he thought, had the swagger of a show horse.

He spoke first. "Hi, sis." When pulling a con, they often pretended to be siblings. "We can catch up on things over a drink. I got you your usual."

The evocative scent of roses and jasmine from her Dior J'Adore followed her to the table. She stood waiting for him to get up and pull out her chair, etiquette he knew she expected from a man meeting her for a drink, whether or not he was one of her paying customers about to get his brains fucked out. Today his meeting with her was for business of a different kind. He remained comfortably slouched in his chair, his eyes meeting hers in a silent stare. He kicked his shoe against her chair, sliding it just the right distance for her to be seated. She chuckled and sat down.

The waitress returned with the drinks; the odor of her working-girl's perfume invaded the airspace like the stale smell of a stagnant pond. Hamilton sensed from the glum look on the young woman's

8

face that she knew she couldn't hold a candle to what his "sister" could offer him and had thrown in the towel. She placed the drinks on the table and lumbered off to take another order.

"So how's the world been treating you, big brother?" Westbrook asked her occasional accomplice, conspirator, and lover.

"I'll know on Thursday."

"What's so important that you made me give up a client this afternoon? I hope you're not looking for repayment of the thousand I snitched from you. Consider it part of my severance package."

"I consider myself lucky you left me with the shirt on my back," Hamilton said while reaching for an envelope from the chest pocket of his suit jacket. He put the envelope on the table, and her gaze diverted to it with a quizzical expression. With a flick of his index finger, he slid the envelope over to her, a skill he'd acquired as a kid playing match-pack football for lunch money on the cafeteria table at school. The envelope came to rest in front of her drink.

She opened the unsealed envelope and drew out a folded note with bullet points under the heading "Things to Remember," a driver's license, a car rental agreement and key, a lawyer's business card, and a wad of crisp one-hundred-dollar bills. She flipped through the bills like a blackjack dealer shuffling a deck of cards, twice to get the count right. The count stopped at thirty.

"There's another three grand for you if all goes well."

It was Tuesday. Hamilton needed her help with the jewelry robbery on Thursday. The plan was for her to park a vehicle in front of the store, cede the spot to him when he arrived, then circle the block and stop in the street just behind his car. That way he could pull away without any traffic blocking his exit.

"If I'm caught, call the lawyer. You're my insurance policy," he continued. "There's a whole lot more coming your way if I ever need to cash it in."

She returned everything to the envelope, put it in her purse, and sipped her drink.

9

He finished his whiskey in one swallow, threw two twenties on the table, and got up to leave. As he walked away, he looked over his shoulder and said, "Be on time ... and wish me luck, sis."

"If you're counting on luck," Hamilton heard her say as he slowly drifted out of earshot, "you're going to need the insurance."

Chapter 2

November 7, 2016

"All rise," the bailiff said. "The Circuit Court of Miami Dade County, State of Florida, is now in session, the Honorable Malcolm P. McKennon presiding."

The jury was typical for a South Florida murder trial: a couple of upwardly mobiles too honest to come up with a bullshit reason for not serving; a few housewives with kids in school; and the rest were unemployed, barely literate, pissed-off underachievers just waiting to strike back at the community from which they felt detached; the kind of mix that made the outcome of a murder trial a crapshoot.

The Miami Herald had followed the case ever since Guy Hamilton had been arrested and later indicted for robbery and murder. Hamilton faced the death penalty if convicted of killing Harold Adler while robbing his upscale South Beach jewelry store. He'd forced Adler to bind and gag his bookkeeper wife and two saleswomen before putting a bullet in the brain of the elderly owner as his reward for pulling a gun from the safe in a feeble attempt to thwart the robbery. After depositing his mask, gloves, gun, and the stolen cash and jewelry in a locker at the bus station, Hamilton had clipped the rear of an empty school bus passing through an intersection. He'd fled the scene and had been arrested by a patrolman ten minutes later.

"Proceed, Mr. Sullivan," the judge said.

Michael Sullivan was an experienced prosecutor with twenty-two murder convictions under his belt. It wasn't the first time he was prosecuting a capital case without a murder weapon or some of the stolen loot found on the accused. He walked confidently to his usual spot in front of the jury—center of the jury box, exactly six feet from juror four.

"Members of the jury, *we* have a puzzle to solve." He intended the pronoun to convey that he wanted to partner up with them in putting a violent, depraved criminal permanently out of the public domain. "We don't have a confession. What we have is a compelling case of *circumstantial evidence*, which can be as strong and convincing as a case in which the defendant has confessed. The only difference is that the confession is in the puzzle pieces the defendant left behind, which, one by one, will complete a picture ... of Guy Steven Hamilton pointing his gun at Harold Adler and shooting him point-blank in the head."

As he spoke, Sullivan made his right hand into a make-believe pistol and pointed it at the head of juror four—just as he'd rehearsed. He pulled back the make-believe trigger with a jerk of his hand, and her head recoiled slightly—just as he'd hoped.

After summarizing the evidence, Sullivan concluded with a warning and a plea to the jury. "The defendant is counting on the men and women on this jury to find reasonable doubt, acquit him, and reward him with a lavish lifestyle only someone like him would kill for. The state of Florida and the victims of his crimes are counting on you to not let that happen." Sullivan returned to his chair.

The judge, looking over the top of his bifocals, addressed defense counsel. "Ms. Roseman, do you wish to make an opening statement, or do you want to reserve until the state rests?"

Roxanne Roseman, an attractive woman in her late thirties, was the kind of lawyer Hamilton needed. She'd graduated from law school with honors, then partnered with her father, a legendary criminal defense attorney known for being long on courtroom skills and short on ethics. He'd taught his daughter well. She was her father's clone. "I'll reserve, Your Honor."

The judge glanced over at Sullivan. "Proceed with your first witness."

Patrol Officer Henley took the stand, and Sullivan got right to the point. "Officer Henley, why did you arrest the defendant on the day of the robbery and murder?"

"I was on routine patrol when I heard the dispatcher report a hit-and-run accident involving a school bus and a vehicle meeting the description of the defendant's car. I pulled him over. As I was walking to his vehicle I heard an APB that a robbery had occurred—"

"An *all-points bulletin*, Officer Henley?" the prosecutor interrupted for the benefit of any jurors not in tune with police lingo.

"Yes, I heard an all-points bulletin that a robbery had occurred at a jewelry store and that the owner had been shot. The description of the vehicle the gunman fled in matched the defendant's car. It didn't take a rocket scientist to figure out why the defendant also fled the scene of the accident with the bus."

"Objection, Your Honor. Speculation on the officer's part, not fact," defense counsel protested. "Unless Officer Henley is also a mind reader, how could he possibly know for a fact what reason Mr. Hamilton had for leaving the scene of his accident with the school bus? It doesn't take a rocket scientist to understand that."

"Sustained," the judge barked. "The jury will disregard the officer's last comment."

Sullivan winced at the judge's rebuke, took a breath, and continued, "And what, if anything, did you find when you inspected the vehicle the defendant was driving?"

"I found a registration form for the rental vehicle in the glove compartment, with a name on it that wasn't the defendant's."

"Did your inspection of the vehicle uncover any weapons?"

"Yes, I found a handgun under the driver's seat, a .38 caliber Ruger ACP pocket pistol."

"Did you find any information in the glove compartment or on the defendant showing that the gun was lawfully owned and registered?"

"No."

Sullivan finished his questioning and sat down.

"Cross examine, Ms. Roseman," the judge said.

Roseman stood and sauntered over to the lectern. "So, Officer Henley, I assume the license number of the car Mr. Hamilton was driving matched the license number of the car that was observed leaving the scene of the robbery."

"Well, no. We had no report of the license number of the vehicle. The man who described the vehicle at the scene of the crime fell off his bike trying to get it. He could only describe the make, model, and color."

"Do you know what the most popular make and model of car sold in the United States, including Florida, has been over the last three years?"

Sullivan knew that perpetrators of serious crimes typically steal or rent popular models, making the vehicle more difficult to find by police responding to an APB. Sullivan hoped for a candid response from Henley. Instead he got the sarcasm of a smart-ass cop.

"Well, I seem to have forgotten, Counselor, but I'm sure you're going to remind me."

"Does the Toyota Camry, with sales of over a quarter -million cars in the United States last year, jog your memory?"

"No reason to dispute that, Counselor," he replied.

Sullivan tensed up. The cop's cocky gamesmanship had cost the prosecution another point with the jury.

"And can you tell the jury what the most popular color of vehicles in the United States and in Florida has been over the past five years?" The cop's hesitation in answering gave defense counsel the chance to add, "Don't worry, we know the answer."

His response fell neatly in place. "White."

14

"The only reason my client was pulled over on the day of his arrest was because he was involved in a minor accident with a school bus."

"That's true."

"So while you were looking for a vehicle involved in a minor accident, neither you nor any other cop on patrol stopped any other drivers of white Toyota Camrys on the road that day, correct?"

"He was the only one stopped."

"Too bad. We might be here today trying the person who actually committed the robbery and murder, instead of my client." Sullivan jumped from his seat to object. But having made her point, she cut him off mid-sentence with a dismissive wave of her hand and said, "Withdrawn, Your Honor."

The judge's steely look at defense counsel was in lieu of an admonition before the jury. "Continue, Ms. Roseman," he said sternly.

"Mr. Hamilton was fully cooperative with everything you asked him to do after you pulled him over, isn't that correct?"

"Yes, that's correct."

"And he showed no hostile behavior toward you or anyone else at any time?"

"That's also correct."

"By the way, he told you why he didn't stop when he ... uh ... nicked the bus going through the intersection, didn't he?"

"Yes, he told me he didn't think he'd caused any damage."

"In your report you described the damage to the bus as *negligible,* correct?"

The cop thumbed through his report until he found where he noted the extent of the damage. "Yes. I described it as negligible."

"And you were using the common, everyday meaning of the word, correct?"

"I guess."

"Don't guess, Officer Henley. A simple yes or no will suffice."

"Well ... yes."

15

Defense counsel picked up the copy of Merriam-Webster's Dictionary she'd brought to the podium for precisely that moment. She opened it to the page she'd dog-eared, put on her reading glasses for the dramatic build-up, and read aloud. "Negligible—so small or unimportant as to deserve little or *no* attention." She didn't wait for a response from the witness. "No further questions, Your Honor."

"Next witness," the judge said.

Detective Frank O'Leary, the chief investigator on the case, got up from his seat at the prosecutor's table and took the stand looking every bit the grizzled veteran homicide detective. Sullivan's questioning of him established that a robbery and homicide had occurred, that Hamilton had used an alias when he rented his car, and that the pistol found under the front seat was unlicensed and unregistered.

"Cross-examine, Ms. Roseman."

Another relaxed and confident stroll to the lectern. "Detective O'Leary, Mr. Hamilton is not on trial for driving a car that was rented under a different name."

"That's correct."

"And he is not on trial for having an unlicensed, unregistered handgun in the vehicle he was driving."

"That's also correct."

"And you don't know if the gun belonged to Mr. Hamilton because no prints were found on it."

"You're right. It had been wiped clean."

"Yes, perhaps by the person who rented the vehicle before him. And, just to be clear, the gun found in the vehicle Mr. Hamilton was driving wasn't the weapon used to shoot Mr. Adler, correct?"

"Yes. The murder weapon, as I testified earlier, has not been found."

"And none of the victims identified Mr. Hamilton as the person who committed the robbery and shot Mr. Adler?"

"That's right. The robber was wearing a mask."

16

"So let's go over the facts uncovered by your investigation. None of the victims identified Mr. Hamilton as the perpetrator. The weapon found in Mr. Hamilton's car was not the murder weapon. No stolen cash, jewelry, or gems were found on him, in his vehicle, or in his apartment. His prints were not found at the scene. That's one hell of an airtight case you have against my client," she said, laughing loudly.

Many of the jurors chuckled.

Sullivan stood to object. "Your Honor, we can do without the theatrics, can't we?"

"Yes. Ms. Roseman, please, questions only."

"Just one, Your Honor. Isn't it true, Detective O'Leary, that you have no *direct* evidence that my client had anything to do with the crimes he's on trial for?"

Sullivan remained calm. He'd anticipated a question from defense counsel summarizing the deficiencies in the state's case, so he'd prepped O'Leary on how to respond.

"You mean other than the *eyewitness* who saw your client take off his mask and speed away from the scene of the crimes in a 2018 white Toyota Camry?"

"We'll see about that, Detective O'Leary," she said, concluding her cross examination.

Sullivan moved swiftly through the remainder of his case. Mrs. Adler, the two saleswomen, and the man on the bike testified in quick succession, their testimony proving beyond any doubt that the crimes had occurred. Roseman's brief cross examinations countered that none of the witnesses could identify her client as the masked man who'd committed them. Her one question to the chief medical examiner, who testified that Harold Adler had died from a bullet through his right eye that put a hole in his brain the size of a silver dollar, was to have him remind the jury that the shot was not fired from the pistol found in the car Hamilton was driving.

The judge called a recess to meet with counsel in chambers. When all were gathered, he stared at Sullivan over the top of his

17

eyeglasses. "So, Mickey, what's going on?" The judge had recruited Sullivan to join the prosecutor's office when he'd been the state's chief prosecutor. He'd known him and his family for more than twenty-five years.

Sullivan was visibly annoyed by the judge's implication. "What do you mean, Your Honor?" he asked.

"Well, you've convincingly proved everything in the indictment except one small but somewhat important point ... that the robbery and murder were committed by Guy Steven Hamilton."

"The next witness, Your Honor, is the key to our case," he answered with the confidence that saw him through many difficult prosecutions. "She saw Hamilton take off his mask and look over at her as he was getting into his white Toyota Camry, then speed away, almost running over the guy on the bike. If that doesn't seal the deal, nothing will."

Roseman perked up at Sullivan's last comment. "I'll remember you said that, Mickey." She looked over at the judge, grinning like the Cheshire Cat.

The recess concluded, and everyone mustered in the courtroom. Sullivan waited for the judge to nod to him and say, "Call your next witness, Mr. Sullivan."

"The State of Florida calls Vera Westin," he announced as the courtroom door swung open and a bailiff ushered the prosecution's star witness to the stand.

She was conservatively dressed, her hair pulled back in a bun. Yet her striking good looks turned the heads of both the men and women in the courtroom. She walked in one-inch heels, four inches closer to the ground than the footwear she was accustomed to wearing. Her plain, black, knee-length, cotton dress couldn't hide a perfectly developed, statuesque figure. Once she was seated, Sullivan brought his witness a cup of water as a server might bring a cocktail to a guest at a party being held in her honor. He strutted back to the lectern to begin his questioning of the witness who would finger the defendant as a robber and cold-blooded killer.

18

After several preliminary questions, Sullivan asked, "Ms. Westin, what brought you to Ocean Drive on the day in question?"

"I stopped at a Starbucks on the block to get a latte and croissant."

"And were you arriving or leaving the area when the crimes were committed?"

"Leaving."

"What happened as you were leaving?"

"I was in my minivan waiting for the red light at the intersection to change when I heard an alarm bell sound from one of the shops on Ocean Drive. A man came out of one of them, a jewelry store. He was wearing a ski mask, the kind that covers your head and face, and carrying a briefcase. He took off his mask as he got into a white sedan … the car in the photo Detective O'Leary showed me at the police station the next day."

"Did you get a good look at the man's face?"

"Yes. As he got into his car, he looked right at me."

"What did he do after that?"

"He drove away, almost hitting a young man on a bicycle."

"And you … what did you do?"

"The light was green by then. I proceeded through the intersection in a stupor. As soon as I collected my thoughts, I turned down a side street to get as far away from the man as I could."

"Ms. Westin, why didn't you report what you saw until the following day?"

"Because before I turned, I saw two police cars approach from the opposite direction and stop at the store where I'd heard the alarm. I figured things were under control. I really didn't want to get involved, particularly after seeing the angry look the man gave me when he got in his car."

"What made you contact the police?"

"I heard on the evening news that the jewelry store had been robbed and the owner shot and killed. I knew then that I needed

19

to report what I saw, regardless of how I felt about not getting involved."

"Very civic-minded of you, Ms. Westin. We thank you for that," Sullivan interjected. He then approached the witness with two photos and handed them to her. "Do you recognize the vehicle in the photographs marked trial exhibits 31 and 32?"

"Yes. They're side and rear views of the vehicle the man was driving ... the same vehicle in the photos Detective O'Leary showed me."

"Did you subsequently attend a seven-person lineup to see if you could pick out the man you saw that day?"

"Yes, the day after, when I reported what I'd seen to Detective O'Leary."

"And did you pick out the man you saw that day from among the seven?"

"I did."

"Is the man you picked out of the lineup and the one you saw on the day of the alleged crimes in the courtroom today?"

The witness paused briefly, looked over at Hamilton, and pointed her finger at him. "Yes, the man I picked out is sitting there."

The judge interjected with the words that brought an adrenaline rush to prosecutors, and Sullivan was no exception. "Let the record reflect that the witness has identified the defendant, Guy Steven Hamilton."

"No further questions, Your Honor."

Sullivan casually looked over to the jury as he returned to his seat. Jurors two and ten, the two middle-aged, Caucasian businessmen, cracked smiles. But it was the head nod he got from juror four that brought a smile to his face. The smile lasted until defense counsel walked to the lectern to begin her cross-examination.

"Ms. Westin, you realize how important your testimony is and the need to be certain about what you remember. After all, the life of Mr. Hamilton hangs in the balance. Do you agree?"

"Yes. I realize that … of course."

"I suppose you got a real good look at the car you saw the man get into, because you followed it for a couple of blocks before turning in a different direction."

"Yes, it was a late-model, white Toyota Camry."

Roseman walked to the clerk's table and picked up exhibits 31 and 32. She returned to the lectern to resume her questioning, putting the photos on top of another photo she had brought with her—a photo of the back of a late-model white Toyota Camry. This new photo showed a license plate.

"Ms. Westin, when Mr. Sullivan showed you the photos of the 2018 Toyota Camry my client was driving, you seemed certain it was the car you saw the man get into. How sure are you?"

"Pretty sure … no, I'm certain. As I said, I followed it for two blocks before turning down a side street."

"But you didn't get the license number of the vehicle, correct?"

"I was looking at the vehicle, not the license plate."

"May I approach the witness, Your Honor?"

"You may."

She picked up the three photos from the lectern, walked over to the witness, and handed her the one showing the license plate. The car looked just like the car in the state's trial exhibits.

"So you can't identify the license plate of the white Toyota Camry in the photo I just handed you as the license plate of the vehicle Mr. Hamilton was driving, is that correct?"

"No, I can't. But I'm sure the car in this photo is the car the man was driving."

"Are you as sure about that as you are that the man you saw get into *this* car was Mr. Hamilton? Take your time. Look at the car in the photo again."

The witness looked at the photo a second time and reaffirmed her earlier testimony. "I'm sure," she answered emphatically. "This is his car."

"Ms. Westin, please turn the photo over and tell us what's printed on the back."

The witness slowly read aloud, "2016, white Toyota Camry registered to Vivian Spinelli, 226 Flamingo Lane, Miami, Florida 33101."

Sullivan felt like a ton of law books had been dropped on his head. He rose to express his outrage. "Objection. Your Honor, defense counsel has tricked the witness by switching the photo marked as a trial exhibit with another photo."

The judge was unreceptive. "Mr. Sullivan, I don't recall defense counsel identifying the photograph she handed the witness as a trial exhibit. She showed her a photo of a white Toyota Camry and asked if she could identify the license plate as the one on the defendant's car. The witness kept insisting the car in the photo was Mr. Hamilton's. I am curious, however, Ms. Roseman; who is Vivian Spinelli?"

"I think Mr. Sullivan knows who she is."

"Well, Mr. Sullivan, are you going to keep us all on the edge of our seats? For the record, who is Vivian Spinelli?"

Sullivan's face flushed. "My secretary, Your Honor."

Laughter came from the courtroom spectators, along with a few more chuckles from jurors.

"Order in the courtroom," the judge bellowed, his admonition directed to those who thought the exercise humorous. The judge had unwittingly become the straight man in defense counsel's comedy act—but all was fair game in a murder trial with a crafty criminal defense lawyer.

"Continue," the judge said.

Roseman asked the witness, "When you attended the lineup, what were you asked to do?"

"To pick out the person who looked like the man I saw on the day of the robbery."

"Who *looked like* the man. So you were asked to pick out the person whose features looked the closest to the person you saw that day, is that correct?"

The witness answered awkwardly. "Well, I knew I was supposed to pick out the person I'd seen, but the person I picked out of the lineup looked more like the person I saw get into the white sedan than any of the others."

"And the others in the lineup, describe them so the jury can understand how they appeared to you."

"Well, one of the men was tall and had sort of reddish hair. Another was short and stocky with a receding hairline. I can't remember the rest of the men in the lineup, but they didn't look to me at all like the man I saw get in the car."

"So you agree that the other persons in the lineup didn't look at all like the person you saw on the day of the robbery and murder?"

"Not to me, they didn't."

Sullivan glared at his chief investigator. Lineups were supposed to include persons who were approximately the same height, weight, and ethnicity as the suspect. O'Leary's vacant stare back and shaking of his head told Sullivan he didn't know what the witness was talking about.

"But how can you be sure that the person you saw was my client? After all, you only had a few seconds to see his face."

"Well, when I saw him take off his mask as he was getting into his car," the witness said reluctantly, "I ... I was drawn to a tattoo on his neck. It frightened me. A black and red swastika, which is why at first I was afraid to report what I'd seen to the police."

Sullivan arched back in his chair. His face lost its color. Tattoo? There was no mention of Hamilton having a tattoo. Witnesses are always asked whether the perpetrator had any scars, moles, tattoos, or other distinguishing marks. He shot another glance at O'Leary with eyes that asked, "What the fuck is she talking about?" O'Leary shrugged, and his ruddy complexion turned a shade darker.

"So this tattoo you saw, was it on the left side or the right side of his neck?"

"It was on the left side, the side I saw as he walked by my car and got into his."

Roseman walked over to her client and stood behind him. She looked at the jury but directed her question to the prosecution's star witness, the one whose testimony was supposed to send her client to the afterlife. She put her hands on Hamilton's shoulders. Then, with the dexterity of a magician pulling a veil off a canary just before making it disappear into thin air, she yanked down the top of her client's turtleneck collar to reveal his neck all the way down to his left shoulder. "You mean like the tattoo on Mr. Hamilton's neck?"

The jury gave a collective gasp. Hamilton's unmarked neck was all the proof needed to undermine Vera Westin's testimony. Defense counsel finished her questioning with the statement she usually made after debunking the testimony of the state's most important witnesses. "Your Honor, I believe we have all we need to know from this witness."

Sullivan got up from his chair with the intention of doing his best to rehabilitate his witness, but before he could ask a question, the witness looked at Hamilton. Giving the appearance of holding back tears, she said, "I was mistaken, Mr. Hamilton. I'm so, so sorry."

Sullivan took a deep breath, exhaled slowly, and returned to his seat, like a sulking fifth grader rebuked by the teacher in front of the class for not doing his homework. It came as no surprise to hear the judge announce a recess and call for the attorneys to assemble in chambers. Ten minutes later, he was back in the courtroom to announce his decision to dismiss all charges against the defendant.

~

The one puzzle piece that didn't fit into Sullivan's case against the defendant was Vera Weston. Sullivan hadn't planned on the "insurance policy" Guy Hamilton had taken out with Veronica Westbrook—a.k.a. Vera Westin. It had been the best decision Hamilton had made in a lifetime full of bad decisions.

Chapter 3

June 28, 2017

Ann Livingston looked over at her husband, Ben, as he drove into
the Bella Vista Country Club located in the rural outskirts of
New Orleans. "Dinner alone with you here on my birthday is the
perfect gift."

Called Belle by its members, the Bella Vista Country Club was
the most exclusive private country club in Louisiana. Two eighteen-
hole, PGA-designed golf courses snaked around six hundred acres
of the most scenic countryside in the state, along with four tennis
courts, two Olympic-size pools, four restaurants, and a conference
center.

"As much as I love coming here," she continued, "I can't help
but feel some guilt enjoying the benefits of your wealth."

Ben Livingston's father had built the club. "I know the feeling,"
Ben said. "When I was in high school, we studied class systems as
they evolved through civilization. There were always the rich and
privileged, and the poor and disenfranchised. It was pure luck I
was born into a wealthy family. It made me feel guilty. But my
father told me there was no shame in acquiring wealth, only in not
sharing it with those in need. And that's when he told me about the
charitable foundations he and my mother had formed and funded."

The Livingston family was well known for their philanthropy,
regularly giving away substantial portions of their wealth to many
worthy causes. "You and your family have been generous in sharing
your wealth," Ann said. "The work of the foundations they created
and the ones you and Emily have formed will continue long after all

of us pass away. I'm so happy you've involved me in the operations of the foundations. It means so much to me."

"Your fundraising events have tripled the number of regular donors. You're an essential part of those operations."

"Your parents would be proud of all you and Em have accomplished," Ann said. "And the way you've run the company since you took over is nothing short of extraordinary. You and your family gained great wealth the good, old-fashioned American way. You earned it."

Benjamin Livingston and his sister, Emily Livingston Simmons, were heirs to the Livingston fortune. Like many fortunes in Texas and Louisiana, the Livingstons' wealth was related to oil. Livingston Industries manufactured drilling equipment and built and operated oil rigs. With Ben running the company, the parent organization and its subsidiaries had an estimated value of two-and-a-quarter billion dollars one year after going public in 2015. The Livingston family still owned twenty percent of the voting shares, a substantial voting block of stock ownership in a publicly held company.

Ben checked his Jaguar XJL with valet parking. Ann caught him glancing at his watch just before he took her hand to walk into the Savoy, the most elegant of the four restaurants at the country club. "What? You have another date after dinner? I thought you were all mine tonight."

"No. It's just that I was expecting a call about the upcoming merger."

"So it's business before pleasure, is it?" she asked playfully.

Ann McMillan Livingston, thirty-three, was strikingly beautiful—movie star good looks with naturally wavy blonde hair, sky-blue eyes, and a lean, firm figure she attributed to the daily exercise routine she followed to nurture five years of professional tennis. Though married to one of the wealthiest men in the country, she was a simple, understated woman. She had been adopted into a middle-class family with parents who both taught public high school. Her father coached tennis. Her mother taught piano. An outstanding student athlete, Ann had won a full scholarship to Tulane University, where she studied fine arts and graduated magna cum laude. Yet as a teenager and young adult, she'd always found time to volunteer in the soup kitchens of New Orleans and tutor children with learning disabilities.

The couple entered the restaurant foyer and were met by Antonio, the maître d'. "Good evening, Mr. Livingston. Your table is almost ready. And you, Mrs. Livingston, you look absolutely fabulous."

"Antonio, how many times have I told you to call me Ann?" The formality of his greeting always induced some lighthearted dialogue between the two.

"As often as I've called you Mrs. Livingston, I'm quite certain of that."

"I'm curious about something. Does your wife, Maria, want you to call her by her married name when you're with her?"

"Only when I'm in her service," he replied as he brought his right hand to his chest and bowed.

She saw Ben glance at his watch again, this time with an anxious look on his face. His cell phone rang. He took the call and immediately told the caller to hold. "Antonio, I know how much you two enjoy these exchanges," he said, "but I need to bring this one to an earlier end than usual to take this call. Please seat Ann. I'll join her shortly."

He walked away and was soon out of sight.

Ann suddenly felt anxious, like something bad was going to happen—a premonition that her special evening out was about to take an unexpected nosedive. Was Ben expecting to wine and dine her as a prelude to lovemaking afterwards?

God knows he's entitled to have sex with his wife, even when we both know it'll never lead to me producing the son he's always wanted.

She opened her purse and was relieved to see the small silver pill case. Inside sat her anti-anxiety medication, three ten-milligram tablets, the maximum recommended dosage for an eight-hour period. The antidepressants and sleeping pills were back home in a kitchen cabinet for her use later. She'd be out on their date for no more than two hours. A single tablet should be enough—and a glass of chardonnay—maybe two.

Whatever it took to help her forget.

She closed her purse and followed Tony into the Elegante Room, where the finest western European cuisine was served in an elegant Mediterranean setting. The lights were dimmed when they entered, but only for a few seconds. Then, as if someone had opened all the shutters and let the sunlight in, the lights came on. A crowd of people, including Antonio, yelled, "Surprise," and then began singing Happy Birthday. Ben followed Ann into the dining room and soon stood by her side. He took her into his arms and kissed her. Applause and some hoots and whistles came from the onlookers.

Ann surveyed the crowded room—relatives, friends, trusted business associates. It'd been a long time since she felt at ease in crowds. Her anxiety spiked, then abruptly eased when her eyes met those of a pretty, blonde-haired, seven-year-old girl holding the hand of her grandmother. Ann gave an audible sigh of relief, her broad smile mirroring the little girl's.

Meg, the Livingstons' only child, calmed her like no medication could.

Meg dashed from her grandmother's side and ran to Ann with a special birthday gift in her hand. She hugged her mother and gave her a drawing she'd done in acrylics on parchment set in a silver frame. A white silhouette on a black background showed a woman with a halo holding the hand of a little girl. Inscribed below the sketch were the words, "My Mom is an Angel."

Ann studied the drawing, leaned forward to hug Meg, and whispered in her ear, "My love, you are what makes me who I am and will always be: your mother, who loves you with all her heart, now and forevermore."

Meg beamed a smile, cupped her hand around her mouth, and spoke softly into her mother's ear. "I love you too, today and for always."

"Ann, let me get you a champagne," Ben offered.

"Not right now. I see Lucinda with my mother. I have a question for them. Do circulate among the guests, dear." She walked away with Meg glued to her side.

Ben's brother-in-law, Dan Simmons, soon joined him. He had a glass of champagne in each hand and offered one to Ben. "You know the best decisions we ever made were to marry the women we married." He tapped Ben's glass in a toast. Simmons, a neurosurgeon, and Ben had been fraternity brothers and roommates during their time as Tulane undergraduates.

Ben nodded. "I know. Em was always trying to fix me up with her girlfriends because I wasn't that interested in finding a mate and settling down. The business consumed so much of my time."

"Your sister was worried you were so set in your ways that no woman would be able to live with you."

"And when you and Em got hitched, she ratcheted up the pressure on me."

"Then, out of nowhere, along comes Ann McMillan. Beautiful. Accomplished. No man could resist her."

"Yeah. I knew instantly I wanted to fall in love with her. It was the first time I put personal pleasure before business. Best decision I ever made."

"Ditto, bro."

Lucinda Alvarez, the Livingstons' housemaid and *au pair* to Meg, stood talking to Ann's mother, Martha McMillan. When Ann and Meg joined them, she said to Ann, "*Feliz cumpleaños*, Ana. You look so pretty and so happy. It make me want to cry." Lucinda's routine presence at family gatherings attested to her special place in the lives and hearts of the Livingston family.

"Lucy, my dear; dear, Lucy," Ann said as she hugged Lucinda tightly. "How were you and Mom able to keep the party a secret?

I mean, you two were so convincing when you suggested at lunch yesterday that Ben and I should have a quiet dinner together on my birthday. And Meg sat stone-faced at the table when you said it."

"*Sí*, but as soon as you leave, the party all she want to talk about. Now you go mingle. We share our Ana with everyone."

"Yes, Ann," her mother said. "We'll take Meg and have a look at your birthday cake." She took Meg by the hand and led her away.

Guests gathered around Ann. Drawn by her pleasant manner and friendly smile, they wished her well.

"So, were you really surprised?" Emily asked when she seized an opening to speak privately to her sister-in-law.

"Completely."

"So, I hear Meg's being recruited to play for the club on the boys' tennis team. She beats all the nine and ten-year-old girls and holds her own against the boys. The apple doesn't fall far from the tree, eh?"

"She loves tennis. I see the passion she has for the game. She's better than I was at her age."

"And your mother has her playing the piano so well, it wouldn't surprise me if she plays professionally one day."

"But stick her in tights in a ballet studio"—Ann sighed—"and it's like trying to tame a wild animal. I'm getting close to letting her decide whether she wants to hang up her slippers."

Absent from the festivities were Ann's father, who'd died from a heart attack shortly after Ann became pregnant with Meg, and Ben's parents, who had been killed in a plane crash two years earlier. Ben's father, an experienced private pilot, had often relieved the regular pilot of his duties and flown the company jet himself. No one could have anticipated the flock of Canada geese that had shut down both engines of the Learjet he was flying that fateful night.

Ann found the evening enjoyable, made easier by the champagne … and the tablets in her pill case.

Ben made sure it ended in spectacular fashion. After the sun completed its descent below the western horizon, he had the guests

31

gather on the lawn and treated them to a fireworks show over the lake at the center of the country club property.

~

Ann sat at her desk in the office adjoining her stately bedroom on the second floor. She and her family lived in a three-story, six-bedroom, Georgian-style home in the exclusive community of Whispering Pines. The home, on twenty-five acres, rivaled the grandest of mansions on antebellum plantations, but it had several modern upgrades: a tennis court, an Olympic-size pool, and manicured walking gardens that stretched from the rear patios of the home to two natural ponds at the back end of the property aptly named Twin Lakes.

Ann, her eyelids heavy with tiredness, looked at the clock on her desk just as the grandfather clock in the foyer began to hammer its eleven strikes, muffled by the distance. Meg had fallen asleep on the way home. After Ann had put Meg to bed and changed into her own bed clothes, she had gone to her office to finish the letter she'd started earlier in the day. She'd wanted the handwritten letter to be perfect, and now, happy with the results, she slipped it into an envelope along with photos of herself and her family.

While she was placing the stamp on the envelope, Ben came in and put his hands on her shoulders. He bent over and kissed the top of her head. "Ann, you looked so beautiful tonight. I thank God every night that you became a part of my life and gave us our sweet Meg. You know, my father told me when I was ten and Em was eight, while we were at a birthday party he gave for my mother, that I'd know I was truly in love with the woman I married when the mere sight of the child she gave me brought a smile to my face and a tear of joy to my eye."

Ann turned to face Ben. He was smiling, and his moist eyes were fixed on the photo of Meg on the desk. Ann got up from her chair, hugged him, and kissed him softly. "Ben, my darling, my love. I, too, am thankful. You and Meg complete me as a person."

32

Ben took Ann by the hand and led her to bed, where he cradled her in his arms and stroked her hair. She looked lovingly into his eyes, smiled, and, with the help of an antidepressant tablet and one of her sleeping pills, surrendered to a deep and dreamless slumber.

Chapter 4

July 23, 2017,
Cumberland County Women's Correctional Facility.

"Hey, Ronnie, what did you think of the shepherd's stew they served tonight? Ever since they started putting cons in charge of weekend dinners, you don't know what's in what you're eating ... but it tastes like shit."

Veronica Westbrook had met Sarah Booth when they became cellmates at Cum-land, the name the inmates affectionately called Cumberland County Women's Correctional Facility, a women's prison located twenty miles west of Baltimore, Maryland. "The reason the stew tastes like shit," Westbrook replied, "is because it is shit. That's why the diet I've been on for the past six months doesn't include eating any meals prepared by cons. By the way, how do you know what shit tastes like?"

"Fuck you, Ronnie. You know what I mean."

"The stuff they put in the food to vent their anger over being here, or to get even with someone, is ridiculous," Westbrook continued. "Two-time Sellers, who pulled dinner duty last month, told her cellmate not to eat weekend dinners because Piggy Peggy Nelson, the cook she worked with, mixed shit in with the ground beef on Meat Loaf Saturdays."

Westbrook and Booth were as close as any two convicts could be. Westbrook was halfway through a two-year stint for befriending and bilking a wealthy widow with Alzheimer's disease out of $150,000. If the widow's brother hadn't discovered a bank statement in a waste basket at his sister's home, the account would have been drained of the remaining $97,000.

34

Booth was a year into an eighteen-month sentence for driving the getaway car at a robbery her ex-boyfriend bungled. She would have done a lot worse had she not fingered her accomplice and turned state's evidence.

"So what kind of shit did she put in the ground beef?" Booth asked.

"I wasn't using the word *shit* metaphorically, I meant it literally. Like in ... *her* shit."

"No shit."

"And she puts her piss in the lemonade."

"Jesus, Ronnie. She's one sick bitch. And I used to like the lemonade. Why didn't you tell me sooner?"

"Because you looked like you enjoyed drinking it so much. Don't worry. It's probably safer to drink than the water out of the tap."

"So what should we do next week on our anniversary? It's been one long year, girlfriend."

They'd come into the prison together and had bonded immediately, like Thelma and Louise but without the car and cliff. Booth, a good-looking thirty-one-year-old brunette, was bisexual. So Westbrook partnered up with her, became her pimp, and bartered her cellmate's marketable skills to lesbian inmates and wannabes in return for cash and contraband, and to several of the male guards in return for special treatment and favors.

It was remarkable how much they had in common. Both were hookers with criminal arrests for prostitution, shoplifting, and petty theft. Both had been expelled from high school: Westbrook, for assaulting another student; Booth, for stealing purses and wallets from students' lockers. Both were sexually involved with adults as adolescents: Westbrook, in the ninth grade with her high school gym teacher; Booth, with her stepdad when she was thirteen. Each confided in the other that they'd initiated the sexual contact and thoroughly enjoyed their experiences.

35

There was one other important common denominator, one that Westbrook knew joined them at the hip, one that explained their instant attraction to and sordid interest in each other, one that meant they could each turn on the other at the drop of a tear.

They were both sociopaths.

"How about we dine out. I'll make reservations for two at the Cum-land Bistro. I hear their meat loaf is to die for."

"Fuck you, Ronnie."

~

The mail and magazine delivery cart passed by every day between three and four in the afternoon. Same dog-eared, months-old fashion and celebrity magazines. Some religious bulletins for the born-agains. Several issues of *Cycle World* and *Popular Mechanics* for the butch inmates.

This day was different.

Westbrook was alone in the cell when the cart rolled into view. "Allie, do you have the issue of *Vogue* I wanted?" she asked.

Allison "Dog Face" Harrelson, a prison trustee assigned to mail duty, was doing five years for manslaughter. A junkie whore, she'd killed her pimp by setting him on fire one night after he'd beaten her for the umpteenth time. The problem was, she'd gotten caught in the fire she'd set. Third degree burns on her face flattened and scarred it. She had the squashed facial appearance of a bulldog. The judge had felt pity for her and strayed from the sentencing guidelines, halving what she should've received.

"Ronnie, there's something else here for you. I put it inside the issue you put your dibs on last week."

"Thanks, Allie. You're a peach." Westbrook reached for the magazine with one hand and exchanged it for a cigarette she had in the other. She respected Harrelson for what she did. Unlike the other inmates, she didn't call her Dog Face—at least not to her face.

The cell doors remained open most of the day. Lockdown was at nine in the evening. Prisoners moved about freely on their floors.

36

Cell doors were typically only locked before nine when someone turned violent or was being disciplined for some infraction of the rules.

Booth was out servicing a client, so Westbrook sat alone in her cell. When she opened the magazine, an oversized envelope fell to the floor. In the upper-left corner of the envelope, a preprinted sticker identified the sender as *Caroline Westbrook, 2012 Covington Lane, Towson MD 21204.* She tossed the envelope on the desk she shared with her cellmate, lay down in bed, and opened the three-month-old issue of *Vogue* to read the feature stories.

The envelope remained unopened on the desk.

~

"Ronnie, this envelope's been here on the desk for a week. It's from your mom. Maybe she's telling you she'll be sending you something nice, like a fruit basket, for your one-year anniversary."

"Sal, why don't you go tickle the twat of some pillow princess," Westbrook said, deadpan, as she sat in bed applying a second coat of polish to her toenails.

"Really, aren't you the least bit curious?" Booth continued, tossing the letter on the bed beside Westbrook.

"If they send me a fruit basket, I'll save the banana for you. You can take it to bed and pretend it's your boyfriend."

Booth laughed. "I love it when you get all warm and fuzzy over your parents and family life. Well, I'm headed out to get felt up by that redhead who's in for her third DUI. Make sure you collect."

An hour passed, and Westbrook figured she'd open the envelope just to relieve the boredom. Inside she found three letters and photographs. The first letter was from her mother.

Dear Veronica,

Dad and I have tried to reach out to you since you were incarcerated, but the times we came to see you, you didn't want

37

*to meet with us. We respect your wishes, even though we don't
understand them.*

*I enclose a letter we received from the adoption agency that placed
you with us thirty-three years ago. The letter advises us that you
have a sister who wants to reach out to you. As you know, we told
you that you had a twin sister, who was adopted by another family.
We offered to assist you in finding her if it was important to you.
You expressed no interest. But your sister has.*

I've enclosed the information we received from the adoption agency.

*Dad and I realize that this is an intensely personal decision for you.
Perhaps if you reconnect with your sister, you can come to learn
more about who you are and who you can be.*

We love you very much, Veronica, and we always will.
Mom

The next letter was from Harriet Cummings, Senior Placement
Specialist with the Maryland Department of Human Services.

Dear Ms. Westbrook:

*Your biological sibling recently contacted our agency and would
like to contact you. Our records confirm that Mrs. Ann Livingston
of New Orleans, Louisiana is your identical twin sister. Mrs.
Livingston authorized our agency to disclose her identity to you
and forward you a letter and photographs that are contained in the
sealed envelope enclosed with this letter.*

*We have not shared with Mrs. Livingston anything that would
reveal your identity or whereabouts, or the identities or whereabouts
of your parents. Whether or not you wish to communicate with your
sister is, of course, entirely your decision.*

Warmest regards,
Harriet Cummings

Westbrook took out the sealed envelope marked "To my sister" and, using a small nail file from the contraband hidden under her mattress, opened the top of the envelope and pulled out the contents: ten photos and a letter.

My Dear Sister,

I hope you receive this letter in good health and read it knowing that I do not want to be intrusive in your life. I respect your right to privacy. But I just can't live with myself if I don't at least reach out to you and see if you might possibly feel the same void in your life that I've felt for quite some time in mine. I'll explain later.

If you want to know about me, I'll provide you with as much information as you want. For now, just know that I am married to a wonderful man and I have a daughter, Margaret, whom we call Meg. Meg is the sunshine of my life. If you have children, perhaps you know the feeling. We live in Louisiana, just outside New Orleans.

I grew up in Louisiana. My parents were both public high school teachers. My father died about eight years ago. He knew he was going to be a grandfather but never had the pleasure of seeing and holding Meg, although I used to hold a picture of him in my hand when I held Meg in my arms. I know this may sound silly, but I always felt we were all connected when I did that.

We didn't have a whole lot of money growing up, but always a whole lot of love to go around, which seemed to get us through the difficult times. My life changed a lot when I met and married my husband, Ben. I hope there's someone in your life you can feel close to and with whom you can share your innermost feelings.

My reaching out to you is something that has been on my mind ever since Meg was born. I was pregnant with twins and knew they were girls. Ben and I, and our families, were looking forward to seeing them grow up together. But problems developed during my delivery, and Meg's sister, whom we named Charlotte, died at birth.

Needless to say, I was so overwhelmed with grief that I lapsed into a deep depression for a very, very long time. I don't mind sharing this with you because I have always felt in my heart a connection to you, ever since I learned that I, like Meg, am an identical twin. I have always known I was adopted, but I didn't know until last year, when I contacted the agency that handled our adoptions, that you and I are identical twins. Charlotte and Meg were also identical twins. So all of us share a common bond.

My purpose is not to burden you with my problems, dear sister, then or now. It's just my way of wanting to know more about you so that I can perhaps learn more about myself.

Anyway, I enclose some photos of me growing up so that you can compare my looks to yours. Please know that you can share these photos with your family if you like. And maybe, just maybe, you may feel comfortable sharing some photos of you and your family with me.

My dear sister, I hope and pray you are healthy and happy, and will always be.

If you wish to respond, or reach out to me in the future, my contact information is: Ann Livingston, 5 Owls Nest Road, Whispering Pines, LA 70112. (504) 227-6995 (home), (504) 562-2020 (cell), Email: alivingston@aol.com.

God bless you and your family and loved ones.
Ann

Westbrook pulled out the photos. An important detail had been written on the back of each photo: photo one, *age 2;* photo two, *first grade;* photo three, *age 13, elementary school graduation;* photo four, *age 18, high school yearbook photo;* photo five, *age 24, wedding photo;*

40

photo six, *pregnant and with my parents (last photo of my dad);* photo seven, *Meg and I when she was born;* photo eight, *Meg, age 2, with Ben and me;* photo nine, *family photo, Meg's 7th birthday;* photo ten, *me, this year.*

She was amazed by how much she looked like her sister. Everyone who knew her, if shown these photos, would believe they were of her. From the contraband beneath her mattress, she pulled out a mirror and held it in one hand, with the most recent photo of Ann in the other. As if reciting a nursery rhyme, she whispered to herself, "Mirror, mirror, in my hand, who's the fairest in Cum-land?"

A neuron sparked in the frontal lobes of Veronica Westbrook's brain, and an explosion occurred in the deep, dark recesses of her mind. She felt strangely excited in a sexual way. She put the mirror back under her mattress, alongside the scissors, cigarettes, narcotics, and shiv. She kept her cash elsewhere—in her pocket during the day, in her pillow case when she slept, and in a plastic baggie when she showered. Some of her money came from inmates who didn't take such precautionary measures.

The wedding photo caught her interest; studying it aroused her. She got out of bed and retrieved Booth's dildo from under her mattress. It was a tool of the trade for her cellmate, but also a mutually shared object for each's solitary pleasure. Returning to her bed, she pulled off her pants and panties, parked the plastic tube in its usual space, and held up photo five, the wedding photo. She looked first at Ann Livingston—her mirror image—and then only at Ben Livingston for the five minutes it took for her to climax.

The next day, she sat at the computer in the prison library with a notepad and pen in hand.

Who is Ann Livingston of New Orleans, Louisiana?

She found dozens of stories and several biographies with details about Ann growing up: her many accomplishments as a scholar athlete in high school and college; her career as a professional tennis player; her community service; and her marriage to Benjamin Livingston, one of the wealthiest men in the country. She learned a lot about Ann Livingston in the thirty minutes of computer time allotted to inmates once a week. When she exited the internet, the screen went black except for the prison logo and the words: *Learn Right. Live Right.*

Westbrook returned to her cell and found a note Booth had left asking her to join her in the community room to watch a movie. The quiet of her cell, however, provided her the opportunity to think clearly about what she needed to do. She sat up in bed, reached for her pen and notebook, and wrote:

Learn everything about Ann Livingston.

Learn everything about Ben Livingston.

Learn everything about everything that is important to Ann and Ben Livingston.

Learn how to be Ann Livingston.

Chapter 5

Westbrook needed to do two things as soon as possible. She needed to end Ann's quest to reunite with her, and that meant yesterday. If Ann's family ever learned about Westbrook's colorful background, they'd surely veto any invitation to the Livingston family reunion. She also needed to move out of her current digs at the earliest opportunity. If she was to learn how to become Ann, she needed to be near her.

The first matter was resolvable by a simple letter. However, prison personnel read letters to and from level-two inmates like her, unless they were between the inmate and their on-file lawyer. She decided to contact the one lawyer she knew she could count on, using the one phone call a week she was entitled to make.

"Roseman and Roseman. To whom may I direct your call?"

"This is Veronica Westbrook. I'm a friend of a client of Ms. Roseman."

"Ms. Roseman is in court. Can her secretary help you?"

"I really need her help, and I only have the one call."

"Let me put you through to her voicemail. It's a new system. You can speak for as long as you want. She accesses her voicemail messages regularly during the day."

Westbrook left a message with all the necessary information, then typed a letter to Ann using the same font and layout of Harriet Cummings's letter. She forged Cummings's signature and post-dated the letter by two weeks to allow time for it to be processed out of the prison, get to Roseman, and be mailed from her office.

Dear Mrs. Livingston,

I regret to inform you that your sister is deceased. The details of her death are, of course, confidential.

Your letter and other items in your sealed envelope were forwarded to your sister's adoptive parents, who opened the envelope and reviewed the contents. They authorized me to inform you that their daughter would have been proud to have known you and your family. They do, however, wish to remain anonymous, and ask you to respect their privacy during this very difficult time for them.

Warmest regards,
Harriet Cummings

The second matter needing her attention required more finesse. She hatched a plan for her get-out-of-jail-early card. But she needed Booth's help.

"Sal, I need to cut some time off my sentence, and I need your help. I want to set up the diesel dyke for a con."

"Are you sure, Ronnie? She's one crazy bitch. Maybe it's best we just stay as far away from her as possible."

"No way. I'm hearing she's been wanting to come after us ever since she was transferred back to our cellblock. We need to be proactive."

"You want to *cut* her again?" Booth whispered.

"No. I have a plan that should be bloodless."

Westbrook was referring to Billy Sue Campbell, the prison bully from West Virginia doing eight years for aggravated assault. A year earlier, she had wanted exclusive rights to Booth. Campbell had beaten a waitress at a trucker's diner half to death for rebuffing her sexual advances. When she got to prison, she'd preyed on vulnerable inmates who were too afraid of her to refuse to be her punk. By two-thirds of the way through her sentence, she had a half-dozen punks. The unluckiest ones were her cellmates. For them it was the equivalent of a sentence of hard labor.

44

"Sal, do you remember how close you came to being her punk and what I had to do to protect you?"

"Like it was yesterday. I've thought about it every time our paths have crossed since she's been back."

Westbrook could see the angst in Booth's face. Or was it fear?

A few months into their sentences, Campbell had decided to have her way with Booth. But Booth was selective even in the confines and closed community of a women's prison, and Campbell was so low on the food chain, it made Booth's skin crawl just being in the same cellblock with her.

Campbell, however, was used to getting her way and hadn't taken kindly to the rejection. She'd left a note on Booth's bunk: *Coming for you. You be my dessert. You be my new bitch. You snitch on me and you be leaving in a box. Billy Sue.*

Westbrook smiled, remembering the events that had followed.

"No worries," Westbrook had told Booth when she'd showed her the note. She knew how to protect Booth. It would give her a chance to use the shiv she'd made out of a plastic soda bottle. She'd cut it into two jagged-edged, tapered pieces and bound them in a very acceptable handle using adhesive tape she'd swiped from the infirmary.

A plan requiring two people is more easily hatched when the two minds are in sync, and Westbrook and Booth's minds were calibrated with the same tuning fork. "Sal, at dinner tonight," Westbrook had told her, "I want you to smile at Billy Sue. Bring a bar of soap and put it up to your nose and sniff it to suggest you'll meet her in the shower tonight."

Booth had looked nauseous when, after she'd done her soap thing at dinner, Campbell gave her a gapped-tooth smile and wiggled her tongue at her.

Back in their cell after dinner, Westbrook had said, "Sal, put on your robe, pull up your pant legs, and throw a towel over your shoulder."

Booth had done as instructed and then sat on her bunk, waiting for Campbell to show up.

Most inmates showered in the morning, but the shy ones and the couples waited until evening when they might be able to shower in privacy. Privacy was exactly what Westbrook needed. Campbell came to their cell naked under her robe, with a towel over her shoulder. Booth forced a sexy-looking smile and said, "Lather up good for me. Be there in five."

As soon as she was out of sight, Booth got out of her robe, pulled her pant legs back down, and went to the infirmary where she checked in with the nurse, complaining of cramps and irregular periods, and demanded a pregnancy test. Something that would take a good twenty minutes.

While her cellmate manufactured an alibi, Westbrook slipped out of her cell and worked her way to the showers. Billy Sue Campbell had paraded herself through the cellblock to the showers, virtually guaranteeing that no one else would be following her in, and anyone seeing her show up would soon leave. Westbrook saw two inmates exit the stairwell a few minutes after Campbell had entered it, one with soap still in her hair and the other dripping water on the cellblock floor.

After the two inmates left the area, Westbrook felt she could safely join Campbell in the shower. No one was in the shower area when she got there, and only one shower was in use—occupied by Campbell.

Westbrook slipped a nylon stocking over her head to disguise her identity and stepped in front of the shower. Campbell had been rubbing soap into her crew cut and had her back to Westbrook. Acting swiftly and purposefully, Westbrook stuck the four-inch blade of the shiv a good three inches into Campbell's left side, then yanked it out. Blood gushed out like water from a hose. Campbell gasped, looked down, and pushed her hands against the wound. At the same time, Westbrook shoved the shiv into and then out of Campbell's right side. Another stream of blood spurted out.

"What the fuck!" Campbell yelled, her right hand flying to the second wound.

Westbrook's *coup de grace* had been to stab Campbell dead center in her back between her shoulder blades. Campbell screamed and spun around, cursing and struggling to grab the shiv that was just out of her reach. Westbrook smiled at the wide-eyed, open-mouthed look of terror on her face.

"It was the shower scene in that Hitchcock movie," she told Booth later.

Leaving the shiv in Campbell's back concerned her, though; the shower water might not wash away her prints. She pulled it out and quickly washed away the visible blood. Campbell slid, moaning, to the floor as Westbrook pushed the shiv into the waistband of her prison-issued trousers. She walked away from the bleeding woman, removed the nylon stocking from her head, and tucked it in her pocket.

On her way out, she heard a couple of inmates walking toward the showers. Her only cover was a large laundry basket at the entrance to the showers, filled halfway with wet towels and washcloths. She jumped in and buried herself under the dirty laundry. When the inmates had passed by, she peeked out just enough to see their backs as they moved to where Campbell lay bleeding in the shower. They were close enough for Westbrook to hear what they said.

"Jesus Christ, it's fucking Campbell," the taller of the two cried out.

"Damn if it isn't," the other one said. "Let's get the hell out of here. We want to get as far away from this shit as possible."

"But if we're seen leaving, we might get blamed."

"But if we report, Campbell will know we were here and blame us."

"You and me got fucked tonight, but in a way we never imagined."

"So I guess we report and hope the bitch doesn't make it."

47

Westbrook saw enough of their faces to watch them trade smiles.

"The bitch, she never looked so good," the tall one said.

Her cellmate chuckled. "I know. Let's give it another five minutes before we call for help."

The tall one spoke last. "Make that ten."

The inmates still had their backs to Westbrook, so she quietly climbed out of the basket and walked to the community room, where Booth—her alibi—waited already, watching a movie with a large group of inmates.

Booth interrupted Westbrook's journey down memory lane and brought her back to the present. "You know what happened to Billy Sue after you cut her in the shower?"

"Yeah, I know. Taken by helicopter to the Maryland Trauma Center in Baltimore. Allie Harrelson heard she lost half her blood. Both kidneys, punctured. Got an infection from some bad blood she got. A month in intensive care. Three more in rehab. Who says there isn't a God? It makes you want to believe."

Booth smiled broadly. "Yeah, a real nightmare for the poor soul." Her tone of voice turned serious again. "But now she's back and gunning for both of us. She knows I wouldn't have the guts to cut her. But everyone knows you stick up for me and take shit from no one."

Westbrook had heard the rumors. Campbell knew who was responsible for cutting her. Booth would never go one-on-one with her. Westbrook, on the other hand, had a reputation in the cellblock for being clever, resourceful, and fearless. She'd gained the respect of the inmates shortly after she arrived. When one of them had come on to her in the shower, she'd jammed a thumb in her eye and stuffed a bar of soap in her mouth. When another talked trash to her in the community room, the inmate found a disemboweled rat under her pillow that night in bed. Another, who repeatedly stole food from the tray of a mentally-challenged prisoner Westbrook stood up for, ended up finding a blood-soaked tampon

48

at the bottom of her plate of pasta one night at dinner. How the rat and tampon got where they were remained a mystery, but who was responsible for getting them there didn't. Within a matter of weeks, Westbrook had earned her reputation as a stand-up inmate and someone you didn't mess with.

Westbrook continued to outline her plan to Booth for an early departure from the Big Doll House. "I have my patsy in Campbell. All that I need is some bait to lure her in."

"What kind of bait?" Booth asked.

"I'm still working on that."

~

The bait arrived the next morning—Molly Stevens, the skinny, plain-looking, nineteen-year-old daughter of a prominent local Baltimore businessman. Freckle-faced Molly looked more like fifteen in her braces. When she first showed up in the cafeteria, she sat alone and as far away from the other inmates as possible, looking like she was about to shit her prison-issued underwear. Westbrook seized the opportunity and went immediately to her table with her cellmate in tow.

"Hey! Do you mind if we sit with you? I'm Ronnie. This is Sal. We're roommates." They sat across from the new girl so as not to intimidate her. "Look, I know you're probably scared crazy, but you'll get through it. I hear you're a short stay. What did you do? Litter in the park?" Westbrook hoped the attempt at humor might break the ice.

Molly opened up. Westbrook knew she needed to talk to someone, to confide in a friend while she counted the hours of each and every day she was in prison. "I—I'm Molly Stevens," she stuttered, staring at her untouched plate of food. "I'm here for thirty days because I let my ex-boyfriend use my apartment to sell drugs to students at the high school I graduated from. One of his customers, a seventeen-year-old boy, overdosed and almost died. The judge wouldn't go along with probation, even though everyone else agreed

49

I shouldn't be locked up with criminals … Oh! I'm so sorry. I didn't mean to call you criminals … it's just that I don't feel like I belong here … is what I meant to say."

Westbrook comforted Molly, much like an older sister might. "It's okay, Molly. You can count on me and Sal to get you through the next month. We'll be your friends and protect you. No need to worry."

Through moist, doleful eyes, Molly looked at Westbrook and said, "I prayed someone like you would be here to look after me." Drops fell on spotted cheeks.

Westbrook sensed it was the first time since she'd received her sentence that Molly's tears were of joy, not fear. Molly had found a friend. Just as Westbrook planned. It helped that Molly had wept, trembled, and been so frightened during her in-processing that the prison director hadn't assigned her a cellmate, believing it might be too traumatic for Molly to bunk with a real criminal. So the sweet, innocent teenager was all Westbrook's for the taking.

~

Knowing that if Campbell didn't bleed to death in the shower, she could eventually be back in their cellblock, Westbrook had saved the note Campbell had left on Booth's bunk. She'd placed it in the drawer of their cell desk for safekeeping, but it was no longer necessary to keep it safe.

She waited until Campbell and her cellmate, whom Campbell affectionately called "my bitch," left their cell for breakfast, then said to Booth, "Sal, I want you to go to breakfast with Cupcake. You know how she's afraid to be left alone."

Cupcake was the name Westbrook had given the sweet thing when she'd arrived in prison.

"I know. She calls you her big sister."

"Tell her I can't join you because I need to talk to the deputy director about what I overheard Billy Sue say to her cellmate last night in the community room."

"And what will you say you heard?"

"That Billy Sue was going to make Cupcake her new punk."

Westbrook then directed Booth on what she was to do. "At breakfast, you and Molly sit at a table facing Campbell. Make eye contact with her … smile, wink, or wiggle your tongue—anything to get her attention. It'll piss her off, and she'll stare you down for sure. She'll be looking at you, but Cupcake will think she's looking at her. Just seeing Campbell look in her direction will scare the crap out of her."

While Booth and Molly were at breakfast, Westbrook went to Campbell's cell and hid under her mattress a shiv, some narcotics, and Campbell's note, which she put in a prison-issued envelope with Molly's name scrawled on the front. An added touch of authenticity was to misspell Molly's last name *Stevins*, to go along with the misspelled word *dissert* in the original note. Her next and last step was to request an emergency meeting with the deputy director to report overhearing Campbell tell her cellmate she was going to make the teenager "my new bitch" and that she'd "cut her up good" if she refused or snitched.

Two guards were sent to search Campbell's cell, where they found the evidence of a crime in the making. Campbell was taken to an isolation cell and charged the next day with attempted sexual assault and possession of contraband, including drugs and a weapon. No one believed, or wanted to believe, she was framed. An eventual plea bargain added a year to her remaining sentence.

Molly was grateful. So was Molly's well-to-do father. He paid a lawyer to file a petition to get Westbrook an early release date for her role in preventing the sexual assault. Six months were cut from her sentence. She'd walk out a free woman in less than four.

Westbrook had accomplished the two things she needed to do. Now she could concentrate on learning how to be Ann Livingston. She used her computer time to take notes from postings on the internet about Ann and Ben Livingston. One video had Ann walking to a podium and giving a speech at an awards ceremony

51

for the work of the Livingstons' charitable foundations. Westbrook began mimicking Ann's slight Southern drawl and walking like her, with a short, quick stride.

"So, what's with the Scarlet O'Hara imitation?" Booth asked as Westbrook's discharge date drew near. "And you're walking like you just got gang banged by the football team. Something's up. C'mon, Ronnie, your secret's safe with me."

"Molly told me her uncle is a television producer working on a soap opera," Westbrook lied. "The main characters are fine Southern women. She and her dad will put in a good word for me to land a role as an extra doing bit parts as a friend or an acquaintance of the regular characters. So there, you have the scoop."

"Hey! Maybe there's a part for me."

"Don't be looking to muscle in on my territory, girlfriend. Besides, you'd never be able to lose that Jersey accent. But if there's ever a part for a bisexual from Hoboken, I'll put in a good word for you."

"You know, Ronnie, the shit that comes out of your mouth could feed the prison for a month with Piggy Peggy doing the cooking."

"Fiddle dee dee! Well, believe me or not. Y'all will just have to get used to the new southern belle while she's visiting the plantation."

~

Booth's natural curiosity got to her. While Westbrook was in the infirmary having her discharge medical examination two days before her release, Booth removed her cellmate's notepad from under the mattress and read what she'd written. She also read Ann Livingston's letter and studied the photographs Ann had sent.

On a prison-issued notepad, she wrote facts about the Livingston family that had been recorded in Westbrook's notes. What immediately caught her interest were four short sentences on the first page, the last of which was: *Learn how to be Ann Livingston.*

But the entries she paid the most attention to, the ones that whet her appetite, and the ones that led her to formulate a plan of her own, were the ones that appeared toward the end of the journal:

Get cash from Molly
Get seed money from cousin Roger
Follow Ann
Say goodbye to Ann
Become Ann
Leave with millions
Buy a Porsche
Find a villa near the Swiss Alps
Live happily ever after

Booth finished copying the important details. But when she got to the end, she added one more.

Cut Sal in on a piece of the action.

Chapter 6

At precisely one o'clock in the afternoon on Wednesday, November 5, 2017, Veronica Westbrook walked out of the Cumberland County Women's Correctional Facility a free woman. Molly Stevens was waiting for her at the prison entrance. Westbrook had written to Molly about how heartbroken she was that her mother was "terminally ill" but that her early release would give her "the chance to be with Mom in her final days."

They had lunch at a nice restaurant in Baltimore. After taking a dozen photos on her cell phone to memorialize the occasion, Molly picked up the tab for lunch, and Westbrook picked up the thousand in cash "Cupcake" got from her dad to help her reunite with a dying parent. Afterwards, they drove to Baltimore's Penn Station. Molly cried when they said their goodbyes. Her "big sister" promised to keep in touch.

Westbrook boarded the Northeast Regional to Charleston, South Carolina, where she planned on meeting up with her cousin, Roger Pennington. She sat back in her seat for the eleven-hour journey into the Deep South, wearing the prison-issued sweats and slip-ons she'd received, complements of the state of Maryland.

Along the way, she frequently daydreamed about her new life as Ann Livingston, and about Ben Livingston and the intimate moments they'd soon be sharing. It excited her. She rustled through her travel bag for the photos Ann had sent her. She found photo five, the Livingston wedding photo, propped it up on the empty seat next to her, and focused on it as one hand worked its way down to the sweet spot between her thighs, the other gripping the armrest. When the special moment arrived, her groin arched up from the seat and three words flowed from her mouth like the spontaneous cheer one gives when a favorite player has scored the go-ahead touchdown. "Yes, Ben, yes."

~

Westbrook motored in her rental car over the Cooper River to Mount Pleasant, a fashionable suburb just outside Charleston, full of magnificent, historic homes.

"Your destination is ahead on your right," announced the fembot in the navigation system when she turned onto Bradford Circle. She parked in front of number twelve.

According to the gold-plated plaque adjacent the door bell, the home, a baronial manor house, was built in 1857 by Colonel Henry T. Mason. A rail-thin, elderly African American woman in a black skirt, white blouse, and apron answered the soft and pleasant chime.

"May I help you, ma'am?" she said in a monotone and without a hint of facial expression.

"Yes. My name is Veronica Pennington. I'm Roger Pennington's—" Before she could finish, she heard him speak from the staircase he was descending.

"Rose, I'll greet our guest," he said as he approached the door, passing the house servant on her way to the center of the foyer to await his further instructions.

Westbrook noticed a lazy regional twang in Roger's speech as phony as his name.

He had a bemused look on his face. "Well, well. Isn't this a pleasant surprise? I thought you were out of the country and not returning for another six months." A subtle reference to the remaining time on the two-year prison sentence she was supposed to serve. "Cousin Roxanne told me you might be stopping by on your way home to take care of your mother, whom I understand is quite ill. So I know you'll want to leave after a short visit." He called out to Rose over his shoulder. "Rose, bring us tea and some of those delicious biscuits you made this morning. We'll take our libations in the study."

He led his guest to a room opposite the kitchen. She sat in one of four upholstered chairs that surrounded an old, slave-carved, walnut coffee table, being sure to cross her legs in the style of a well-mannered, prim and proper southern lady. He sat in the chair directly across from her. The playacting was temporarily suspended. He was blunt.

"So, how much do you intend to blackmail me for? I don't want you fucking up the hard work I've put into this gig. I'm the financial consultant and confidante to Miss Isabelle Avery, the last *dying* descendant of Colonel Henry T. Mason. We celebrated her last birthday in the hospital just last week. The finish line's in sight."

"By the way, what did you end up with after your last gig when all was said and done?" Westbrook asked.

"Not that much. Fencing the jewelry got me ten percent of market value. I dumped it pretty quickly. The cash wasn't as much as I thought it'd be. After lawyer's fees … and the twenty-six grand I paid you … a couple hundred thousand. And most of that's been invested in my current project. There's not much left." He sighed unconvincingly. "But I can be reasonable if you can be sensible."

She knew her occasional lover and former business associate was bullshitting her. His take was more. Her guess, a lot more. And she didn't need him to tell her what Roger Pennington was up to. She'd tried to do the same thing on a smaller scale two years earlier and had gotten caught.

Rose entered with a serving tray and placed it on the table. Roger said he'd pour and dismissed her. Once the door was closed, Westbrook got right to the point.

"I want ten thousand dollars, half in hundreds, half in fifties. I need two sets of passports, socials, birth certificates, and Louisiana and Swiss driver's licenses. I'll be back tomorrow with the names, addresses, and other information you'll need to prepare the documents, as well as the photos for the passports and licenses. I need to have the money and documents by the end of the week. See how easy that was? And then you can continue providing financial

56

advice to the mistress of the house on how she should be investing her … uh, excuse me … *your* money."

He poured tea for his guest and for himself, then put milk and two lumps of sugar in his cup. "Cousin Veronica," he politely asked, "how would you like your tea? With milk and two lumps of sugar?"

"No, dear cousin, I'd like mine with ten grand and two sets of identity documents."

Hamilton couldn't contain a smile. "Then I'll see you to the door and bid you a fond farewell until later this week."

Westbrook returned to her hotel room, stopping at a mall to shop. She bought a short black wig, poker straight, the antithesis of her mane of naturally wavy blonde hair, and a color stick and mascara to darken her eyelashes and brows to match the color of the wig. New, frumpy looking clothes came next: flat shoes, slacks, no skirts, nothing to reveal her shapely legs.

Once safely back in her room, she removed her makeup, put on the wig, and dressed in her new clothes, then walked two blocks to Walgreens and had her passport and driver's license photos taken in her new disguise. Two gum balls placed in her cheeks gave her face the fuller look of someone slightly plump. She didn't smile in the photograph and kept her mouth shut tight, hiding another hint of her true identity, her perfect teeth.

She looked at the four photos and smiled. The women in the photos were not Veronica Westbrook. The women in the photos were Mary Smith and Laura Mueller.

She then drove to twelve Bradford Circle and slipped an envelope into the mail slot containing the photos, the bogus information needed to prepare the documents, and a note: *Be back at noon on Friday. Your cousin, Veronica.*

Hamilton gave Rose the day off and answered the door when Westbrook arrived looking like the women in the photos. "Well, who do we have here?" he said. "Is it Mary Smith responding to the ad for the position of housemaid, or Laura Mueller asking for a donation to the Widows and Orphans Fund?"

She walked by him and into the study with a smirk on her face. They sat in the same chairs as before. A small gym bag sat on the floor beside him. He put it on the table and unzipped it. When she leaned forward and looked in, she saw piles of hundreds and fifties. She flipped through each pile.

"Don't fret, cuz. It's all there. I wouldn't stiff a relative."

"You'd cheat your disabled old grandmother out of her life savings if you thought you'd get away with it."

"It was my disabled old grandfather, God rest his soul."

She reached in and took out the identity documents. There were two sets, with rubber bands around each set. She opened the first set—for Mary Smith—then the second set—for Laura Mueller— and smiled. *Nice work.* Her facial expression showed that she was pleased.

"What's with the identities?" he asked. "I mean, how many different persons do you want to be? But I've got to admit, you are *not* Veronica Westbrook." He paused a moment, then added, "You know, the documents cost another grand. I should make you reimburse me out of what's in that bag."

At that moment, she became the woman she was, and he became the man she knew him to be. The sounds of zippers opening and closing pierced the sudden silence: she, closing the zipper on the duffle bag; he, opening the zipper on his trousers. She got up, walked over, and knelt down in front of him. He slouched back in his chair. She pulled out his manhood. His breathing grew rapid. She gently kissed the head of his erect penis while she slowly stroked the shaft.

Her last words before payment was delivered in full were, "So, Roger, who do you want me to be … Mary Smith or Laura Mueller?"

Chapter 7

Five months earlier

After the stillborn death of Charlotte, Meg's identical twin, Ann's visits with her psychotherapist, Dr. Trevor Moore, occurred weekly for six months. Monthly visits followed for another year. After that, she saw him as needed.

The need continued.

"I've reached out to my identical twin," she announced, opening the session. "Like me, she might feel a special bond between us and want to connect."

"And if she does, what do you hope to learn?" Moore asked.

"Do we feel the same way about things? Do the same things? Cry reading love stories? Feel a real kinship with our adoptive family? Trust in the goodness of others? Long to know more about our birth parents and ancestry? Hope to find the same kind of happiness in life? Sounds deep, I know."

"There's a natural curiosity to know such things," he interjected.

"And they are just some of the questions I hope to have answered."

Moore nodded. "Have you thought about coping mechanisms, if your sister wants to maintain her privacy?"

Ann shifted uneasily in her chair. "I'll assume she has a very good reason for not wanting to establish a relationship," she lied.

What she wanted to tell him was that her stomach churned and head throbbed whenever she thought how she'd react if her sister rejected her. She could easily go off the deep end … again. Fall into another black hole of despair and self-pity. More frequent therapy visits. A higher dose of her antidepressant. A pill at night for sleep.

She decided to hold back and avoid appearing too fragile. "I will accept her decision," she added. Another lie. How do you accept being rejected by the person who shared the same egg in the same womb as you … your identical other self?

"If she's anything like you, Ann," Moore offered, now speaking as her friend of the past seven-and-a-half years, "your sister will jump at the opportunity of getting to know you." Changing the subject, he asked, "Have you and Ben decided to go forward with the adoption?"

"Yes. We're excited about Meg having a brother or sister. And, if we end up with a boy, Ben will have the son he's always wanted. He says it doesn't matter. But I know differently. It's natural for a father to want a son."

"Regardless, the child you adopt, boy or girl, could not have chosen better parents."

When the session ended, Ann left Moore's office feeling ambivalent about the future.

~

"I talked to Meg," Ann said, lying back in bed with a half-read hardback novel opened and resting on her chest. She hadn't turned a page in five minutes. "She's excited about having a sister or a brother, or both. She's just as happy if they're infants, so she can be a second mommy, as she is if they're older, so she can be a best friend."

"What did you tell her about the timeline?" Ben asked.

"That it could take a year."

"Does she know we requested twins?"

"No, I didn't want to get her hopes up."

"How often are twins available?"

"Infrequently. And rarely are identical twins available. When I told the placement specialist at the agency that I was separated at birth from my sister, she told me she'd never heard of separating twins. 'Just isn't done,' she said."

"What reasons did she give other than the obvious one that it's inherently stupid to separate them?"

"Public and private adoption agencies both believe it's in the best interest of twins to grow up in the same family. The birth mothers usually insist on it. Twins often share the same physical conditions and have the same health issues ... more so, if the twins are identical."

"Any reason given why your birth mother permitted it?"

"No. It's all confidential. The placement specialist said the people involved in the adoption must have felt it was in our best interests to be separated."

Ben put aside the financial report he was reading and looked over at her. "I look forward to adopting a son, or another daughter, or both. You know that. But I want you to be sure now is the right time. We can wait a little longer, or a lot longer, if you feel you may not be ready."

"No. I think I'm ready. I've come a long way in discovering how I feel about myself, our lives together with Meg ... and enlarging our family. I was so obsessed about Charlotte's death, I forgot how to live my life to the fullest. I needed to blame someone, anyone, everyone, for what happened to her."

"No one is to blame, Ann. Things happen in life we have no control over. What were the chances my dad would fly into a flock of geese landing his plane two years ago? Fate? God's will? Who really knows why things like that happen?"

"You know, when I delivered, I held back on the normal dosage of drugs because I wanted to experience firsthand the birth of our baby girls. I could hear snippets of the conversation between you and my doctor. I heard him tell you there were complications that threatened my life if I delivered a second baby after Meg was born."

"I didn't think you could hear what he was saying. I was so worried about you that even the sound of Meg's beautiful cries couldn't suppress my fear of losing you."

"I know now that you, more than me, were dealt a very bad hand. You had to make the decision between saving me or maybe saving Charlotte."

"It was the very best and very worst day in my life."

"I heard the doctor warn you my blood pressure was so low that if I required resuscitation, I probably wouldn't make it."

"The pressure on me was overwhelming. It was like I was on a cliff and Charlotte was a child, and you and Charlotte fell off, each holding on to the edge for dear life. I had a split second to reach for only one of you. My mind told me to save Charlotte, who had her whole life ahead of *her*. My heart told me to save the only woman I could ever love in the life I had ahead of *me*."

"Afterwards, I blamed you for saving my life. But it was you who gave me the opportunity to experience the love a mother feels for a child. Because of what you did for me, I will see Meg grow up, get married, and someday be a mother."

"When I heard Meg's cries, all that I could think about was her growing up without you … motherless. I thought about how all of our hopes and dreams would die with you in the delivery room. It was an out-of-body experience for me. I stood there frozen by fear … and heard someone say, 'Save, Ann. My God, save my wife.'"

Ann grew somber. "Afterwards, when I developed the infection and required the hysterectomy, I not only felt responsible for losing Charlotte but also worthless as a wife. I wouldn't be able to give you a son someday."

"Trevor helped you get through some difficult days."

"I know. He made me realize it wasn't anyone's fault and that I had a lifetime of happiness ahead of me with you and Meg. But it was you, my dear sweet husband, who reminded me how much happiness I brought my parents, and that our adopting a child would do the same for us."

"And meeting your sister is something I know you're looking forward to."

"It's important to me, Ben ... more than you can know. Meg will never know what it's like to be a sister to Charlotte because she was taken from her ... God's will, I suppose. But now I've been given this opportunity to know my sister. It will make me a more complete person to have a connection to her. Knowing more about her will help me know more about myself."

"How long has it been since you sent your letter?"

Ann hesitated before responding, allowing a flash of anxiety to pass. "A month," she said. "I dated the letter on my birthday and posted it the next day. I was hoping to hear from her by now."

"I believe she'll want to meet you," he said. "And when she does, she'll embrace you as a sister."

Ben closed Ann's book, put it on the nightstand, and turned off the light. He put his arm around her and gently pulled her close, her head nestled under his chin.

"Ben," she whispered as her eyes closed.

"What, dear?"

"I hope ... and pray ... you're right."

~

Ann dropped Meg off at school and went directly to Christ Cathedral Episcopal Church. She'd followed the mid-week routine since her pastor had counseled her that Charlotte's death was "God's will," and that praying would bring comfort. The church was empty as usual, except for two elderly women in a pew three aisles from the altar; prayer beads dangled from their hands. Ann lit a candle and sat in the first pew, her customary spot. She pulled out her prayer beads and a hanky, looked up at a statue of Mary holding baby Jesus, and prayed for half an hour.

When she returned home, she called her mother and asked her to pick up Meg from school and the family's pet from the groomer, and to stay for dinner. She hung up just as the doorbell rang twice, the postman's signal that mail had been delivered. Lucinda had the day off, so Ann collected it from the mailbox and, following

63

her routine, poured herself a cup of tea and went to her office. She leafed through the letters delivered that day, stopping when she saw it. Her heart began to race. She felt the envelope. Whatever was inside was thin, nothing like the bulky materials she'd sent the Maryland Department of Human Services to be forwarded to her sister. Using a letter opener, she very carefully cut a clean seam at the top of the envelope and pulled out the letter. It was from Harriet Cummings. She read it, twice, then put the letter on her desk and went to the kitchen where she kept her antidepressant medication.

The label read, "One tablet at bedtime as needed," and warned, "Do not exceed the recommended dosage." Eight tablets remained. She swallowed them all with a glass of water, walked upstairs to the bedroom, and sat on the edge of the bed, staring at the wall.

Ten minutes later, she became drowsy, and a sense of dread suddenly overwhelmed her. She picked up the phone and speed dialed Trevor Moore. No answer. She slurred a message on his voicemail. "Trevor, I need to see you. I hurt real bad inside." The phone became too heavy to hold. It dropped from her hand. She slumped back on the bed and, for Ann Livingston, day became night.

Chapter 8

"So, Eugene, how have you been coping this past week?" Moore asked. He opened the therapy session the same way he had the previous two. The client, a balding, overweight, middle-aged man, was recovering from major depression following the loss of his twenty-year job as a plant manager. It didn't help that his wife skipped out on him after a twenty-five-year marriage. She left him for his boss. It was a double whammy.

"Not too good, Dr. Moore. I thought Donna was happy to be married to me. I thought Phil, my boss, was happy with the way I was running the plant. Hell, I thought I was happy."

Moore had to admit that Eugene's wife was a piece of work. After seducing his boss at the company Christmas party, she'd drained their joint accounts of all available cash and filed for divorce. The property settlement gave Donna the seed money to fund a new and exciting life. Eugene got the ten-year-old pickup truck with a transmission as bad as his back. His new start in life was to deliberately drive it into a concrete wall at sixty miles an hour. The physical injuries eventually healed. The mental and emotional ones didn't. He'd be in therapy for a while.

When his patient left, Moore accessed his voicemail and heard Ann's message. His return call went to voicemail. He immediately phoned Ben Livingston, but his secretary told him Ben was out of town on business. Fearing the worst, Moore ran to his car and raced over to five Owl's Nest Lane, but his doorbell ringing, banging, and yelling received no response. He bolted to the back of the house, broke a pantry window with his fist to unlock it, and stumbled his way in, calling out to Ann as he darted from room to room. A deathlike silence covered the airspace like a wool blanket. Only the echo of his shouts reverberated in the hallway.

If she's home, why isn't she answering me? If she's asleep, surely my yelling would wake her up.

Then he saw it.

In the kitchen.

The uncapped, empty container of Ann's antidepressant medication.

His heart beat hard and fast. He felt hot and sweaty. A two-steps-at-a-time sprint up the staircase to the second floor led him to the bedroom where Ann lay motionless on the bedspread.

"Ann! Ann! What have you done?" he screamed while shaking a body as listless as a rag doll. Her breathing was indiscernible. She barely had a pulse. He picked up the phone from the floor, hurriedly dialed 911, and pleaded for an ambulance. Then he stared into a face as lifeless as the dearly departed at a viewing, and held unresponsive hands that were cool and dry. And he prayed that he was not too late.

~

Ann received resuscitative drugs through an IV in the ambulance and at the hospital. Moore stayed with her until Ann's mother arrived. The report he gave the paramedics was an accidental overdose. Ann was fully revived within an hour, but sedated. Ben was on the first flight out of Galveston, Texas and in the hospital by eight that evening. When he arrived, Martha was reading in a chair and Ann was sleeping.

"How is she, Martha?"

"Stable. Trevor said she called him quite upset. He went right to her. Thank God he did. Ben, she took too many of her antidepressants."

"Do you know why?"

"I haven't had a chance to talk to her. She's been sedated."

66

They held their conversation in hushed tones but loud enough to awaken Ann. She stared at the ceiling and then turned her head in the direction of the voices. "Ben?" she said softly.

He immediately went to her, sat on the edge of the bed, and held her in his arms. The only woman he'd ever loved cried on his shoulder.

"She's dead, Ben," she said between sobs. "My sister's dead. When I read the letter from the adoption agency, all that I could see in my mind was Charlotte's face in the photo of Meg on my desk. All that I could think about was how much I wanted to look into the face of my twin and see someone who was as happy to see me as I was happy to see her. I felt like a part of me died, just like I felt when I learned that Charlotte died the day Meg was born."

She stuttered her words through choppy breaths. "I ... I really didn't want to die. I love you and Meg too much to ever let you go. I just wanted to go to sleep and not think or dream." She paused to catch her breath and pulled away from Ben so she could look into his eyes. "Ben, am I mentally ill? I don't want you or Meg to suffer because of me, because of my mood swings and the dark thoughts I sometimes have about myself." She burrowed her face into Ben's shoulder, allowing his suit jacket to absorb her tears.

He whispered softly in her ear. "My dear, sweet Ann. I'm here for you. Mom and Meg, too. We'll always be here for you."

His tenderness was like a salve on an open sore. Her eyes fluttered shut. She went limp in his arms. He laid her back, carefully resting her head on the pillow, and kissed her forehead. For the next hour, he remained next to her on the edge of the bed, holding her hand.

A month passed before Ann resumed all of her usual activities. Her therapy sessions with Moore helped her come to terms with the death of her sister. She immersed herself in her work of organizing fundraisers for the Livingston foundations and arranging field trips at Meg's school. She and Meg were inseparable, like sisters and best friends. They shopped, sketched, played duets on the piano,

67

and read together at night. She resumed playing tennis, mostly with Fernando Salmos, who'd coached her when she'd played professionally. Ann and Ben were once again intimate, lovemaking that was restrained, respectful, and seemingly enough to satisfy them physically and emotionally.

She also resumed her nightly talks with Ben about adopting a sister or brother for Meg. "There's way too much love in our home and hearts not to share it with others," she told him.

By early December, Ann and Ben were looking forward to the end-of-year holidays and Meg's eighth birthday. The future looked good for the Livingston family.

Or so they thought.

Chapter 9

Westbrook waited patiently in her white Mercedes Benz SUV parked up the road from the Livingston home. She'd arrived at seven in the morning, wanting to see if Ann drove her daughter to school. The late-model, high-end rental was a necessary upgrade if she was going to shadow Ann Livingston. At precisely twenty-four minutes after seven, a blue Lexus LX 570 SUV pulled out of the driveway, turned right, and proceeded down Owl's Nest Lane.

"It's show time," Westbrook said to herself. "There's no way Ann's daughter is not in that mommy car." Maintaining sufficient distance from it so as not to be conspicuous, she followed the vehicle, which entered the expressway and crossed the bridge over the Mississippi River into New Orleans. At ten minutes to eight, the Lexus pulled into the circular driveway of St. Alban's Academy. Westbrook parked across the street near the corner, where she had a good view of the front of the school.

As each vehicle in line pulled up to the entrance, passenger doors opened, children got out, and a nicely dressed school representative with a glued-on smile greeted them warmly. St. Alban's was a private school for wealthy kids. Fenced and gated, the oversized towers at each of the four corners of the rectangular building gave it the appearance of a fortress.

So far, the drivers in the vehicles in front of the Lexus had remained in them when the children got out. "Come on, Sis, don't disappoint me," Westbrook muttered. "Get out of the car. Bring her the Cinderella lunchbox. Give her a hug and kiss." Sure enough, as though on cue, a woman who looked like her double got out of the Lexus. The child who got out the other side wore a school uniform with a book bag draped over one shoulder. Her thick, wavy locks were identical in length, color, and style to her mother's. The woman straightened the girl's collar, gave her a kiss, and didn't drive away until her daughter had hurtled up the stone steps and skipped into the school.

Veronica Westbrook's on-the-job training to become Ann Livingston had begun.

~

The dilapidated clapboard cottage with the peeling paint and grassless front yard looked perfect. Westbrook had found the dump online. Located in a mostly neglected rural area outside New Orleans, the place gave her good vibes as soon as she met the guy who took her money.

"So, missy, I can give it to you for eight hundred a month, cash only ... upfront," he said.

"I want to stay for three months," she said. "Do we need to sign a lease?"

"Lease? Hell, no. Don't expect no receipt neither. Just the key. We deal in trust here."

"Security deposit?"

"Nah. No sense to it. It'd take a lot to make the place worse than it already be. Just leave the key on the kitchen table and slam the back door shut when you leave. Deal?"

"Deal."

No lease. No security deposit. No questions. Not even a handshake. The perfect rental for someone who was parading around as Mary Smith and didn't want anyone to be able to trace her to the place that would be her residence and workshop over the next couple of months.

She pulled off her wig and tossed it on an uncomfortable-looking chair, opting to sit on the soiled, lumpy sofa. With her feet propped up on a coffee table that had its best days behind it, she reflected on her first day of tailing Ann Livingston. She figured she'd need two or three weeks of shadowing her to fully understand her daily routine.

Over the next several weeks, Mary Smith did just that, making notes in a nice leather-bound journal she kept in her car. She followed Ann to and from Meg's school, to church, to the grocery store, to the country club and mall, always deliberate and careful in her interaction with Ann. Only once did they meet face to face.

It happened at the fitness center about three-and-a-half weeks into the surveillance. She followed Ann in, bought a day membership, and while she walked at a leisurely pace on a treadmill, she watched Ann do a rigorous cross-training exercise routine. When Ann finished her workout, she left the gym, and Westbrook followed. Ann unexpectedly turned back, and they chest bumped, causing the Gatorade she was holding to spill on Westbrook's white cotton exercise top.

"I'm so terribly sorry," Ann said. "I just wasn't thinking. I've ruined your shirt. Please let me pay for a new one."

"No, it's all right," Westbrook said. "It will come clean in the wash."

Ann squinted into Westbrook's face, making her feel as if she'd been placed under a microscope. "Have we met before?" Ann asked. "I feel like I know you. My name is Ann, Ann Livingston."

"I don't think so. I just moved to New Orleans." Westbrook wanted to slam the brakes on further conversation; otherwise, her sister would be inviting her out for a latte and danish. "Sorry, I've got to run. Doctor's appointment. See you around."

Mary Smith decided to end the surveillance for the day and took off in her car. She couldn't chance another encounter with her sister. Her on-the-job training was over.

She would become Ann Livingston on Friday.

Chapter 10

January 4, 2018

Westbrook found it at Sam's Fish and Tackle Shop at the marina on Thursday. The insulated cooler—six feet long, three feet wide, three feet deep, and lined with a refrigerant—was the perfect size and shape for half a dozen thirty-pound tuna from the Gulf ... or a five-foot-eight, 125-pound woman from Whispering Pines. The chest cooled to a temperature of thirty-five degrees Fahrenheit and was the largest and most expensive cooler at Sam's, and worth every penny of the $275 she paid for it.

Next, she stopped at the hardware store across from the marina and purchased an eight-foot burlap sack, the kind commonly used to cover tall shrubs when major storms off the Gulf struck the area. She also picked up fifty feet of flexible garden hose and some duct tape.

Lastly, she walked into Grissom's Dive Shop. Gris Grissom—a short, lean, fifty-year-old man with uncooperative salt-and-pepper curly hair—was more dark-skinned than any other Caucasian man she'd ever seen.

"Well, pretty lady," he said with a friendly, flirtatious smile. "How can I satisfy your needs today? Are you interested in purchasing gear, scheduling lessons, arranging a dive? Please tell me it's all three and make my week!"

Westbrook always liked men's attention, and because of her striking appearance, she frequently got it. "Just looking for a diving mask to replace the one a shark took off with last summer," she fibbed. "And if you sell me one, you'll be batting .333, which just might get you into the Hall of Fame." She couldn't resist engaging him in playful banter.

She loved role playing, and she had a gift for it. Thanks to her job as a successful high-end hooker, she knew more things about men than most women, and many men. The escort agency had always sent a client profile to familiarize the escort with the client's background, likes, and dislikes. She had taken getting to know her clients seriously, regularly going on the internet to do research on their favorite athletes, movies, books, and pastimes. "Vera," as she had liked to be called, always made good conversation with her clients. It had eased any tenseness on their part, made for better sex afterwards, and turned first-timers into repeat and regular customers.

"Let me see what I can do for you. Who knows? Maybe I'll connect on a good pitch and hit one out of the park," Gris said behind a devilish grin.

She laughed. After trying on a couple of masks, she settled on one that fit her nicely and cost $125. If it fit her, it would fit the person she bought it for. He knocked off twenty-five dollars at the register, probably hoping to get another chance to bat sometime later in the game. She led him on by promising to return with her girlfriend to arrange a dive and what she referred to as "a Grissom threesome."

She left the dive shop with a discounted mask, leaving Gris with a pulsating hard-on.

~

The cabin she'd rented sat back in a wooded area at the end of a one-lane, pot-holed, thinly graveled road. To get to it, one had to pass two equally shabby-looking dwellings, but they were far enough down the road to not interfere with what she'd be doing tomorrow, and the rusty old pick-up truck parked in front of one of them hadn't been moved since she'd arrived. Not another living soul in the area. Her plan was to keep it that way.

73

She parked on an assortment of stones, shells, and broken bottle glass that served as a patio in the back of the cottage. She didn't want some pain-in-the-ass resident to notice her luxury car and come over with a fruit cake to welcome her to their lovely neighborhood.

Westbrook put the inside of the cabin in good order. She dragged the chest to the bedroom and placed the neatly folded burlap sack on top of it. The rock she'd collected in the brush alongside the cabin went into a bag on the dresser, along with a large sponge, a vial of chloroform, and an industrial-grade particulate respirator used to avoid inhaling noxious gases and infectious agents. The hose, diver's mask, and duct tape, she placed on the bedroom floor in a corner.

Each item had an important purpose in what she'd planned for tomorrow.

Chapter 11

January 5, 2018

Westbrook looked in the bathroom mirror on Friday morning, and for the first time, she saw Ann Livingston looking back at her, complete with flowing sunrise-golden hair the same length as Ann's. She went easy on the makeup, just a touch of eyeliner and some lip gloss.

She'd written "To my sister, Ann Livingston" on the front of an envelope in the same handwriting style as Ann's—the more similarities, the better—and had enclosed a letter and several photos of herself, including two that Molly had taken the afternoon of her release from prison. As Ann had done, she'd provided an important detail on the back of each one: photo one, *with my sister, Molly, in Baltimore*; photo two, *another of Molly and me*; photo three, *Vera with her new Mercedes (love that car)*; photo four, *visiting Roger in Charleston, SC (our rich cousin)*. Photos three and four were selfies, the last one taken in front of the now *former* residence of Isabelle Avery.

In the letter, she wrote:

My Dear Ann,

I am your sister, Veronica Westbrook, and the woman you bumped into at the gym. My disguise had a purpose. I'll explain.

I'm in stage four renal failure and on a waiting list for a donated kidney. My doctors tell me that my kidneys are somewhat unique, so it may take longer for a match to be made. At first, I didn't want to respond to your beautiful note to me because you might have felt some obligation to offer me one of your kidneys. I could never allow you to do that. But I couldn't keep from meeting you before my kidney disease might take me from you.

I need to leave today for the University of Miami Medical Center, where I will receive dialysis and have further consultations with specialists. I remain upbeat and optimistic about the future. I pray a lot, too. It helps me get through the difficult times.

If you want to see me, I've drawn a map showing you how to get to the cabin where I'm staying. Don't be too put off by its appearance. An acquaintance of mine has a friend who uses the cabin when he fishes in the bayou. I was just grateful for his generosity in making the place available to me so I could come here and be close to you.

My parents have a lovely home in Towson, Maryland, where I grew up, and I have a nice condo in Baltimore with a view of the harbor. I was married to a Marine officer who died in Kuwait, but we didn't have a chance to have children. I work as a hospital administrator and am on medical leave while my kidney issues are being addressed.

I leave in a couple of hours. If you can come right away, that would be very special for me. I had my sister, pretending to be our mother, write a letter to the adoption agency indicating that I was deceased. She did that for me so you'd end your search to find me. But when I saw you, dear sister, and you seemed so friendly and approachable, my heart told me that we should meet.

If you can't come to me, I'll understand. I've enclosed several photos of me and my sister, Molly, who, like you, was adopted into a wonderful family.

Your sister,

Veronica

~

76

Westbrook parked her car on a side street across from Christ Cathedral Episcopal Church and slouched down in the backseat enough to make it appear empty while still retaining an unobstructed view of Ann's Lexus. She'd get a good look when Ann read the letter.

Ann emerged from the church and was drawn to the envelope tucked under her windshield wiper. To Westbrook, Ann's eyes appeared fixed on what was written on the front of the envelope. When Ann gave a quick one-eighty rotation of the head, Westbrook dropped to the floor of the rear of her vehicle. Peeking over the front-seat headrest, she saw Ann unseal the envelope, read the letter inside, and study the photos one by one with the care of an art critic, while Westbrook's identical pair of eyes watched from a distance. Ann fumbled for the hanky in her purse and, while dabbing at tears, returned all but the map to the envelope. Then she started her car, drove down the street, and made a right turn at the next intersection.

Just as the map indicated.

Westbrook smiled. The most important step of her plan to become Ann had been taken, and there was no going back.

~

Taking a more direct route, Westbrook arrived at the cottage a full ten minutes before her sister. She combed out her hair and slipped into a black dress that had served her well in the past. The garment's shelf life was about to expire. When she next left the cabin, she'd be wearing an entirely new outfit, compliments of Ann Livingston.

A kettle she'd placed on the stove soon whistled, and Westbrook poured the hot water into a ceramic teapot where four teabags waited. She spread pastries out on a platter and hummed a tune under her breath as she waited for her sister's visit.

"Just tea for two and two for tea. Just you for me and me for you ... mm ... mm, mm ... mm mm, mm mm ... nobody near us,

77

to see us or hear us, no friends or relations, or weekend vacations ... mm ... mm mm ... mm mm, mm mm."

Role-playing—a requirement in her profession as a high-end hooker—was second nature to her: the southern belle being seduced by the gun-running Confederate gambler; the trailer-trash waitress getting humped by the redneck biker; the teenage cheerleader losing her virginity to the captain of the football team. She played them and others. Some clients even brought clothes for them to wear to create the right mood. But playing the loving sister and getting all teary-eyed was not her cup of chai. Emotions such as compassion, empathy, and love were foreign to her. She couldn't remember the last time she'd cried, or if she ever had.

But she needed a five-star performance today.

Westbrook parked her Mercedes out front. She didn't want her sister intimidated by the backwater appearance of the place. When she arrived, Ann parked her Lexus next to the rental car. Westbrook waited by the door. When Ann stepped out of her car, Westbrook walked slowly toward her, matching her sister's pace step for step, like two spies in a prisoner exchange meeting halfway.

Ann's tears dropped like an April rain shower. Westbrook resorted to sniffling air into a hanky and dabbing at dry eyes. The prop helped legitimize a powerful moment for Ann, who opened her arms and hugged her identical twin—her mirror image.

"I prayed you would come," Westbrook whispered. "Now come in and have some tea, and we can get to know each other."

They walked into the cabin holding hands. "Sit here, please," Westbrook said, directing Ann to the only chair in the living room with its back to the bedroom. She poured two cups of tea and placed them and the pastries on the table.

"Veronica, do you have a nickname your family and friends call you by. I saw Vera on one of the photos."

Westbrook nodded. "They call me Vera." She used the name professionally and when she was playacting, like at Guy Hamilton's trial. "Please call me Vera."

For an hour, the two exchanged personal information about their families, childhoods, school years, marriages, and their likes and dislikes. They were alike in many ways. Westbrook made sure of it. She dominated the questioning, learning things about Ann that could be useful to her later. What Ann learned about her sister was ninety percent lies and ten percent wishful thinking.

When matters of health were raised, Westbrook probed for more information about Ann's depression. "How have you managed it, if you don't mind me asking?"

"I see a psychotherapist. He monitors my mood swings. Sometimes I go through dark periods. I felt a lot of guilt over Charlotte's death for a long time. But Trevor, my therapist, helped me through that."

She wanted to know more about Trevor. Their paths would likely cross. "Trevor, what's his last name? I bet he's a good-looking Englishman. We can share this personal stuff. We're sisters."

"Dr. Trevor Moore is his name, and yes, he is very good looking. Even if I'm not his type." Ann paused to giggle, a sure sign to Westbrook that her therapist was gay. "But we've become close friends," she continued. "He's like the brother I always wanted." Ann's expression turned serious. "Vera, I have every intention of following you to Florida and being tested to see if one of my kidneys will be of use to you."

Westbrook shook her head. "I can't let you do that for me."

"I'm not only doing it for you, dear sister, I'm also doing it for me. By allowing me to share something I have with you, you're helping me mend something that's been broken inside me for a long time. Please let me into your life," Ann pleaded, "just enough to do this for you ... to do this for us." Ann reached for her sister's hand and gripped it tightly.

Westbrook squeezed back hard.

Their eyes locked. One pair moist, the other bone dry.

"Bless you, Ann," she said, wiping at make-believe tears with her hanky. "With a part of you inside me, it'll be as though the two

79

of us have become one." She pretended to fight off an all-out crying spell. "Oh, my. I need to gather myself. Please excuse me for a few minutes." She made a beeline to the bedroom.

A few minutes later, she came out of her bedroom wearing the particulate mask and holding a sponge in a gloved hand. The smell of chloroform in small quantities is sweet, in large quantities pungent. The sponge had a distinctly pungent smell.

Ann's back was to Westbrook as she approached, but the foul odor caused her to turn. Her face froze in terror as Westbrook, cold-eyed, calm, and determined, came at her with hands outstretched. Catching her completely by surprise, Westbrook quickly smothered her nose and mouth with the sponge. Ann's struggle to remove it proved futile, her sister's hold too tight. Ann's rapid breathing meant her inhalations came quickly. In less than a minute, her body went limp, and she slumped back in her chair.

Westbrook had no more than twenty minutes to get things ready before the anesthetic wore off. She put the sponge back in its plastic bag and took off her mask, the vapors no longer a threat to her. After pulling her Mercedes around back, she secured one end of the garden hose to the tailpipe—she'd already attached the other end to the diving mask. The cooler hummed along at a chilly thirty-five degrees.

Ann's weak pulse meant she was still alive but hovering somewhere between New Orleans and La La Land ... but not for much longer. After laying Ann's body face up on the floor, Westbrook removed her clothes: tan-suede, two-inch heels and stockings; mid-length floral skirt; lavender silk top; bra and panties. Then came the jewelry: Akoya pearl earrings and matching necklace; diamond-studded Rolex; ten-karat diamond engagement ring and wedding band. She laid out everything neatly on the bed, then spent a moment inspecting Ann's remarkably familiar, near perfect body.

Differences were negligible. Ann had more defined calves and biceps—the product of years on the tennis court and in the gym. Westbrook's calisthenics, conversely, took place between sheets, and the men did the push-ups. Ann didn't bikini wax but was neatly groomed. Westbrook had planned for that by growing out her coverage, but a trim later would be necessary in case Ben was the observant type with a good memory for details. Hot-pink polish covered Ann's fingernails and toenails—the color among the nail polishes Westbrook had purchased the week before.

Once she had the diving mask and respirator on Ann, Westbrook went back to the Mercedes and turned on the engine. The smell of gas couldn't be prevented. It oozed from the mask on Ann's face. Her chest heaved as her lungs absorbed the carbon monoxide. Brain cells were dying. When enough did so, she'd go into respiratory arrest, stop breathing, and die.

And so it happened for Ann Livingston that Friday morning at twenty-five minutes after eleven.

Or so it appeared to the new Ann, who felt no pulse.

Westbrook turned off her car and removed the hose from the tailpipe and the mask from Ann's plum-colored face. She rewound the hose and put it in a large trash bag with the mask and respirator, to be disposed of later, then placed Ann's arms by her sides and worked the burlap sack over her head and shoulders, all the way down to her feet. After tightening and tying the drawstring at the bottom, she grabbed hold of Ann's ankles, dragged her to a position parallel to the chest, and manhandled her into it. A green light on the electronic panel read *35F set.*

With the window shades drawn throughout the cabin, the filtered late-morning sunlight made it dusk-like inside. Only the muffled sound of Westbrook's exhausted breathing broke the silence. She knelt beside the chest to lower and lock the lid, but as she did, Ann's body shook violently. Her torso rose up so abruptly that Westbrook fell backwards on the floor. She glared at the upright body in a state of shock. A few seconds later, it slumped back in its original position.

Westbrook wasn't sure if Ann was alive or dead, and she had no interest in finding out. She slammed down the lid, knowing one

81

thing for certain as the lock clicked shut. Ann Livingston would be dead when the chest was next opened.

She was sure of that.

Dead sure.

~

Westbrook stood beside Ann's Lexus behind some dense shrubbery on a grassy knoll on the road to Belle, the heels of Ann's shoes sinking into the soil. She leaned back against the side of the car, and with the smooth side of the rock gripped firmly in both hands, she slammed it into her chest. She cursed loudly. When the initial pangs of rib-bruising pain eased, she took the rock in her right hand, grasped the luggage bar on the roof with her left hand, and smashed the top of her left hand with the rock. Another string of obscenities followed.

Westbrook stumbled her way into the car and drove off. A half mile later, she pressed speed dial on Ann's cell phone. "Good afternoon. St. Alban's Academy. How may I help you?" were the last words she heard before she yelled, "Oh my God," and drove off the side of the road. The vehicle descended the embankment, picked up speed, and crashed into a stately looking oak tree fifty yards from the road. She felt the jolt from the impact behind closed eyes, and the blast from the airbag exploding took her breath away. The engine stalled. Dazed, she went limp in her seat.

When she'd returned to full consciousness, she unbuckled her seatbelt and used the rock to crack the driver's door window. With its jagged edge, she slashed the left side of her scalp at the hairline above the left eye. A line of blood coursed down her cheek, and she smeared some on the window at the location of the crack. After opening the door to toss the rock, she closed it again and reached for her cell phone.

The first words the new Ann Livingston spoke that day were stuttered haltingly, as though spoken by a woman with her dying breath, to a 911 dispatcher. "This is Ann … Ann Livingston. Help me … Please help me."

With the back of her head pressed firmly against the headrest, she allowed her mind to wander, but only for a moment. Then she slammed her head as hard as she could against the doorframe, knocking herself out.

PART TWO

And some that smile have in their hearts,
I fear, millions of mischiefs.
William Shakespeare

Chapter 12

"**A**nn, please rest. Everything will be all right. None of your injuries are serious. You'll be fine in no time."

Westbrook heard someone's voice and wondered whether it belonged to the person holding her right hand. She opened her eyes and turned her head. The person, a woman with a friendly face and pleasant smile, she remembered from a photo Ann had sent her. It was Ann's mother, Martha McMillan.

"If you don't feel like talking right now, that's fine, just go back to sleep," she said. "Ben's on his way. Lucinda picked Meg up at school. I'll go get her later. She can stay with me until you're home and back on your feet."

This was her opening scene. The actress playing Ann Livingston was center stage and prepared to give her opening lines. "I recognize you, but I don't remember who you are," she said haltingly, sniffling into the shoulder sleeve of her hospital gown.

Martha brought her some tissues. "Don't worry. You will in time. You must have suffered a concussion in the car accident. Dan reviewed your CT scan and said it was entirely normal, but he also said that concussions don't typically show up on those tests. Do you remember your name?"

"Yes, I … I am Ann," she replied in an uncertain manner and only after a period of reflection.

"Well, you remember something. That's a good start."

"Not really. It's what you called me," came her cleverly-worded response.

"Oh! My dear, you really don't remember anything."

Martha spent the next half hour summarizing her daughter's life with amusing anecdotes thrown in for good measure. She talked

87

about Ben, Meg, Lucinda, whom Ann affectionately called "Lucy," and Emily and her family. As she was telling her about the family trip to Disney World planned for early February, a Hollywood-handsome man in a business suit entered the room. Tall with thick, black, curly hair, neatly trimmed and brushed, he wore tailored clothes that showed off a lean and muscular physique.

Ben Livingston looked at Westbrook with concern in his piercing blue eyes. He walked immediately to her and kissed her gently on the forehead. "Thank God you're all right. When I received the call from the hospital, I was at a board meeting with Em to discuss the merger." He took off his suit jacket, revealing a fitted shirt clinging to an athletic build. "I left right away, but got hung up in a roadblock for half an hour. Someone found an explosive device in a trash receptacle at Jackson Square. It's been bedlam in the French Quarter. How do you feel?"

Martha spoke for her daughter. "Ben, Ann has amnesia and doesn't remember much right now."

"Ann" knew she had to say something, but was in a state of shock over how good looking her *husband* was. "I know who you are," she uttered meekly, pausing to reflect on what next to say so the dramatic moment could play out. "You're my husband, Ben, and we have a daughter, Margaret." Ann looked over at Martha, dabbed a dry eye socket, and continued. "My mother told me about you and our daughter. What I learned tells me I'm very blessed to be who I am."

Ben sat at the foot of the bed and patted her leg. "I spoke to the ER nurse. She let me read the paramedics' report. You lost control of your car coming from Belle, went down an embankment, and struck a tree. Dan called me on the way over. Bruises and abrasions. Nothing serious. Your CT scan was perfectly normal."

Martha looked at her watch. "I'm off to pick up Meg. Lucinda wants to visit this evening, and Emily texted she'll stop over later, too."

More family members with visitation rights. A mild protest was in order. "I'm tired and would like to rest," Ann said, shaking her head. "I don't think I can handle seeing another person I don't remember."

Ben stepped in. "Yes, you should rest. Martha, tell Lucinda and Em to hold off on visiting. And don't tell Trevor what happened. He and Devon are headed to Vail tomorrow for two weeks. Ann needs her privacy right now. I'll stay with her until they kick me out."

Martha smiled at Ben and Ann, then left.

Ben was easy to manipulate. With the amnesia as a cover, it was a good time to find out how rich they were.

"I wake up in a hospital this afternoon not knowing who I am and find out I have a husband and an eight-year-old daughter I can't remember … and that I've married into a wealthy family." To hide her excitement, she winced in pain as she repositioned herself in bed. "How wealthy are we?"

Ben laughed. "You want net worth or annual income over the past five years?"

"I'm just trying to fill in the blanks," she said timidly, rubbing her temple as though his sarcasm had brought on a headache.

"You really don't remember, do you?"

"If you think I don't need to know, that's okay." She pouted, dropping her eyes to her chest.

"Ann, I'm sorry. But you know everything because I share everything with you. It's just that you don't remember right now. There are assets in a family trust my father created that will pass down to Meg and to Emily's boys. We have a net worth of approximately 125 million dollars. Roughly half of that comes from our personal shares in the company. The trust shares are separate. The rest is in real estate and investments with several brokerage firms. I made it a point of giving you access to the accounts soon after we married. We use several of the accounts to fund the operations of our charitable foundations. You've been an important part of those operations, particularly our fundraising."

89

Ann was directly involved in the operations of the foundations, so Westbrook figured it wouldn't be questioned if she liquidated an asset or two, or transferred funds.

Not wanting to appear overly interested in their wealth, she changed the subject. "Ben, if I could see photos of the people who are important in my life, it might help me remember them."

"We have lots of photo albums. I'll make sure you see the video of your birthday party last summer. Most of the people important to us are in the video. We'll eat popcorn. I'll narrate."

Ann laughed uneasily.

"We'll go gradual on this. For a while, just immediate family, Lucinda, and, of course, Buddy."

That piqued her curiosity. Martha hadn't mentioned Buddy, but it could've been because Ben had arrived before she'd had a chance to bring him up. "Who's Buddy?"

"Buddy is Meg's brother."

"Brother?"

"You picked him out of a litter of puppies at the animal shelter for Meg's birthday present when she turned five. You trained him. He sleeps at the foot of Meg's bed most nights."

Over the next two hours, Ben took up where Martha had left off. He told her one amusing story after another until the pain pill she received from the night-shift nurse after dinner caused her to become sleepy. Ben went to kiss her goodnight—a not-too-intimate kiss on the forehead.

She had other ideas.

She put her one good hand on his face, looked into his dreamy blue eyes, and kissed him hard on the lips. She watched for his reaction. It surprised him, but pleasantly so.

Ben returned the following afternoon to take Ann home. Her blood work was normal. Her vital signs were stable. Her left hand was in a soft cast. All in all, Ann's injuries were minor and expected to be mostly healed in a week, about the same time her doctor assured her that her memory would completely return to normal.

Chapter 13

Ann sat back in Ben's Jaguar, occasionally looking over at him with a worried expression. Finally, she spoke. "I'm scared, Ben. I don't know what I'll encounter when I'm home. How do I interact with Meg? How can I be expected to hold her and kiss her and be the mother who has loved her all her life when she'll feel like a perfect stranger to me?"

"I talked to Meg last night," Ben said. "I told her you hurt yourself in a car accident and may not be the mommy she's known all her life, at least, not for a while. She told me she'd be your nurse and help you get better. I wouldn't worry about her. She's more perceptive than you can now appreciate. She'll understand if you're reserved around her for a while."

He pulled up to the front entrance of the Livingston mansion and helped her out of the car. Martha, Lucinda, and Meg stood at the front door. Meg bolted from the doorway and sprinted to Ann with her arms outstretched, wrapping them around her waist. She looked endearingly into her mother's eyes.

"Mommy, you're home," she said excitedly. "Now I can take care of you. You'll be well soon, I promise."

"Mommy" forced a smile. "My dear Meg. I'm having some difficulty appreciating how sweet and wonderful a daughter I have, but I will in time. Will you promise to give Mommy some time to herself to heal so she can once again be the mother who loves you so much?"

Meg's eyelids drooped. "Yes, Mommy, I promise."

They walked into the Livingston home with Meg holding the hand of a total stranger, a woman about to leave a hard-knock life behind her, about to enter a new world and begin a life any woman would die for, but only a very special kind of woman would ever kill for.

"Mom, Lucy, I hope I won't be too much of a bother to you while I get better," she said, not stopping so she could avoid more awkward displays of affection. Feigning dizziness, she retired to her bedroom with Ben by her side, surveying some of the large and elegantly decorated rooms on their way. She couldn't believe people lived like this—dazzling paintings, sculptures and busts strategically placed to be viewed from the sofas, chairs, and cushioned benches that filled but didn't clutter the rooms and entrance hall. Yet, despite the lavish accoutrements, the home had a warm, lived-in feel about it.

"I feel comfortable being here," she said as they entered the bedroom. "Now, if I can just get some rest."

"I'll make sure you get some privacy and peace and quiet," Ben said. "We'll all stay downstairs. Now go lie down."

Ann had other ideas. As soon as the sound of footsteps descending the staircase grew faint, she snooped around, opening closets and drawers of dressers and nightstands. Barefoot, she left the bedroom to reconnoiter, moving stealthily from room to room on the second floor like a lioness on a hunt. She found Ann's office, where a stack of unopened mail lay by her computer, the perfect place for the new Ann to conduct the business that would make Veronica Westbrook—former convict, con artist, call girl, thief, and recent murderess—an independently wealthy woman.

Meg's room was close by. Warm and comfortable, it had all the amenities you'd expect for a rich kid.

The guest bedrooms received a passing glance on her way to the third floor for a quick tour. There she found additional guest bedrooms and an artist's studio with oversized windows that overlooked the sunrises and sunsets captured by the paintings that hung on the wall. The multiple portraits of Meg and Ben strongly suggested that the gifted painter was Ann.

Yet another of Ann's many talents.

Westbrook's only expression of artistic talent was a note she gave to Billy Sullivan in seventh grade, a sketch of a penis below which she'd written, "After school behind the gym. Ronnie." She'd drawn it so poorly that Billy hadn't known what it was. He'd found out later when he'd met up with her and she'd stroked the thing she'd drawn.

On her way back to her bedroom, the one family member she hadn't yet met greeted her. Buddy sat on his haunches in front of the bedroom door, staring at her. He growled as she drew near.

Not good.

The dog she'd picked out for Meg. The dog she'd trained. The dog who was her daughter's best friend.

The dog who now didn't know who the fuck she was.

Time to use her dog-whispering skills. "Hey, Buddy … it's Mommy. I've missed you so much. Did you miss me?"

Buddy growled again, turned, and took off for the first floor to be with people he knew.

The new Ann remained in the sweatpants and Tulane t-shirt Ben had brought to the hospital for her to wear home. She took two Percocet, twice the prescribed dosage, and nestled under the covers. Sleep came quickly.

~

The new Ann awoke to the stare of an eight-year-old girl sitting on the bed in a blue chiffon dress with a thermometer in her hand. "Daddy said I need to take your temperature to be sure you don't have a fever. Open up."

Ann instinctively opened her mouth, and Meg placed a thermometer under her tongue.

Ben entered the bedroom dressed in gray slacks, a light-blue shirt, a striped tie, and a charcoal blazer, perfect for the family's

Sunday routine of Mass at Christ Cathedral Episcopal Church followed by brunch at Belle. "Honey, I let you sleep alone last night," he said from the doorway. "I bunked with Meg and Buddy. I figured you wouldn't want someone moving about in bed and waking you up."

He couldn't be more wrong. If it were up to her, she'd have wanted him to come to bed naked, with his flag at full mast, and make the bed frame rattle.

"Lucinda's coming over. She'll help you with whatever you need until we get home. We're going to skip brunch out and have breakfast here with you. How do you feel?"

True answer? Impressed by all the attention she was getting.

Before replying, she took the thermometer out of her mouth, looked at it, and gave it back to Meg. "Normal. But I do feel sore all over, particularly my chest. I took a pain pill last night and was out like a light."

"You may have bruised a couple of ribs. It hurts just breathing, I know. I bruised some playing football. Missed a game. Dan's concerned about you developing an infection. He wants your temperature taken three times a day over the next couple of days. I put Meg in charge to be sure you're a compliant patient."

"Don't worry. I wrote it down," Meg said while nodding her head. "Again at two, and just before Mommy goes to bed."

"I put a photo album on the desk in the study. Meg and I made notes on the photos last night to identify who everyone is. We can watch the video of your birthday party this afternoon, if you like. But we'll do things at your pace, okay?"

"Yes, Ben. Let's go slowly, if you don't mind. And thank you, Meg, for being such a good nurse."

As soon as Meg and Ben left the room, Ann got up, showered, and washed her hair, pulling it back into a ponytail when it'd dried. She knew the slacks and blouse she found would fit perfectly. It was too soon for lip gloss or blush. Best her bruises and scabs be on display.

94

Lucinda was baking a quiche and had pancake batter in a bowl when Ann arrived in the kitchen. She opened the conversation. "Good morning, Lucy. Thanks for coming over. But you shouldn't be coming over on weekends. You should be with your family."

"Ana, you know I not mind," Lucinda said. "I stay as long as you need me."

She needed to gain Lucinda's trust. Allay any concerns she might have if Ann acted strangely. "Lucy, I suffered a concussion in my car accident. I'm having trouble remembering things. If I appear different to you, please know it's because of my injuries. I just need some time to myself to get better. While I'm healing, I may need to rely on you to take care of more things for me, at least for a while. Will you do that for me?"

Lucinda was too choked up to speak and instead moved toward her Ana. From the moist, doe-eyed look on the woman's face, the new Ann sensed an embrace coming. Such expressions of affection—unrelated to paid-for sex, anyway—were rare in her life, discouraged by her, and never returned in kind. Yet she found something strangely comforting about the woman's genuine feelings of affection for someone she obviously loved. She accepted the hug.

Ann felt satisfied with her performance on the first day home. When Ben, Martha, and Meg returned home from Sunday service, she felt comfortable integrating herself into the life of a family she didn't know, couldn't understand, and would never care about.

~

Westbrook couldn't believe it. She deserved an Oscar in her lead role as Ann Livingston. The first week couldn't have been scripted any better. As Ann, she played the innocent victim of a terrible accident; everyone else played a supporting role. With Ben at work, Meg at school, and Lucinda on errands, she roamed the house like a cat spraying to mark its territory. She rummaged through her own office as well as Ben's, where she uncovered a gold mine: financial reports, quarterly statements, and stock holdings. The overwhelming wealth was all there in black and white.

Westbrook got Ann's username and passcode from Ben and read her emails. Many were requests for financial help from individuals and organizations. The email exchanges portrayed a woman generous to a fault, who took no credit for helping others out of jams. Westbrook had to admit, the woman was a genuinely giving person who did good things and expected nothing in return.

Sitting there alone in her sister's office put the new Ann in a frame of mind to reflect on whether her life had any substance, any real meaning. Ann's life had been full of substance and meaning. She knew that from the way Ben, Martha, Meg, and Lucinda treated her, the person they believed was Ann. They loved Ann because she was good, kind, and caring. She gave their lives substance and meaning, too.

The new Ann reflected on how different she was from her sister and sensed there must be something in the makeup of people that bonds them together, makes them rally around family members, friends, and even total strangers who need help, just as they did for the person they believed was Ann after her car accident.

Would anyone care if Veronica Westbrook were injured in a car crash? She tried not to think about it. But she knew the truth. No one would care the least bit.

How different things would've been if she'd been taken to the hospital instead of Ann Livingston.

No woman would've been holding my hand and comforting me when I woke up in the hospital. No man would've come to be with me and promise to be by my side while I recovered from my injuries. No one would've reassured me that all would again be good and wonderful in my life. No one would've told me they loved me.

She put down her cup of tea and picked up a photograph encased in a golden frame on Ann's desk—a photo of Meg. A broad, toothy smile consumed the girl's face. A photo undoubtedly taken by Ann to capture how happy Meg had been at that moment in time. She studied the face, a face she recognized because it looked just like she had at Meg's age. But she didn't recognize the smile.

Why didn't I smile like that? My parents were always good to me. They always stood up for me. When I got into trouble, they told me not to worry because we all make mistakes, but we learn from them and move on with our lives.

Memories swirled around in her head, buzzing like hornets in a nest. When she'd been accused of her first crimes, her parents had been there to post bail and write a letter to the judge reassuring him that Veronica was a good person who just needed more family support and perhaps some court-ordered counseling. But she'd felt no emotional connection to them, expressed no gratitude for their concern for her. She'd given back nothing.

Her eyes remained fixed on the pretty little girl in the photograph. Would she grow up to be like Ann, the mother she knew, or like Westbrook, the mother she'd now come to know? Was it all about DNA? Genes? Chromosomes?

Why did Ann turn out to be the person she was, and I turn out to be the person I am?

Both had parents who were good and kind to them. Yet Ann could return their love. Westbrook could not. Sitting there alone in the quiet of her sister's office, she thought for the first time that perhaps she would've liked to have done so.

Her childhood memories were few and barren of sentimentality. Nothing like the abundant photos in the family albums she'd been given to help Ann remember: of birthday parties, family vacations, and holiday celebrations; of bear hugs, handholding, smiles, and kisses. Westbrook's flashbacks were about material things she'd gotten and actions she'd gotten away with: shoplifting sprees, the bike she'd stolen, cheating on exams, spiteful messages on social media, blaming others for bad things she'd done. Reflections about her childhood made her feel strangely empty inside—like she'd somehow missed out on something better. Something *good.*

She sat there paralyzed, unable to turn her head away from the framed photo of Meg, unable to break her trancelike stare into the eyes that were windows into the little girl's heart. She had a flashback of Meg giving her a hug and kiss that first morning when she'd awoken, a stranger in Meg's mother's bed. She'd been unmoved by Meg's acts of affection. Felt nothing. Not then.

But as she looked into the face of the little girl in the photo, she could see and almost feel the love and affection in her eyes, and Veronica Westbrook had something happen to her that had never happened to her before, not once in her life. Not ever.

She cried.

Chapter 14

Thomas Joseph Crowder was the name she was supposed to have. Her daddy picked it out himself. Thomas and Joseph were his brothers' names. The name had to change when she showed up without the necessary hardware. Her momma named her Tamitha. The Joseph stuck. Daddy insisted. The consolation prize for his initial disappointment.

Tamitha morphed into Tammy, about as close as her daddy could get to brother Tommy's name. Tamitha Joseph Crowder soon became Tammy Jo Crowder, and then simply Jo to her daddy, to everyone else in the family, and to many of the folks who lived in Breaux Bridge, population 8,462, in the heart of Cajun country, where she grew up.

Jo Crowder knew early that she wanted to work in law enforcement.

Her father had served twenty-five years with the Louisiana State Police, retiring at the rank of captain, and was twice elected Sheriff of St. Martin Parish. Her uncles were both cops with the Lafayette PD. Her maternal grandfather was a career MP with the U.S. Army, and two of her mother's sisters were married to cops.

"There were more firearms at family reunions than at an NRA convention," she'd told the recruitment officer when she'd applied to the police academy.

An athletic scholarship to a community college had earned her accolades and a degree in criminal justice. She'd finished second in a class of thirty-five cadets at the police academy, one of only five women in the class.

Patrol Officer Jo Crowder wasn't a good cop.

She was a *very* good cop. It came to her naturally.

Her very first arrest was a legendary success. She'd responded to the attempted rape of an eleven-year-old girl in an alley of a neighborhood known for such things and worse. She'd arrived at the scene on foot while the perpetrator was still with the girl, but just in time to save her. The perpetrator had seen the cop and had taken off down the alley. She had gone to the girl, who was crying hysterically, ripped off her badge, and had given it to the girl to hold. "You're all right now," she'd said. "Help is on the way. My badge will protect you until they get here." The young officer's words had comforted the girl, and, with the badge pressed tightly to her chest, she'd stopped crying and calmed down.

When her backup had arrived, the rookie cop had left the girl in order to track down the perpetrator. She'd cornered him in a backyard two blocks away. The stocky, tattooed, bandana-wearing Caucasian male in his late twenties had pulled out his switchblade and mockingly yelled, "I'm coming for you, bitch. I'm going to cut you up good, real good."

The young cop, a martial arts black belt, had charged the punk. Her sliding side kick to his groin was all that was necessary to take him out.

Patrol Officer Jo Crowder had received special recognition and a citation of merit from the department for the arrest, one of several she would receive.

She had advanced rapidly in law enforcement: patrol officer to corporal to sergeant in three years. A master's degree in criminology and advanced study of criminal forensics had opened up more opportunities and a promotion to lieutenant. She'd received her gold shield as a detective in the homicide division by the ripe young age of thirty-one. In her five years with the homicide division, she'd solved eighty percent of her cases, a statistic reserved for the very best detectives in Louisiana law enforcement.

On the home front, Jo had become a surrogate mother and role model for her three younger brothers when her mother had died in a car crash when Jo was sixteen. Two of her brothers were now police officers, the other a prosecutor in the Orleans Parish District Attorney's Office. When their father had passed away from cancer during her time as a rookie cop, she had become the head of a family dedicated to public service and the administration of justice.

Detective Jo Crowder wouldn't have it any other way.

~

Sergeant Sidney Steele leaned on the wall in the police academy gym where the officers worked out and the cadets received their training. His partner was giving the punching bag its usual beating. The five-foot-five, 120-pound woman looked strangely out of place among the dozen male cadets in the gym, who were engaged in hand-to-hand contact training in the ring in the middle of the gym.

Lieutenant Miles Jeffreys, a middle-aged African-American police officer, was the police academy's training officer and weapons instructor. He knew Steele's partner well. They'd previously been partners and, both being black belts, worked out regularly in the gym to spar and practice their martial arts techniques.

Jeffreys had taken two slugs in the chest five years earlier. One had blasted a hole in a lung. He would've taken more if his partner hadn't put a bullet between the eyes of the perpetrator who was shooting at him. He'd lost the lung, but not his nerve, nor his zeal for police work. Offered early retirement at full pay, he'd chosen to stay and work with the recruits at the academy instead.

Jeffreys stood in the ring with two recruits to referee their contest. The larger of the two, a muscular young man with a crew cut, jumped the whistle and kicked the other recruit in the head. It was obvious to everyone that the cadet had martial arts training and equally obvious that he had deceptively used it against someone who had no clue what he was up against.

Jeffreys went to the aid of the dazed cadet and helped him up and off the canvass; the other he told to remain in the ring. "So, you appear to have some training in martial arts, Cadet Ramsey," he said to the recruit.

"Yes, sir. I'm a brown belt," he boasted.

"Your special training is good to have. But if the perpetrator was a woman, would you apprehend her in such an aggressive manner?"

Ramsey couldn't contain his cockiness. "Yes, sir. If I'm confronted in an aggressive manner, I'll take out the assailant, whether it's a man or a woman."

"Well, perhaps you can demonstrate that for all of us here. Lieutenant Crowder, can I borrow you for a minute?" he shouted over to the young woman who'd stopped punching the bag when she'd seen the cheap shot Ramsey had given his fellow cadet.

Crowder joined him in the ring. Jeffreys tossed her the headgear she'd need to wear to engage Ramsey in the contest.

"Sir, I can't be responsible for hurting this woman," Ramsey said. "Do you really want me to take her out?"

"Lieutenant Crowder, perhaps he's right. I know you received training here a while back, but are you able to take on a perpetrator who has martial arts skills like Cadet Ramsey? I mean, how could you defend against such maneuvers?"

"Well, sir," she responded timidly, "I'd like to give it a try."

"Sir, do you want me to go slow or at full speed with my techniques?" Ramsey asked.

"It's all right," he assured the cadet. "I want you to go full speed, as you did with Cadet Larson."

"Okay, sir, but it's her funeral."

The two paired off in the center of the ring with Jeffreys standing beside them. He separated them as he'd done with Ramsey and Larson and put the whistle in his mouth. Ramsey shifted his weight to his left leg, freeing his right foot to kick, a subtle movement not likely to be seen or appreciated by untrained eyes.

Steele watched from the wall, chewing on his coffee stirrer.

His partner stood erect with her arms by her sides, looking defenseless. Although she fixed her gaze on Ramsey's eyes, she had panoramic peripheral vision. She could sense whether an attack was a hand technique or a kick by her opponent's slightest flinch.

Ramsey was ready.

Crowder was more ready.

The musclebound cadet stepped into his backspin, and his right leg whipped around in a 180-degree arc, with his right foot on a trajectory to Crowder's left temple. Simultaneously, Crowder reacted by see-sawing with her shoulder nearly touching the floor, and she delivered a full-extension side kick to Ramsey's groin as his foot passed harmlessly by.

"Ouch!" Steele uttered under his breath while the cadets who surrounded the ring let out a collective groan. Ramsey collapsed hard to the canvass in a fetal position, coughing in pain, spittle dripping from his mouth. He cupped his hands tightly over his private parts.

Jeffreys motioned to the cadet Ramsey had cold cocked. "Cadet Larson, will you kindly assist Cadet Ramsey off the canvass? And please be gentle with him." Larson was all smiles as he helped Ramsey limp from the ring.

The grin on Jeffreys' face was all the affirmation Crowder needed to know she'd done exactly what she was supposed to do.

"Thank you, Lieutenant Crowder. See you Thursday at the gym. Usual time."

Crowder left the ring, grabbed her towel, and walked over to Steele, who said, "Think the jerk was wearing a cup?"

"Doubtful," she replied. "The department doesn't issue protectors that small. So what's up?"

"Cap wants us to investigate a one-car crash that happened on the road to Bella Vista Country Club last Friday." "Cap" referred to Captain Francis O'Malley, thirty-two years on the force and head of the Violent Crime and Homicide Division of the New Orleans Police Department. A stand-up guy in the opinion of most officers, including Crowder and Steele. "A woman drove off the road and head-butted a tree. She has amnesia and doesn't remember anything."

"What's homicide doing investigating a car accident?"

"Two reasons. First, there's the possibility she was run off the road. The cop who investigated the accident couldn't rule it out. Cap wants some forensics on this." Steele paused a moment.

Impatient, Crowder broke the silence. "And the second reason?"

"The woman driving was Ann Livingston."

Captain O'Malley was being careful about the investigation. The Livingstons were important members of the community. Livingston Industries owned and operated two manufacturing plants in Louisiana that employed thousands of workers. The family's charitable work was well known throughout the Gulf Coast states. Ben and Ann Livingston were socialites.

"Let's take a look at the scene. Did you bring the police report?"

"It's in the car with the photos the investigating officer took."

It was Monday, and there'd been no precipitation over the weekend. Skid marks, if there were any, would still be present. Crowder looked at the report and photos on the way over.

She inspected the road surface when they arrived, as well as the two-foot shoulder and the dirt and vegetation in the path the car took before it crashed into the tree.

"Not a mark on the road," she said. "Drivers instinctively grip the steering wheel with both hands and slam on their brakes. The car traveled almost fifty yards after she left the road. No effort by her to stop or turn. The dirt's undisturbed. The foliage is flattened, not ripped out like you'd expect if she braked. She drove right into the tree."

"How fast do you think she was going?"

"At least thirty, which is the minimum speed needed to activate the airbags. The front-end damage shown in the photos is consistent with what you'd see in a head-on collision at thirty, thirty-five miles an hour." Crowder walked back to the car. "Let's take a look at her vehicle."

104

The detectives found the vehicle in the police lot where seized vehicles were impounded. While Steele checked the glove compartment, rear seat, and trunk, Crowder inspected the driver's seat, seatbelt, headrest, and foot pedals. She noticed grass clippings and dirt on the carpet in front of the foot pedals. She sat in the driver's seat, buckled the seatbelt, and gripped the steering wheel, looking at the cracked door window to her left. "Not possible," she said.

Steele's gaze bounced from the front-end damage to Crowder. "What's not possible?"

"No possible way her head cracked that window."

"Why not?"

"The airbag deployed a half second after impact, making movement to the left far enough for her head to strike the window and door highly unlikely and, if her seatbelt was buckled, impossible. Was her seatbelt fastened?"

Steele thumbed through the report. "The report only mentions it was not in use when first responders arrived."

"So why would Ann Livingston not be wearing her seatbelt?"

"Maybe she unbuckled it after she struck the tree," Steele suggested.

"If that's true, the investigating officer is wrong in concluding she was knocked unconscious when her head struck the window."

"I see what you mean. If she's unconscious, she wouldn't have been able to unbuckle her seatbelt and, if it was buckled when she struck the tree, her head wouldn't have hit the window."

"The crack in the driver's side window also makes no sense," Crowder continued. "The force needed to crack the window is so substantial, she'd likely have suffered a serious head injury. She was discharged the day after the crash, according to the report. How serious a head injury could it have been?"

Crowder noticed something else. "Sid, let me have your pencil light." He handed it to her. "See the dark-brown stains on the doorpost?"

Steele moved closer. "Dried blood."

Crowder looked at Steele. "Let's see what's in the evidence locker."

~

The large room was accessed through a locked chain-link door, but only after a police official logged the names of the officers who requested entry.

The evidence locker contained a handbag, cell phone, and a tan-suede, spiked, two-inch heeled shoe—all taken from the vehicle. Crowder picked up the shoe and studied it. "The shoe probably came off when the paramedics removed her from the vehicle. The dirt and grass on the heel, sides, and toe had to be on it before she got in her car. It's hard to believe she'd be traipsing around on grass and dirt in heels."

"So what's your take on this?

"Right now, there are two possibilities. The first is an accident. She's not wearing her seatbelt and is on her cell phone when, distracted by something, she veers off the side of the road. She's startled and doesn't brake. She defies the law of physics and is somehow thrown sideways, striking the window hard enough to crack it. She's got a head as hard as rock and avoids a serious injury. But the forensics make no sense."

"And the second?"

"The second is intentional. She's wearing her belt and purposefully veers to the left and drives off the road. She doesn't brake and makes no effort to reduce her speed or turn to avoid striking the tree. Because she's belted and the airbag deploys, she suffers only minor injuries. She comes to her senses, realizes what's she's done, calls for help, and knocks herself out. The forensics make perfect sense."

"Why would Ann Livingston want to hurt herself?"

"That's what we'll try to find out when we question her."

Chapter 15

On the Tuesday after the collision, a few minutes before noon, Steele drove the four-year-old, unmarked police car with a hundred thousand hard miles under its fan belt through the gates of five Owl's Nest Lane, leaving behind a cloud of exhaust and engine soot. They had scheduled a meeting with Ann Livingston.

Crowder knew she'd win no beauty contest with Ann Livingston, but she was pretty with short, pixie-styled, dark-brown hair and eyes, and a lean, firm figure. In contrast, Steele was six-foot-three, skinny as a rail, with shoulder-length hair pulled back in a ponytail. The style fit her partner's hobby—he played electric guitar and was lead singer in a band with three other cops that performed on weekends at the local bars and clubs.

Steele's good looks rarely left him companionless. He fell in love at an alarming rate. The romances usually lasted only a few months, although the nurse he was currently seeing had been his steady for almost a year.

Crowder's love life, conversely, was in the proverbial shit can. She never dated another cop. Sexual relationships between cops violated departmental policies. She'd been in and out of relationships with a few prosecutors and even a criminal defense lawyer. Her longest relationship had been with him—almost two years. The sex had kept them together. She'd liked the cuffs on him. So had he. They'd broken up over professional disagreements. He wanted to get sex offenders and drug dealers off, or cut a break at sentencing. She wanted to cut off their dicks and balls. Crowder was never interested enough in any man to share a residence with him. The only one currently sharing her bed was Fred, a stray dog of unknown age and breed.

Crowder made no fashion statement by the way she dressed. She owned two dresses she never wore, preferring slacks and pullovers to skirts and blouses. She shopped for clothes at K-Mart and Target. Off duty, she mostly wore department-issued t-shirts and sweats, with N.O.P.D. logos on them.

For her, old habits died hard, if at all. During her childhood, if someone was playing a pick-up game of football or baseball in the park, she'd wanted to be picked to play—not likely if she looked or acted like a girl. And Jo Crowder had always been picked by the boys, not first, but never last, and she'd always played to win.

She played being a detective the same way. It was her life. She lived it day and night. "Lawfully avenge the victims of crime, and you make the world safer for everyone else," her father had told her as a child. "Someone has to slay the dragon to make the kingdom safe. Why not you?"

Crowder knew she was different. It wasn't because she drove a pickup, competed in martial arts, boxed, rock climbed, and hunted buck and bear. And it wasn't because she *thought* she was smarter, more determined, more resourceful, and braver than everyone else.

It was because she *was*.

~

Lucinda led the detectives into the study, where she'd laid out a pot of hot water with a variety of tea bags and a matching pot of coffee with sweeteners and milk. Upstairs, Ann had spent the last ten minutes getting ready. She'd removed all evidence of makeup, pulled her hair back in a ponytail, re-taped her scalp wound, and put on the hand splint she'd stopped using a day after her discharge. Wearing the same sweatpants and Tulane t-shirt she'd worn home from the hospital, she grabbed her container of Percocet and headed to the study to receive her guests.

She limped slightly when she entered and walked guardedly toward the detectives. "Good afternoon, Lieutenant Crowder," she said, using a weary tone.

"Thank you for seeing us, Mrs. Livingston. This is my partner, Sergeant Steele. We hope you're making a good recovery from your injuries."

The splint on one hand and pill container in the other prevented any handshaking. Ann didn't return the detectives' department-issued smiles and immediately set the stage for a short interview. "I hope I can help you. But I'm having difficulty remembering things. I'm told the amnesia is from my head injury. I'm starting to recall a few things, but nothing about how the accident happened. At least, not yet. Please have some coffee or tea."

Steele did the pouring.

Crowder did the questioning. "If you don't remember something I ask you about, it's all right to tell me you don't remember. Do you mind if we record our interview? It helps when we prepare our reports."

The request caught Ann off guard. This was a car accident, not a criminal investigation. She stifled a look of surprise. "No, of course not," she deadpanned with a touch of the southern drawl that was now an integral part of her speech.

Steele pulled out a handheld recorder, turned it on, and placed it on the table. After some preliminary statements and questions, Crowder got right to it. "Do you recall anything you did the day of the car crash?"

"No, nothing. Just waking up in the hospital."

"Well, you must have tried to reconstruct what you did and were going to do that day from talking to your husband or others. You were dressed like you were going to a business meeting."

"Yes, apparently I was on my way to a meeting downtown to discuss plans for a fundraiser we're having this summer."

"What time was the meeting?"

"Twelve thirty. It was supposed to be a lunch meeting."

"The accident happened around twelve-forty. It's about a twenty-minute drive from Bella Vista Country Club to your husband's office. Did you call to say you'd be late for the meeting?"

"I don't remember. I may have figured they'd have lunch, and I'd join them later."

"What took you to the country club? You must have some idea."

"I've been told I'm a tennis player and that my former coach, Fernando Salmos, is the club's tennis pro. I may have wanted to see him to arrange a time for us to play."

"Why not call him and avoid a trip to the country club on a day you had a business meeting?"

"I don't know," she said, feigning a blank stare. "I didn't remember what my coach looked like until my husband pointed him out to me in a photo." She uttered the words defensively to exhibit the frustration of an amnesiac.

"Your husband's not here with you. Did he know we were coming?"

"No. I didn't tell him."

"Why not?"

"Because I knew he'd want to be here, and I didn't want to keep him from his work. He's currently involved in some very important business for the company."

"Medications. Did you take any on the day of the accident?"

"I did see a prescription bottle of a medication prescribed for bedtime. I don't remember if I took it the night before my accident. I know I take vitamin supplements and fish oil because my husband told me I do."

"There was grass and dirt on the carpet in front of the gas and brake pedals, and on a shoe that was found in your car. Any idea how it got there?"

The grassy knoll.

"No," she replied, straight-faced.

"Do you use your cell phone while driving your vehicle?"

110

"I know you shouldn't use it while driving, but I'm sure there have been times I have. Perhaps that's why I lost control of my car," she hinted.

Crowder was winding down the interview. "Mrs. Livingston, do you normally fasten your seatbelt? Yours was unbuckled when the first responders showed up."

"I know how important it is. I guess I could have unbuckled it to reach for something in the car."

It was time for her to take her narcotic pain medication. She struggled a bit to open the pill container and took two tablets—twice the recommended dosage—each with a separate swallow of water. The detectives shot glances at the container when she put it on the table with the label facing them.

"Well, they're all the questions I have for you," Crowder said. "Do you have anything, Sergeant Steele?"

"Just one thing, Mrs. Livingston." He pulled out a medical authorization form. "If you sign an authorization, we can access your hospital records. There might be information you gave the paramedics and ER staff that you can't remember now. It might help us figure out what happened."

Another surprise.

Probably looking for my knee-jerk reaction.

What they got was a dispassionate response. "I'm sure it will be all right, but my husband would want me to discuss the matter with him first. Just leave the authorization with me."

"Do you have any questions for us?" Crowder asked.

"Do you have cards? If I remember something, I'll call you."

They pulled out their cards and placed them in her outstretched good hand. She glanced at them and saw that the detectives were with the homicide division.

"Oh, my! I guess I do have a question. Why, Detective Crowder, are two homicide detectives investigating my car accident?"

"Ma'am, the crash was unwitnessed. You don't remember what happened. The police officer who did the initial investigation

111

couldn't rule out another motorist running you off the road and leaving the scene. We're still investigating the possibility. Do you know anyone who would do something like that to you?"

"No," she said, "I don't know anyone who would want to hurt me."

Chapter 16

Ann had two pressing matters. She needed Ben to get the police off her back, and she needed him on his back in bed so she could consummate their marriage. The second matter became her top priority, and was something the new Ann was good at.

Ben was about to find out how good.

The first two nights at home, he slept elsewhere, not wanting to disturb her while she was healing. The third night, he began closing the distance between them. He quietly crawled into the opposite side of the bed around midnight, rising just as noiselessly to leave it by six. By the fifth night, she was fed up with being treated like a bunkmate at Boy Scout camp. His self-imposed code of honor was about to be broken, and in ways he wouldn't soon forget.

He came to bed as he had the night before—around twelve and maintaining as much distance between them as a king-size bed would allow. After he'd fallen asleep, she slid out of bed, tiptoed into the bathroom, brushed her teeth, and spritzed perfume to give her body the scent that would attract him to all the right places. Back in bed, she cuddled up close. He lay on his side with his back to her. She ran the fingers of her good hand down his back and then reached around his muscular chest and gently rubbed it. Instantly aroused, he shook off his sleepiness and turned to see his wife staring at him.

"Darling, you, you look so …" he stammered, unable to complete the sentence.

"It's all right, I'm your wife. I want to remember you. Please help me remember."

She saw him studying her naked body as if he hadn't seen it before. A good Episcopalian wife is modest in her lovemaking and responds to her husband's urges; she only initiates when childbearing is intended. That's what several clients had told her about their good Episcopalian wives.

Ann didn't have the time or inclination to be a good Episcopalian wife.

She kissed him once and then again—soft, moist kisses. He seemed reticent at first, but when she licked his lips and entered his mouth with her tongue, he responded in kind. Their kissing became passionate, as if each other's tongue were an ice cream cone and they competed for the last lick. Their bodies tingled with each other's slightest touch. Ann remained in control.

She acted.

He reacted.

It was what she was trained to do, what she liked to do, and what defined her as a person.

"Baby, are you sure it's okay?" he stuttered between kisses. "I, I don't want to hurt you. Your injuries … I might …"

She soon had him multitasking: kissing, pulling off his t-shirt, and kicking down his boxers. He acted like an overheated teenager in his high school sweetheart's bed after she'd just said, "Hurry! My parents will be home any minute." Her training, however, meant she could arouse him gradually so they could share equally in the pleasure of their sexcapade.

After gently pinching at his nipples, she reached down to take hold of his manhood for a reading of his barometer. He was rock hard. She immediately released her grip, knowing not to prematurely end their adventure together. Slithering around like a snake, she slowly worked herself down to where she needed to be, and he did likewise. Ann knew she could best maintain control by being on top, which allowed him to satisfy her need to climax, something that came to her early and often.

Reversing her position and kissing him hard on the lips signaled that she needed him to enter her. She knew to raise and lower herself on him slowly at first, and then gradually pick up the pace.

Finally, while riding him full stride, his body tensed up for the final thrust. "Yes, Ben, yes," she moaned as their lovemaking came to a crescendo.

She collapsed into his embrace.

When he softened, she lay back on the bed beside him. She heard him swallow air to normalize his breathing and saw him gaze into the darkness of the ceiling as if waiting for Halley's Comet to appear in a cloudless, star-filled sky.

"I love you. I love you so much," he said softly as if in prayer.

"I know, Ben. I know. I felt like I belonged to you and you belonged to me."

Not wanting to overplay the moment, she moved to her side of the bed and pretended to fall asleep. Ben's satisfaction, she knew, would be short-lived. He'd be back tomorrow night for a sequel. She could pretty much guarantee that, and she had every intention of giving an encore performance. But tonight, the most pressing matter had been taken care of. An important one. The marriage between Ben and the new Ann McMillan Livingston had been consummated. Ben Livingston was precisely where she needed him to be.

Between a rock and a hard-on.

The next morning, he greeted her with a kiss and a cup of coffee while she lounged in bed. She extended the kiss just long enough to signal to him that their lovemaking adventure had been real and that their erotica would continue for another night.

"I wanted you to sleep," he said. "Meg's up and ready to go. I'll drop her off at Belle on the way to the office. Your mother wants to see her tennis match and will be taking her out for lunch afterwards."

She seized the moment to broach the subject of the police wanting to look at her medical records. "Ben, I didn't tell you, but the police came to the house to talk to me about my accident. They were concerned someone might have caused me to crash, you know, like a hit and run."

115

"It's hard to believe someone wouldn't stop and call for help, whether or not it was the person's fault," he said.

"That's how I feel, too. I think the accident was my fault. I must have been distracted by something and lost control of my car. They're making such a big deal about it. They even recorded my statement."

"It's very annoying for them to pester you when you don't remember what happened."

"They asked me to sign an authorization. They want to review my medical records and talk to my doctors. I don't want them prying into my personal life. It scares me to think the police would know more about me and my health issues than I can remember."

He responded as she knew he would. "There's no way you'll be signing any authorizations. Who asked for it? I'll contact him today and tell him to back off."

"Yes, dear. The card's on my dresser. Sergeant somebody or other."

"Done, baby. I'll call you later." Ben took the card off the bureau, kissed her again, and left.

She propped up her pillow, lay back, and sipped her coffee.

She was in control, and her plan was unfolding as expected.

Chapter 17

"I just got off the phone with Ben Livingston," Steele said when he walked over to his partner's desk. "Mrs. Livingston won't be signing the medical authorization. Mr. Livingston wants the investigation concluded as soon as possible."

Crowder looked up from her computer screen, staring over it at nothing in particular. She leaned back in her chair and took a sip of her coffee. "Ann Livingston's hiding something. Let's talk to Fernando Salmos. See if she went to see him last Friday. And one other thing?"

"What's that?"

"Ask Jenny to take a look at her records."

Crowder knew that Steele's girlfriend could get fired for snooping around in a patient's confidential medical records, and Steele and Crowder could be brought up on charges for asking her to do it. But Crowder had to protect Ann Livingston, even if it was from harming herself.

"She has a shift tonight," said Steele. "I'll fill her in on what to look for."

The detectives drove out to Bella Vista Country Club. They stood under a tree near the tennis courts and watched Salmos giving a lesson to an uncoordinated, pale-skinned young woman. From the puzzled look on her face, he might as well have been speaking to her in Greek. She proceeded to hit a bucket of balls all over the court, but rarely over the net and within bounds.

"I give her one or two more lessons before she quits and finds a quilting class," Crowder said.

Steele chuckled. "Wouldn't surprise me if she pokes an eye with a quilting needle."

The meeting with Salmos added no support for Ann Livingston's speculation that she had met with him at the club shortly before the crash. "Ann and I had a regular time to play," Salmos told them. "Every Wednesday after she dropped her daughter off at school. I wasn't even at the club on the day of her accident. I was playing a match in a tournament in Shreveport."

The detectives returned to the district headquarters to do paperwork on other cases.

The next morning—a Saturday—a ping wakened Crowder. A text message from Steele read:

Be over in twenty minutes.
Breakfast is on you.
I have something important to show you.

The usual morning routine followed: zap what remained of day-before coffee; sip it while Fred watered his favorite tree in front of the apartment building; fill the kibble and water bowls; quick shower; brush and gargle; dab of hair gel; dress. All in under fifteen minutes.

A few minutes after she slipped into her workout sweats, she heard the distinctive blare of Bugsy's horn. Steele had bought the vintage '68 VW Beetle five years ago and had nursed it back to health as if it were a sick family member.

They drove to Trixie's Cajun Diner on Harrison Avenue in the Lower Garden District, where cops were regular customers. On the way over, Steele handed his partner six pages of medical records that Jenny had copied after breaching hospital confidentiality rules and reviewing Ann Livingston's medical records: two pages of emergency department records for January 5, 2018, and four pages of records from a July 2017 hospitalization. Crowder made mental notes as she read them. She started with the ER records from the day of the crash.

Under Medical History:

Mother arrived at ED to provide history. Patient is 33 years old, adopted, married, one child whose twin died at birth. Hysterectomy and bilateral oophorectomy in August, 2010. History of depression. Under Physical Examination:

Awake upon arrival. Became agitated during examination. Sedated. Tenderness in the abdomen and left rib cage. Chest/ abdominal x-rays and CT of brain ordered.

Next she looked at the records from the hospital stay six months earlier.

Under Medical History:

Arrived by ambulance. 33-year-old Caucasian female. Unconscious. Vital signs stabilized by EMTs. Patient's friend/therapist provided history. He received a voicemail message from patient. She sounded distraught, so he drove to her house and found her unconscious in bed. Called 911. Found empty bottle of her antidepressants on kitchen counter with the top off. He believed she may have "accidentally" overdosed.

In a psychiatric evaluation the next day, the psychiatrist reported:

Patient, who is adopted, received a letter informing her that her identical twin sister had died. She was overwhelmed by her sister's death and took all of her antidepressant medication. Seven or eight pills. "I only wanted to go to sleep and forget about my sister's death." She called her therapist just before passing out. Patient is suffering from major depression following her suicide attempt. She will need a medication regimen that addresses her depression, anxiety, and sleep issues, as well as psychotherapy and family support.

The detectives sat in a booth. Mimi, a heavyset African-American woman, came right over and poured two black coffees. No creamers. No menus. The order was placed in the usual way—by telling Mimi, "The usual."

"You're right," Steele said after that. "She intentionally drove off the road and into the tree. The amnesia is a cover."

Crowder nodded. "Let's give it another week. We'll make an unannounced visit. If her memory hasn't improved, we'll know better that she's lying to us about not remembering things. Then we'll talk to Cap. See what he wants to do."

"He'll want to do what Ben Livingston wants us to do. Bring the investigation to a quick and simple end."

"I know, but doesn't Ben Livingston have the right to know his wife's accident may not have been an accident and may have been another suicide attempt instead? Otherwise, how can he help her? What if she does a swan dive off the Crescent City Connection into the Big Muddy, and we withheld the information from him? I certainly don't want to live with that."

"Putting it all together like that, Jo, neither do I."

Chapter 18

Ben Livingston looked handsome in his dark-brown, hand-tailored, fitted Corneliani suit and his lime-colored, open-collar Amina Rubinacci shirt. He could have passed as the cover for GQ.

His wife looked even better.

A figure-fitting black mini-dress purchased earlier in the day provocatively showcased her physical attributes. Her hair had been styled at a downtown salon where cosmetics had been applied as though she were attending an awards ceremony in her honor. She glittered in gold and diamonds.

Earlier that evening, while they were dressing for their Saturday night date, Ann had found the perfect opportunity to gain access to the wall safe she'd discovered while snooping around the day before. Looking into the jewelry box on her dresser, she'd said, "Why do I feel like I have other jewelry to wear that might go better with my dress?"

Ben picked up on the comment. "Why don't you get something out of the safe?"

"What safe?"

"Oh, I'm sorry. You don't remember. It's behind the mirror. I'll write down the combination for you later."

He opened the safe while a pair of coral-blue eyes peered over his shoulder like a camera lens. They photographed two piles of documents on the upper shelf and, on the shelf below, a large, leather-covered, gold-leaf embroidered box with the initials *AML* embossed on the lid. On the bottom two shelves sat bundles of one-hundred-dollar bills stacked neatly in rows.

The jewelry Ann wore that evening came from the box in the safe. The money she'd be leaving with in the not-too-distant future would come from the cash on the shelves just below.

She insisted on going to a restaurant where they wouldn't be recognized. Ben chose an upscale one that had recently opened just outside New Orleans. She knew it fit right into his plan for a quiet dinner and no-limits sex afterwards.

Ann, a good Episcopalian wife, had been accustomed to downplaying her good looks and shapely figure, wearing conservative dresses and being moderate with makeup and jewelry. The new Ann was alluring and seductive. A creature of habit, she couldn't resist the urge to dress like the professional woman she was—a five-star call girl. And if she played her cards right, her payday would be her biggest ever. Figuring that Ben had spent most of the day daydreaming about their lovemaking the night before, she aimed for him to feel lust for his wife—something a good Episcopalian husband was supposed to shun.

She tortured him with foreplay: the salacious way she looked at him, the sexy giggle in her voice, the way she stroked his palm when she held out her hand for him to hold, the shoeless foot that found its way between his thighs when he ordered dessert. She heard his sigh of relief when she suggested they forgo dessert and head directly home. Her toes felt him go stiff again when she said they would have dessert in bed.

~

Ben's foot sat heavy on the gas pedal on the way home. He parked the Jaguar at the front entrance and rushed to open her door. They entered the house and were soon in the bedroom, walking softly so as not to cause Buddy to bark and wake Meg, or Martha, who was spending the night.

Ben pulled Ann into the bedroom, closed the door, and, holding her in his arms, kissed her passionately, the kind of wet, sloppy kisses expected of teenagers in the backseat of a car in the parking lot of the mall after a movie. Then he shed his clothes as though they were on fire—jacket, tie, shirt—kicked off his shoes, unbuckled his belt, and stepped out of his trousers and boxers.

While he performed his Chippendale routine, Ann did her version of a strip tease.

She stepped away from him and, while he stood there at full mast in his birthday suit, she unzipped the back of her dress and let it slip to the floor.

His eyes widened, surprised at her skimpy undergarments, and took a moment to study her near-perfect body. She hadn't worn stockings, and her thong was barely visible. She undid her bra and in a matter of seconds stood before him practically naked.

Lifting her into his arms, he carried her to the bed, where he hoped that all would be good again. He thought that maybe, just maybe, his wife's unfortunate accident was God's way of righting a ship that had seemed destined to strike a shoal during a storm of depression, and then break up and sink to the bottom of the sea. He didn't hold back. Nor did she. He gave everything he had, but when his tank was empty, he felt as if hers was still full.

He awoke early the next morning. Ann, still naked, slept beside him under the sheet. He lay there aroused and incredulous. How did she know the things she knew? She made his desire to climax ebb and flow like the ocean between high and low tides. When the time had come for his gratification to be fully achieved, it was like he'd already climaxed several times over.

On his way to his office, he reflected on the events of the past two nights.

It was almost as if she had become another woman.

Chapter 19

"**D**o you remember anything at all about that wonderful woman we know to be Ann Livingston?" Trevor Moore asked when he visited Ann at her home on Sunday more than two weeks after the car crash.

"I wish I could, but I don't," Ann replied. "When I look at you, I sense your face is familiar to me. It's just that I don't know who you are or why you're important in my life."

"That's okay," he said behind a friendly smile. "It's only a matter of time before everything comes back to you." He paused momentarily, then leaned forward in his chair. The expression on his face turned serious. "Ann, the cause of your amnesia is obscure to me."

"What do you mean?"

"Amnesia is a rare condition, doesn't last long, and is almost never complete. A mild concussion of the type you suffered would not have injured the hippocampus, which lies deep inside the medial temporal lobe of the brain. Or the cerebral cortex, which is well protected from minor head trauma."

"Are you saying I'm imagining my memory loss?" she said, as though hurt that a friend would suggest such a thing.

"No. No. What I mean is that amnesia isn't always explained by a physical injury. Sometimes there are psychological and emotional causes of amnesia. To the patient, the memory loss is just as real."

"So you think it's all in my head. That I don't want to remember Ben, my mother ... Meg." She pulled out a hanky, the same prop used in other scenes where the script called for her to tear up.

"Will you give some thought to seeing a neurologist? I know two very capable ones, specialists in head trauma and amnesia.

125

Until you do, we can explore other potential explanations for your memory loss."

"Yes, Trevor," she said between sniffles, "I will consider your suggestion. I want to remember, I really do."

"Then we have a plan. I'll see you in the office as soon as you feel up to it. Agreed?"

Ann looked up from her hanky. "Agreed," she replied, standing to signal an end to his visit.

When Trevor left, she went immediately to Ben's office to study the incorporating documents for the Second Chance Foundation. Ben and Ann Livingston had set up the foundation five years earlier to provide services to drug addicts. It operated methadone clinics and drug rehab facilities at various locations in New Orleans, Shreveport, Baton Rouge, and Lake Charles. The initial funding of five million dollars had come from the Livingstons' personal investment account with Smith Reid Investment Advisors, which had in excess of thirty-five million dollars of their personal wealth under management.

An hour later, she found back-and-forth letters in Ann's correspondence file between Ann and a public-interest group requesting financial assistance. The organization's mission statement was to provide financial aid for American families who'd adopted special needs children from Eastern European countries. The program was the perfect blueprint for Ann's new foundation. All she needed was a lawyer to form the nonprofit and a request for the bank to transfer five million dollars to fund it.

~

"Ann Livingston's car crash was no accident," Crowder announced to Captain O'Malley. "She was trying to hurt, even kill herself. The physical evidence doesn't fit an accident. When she didn't die in the crash, she had no choice but to make it look like an accident. The amnesia's a cover for not having to explain what happened."

"What makes you believe the crash wasn't accidental?" O'Malley asked, his tone suggesting to Crowder that he was annoyed the matter couldn't be resolved without controversy.

Crowder set her coffee down and briefed O'Malley on how nothing on the forensic side made sense: no effort to stop, the cracked side window, the blood on the doorpost, the dubious amnesia, and the refusal to sign a medical authorization.

Crowder had anticipated that O'Malley would have a hard time buying into a suicide attempt. He asked, "Why would a beautiful woman, married to one of the richest men in the country, who lives the life of a princess, want to kill herself? It makes no sense."

She couldn't share what she knew about Ann's medical history of depression and a prior suicide attempt because the information was obtained illegally. A different approach was needed. "Sir, I believe we should tell Ben Livingston our investigation doesn't support an accident and let him decide what to do with the information. We can ask him whether there's anything in his wife's past that might indicate some tendency to want to hurt herself in the crash."

"Imply his wife's a mental case," O'Malley said sarcastically. "Are you serious?"

"At the very least, we can suggest he look into whether his wife had a reason to make the crash look like an accident. Then, if Ann Livingston were to jump off a roof or throw herself in front of a train, the department will be protected."

"I see where you're going with this. You're right. We need to protect the department. If we don't bring it up, it could come back to bite us on the ass if she does have a death wish." He agreed with Crowder as to what they should do. But as his detectives turned to leave, he warned, "Don't piss him off. The last thing we need is Ben Livingston thinking we think his wife's crazy."

Chapter 20

Ben Livingston's office was on the top floor of a quaint, historical, three-story brownstone in the central business district of New Orleans. The company had purchased the building, once the largest bank in Louisiana, in a fire sale when the bank had gone bust during the Great Depression.

To describe his workplace as lavish would understate its appeal. It had an adjoining exercise room and full bath; chandeliers and oriental carpets; a leather sofa and upholstered chairs arranged around ornate, hand-carved tables; walls adorned with an eclectic collection of original artwork by Jackson Pollock, Charles Russell, and Andrew Wyeth; a large mahogany desk and matching judge's chair in the center of the room; a framed, fifty-five-inch, full-HD, 3D plasma TV, and a built-in bar stocked with bottles of top-shelf scotch, bourbon, and brandy. Just the kind of office expected for the head of a company with a rich tradition of being well run and profitable.

"Mr. Livingston, detectives Crowder and Steele have arrived for their ten o'clock appointment," Elizabeth Sanders said when she phoned him from her desk. Livingston's personal secretary, a spry, spunky seventy-year-old, had started out working for his grandfather at seventeen. He'd inherited her when he'd become the company's CEO, as had his father before him.

"Yes, Elizabeth, I'll see them now."

The detectives followed Elizabeth into Livingston's office, where she showed them to chairs around a marble-top coffee table—the round, politically correct kind intended to equalize the status of all who sat around it. Livingston was already seated, but stood to shake the detectives' hands.

Crowder got right down to business. "Mr. Livingston, I believe you're a man who likes it when someone gets to the point of a visit."

"Of course. I'd expect nothing less from you."

"The physical facts don't fit an accident. Since your wife can't remember what happened, we had to rely on the physical evidence and forensics."

A surprised, quizzical look appeared on Livingston's face. "What do you mean, the facts don't fit an accident?"

Crowder leaned forward in her chair to close the distance between them and then outlined the forensic evidence as compassionately as she could. She then went on to explain the incongruity between Ann's situation and the limited, temporary memory loss of most amnesia sufferers. She paused to allow him time to digest the facts.

Livingston's back straightened. His grip on the arms of his chair tightened. "Are you suggesting my wife intentionally drove off the road and into that tree? Why would she do such a thing?"

Crowder paused a moment, allowing his question to linger a while. "That's something we hoped you might be able to tell us."

"What you're suggesting is that Ann intended to hurt herself. Then made it look like an accident."

The silent treatment continued. Crowder hoped he was reflecting on Ann's history of depression, her past suicide attempt, and her unlikely amnesia.

"If it was impossible for Ann's head to have cracked the window, how did it get cracked?" he demanded to know.

Crowder kept her finger on the mute button.

Finally, he spoke—haltingly, like he was coming up with his answer while still reflecting on the question. "She broke it afterwards to make it look like her head had struck the window ... to explain her amnesia ... and not have to talk about what really happened."

Crowder offered him hard evidence for the conclusion he'd reached. "There was blood not only where the window was cracked, but also on the metal doorpost. The blood got there by Ann's head coming in contact with the metal post."

Another puzzled look. "I thought you told me that was impossible because the airbag deployed."

You could have heard a mouse squeak.

Livingston slumped back in his chair, a look of exasperation on his face. He said in a hushed tone, as if alone and whispering to himself, "She struck her head on the doorpost after the crash to knock herself out."

Crowder, sensing his exhaustion, finished up. "We're suggesting no changes to the report of the investigating officer who concluded the crash was an accident. We know you'll do what's in your wife's best interest."

Crowder had done what she'd needed to do.

It was now in Livingston's hands.

~

"I need to be alone for a while," Livingston said to Elizabeth after the detectives left.

He went to the bar and poured himself a bourbon, then sat in the chair behind his desk, thinking. He finished the drink in two quick swallows, then went back to the bar to refill his glass.

He thought some more.

Ben Livingston had a difficult time wrapping his head around what he now believed to be true, about what it all meant. It meant that Ann had wanted to hurt herself in the car crash. The amnesia was her way of rejecting her former self. She didn't believe she was Meg's mother. The woman who made love to him didn't believe she was his wife.

Ann had assumed another personality and an entirely new identity.

Which meant that ...

Ann might be mentally ill.

Chapter 21

"So, Sarah, what are your plans now that you've been given a second chance?" The director of Cumberland County Women's Correctional Facility had asked that question at every exit interview since he'd arrived at the facility ten years ago.

Booth slouched in a chair between the director and the prison chaplain in the director's office. Her words flowed smoothly from a crooked smile. "I want to go back to school and get a college degree in social work, then get a job counseling young women who've gotten into trouble. My mom and stepdad want me to move in with them until I can afford an apartment of my own." She remembered the little speech Westbrook had told her she'd be giving at her exit interview. Why reinvent the wheel? Booth adopted the lies verbatim.

For the director and the chaplain, it was déjà vu, all over again.

An inmate's ex-boyfriend picked up Booth and gave her a ride to her sister's house just outside Richmond, Virginia. The dude figured he'd get laid for the favor. She promised to make it worth his while, and she did, but only after hitting him up for fifty bucks.

The bittersweet reunion with her sister was the third in five years. Whenever Booth needed a safe house, she turned to Carrie, who was married to a plumber and had three sons destined for Vo-Tech schooling and jobs in the trades.

"How long can you stay?" Carrie asked, forcing a smile.

"Just a week," Booth said. "I'll be heading to New Orleans and meeting up with a friend. It's a fresh start for me." They exchanged a quick, weak hug. "I really appreciate you letting me bunk with you guys while I recharge my batteries. How are my favorite rug rats?"

Carrie's boys loved it when Aunt Sal stayed over. She'd sit on the couch with them, eating popcorn and potato chips, playing video games, and watching movies. They'd crawl in bed with her at night to hear stories she made up, scaring them and making them scream. It was like there were four kids living at the house.

"I've got plans," she told her sister. "I think I can turn my life around. It's just that I need a few bucks to get me started. Can you help me?"

"Sure, Sal. When you're ready to leave, Ed and me want to help you out."

Carrie always tied her sister's paydays to the ends of her visits.

Booth had plans, all right. She was moving to New Orleans for a reunion with her best friend from high school. Being a college friend from Tulane would have been a stretch, but she thought she could handle playing a BFF from St. Martin Episcopal School, the high school Ann McMillan had attended. Carrie charged the $199 for a one-way ticket to New Orleans on her only credit card and strained the budget for the $200 cash to help her sister get settled. Booth always promised to pay her sister back, promises as hollow as her chances of turning her life around.

She boarded the Amtrak regional train at eight thirty on Sunday morning for its nine-hundred-mile trek to New Orleans. It took a full day to reach Union Station on Loyola Avenue, arriving Monday just after ten o'clock. She checked in to a cheap motel near the train station at $69 a night, spruced up a bit, and took a cab to five Owl's Nest Lane in Whispering Pines.

She told the driver to wait.

Leaving without some serious cash in her pocket wasn't an option. She had two days before Carrie's money ran out. When it did, she'd be trolling the bars on Bourbon Street, turning tricks.

She'd prepared a letter to Ann Livingston from "your old friend from St. Martin Episcopal (Go Angels!)," who just happened to be returning to New Orleans after living in Baltimore the past fourteen years. She gave her friend an account of her life since she'd moved to Baltimore: "Got my degree in social studies from the University of Maryland (Go Terrapins!) ... was employed as a social worker for the state of Maryland ... my husband, a marine, was killed in action in Iraq ... I lost the baby, a girl we were going to name Veronica ... sadly, my parents recently died in a boating accident ... will be applying for a part-time receptionist job at your husband's company, and a good word from you would be appreciated." The letter ended with an invitation for a lunch downtown "to catch up on what we've been doing and what the future may hold for us."

Lucinda answered the door. "Good morning, may I help you?"

"Yes, I'm here to see Ann Livingston."

"Is she expecting you?"

"No, but she'll want to see me."

"Who do I say is here?"

"Tell her I'm an old friend from high school. We were bunkmates at Cumberland Girl Scout Camp."

She'd read about Ann Livingston's car crash on the internet. There was little risk the woman greeting her would be the real deal.

~

Ann was finishing her letter to her lawyer, Jared Hochstein, when Lucinda knocked on the door to her office and announced the arrival of her visitor. She stopped what she was doing and sat back in her chair. "The bitch must have read my notes," she muttered under her breath. "Keep your cool, Veronica. See what she wants, and give her what she deserves." She turned and said to Lucinda, "Lucy, put her in the study. Don't offer her anything. She won't be here long."

The new Ann strolled into the study casually dressed in clothes from the best shops in New Orleans: fitted, soft denim jeans; a comfortable, canary-yellow, cotton V-neck top with medium-length sleeves; pearl earrings; and the Rolex watch Ben had given Ann for Christmas. What stood out, however, was the engagement ring that

133

sparkled its magnificence in the sunlight that streamed through the windows of the study.

"Ann, don't you look grand," Booth said when Ann entered. "Now I know why you were voted 'Most Likely to Succeed' in our senior year."

Westbrook waited until Lucinda closed the door on her way out. "So, Sal, why don't you get to the point of your visit?"

"I need money. I need a job. I need a place to stay."

"Anything else on your Christmas wish list, little girl?"

"Yes, I want a slice of the pie you're baking. But for now, I'll take ten thousand dollars."

"Yes, of course. The money grows on the trees in the garden. They're between the apple blossom trees and the rubber tree plants. Take as much as you want."

"Very funny, rich girl. With your kind of money, it wouldn't surprise me if you print it on machines in the basement."

"Rich people don't deal in cash, stupid. They deal in plastic or simply say things like 'put it on the account' and 'bill me later.'"

"Rich people always have a lot of cash lying around," Booth countered. "You know, the pocket change that doesn't get reported to the feds. I have a cab waiting. Make it happen, Ronnie. I know you can."

She could easily make it happen. Using the combination Ben had given her, she'd counted the $220,000 in the safe the very next day. She had to give Booth some money. Her plan would collapse around her in a heart palpitation with a single phone call from Booth.

"I'll have to take the money from the cash we keep here at the house for emergencies. I'll drain most of it. There's only about five thousand. If I take it all and Ben finds out, I'll have a hard time explaining things, just as I'll have a hard time explaining who you are if someone comes home and sees you here." She knew Booth was too smart to kill the golden goose. A down payment would keep her happy; a promise of more to come would keep her quiet. "Take four thousand and leave. We can meet later and talk about the future. Agreed?"

"Well, what are you waiting for? Bring me my lunch money, and I am outta here."

Westbrook went to the bedroom, took four thousand dollars from the safe, and stuffed the money into a Louis Vuitton handbag she found in Ann's closet. She returned to the study and gave it to Booth. "The handbag's a gift. Now, where will you be staying if I need to reach you?" she asked, thinking she may want to pay her former cellmate a visit and put an end to their business dealings sooner rather than later.

"Don't know just yet," Booth said. "Give me your cell number and email address. When I get settled, I'll contact you, and we can meet to go over the terms of our partnership agreement."

Westbrook opened the drawer in the study desk to get a pad and pen. A letter opener lay there, and she reached for it without thinking. It had a long metal spear, perfect for opening all kinds of mail, and for penetrating the jugular vein in someone's neck. Reluctantly, she put it back and picked up the pad and pen instead, but the sweet thought lingered. She wrote down the information Booth wanted and gave it to her, signaling the end of their meeting.

When they left the study and entered the foyer, Martha appeared as if out of nowhere. Westbrook had no choice but to introduce Booth. "Mother, you probably don't remember Sarah Booth from my high school class. I didn't, of course. I explained why to Sarah, and she understands. She just returned to New Orleans for a brief visit and thought she'd stop by and see me."

Booth chimed in as though she remembered Martha from the past. "Hello, Mrs. McMillan. I'm so sorry to hear about Ann's accident. I hope to talk to her later when she's feeling better."

Westbrook slipped by Martha and led Booth to the door. When she opened it, Booth discreetly handed her the letter she'd prepared. Westbrook folded it and stuffed it in the waistband of her jeans. After she closed the door, she turned and walked with Martha to the

135

kitchen, where she knew she'd be compelled to chat over a cup of tea.

"I don't remember Sarah Booth," Martha said, sitting at the kitchen table across from Ann.

"Booth is her married name. She mentioned her maiden name, but I can't remember what she told me. When she began talking, I interrupted her to tell her my memory was impaired from my injuries. She apologized for disturbing me and immediately agreed to leave. She gave me her number. I doubt I'll ever call her. There's really no point." She let out a sigh to garner some sympathy from Martha, who moved on to another subject. One that related to a very special event in Meg's life.

"You know how much Meg is looking forward to the trip to Disney World in February. I hope you feel up to going. But if you don't, we can always reschedule. Meg will understand."

"I would never disappoint Meg. I'll stay home if I'm not well." She couldn't milk her injuries much longer. One thing was certain. The trip to the Magic Kingdom could not be postponed; it was the linchpin of her exit strategy.

On her way out of the house after lunch, Martha remarked to Ann, "You know, your friend has good taste. She has the same Louis Vuitton handbag I gave you for your birthday last summer. And to think the salesperson told me it was one of a kind."

Ann needed the afternoon to take care of important business. Her letter to Jared Hochstein followed an earlier call to him in which she'd outlined her project and instructed him to form the nonprofit corporation that would run her foundation. She'd told him she wanted to "branch out" on her own and not always be tied to her husband's philanthropy. "He has his special projects, and I have mine," she'd told him. She knew Hochstein was salivating over getting legal business from a Livingston. He promised to personally supervise the effort and have the documents prepared and filed within a week. They'd scheduled a conference at his office to sign the paperwork for eleven o'clock, Friday morning.

~

After dinner, Ben and Ann retreated to the study. He poured a glass of chardonnay for her and a brandy for himself. A few sips into their drinks, she became sexually aroused. But she sensed some reserve on Ben's part, as if he needed to get something off his chest.

"Do you still not remember anything about yourself?" he asked. "About the person you were? About the people who are your family … me, Meg, your mother?"

"Just an occasional flashback. I may see one of you in a memory, but I don't see me interacting with any of you."

"Do you ever feel you might be suppressing things that happened to you in the past, things that made you feel sad?"

She moved uneasily in her chair, unsure where his questioning was leading.

He continued, enumerating the events in Ann's life that had brought on bouts of deep depression: Charlotte's death, the hysterectomy, the death of her identical twin, and the overdose.

She said nothing while he spoke, freeze-framing the blank look on her face to process what he was telling her. *You OD'd on meds because of the letter I sent you. Jesus, Ann, you were sensitive as well as sentimental.*

"I feel like you've changed," he blurted out, "and it's not just because you can't remember the person you were before," he hesitated, "your accident. It's something about you on the inside that's different. I feel like you're not allowing any of us back into your life, into your heart, because you believe in your mind that you're not Ann."

If he only knew how right he was.

It was time to put an end to Ben's psychoanalysis. Westbrook pulled out her hanky and wiped away make-believe tears. She'd go along with his impression that his wife believed she was someone else.

Better he thinks I'm a nutcase than an imposter.

137

Ben's monologue continued. "If you feel like you're afraid to reconnect with me, Meg, and others who care about you, maybe something has happened to you that's causing you to resist being the wonderful wife and mother you were before you were injured. Do you think that's something you'd like to talk to Trevor about, and perhaps even a psychiatrist?"

She'd already been down that road with Moore. She'd promise to see the shrink right after she saw the neurologist, but not until they'd returned from the family trip to Disney World. She had her reasons. Until then, a visit with her psychotherapist fit neatly into her plans. "Yes, Ben. I should see Trevor. I'll call him tomorrow."

She got up to go to her bedroom. There would be no lovemaking with Ben that night, or ever again. She needed to return to being the emotionally fragile Ann, who was unable to shake past sorrows. The belief that her amnesia was due to mental illness wasn't a bad thing. Trevor Moore had already come to that conclusion over casual conversation and a cup of Earl Grey. It played right into the story she'd be pitching. Trying her best to appear overwhelmed and vulnerable, she told Ben she'd be taking a sleeping pill to "shut out the world and everything in it, if only for one night." She spoke dolefully so he'd feel guilty for suggesting his wife had gone mental.

"Yes, darling. You get ready for bed, and I'll bring you your medication."

He's worried about me overdosing on my meds again.
Good.

But she had another reason for calling it an early evening. When he'd mentioned Ann's hysterectomy, a neuron had sparked a memory. She'd had abdominal x-rays taken on the day of her accident, and she understood enough about anatomy and x-rays to know they could show her reproductive organs. She needed a plan to guard against the discovery of the one piece of evidence that would conclusively prove she was an imposter.

Chapter 22

Westbrook walked into the main entrance of the hospital where her x-rays were waiting to be found by two inquisitive police detectives. She removed her baseball cap and sunglasses and approached the information desk. "I'm here for copies of my x-rays, and I was told I can pick them up in the radiology department," she said to one of the women working behind the desk.

"Let me call them," the woman said, reaching for the phone. "If they're ready, someone can bring them down. What's your name?"

"No, please don't. It's best I go there and explain which ones my doctor wants me to bring to my appointment. It's in half an hour, so I'm in kind of a hurry."

"Sure," the receptionist said. "Take the elevator to the second floor. Left off the elevator. Second corridor, take another left. The records custodian's office is on the right."

Westbrook arrived on the second floor and wandered past the glass door of the custodian's office. Two women sat behind a counter, busying themselves with paperwork. Down the corridor on the left, a solid wooden door had the words "Records - Radiology" inscribed on it. She found it unlocked and slipped inside.

Rows of file cabinets filled the room, the files organized by patient number. Using the number on her discharge instructions, she navigated her way down the rows until she came to the row with her file. She put on her latex gloves, removed the four radiographs and original reports from her file, then lowered the zipper on her exercise jacket and stuffed the radiographs, reports, and gloves inside. Once zipped back up, she headed for the door.

The door opened, followed by the sound of a man and a woman whispering. Westbrook froze, held her breath, and slowly stepped backwards, stopping at the end of the row.

"Come on," the man said excitedly. "Pull down your scrubs. They're waiting for us in the OR, and I'm ready to explode."

"Hold on," the young woman said. "Your patient who had the heart attack doesn't want his surgeon having one, too."

Westbrook sneaked a look. The hospital employees remained vertical with their backs to her, so it was safe to watch. The man's blue surgical pants slid midway down his legs; the woman's matching ones fell to the floor. He thrusted in and out of her from behind, rotating his hips like Elvis, while she, bent over with her hands on the door, panted heavily. With a chest full of x-rays, the former patient turned thief went along for the ride, stuck there until he got his rocks off or someone else entered the room, whoever came first.

Debbie Does the Doctor.

She'd played the role before, and it aroused her. Her honeypot quivered. Unable to resist the urge to participate, she reached down inside her panties until her fingers found her sweet spot. Massaging it, she tried to time her panting to Debbie's. Like synchronized divers, they hit the water together, their groans of satisfaction conjoined. The doctor evoked the name of God's son on the way down.

The couple regained their composure, pulled up their scrubs, and made time for a single kiss. After cracking open the door and seeing no one, they took off. Westbrook quickly followed them to the door and opened it slightly. Hearing the clamor of shoes striking the corridor floor, she gently closed it again. The footsteps grew louder and then softer until quiet returned. With the coast clear, she left to dispose of her radiographs in the privacy of her home.

Back in her office, Ann was reading Booth's letter for the third time when she received a call from Rachel Hathaway, Director of Human Resources at Livingston Industries. "Yes," Ann said in response to Hathaway's query as to whether the company should hire her friend. "Let's hire Sarah Booth. She's seeking only temporary employment. She won't be around very long, I'm quite certain of that."

Chapter 23

Crowder lay motionless in bed, one eye open, the other glued shut, her head a bowling ball on the edge of a crumpled pillow. The open eye watched a digital clock on the nightstand change from 8:22 to 8:23 to 8:24, like a countdown to take-off. A ping interrupted the countdown at 8:25, scrapping the mission.

Mustering the scintilla of strength left in her body, she reached for the cell phone on the nightstand. Her hand got halfway there before it dropped over the edge of the bed. She was afraid to move her head; if she did, it might roll off. Her mouth felt bone dry. She'd wanted to take a glass of water to bed with her when she'd gotten home at two in the morning, but a beeline to her bedroom without puking on the way had been the better option at the time.

Another ping.

Another unsuccessful attempt to reach for the phone.

She reflected on her Saturday evening out. Sid and Jenny had picked her up at seven thirty. Steele's band did two sets at the Bayou Club on Bourbon Street in the French Quarter as the introduction to the main act—the warm-up, when voices get louder and drinks get drunk faster.

She'd sat with Jenny and a couple of single cops with dates. She was the only loner at the table—what cops called the persons on a night out who had no date or prospects of meeting up with someone they could leave with. Crowder called people like her by what everyone thought but didn't openly say—*losers*.

But Crowder wasn't the type to go looking for a man. It just wasn't her style. Call it pride. Call it a lack of self-confidence. Call it a fear of commitment. Call it any damn thing you wanted. "It's just not me," she'd told Jenny after draining what remained of her third Budweiser.

She'd had a heart-to-heart with Jenny who, at twenty-six, was ten years her junior. "When I turn forty," Crowder had lamented, "who'll want to pair up with a cynical, street-stalking, alley-cat homicide detective like me and start a family? Ten years ago, when I was in my mid-twenties, it was a bull market. There were plenty of single prosecutors and defense lawyers out there."

"What held you back? Then, I mean," Jenny had asked.

"Nothing did. I sampled what was out there from time to time. But nothing was satisfying enough for me to give up my independence."

"Jeez, Jo. It's not the end of the world. Get back into the game. It's never too late."

Still in the doldrums, she'd stared glossy eyed into an empty mug. "Now those single men are married and starting families. They're already mortgaged. What's left are the re-fi's. Dudes who divorced the first one because they couldn't hack married life, with or without children. It's like a resale store out there. Used, worn-out stuff likely to break after a year or two."

"You need someone to give you comfort and companionship."

"I do. I have Fred."

When Crowder broke her two-drinks-only rule, she didn't just break it, she obliterated it. By the time Steele had finished his second set, she had finished off two glasses of chardonnay, four Buds, and a couple shots of whiskey. After that, it was anyone's guess.

The ringer on her cell phone replaced the ping. This time she answered.

Steele didn't wait for her to speak. "You got sauced last night, partner. Take some aspirin. Breakfast is on you. I may have some news that will knock your sweat socks off. Pick you up in twenty minutes."

She struggled her way out of bed, went to the kitchen, and took three 325 milligram aspirins, gulping them down with orange juice directly from the spout of the quart container. Then she took a cold, soapless shower, dabbed herself dry with a hand towel, put on her department-issued sweats, and waited to hear the blare of Bugsy's horn.

~

Mimi brought coffee to their booth right away. "Sweet Jesus, Jo, you look like something Fred dragged home."

"Believe me, I feel a whole lot worse than I look," Crowder said.

"The usual," Mimi declared, then left to place the order.

"So," Steele said, "Jenny and I are in bed last night. It was like three in the morning, and she yells 'God! Oh my God!'"

"Really? I'm sure that's something you've heard hundreds of times this past year," Crowder said, rubbing her eyes as though doing so would return them from red to white. "What do you say when you climax? *Gesundheit?*"

"Very funny. But it woke me up. Jenny told me she couldn't believe she hadn't picked up on it when she'd looked at Ann Livingston's medical records. She wanted to check something first to be sure. Said she'd text me during her nine o'clock break."

Steele's cell phone pinged. He opened the text from Jenny, read it, and handed his phone to Crowder. She read:

I was right. Her abdominal x-rays reportedly show an ovarian cyst. But that can't be true. Ann Livingston had her ovaries removed eight years ago.

Crowder looked up. "You know what this means?"

"Yes, Jo. I know what this means. Ann Livingston is someone else, and the someone else is a dead person."

"This puts an entirely different spin on everything that's happened, beginning with the car crash. But I suppose it could be a mistake."

"You mean, like the x-rays were misread?"

"That, or the radiographs are of a different patient and got mixed up with Ann Livingston's."

"The only way to be sure," Steele said, "is for the woman who might not be Ann Livingston to have an abdominal x-ray to prove her identity. That'll never happen."

"Or," Crowder suggested, "we have a physician look at the films. Compare the most recent radiographs to her earlier ones. She must have had postoperative abdominal x-rays after her hysterectomy."

"Which will require a signed medical authorization from the woman who'll never give one, for the same reason she'll never voluntarily submit to an abdominal x-ray. So, what do we do with the information? We can't go to Cap with it. Our asses will be up on charges, and Jenny could get fired."

The resumption of police work cleared Crowder's head of the remnants of her hangover. "Hypothetically speaking, suppose someone who works at the hospital saw the discrepancy in the medical chart and anonymously mailed copies of selective records in a plain envelope to Ben Livingston. The important parts of the records could be highlighted. If posted for overnight delivery to his office, he could receive the records as early as the next morning."

"And, hypothetically speaking," Steele interjected, "if Ben Livingston were harboring suspicions of his own, he just might want to bring us into the loop."

"Right. And if he did, we could do what he can't do without the risk of offending his wife. We can find out for sure whether the woman living at the Livingstons' home is Ann Livingston or her *deceased* identical twin sister."

~

"She seems so different," Ann's mother confided in Ben Livingston as they sat in the study after dinner. Ann had retired early to bed, this time with a headache.

"I know," he said dejectedly. "It's what ... almost three weeks since her accident? She looks fine. Yet she still complains of this and that. It's like she doesn't want to get better."

"I know my daughter. This isn't like her. She's ice cold toward Meg. She expresses no interest in what she's doing in school, or in what you or anyone else is doing."

"What's strange to me," he offered, "is that she hasn't tried to challenge herself. Can I still play the piano? Paint? Play tennis? It's as if she doesn't want to remember. Lucinda says she stays in her office most of the day with the door closed. She never did that before. Buddy was always in and out of her office. Now she doesn't want the dog anywhere near her."

"I think the feeling's mutual, Ben. Buddy growls at her when their paths cross. And something else: Ann went shopping on Thursday. She put her shopping bag on the kitchen table. It was half open when Meg and I went into the kitchen for a snack after her piano lesson. Inside the bag were tampons and morning-after contraceptive pills. Why would a woman who can't get pregnant and hasn't had a period in eight years need them?" She paused to let out a sigh. "Ann's in denial, fantasizing she's someone else. I think we should encourage her to see a psychiatrist."

"I've suggested she see Trevor for a referral. But you can only lead a horse to water."

The grandfather clock in the hallway chimed. "I'll be with Meg," Martha said, leaving the room. "She'll want to read some before she goes to sleep."

"Tell Meg I'll be up to kiss her goodnight. And Martha ..."

"What, Ben?"

"Ann may not appreciate how important you are in her life right now. But Meg and I do."

Buddy showed up in the study a few minutes later, his way of saying it was time for his evening romp. Ben let him out a back door, returned to the study, and poured a bourbon. He let his mind wander. Was Ann experiencing a split personality, stuck in

146

an entirely different person? A person who was single, emotionally detached, with no important relationships in her life. Someone with the personality of a vivacious, sensual woman experienced in matters of sex and unafraid of showing it. Nobody, least of all himself, was able to relate to the person Ann had become.

When his meditation ended and he was staring down at an empty glass, he went to the door to let Buddy in. The dog scampered up the stairs to Meg's room, a signal to him to go to her.

He met Martha at the bedroom door on her way out. "Meg's reading is improving each day," she said. "I told her she could continue reading to Buddy. She reads stories to Buddy from a different book. What's it called, Meg?"

"*The Misadventures of Samson, the Biggest Little Chihuahua in the Litter*," she answered. "And we're on chapter six, 'The Little Dog that Stole Christmas.'"

Livingston sat on the bed. He wanted Meg to open up to him. "Honey, before you read to Buddy, I want to talk to you about Mommy. Remember what we told you? That she hurt herself in the car accident and her memory has gone away for a while. Even though we know she loves us, she still needs time for her mind to heal and for the memories she has of us to come back to her."

"I know, Daddy. Mommy hurt her head on the inside, not just on the outside. You know, where you remember things. Like who you are and what's your favorite ice cream. But she'll get better and remember us again, don't worry."

"How did you feel when Mommy couldn't come to school for Mother Appreciation Day? You can tell me. Sometimes my mom couldn't do things with me because she got sick, and it made me sad."

Meg fixed her eyes on his when she spoke. "I know Mommy was as sad as me that she couldn't be with me at school. But Nana was there, and she's a mother to Mommy and a grandmother to me. I brought the picture I drew of Mommy for her birthday, and it made me feel like she was there with us."

Livingston smiled. "You, Nana, and I need to be strong for Mommy right now. Will you continue to be strong for her, too?"

"Yes, Daddy. You can count on me; cross my heart." After she drew a cross over her chest with her finger, Ben fluffed her pillow and repositioned her comfortably in bed. He kissed her goodnight and paused at the bedroom door to hear her sweet voice read to Buddy.

"Chapter six. Andy woke up early. There was snow on the window sill. He yawned. He stretched out his arms. He rubbed the sleep from his eyes. Today was a very special day. It was Christmas. Andy ..."

Meg's words trailed off as he walked away from her room. Her door was always left partially open so Buddy had a way of coming for them if Meg had some problem. The door to the master bedroom was closed when he passed by it—another change in Ann's behavior. Before the accident, she'd always left it ajar for the same reason.

He opened it slightly and looked in, hoping she was awake so he could speak to her again about seeing a specialist. He spoke softly, not wanting to wake her if she was asleep. "Ann, are you awake?" Hearing no response, he closed the door and returned to the study, knowing it would be another night on the sofa after he finished off what was left in the bottle of bourbon.

Chapter 24

"**Y**es, I'm certain you'll be able to fund the foundation next week," Hochstein assured Ann when she called him. "The paperwork will be filed on Friday after you sign the documents here at the office."

"Thanks, Jared, for working so hard to get everything done," she said, insisting on a first-name relationship with her lawyer.

She needed a paper trail. Something showing that a relationship existed between Ann Livingston and Mary Smith. She used the word processing equipment at the public library to prepare back-and-forth correspondence between them. Smith touted the importance of the work of the foundation. Ann promised the funding.

It all fit in with her plan.

~

She had much to do before her meeting with Hochstein at eleven, and it was best handled by Ann's other self. After dropping Meg off at school, she drove to the cabin. The dented old pickup with its half-flat recycled retreads was still parked in the same patch of weeds. She pulled around back.

On her way to the cabin, she had put on her black wig and stopped at the hardware store to pick up another burlap sack, a hatchet, heavy-duty pruning clippers, and a pair of garden gloves. Now, she placed the items on the bedroom floor next to the chest, which was cooling like a reliable Frigidaire.

After losing the wig, she drove to the offices of Jared Hochstein to sign the documents that created her foundation and made Mary Smith a co-director with an office in Zurich, Switzerland. On her way home, she mulled over what to do about Booth, who would

149

want their future meetings to be in a public place during the middle of the day. No clandestine parleys in the middle of the night or at some secluded location like a cabin in the woods.

Booth's call came in the late afternoon after Meg had arrived home from school. Westbrook was safely holed up in Ann's office.

"Hey! Let me see if I can guess why you're calling," she said, sarcasm dripping off every word. "You want to know what I'll be wearing to our high school reunion."

Booth cleared her throat. "At least I know what bag I'll be carrying. Someone very special gave me a handbag that goes good with any outfit."

"When and where?"

"Monday. One o'clock. The dining room at the Essex House. It's two blocks from where I'll be working. I think you know the company. I start Tuesday."

"Okay, but let's make it eleven. I don't want anyone from Ben's office coming in for lunch and seeing us together."

"Eleven, then. Oh, one last thing. Bring ten thousand dollars, and no bullshit about the piggy bank being down to nickels and dimes." Booth didn't wait for a response and hung up.

Veronica Westbrook wasn't angry. She seldom got angry, but often got even.

~

Monday was a busy day for Ann Livingston and an even busier one for Veronica Westbrook.

Ann dropped Meg off at school, but it was Westbrook who returned home to crush three 100 milligram tablets of Ann's sleeping pills and put the powder in a small vial. She'd stockpiled them over the last few days because Ben counted her pills daily to be sure she wasn't overmedicating. One tablet was all someone of Booth's weight needed to bring on sleep in half an hour. Three tablets made certain she'd be nodding off in ten minutes, fifteen tops.

Next, Westbrook visited the safe and placed the ten-thousand-dollar cash withdrawal in one of Ann's shoulder bags. She put the bag, and a hammer she'd found in Ben's workshop, under a blanket in the backseat of her Lexus.

She arrived at the Essex House at ten minutes to eleven and parked in the hotel's rooftop garage in a parking place three spaces from the elevator. She found Booth sitting at a table for two in the dining room, wearing the proverbial shit-eating grin. Westbrook wanted to bitch-slap the smile right off her face. Instead, she played along.

"My dear friend Sarah. So nice to meet up with you for lunch. I've been so looking forward to it."

"Yes, Ann, but I bet not half as much as I," Booth said cockily.

She'd already ordered a drink, the lime slice and effervescence strongly suggesting a gin and tonic.

"Let's cut the crap," Westbrook said in a hushed, gruff voice when she took her seat. She placed the shoulder bag on the floor beside the table and kicked it over to Booth. "Count it. I don't want you saying I stiffed you for a couple hundred off the top."

"You mean here?"

"No, stupid. I mean in the ladies' room. I'll get a drink while you play the queen sitting on her throne, counting her money, and I play Miss Muffet in the parlor eating bread and honey." Westbrook sensed that Booth couldn't wait to flip through the pile of hundred-dollar bills in the privacy of a bathroom stall. "We'll toast to your good fortune when you get back."

As soon as Booth left the table, Westbrook waved to a server. "I'll have a Grey Goose cosmopolitan. And please bring it right away," she told him. When he'd walked away, she got the vial out of her purse, casually reached across the table for Booth's glass, stirred in the powder, and returned it to where it'd been.

Booth took longer than expected. The conniving little bitch was probably counting it more than once while pinching herself to be sure she wasn't dreaming.

151

The waiter brought Westbrook's drink just as Booth returned to the table. With her glass raised, Westbrook looked into Booth's bugged-out eyes and said, "Here's looking at you, kid."

Their glasses tapped. Each took a long, slow sip of her drink, and then another.

Booth got down to business. "I want fifty thousand dollars, half in hundreds, half in fifties. The amount is non-negotiable. I get the cash, and it's bye-bye, Sarah. I return to my life's goal of a college degree and a career as a social worker helping wayward girls like you. The drop will be in a public place at a time I say."

"How do I know you won't look me up later, perhaps at next year's reunion, and hit me for more money?" Westbrook asked, knowing that if all went as planned, Booth would be in the in-memoriam section of the reunion bulletin.

"Because you and I are too smart for that," Booth said smugly. "Once you score, we'll both be outta here. I don't see you living as Ann Livingston much longer."

And I don't see you living as anybody much longer.

Booth snickered. "You must have an exit strategy in place. I wouldn't even know where to find you."

Westbrook knew she'd seen her notes and could track her to Switzerland. The gold digger would most certainly be back with pickaxe in hand, wanting to mine more from the motherlode.

I'd do the same.

They sipped their drinks until their glasses were empty. Booth began to show telltale signs of sedation. Yawning. Fluttering eyelids. Slurring words. "I, I need some coffee," she stuttered to the waiter.

"No," Westbrook interrupted, "my friend and I are about to leave. She needs a nap, a very long nap. Here's a fifty. That should cover things." The waiter smiled, snatched the fifty from her hand, and walked away.

Booth began to go limp in her chair. Westbrook put Booth's handbag in the shoulder bag with the cash and placed the strap over her shoulder, then went to help Booth out of her chair.

"I want a Porsche, too, Ronnie. I really do," Booth slurred. "And a villi in Swittzerlinger in the Swittzerlinger Epps." She walked to the elevator with deliberate steps, like a tightrope walker on a high wire at the circus, except her unsteadiness wasn't part of the act. Westbrook rested her upright against the wall and pressed the button for the elevator.

When the door opened, a bellhop wrestled a luggage carrier out of the elevator with a full load of suitcases and a bratty five-year-old boy hanging off the back. Westbrook pushed Booth into the elevator and pressed the button for the garage on the top floor.

As the door began to close, an Englishman shouted, "Be so kind as to hold the lift."

Westbrook reached for the close-door button and pressed it repeatedly. The door had nearly shut when an umbrella speared its way into the elevator and the door shuddered open. A middle-aged, gray-haired man with a neatly trimmed handlebar mustache entered the elevator, visibly miffed.

"Oh! I'm real sorry," Westbrook said apologetically. "I must have pressed the wrong button when I heard you call out."

The gent pushed the button for a floor midway to the top.

Booth continued to babble, now mumbling a tune. "Mon ... key makes the world go round. Mon ... day makes the word go down." The mixture of sedative and liquor made her gay, almost sloppy drunk. The Brit left the elevator on the third floor. Just as the door closed, Booth collapsed to the floor in a sitting position with her back against a wall and her legs straight out.

Westbrook knew things could get dicey if someone was there when the elevator door opened. Her heart thumped in her chest as the elevator vibrated and jarred to a stop. The door opened lazily out of spite. No one was there. She pulled the stop button, putting the elevator temporarily out of use, then tossed the shoulder bag in the direction of the Lexus. Her aim was off. The underhanded throw got it only halfway there. It struck the back of a minivan, landing near the rear tire. Grabbing hold of Booth's wrists, she dragged her from

153

the elevator to the rear passenger door of the Lexus, stopping twice to catch her breath. She manhandled Booth's flaccid body onto the backseat floor and covered it with the blanket, then sprinted back to release the stop button.

Just as she left the elevator and the door was closing behind her, two men exited the stairwell. The dash to her Lexus left no time for her to retrieve the shoulder bag. She crawled into the backseat. From her kneeling position on the seat, she peeped out the rear window and saw two men walking to the elevator, mumbling to one another. They drew close enough for her to hear what they were saying.

"It figures. We walk up seven flights, and the fucking elevator isn't stuck after all," one of them said.

"Well, at least we don't have to walk down," said the other, pressing the button for the elevator.

Westbrook, tired, hot, and sweating, remained crouched on the back seat. The party was over if they saw the shoulder bag and looked in it. Booth's purse and the cash would be impossible for her to explain. The elevator took forever to get there. A single minute suddenly felt like two.

The two men got into a cussing match about football while they waited, their eyes fixed on the elevator door.

"When Drew Brees retires, the honeymoon's fucking over. Nobody can replace him ... no one. No fucking way."

"You're so fucking right."

"The team will be fucked."

"The fans will be fucked."

"You're so fucking right."

"You can say that again."

"You're so fucking right."

Just then, Booth moaned. The blanket covering her face caused her body to want air. She began to squirm. Westbrook slid on top of her, but Booth reacted by pushing on her chest.

"Get off me. I need air," she hollered, her voice partially muffled by the blanket. "Get the fuck off me, bitch." Her voice rose an octave.

Westbrook looked over the seat. The men turned their heads in her direction just as the elevator door opened. Westbrook put her hand over Booth's mouth to stifle her wailing, but her ex-cellmate thrashed about and bit down on Westbrook's hand. She responded by punching her in the face. Twice. And then, with one hand clutching Booth's throat, she reached for the hammer with the other and landed a blow dead center to the top of her head.

The covered body lay still.

Another hard strike followed to keep it that way.

A glance at the elevator saw the men stepping aside to allow a couple to get off. To her unpleasant surprise, they had with them the bratty kid who'd been riding the luggage cart earlier. On their way to their car, the annoying little imp saw the shoulder bag, went over to it, and held it up with both hands. "Daddy, Mommy, look what I found," he said excitedly.

By then the parents were standing directly behind the Lexus. They turned to look. Four sets of eyes focused on the bag, one waiting anxiously in the backseat of the Lexus for the scene to play out.

The threat ended when the father yelled, "Billy, put the bag back where you found it and get in the car, and I mean now. Whoever left it there will be back for it."

Seldom were truer words spoken.

Tension mounted again when the family walked to the station wagon parked next to the Lexus. Billy's mother got in first while Westbrook and Booth lay on the floor, both perfectly still but only one still breathing. Billy the brat followed his mother, but he flung open his door, slamming it against the rear door of the Lexus with a bang so hard and shrill that Westbrook lurched in surprise.

"Billy, I hope you didn't dent that car," the pesky boy's father hollered angrily. "Get in and put your seatbelt on." The man walked

155

around the back of the station wagon. "Let me see if you caused any damage," he grumbled out loud on his way.

He'd surely see her when he inspected the door. In one move she rolled onto the rear seat, pulled the blanket off Booth, and threw it over herself as she rolled back to the floor on top of Booth, the blanket now covering both of them. With her cheek pressed firmly against the face of a dead woman, she heard the man's grunting; he stood that close while inspecting the door.

Her late morning nightmare finally ended when she heard him say, "Well, I don't see anything I need to report. Billy, you're one lucky kid."

That made two lucky ones.

Westbrook emerged from beneath the blanket once the station wagon had left. She retrieved the bag and drove to the cabin.

Chapter 25

"Mr. Livingston, an envelope just arrived for you marked personal," Elizabeth said in an accusatory tone of voice. She handed it to him as if it were laced with anthrax.

Livingston couldn't remember the last time he'd received an envelope his secretary didn't open. Did she think it was a blackmail letter with photographs of him in compromising positions? Elizabeth was old school. She adored Ann Livingston. She'd give him an earful and quit on the spot if he ever cheated on Ann.

He studied the envelope. Posted yesterday for overnight delivery. Return address, none. Marked personal and confidential. He opened it. Medical records. No letter. He focused on what was underlined.

Operative report ... uterus evacuated ... Fallopian tubes and ovaries identified ... necrosis seen ... bilateral oophorectomy performed ... Date: 01/02/10.

"Tell me something I don't already know," he muttered under his breath, knowing that a bilateral oophorectomy was surgery to remove both ovaries.

X-rays abdomen and chest ... normal studies with the exception of a benign cyst on right ovary ... Date: 01/03/18.

Livingston frowned. "Ovary? How can that be?" He read the final record.

Psychiatric consultation ... Patient, who was adopted, received a letter from the adoption agency advising her that her identical twin sister had died ... Date: 07/13/17.

Livingston folded the records and returned them to the envelope, then opened his desk drawer and pulled out the card he'd been given the week before. He picked up the phone, dialed the number on the card, and waited for the person he'd called to pick up.

"Homicide Division, Detective Crowder speaking."

~

"We'd have come to your office," Crowder said after Ben Livingston took a seat around the table in an interview room at district headquarters.

"I didn't want to arouse suspicion. It's best I come to you." He hesitated a bit and then continued, "I have information that suggests to me that my wife … well … may not be my wife. Someone at the hospital who was probably involved in Ann's care on the day of her accident picked up on a discrepancy in the hospital chart and sent the records to me." He handed the envelope to Crowder. "Here, you look at them. You'll see what I mean."

She looked over the envelope carefully, like she was looking for evidence of who sent it. Very carefully opening it, she pulled out the medical records and pretended to read them, passing them one by one to Steele for him to do likewise. "I see what you mean," Crowder said. "But it could be some kind of mistake."

"Don't you think I considered the possibility of a mistake? I'm certain Ann's ovaries were removed when she had her hysterectomy. I was with her when the doctor discussed the surgery, because of the implications on childbearing. I knew that x-rays were performed in the ER on the day of Ann's accident. But I only discussed the CT scan of her brain with her doctor and my brother-in-law, who's Chief of Neurosurgery at the hospital."

"Maybe your brother-in-law can take a look at the x-ray films and discuss them with the radiologist who issued the report," Crowder suggested.

"I intend to. The problem is, he's vacationing with his family in Africa, of all places, and won't be returning until next Friday. Ann and I are leaving on a weeklong trip to Disney World with

158

my daughter and Ann's mother next Wednesday. So I really can't confirm things until my brother-in-law returns and—"

Crowder interrupted. "Mr. Livingston, the questions raised have serious implications for you and your family. If we can just get a medical authorization, we can check Ann's records and talk to her doctors."

"Getting her to sign a medical authorization is out of the question," he said, his voice quivering. "If there's any explanation for all this, it would crush Ann to know I believed she was an imposter."

Crowder saw the angst on Livingston's face. She felt herself reading his mind. The only other person the woman could be was his wife's identical and supposedly dead twin sister. If the woman was an imposter, where was Ann, and how safe was Meg?

With his head hung, he spoke to the detectives without looking at them. "I sensed some things were different about the woman, almost from the beginning. Ann was warm, affectionate, kind, and engaging even when she was having her dark moments after the death of our daughter, Charlotte, and then the death of her sister. If the woman is Ann's sister, she must be one sick …" He didn't complete the sentence.

Crowder said, "This matter has to be handled delicately. There are a lot of moving parts. I want to contact the adoption agency that informed your wife of her sister's death. If Ann's sister is deceased, we'll have an early answer and can close out the investigation. Until then, you need to be sure all of you are safe." Livingston stared at a blank space on the wall, reminding Crowder of a lost little boy unsure of what to do. "Mr. Livingston. I know you must be feeling all kinds of emotions right now and are worried about Ann and your daughter. But you did the right thing, the only thing you could do, and that was to bring us into it."

Livingston got up slowly from his chair and, like a dead man walking, left the conference room without saying a word.

Chapter 26

"**D**etective Jo Crowder to see Harriet Cummings," she announced to the clerk, flashing her badge and acting like Cummings was expecting her. "She's a senior placement specialist with the department. I have a letter from her that I need to speak to her about."

Five minutes later, Crowder sat in Cummings' office explaining why a police officer from the New Orleans Police Department had traveled all the way to Baltimore to see her. "Ma'am, the Livingston family is a very important family in Louisiana. Ann Livingston is married to Ben Livingston, one of the wealthiest men in the country. They're good people, very connected to the citizens of our state. We have reason to believe the woman who is holding herself out as Ann Livingston may be her identical twin sister."

"What you've told me, what does it have to do with this agency and me?"

"Ann Livingston and her twin sister were separated at birth and adopted into separate families. Your agency handled the adoptions thirty-three years ago."

"What is it you believe our agency can provide you?"

"Ann wanted to reach out to her twin. Letters were exchanged between you and Ann. You sent her a letter informing her that her sister had died. We need to verify the information you have about her sister's death."

"Detective Crowder, the information in our files is confidential under Maryland law. I can't give you any of the records or disclose information in them without a subpoena."

"I have one that addresses the matter." Crowder handed her a subpoena from a Louisiana court, hoping that she might overlook its jurisdictional invalidity.

After reading it, Cummings said, "This subpoena has no effect in Maryland, not without a Maryland court authorizing the release of the records."

Crowder wasn't about to give up on Cummings, who wore a wedding band and looked to be in her late thirties or early forties. The adolescent children in the photo on her desk were undoubtedly hers. "Do you have children?" she asked.

"Two sons and a daughter."

"Ben and Ann Livingston have an eight-year-old daughter. She may be in danger if we are correct about our suspicions."

Cummings told the detective to wait while she retrieved the adoption files for Ann McMillan and her sister. She was gone about five minutes and returned with two folders.

"You know I can't give you any records. Why don't you ask me specific questions that might help you in your investigation? I'll answer them as long as I'm not divulging confidential information."

Crowder let out a silent sigh of relief. "Was Ann Livingston's letter sent to her sister?"

"We had no address in our files other than the address of her adoptive parents. So we sent it there."

"Were there any responses from Ann's sister or her parents?"

Cummings leafed through the two files in front of her. "No."

"Then why would you send a letter to Ann Livingston informing her that her sister was dead?"

Crowder gave Cummings the letter she'd supposedly sent. Cummings studied it and said, "I didn't."

Crowder was taken aback by the response. The signatures of Harriet Cummings on both letters appeared to be identical.

"I know the signature looks like mine," Cummings continued. "But I'm positive someone else signed this letter."

"How can you be so sure?"

161

"Because the two i's in my name are dotted. I never dot my i's. It just isn't something I ever do in writing my name. Growing up, my parents often reminded me of it when scolding me for not fully completing my chores. They'd say, 'Harriet, she always crosses her t's but never dots her i's.' I guess I did it out of protest. Another thing, this letter was sent only last summer. I'd remember writing a letter like this to someone."

Crowder was putting a puzzle together, and she needed Cummings to share some of the puzzle pieces with her. She confided in her as though they were friends. "Harriet, if you didn't write it, Ann Livingston's sister must have written it to end Ann's search for her and have everyone believe that a dead sister makes an unlikely imposter." Crowder stopped talking.

Cummings remained silent for a while, then spoke. "I'm adopted, Detective Crowder. My parents are good people. They encouraged me to reach out to my biological parents and siblings. I did when I was sixteen, the same age my mother was when she had me. I received a letter from her in response to my inquiry. She was married with two boys. Her husband was in the navy. They were stationed in Hawaii and loved it there. We exchanged letters and photographs, then sort of drifted away.

"About ten years later, I received a letter from her with photos of her eldest son graduating from the Naval Academy. It's strange. I was genuinely excited for what he had accomplished, as though he was a brother I'd known all my life. I wrote back to my birth mother and told her how proud I was of him. After that, we exchanged letters and regular updates on Facebook. Detective Crowder, I think I know how Ann Livingston felt when she reached out to her sister. There was a void in her life she hoped to fill."

Cummings reached for something on her desk and knocked over her coffee cup. She began moving files away from the coffee that had puddled on her desk. She put the two folders she'd been looking at on the end of the desk closest to the detective and turned the two files around so the detective could see the covers. One was labeled "Henry and Martha McMillan," the other "William and Caroline Westbrook."

"Oh, I've made a mess. Let me leave for a few minutes and get a paper towel." Cummings got up and left the office, closing the door behind her.

Crowder opened the jacket of the Westbrook folder and jotted down the information she needed.

Parents: William and Caroline Westbrook, 2012 Covington Lane, Towson, MD 21204. Child: Baby girl, born June 28, 1984; Adoptive Name: Veronica Lynn Westbrook. Biological Mother: Monica Millings c/o Maryland Hospital for the Mentally Ill.

She flipped open the McMillan folder and saw the birth information for another baby girl born June 28, 1984, whose biological mother was also Monica Millings. She returned both files to where they'd been and sat back in her chair.

When Cummings returned to her office, Crowder stood. "Ms. Cummings, I fully understand your inability to assist me further. I want to thank you for your cooperation."

The two exchanged smiles, Crowder's lasting until she was all the way to the parking lot and back in the car she'd rented at the airport when she'd arrived that morning.

Crowder called Steele from her car. "I have her name. Don't ask me how I got it. It's a long story, but with a happy ending. Run a criminal background check on Veronica Lynn Westbrook, date of birth June 28, 1984. Parents are William and Caroline Westbrook of Towson, Maryland. I want to know if she jay-walked, pissed on the sidewalk, or got a parking ticket. Maybe she's squeaky clean. Maybe not.

"I'm heading over to her parents' home. It's about a half-hour drive. I want to know more about their daughter before I talk to them. I don't want them thinking I got their names from the adoption agency. If there's any significant criminal history, the parents' identities and contact information will be there."

"I'm on it," Steele said, and hung up. Crowder knew he would immediately access the FBI criminal database to collect any available information.

Crowder had her laptop with her and decided to do some internet research on the Maryland Hospital for the Mentally Ill before driving to the Westbrooks' home. She periodically read aloud as she perused some of the many articles posted. "Located in Frederick, Maryland ... built in '42 ... an asylum for the criminally insane ... renamed in '75 ... for criminals too violent and dangerous to be incarcerated in prisons .... treatment modalities: straitjackets, anti-bite mouth locks, leather strap bed restraints, shackles, electric shock therapy, padded cells, and experimental mind-altering drugs."

Nice place. But where else can you send them? How else can you control them?

Crowder closed her computer, started her car, and headed to the Westbrook residence, hoping to learn more about the offspring of a mother who'd ended up in an asylum for the most violent, mentally unstable criminals.

Fifteen minutes later, Steele called back. "She's got a rap sheet that's pretty impressive for someone thirty-three. A juvenile record, but that's sealed. Arrests for prostitution, shoplifting, petty theft, assault. A conviction for grand larceny. Did six months for that in Texas. Another, two years ago, for elder abuse, fraud, and theft. Did eighteen months in a women's prison in Maryland. Given an early release last fall."

"Do you have a current address?"

"Last one she gave her parole officer was in December of last year. Towson, Maryland. 2012 Covington Lane."

"I'm headed over there now, and I'll bet next year's salary Veronica Westbrook won't be answering the door."

~

The home of William and Caroline Westbrook was a nice brick house in a suburban subdivision of two-story homes with two-car garages on quarter-acre lots. A typical middle-class, white-collar, white-face neighborhood. Mrs. Westbrook, a soft-spoken, pleasant-looking woman in her mid-sixties, answered the door. When Crowder introduced herself and told her she wanted to speak to her about Veronica, the woman's friendly smile transitioned to a blank stare and the facial droop of a stroke victim, a sure sign to Crowder that she wasn't the first law enforcement officer to pay her a visit about her daughter.

Mrs. Westbrook led her to the kitchen and offered her a cup of coffee. Crowder didn't speak until both had their coffees in front of them. "Mrs. Westbrook, we're investigating the possible disappearance of Ann Livingston, Veronica's biological sister. We have reason to believe your daughter may have recently been in communication with her. I wish I could give you more information but that's all I'm permitted to say right now. Is your daughter living with you?"

Mrs. Westbrook sat there, expressionless, sipping her coffee as though she hadn't heard what the detective said.

Crowder took a swallow of coffee, and another, waiting for the silence to break.

"Her father and I have seen Veronica twice in the past six years," Mrs. Westbrook said matter-of-factly. "Each time was the day she was sentenced for crimes she'd committed. Veronica asked us to write the judges and speak on her behalf at sentencing, and, of course, we did. But after that, she refused to see us when we came to visit her in prison."

"I'm sorry to hear that, Mrs. Westbrook." Crowder continued to probe, hoping for a few more puzzle pieces. "What was she like growing up?"

"Veronica was the most beautiful little girl," Mrs. Westbrook reminisced. "So pretty that when she was twelve, a professional photographer contacted us about having her audition as a model for children's clothing. It was all on the up and up. She entered a modeling competition and won hands down. She was going to

165

be paid almost ten thousand dollars to model children's clothing for several large department store chains. We figured we'd put the money away for college, and we signed a one-year contract.

"At the first photoshoot, Veronica got mad at another girl because she had on the dress Veronica wanted to wear. She demanded the two trade. When the girl refused, Veronica stuck her in the cheek with a ballpoint pen. The poor girl was so traumatized by what happened that she never came back to model for the agency. My daughter's contract was canceled, of course."

"What about in school?"

"She was in trouble a lot, accused of stealing things, although only once did they catch her with another student's purse. Her father and I often found money in the dresser in her bedroom. We had no idea where she got it. We were careful not to leave cash around the house because there were times we knew she took it out of her father's wallet or my purse. When she was nineteen, she moved out and left the area with an older man we only met once. She left with my husband's rainy-day fund, close to four thousand dollars, and most of my jewelry."

"What about friends?" Crowder asked. "Did she have any close friends she continued to see after high school?"

"Not really. She didn't have any girlfriends who saw her regularly, at least none we were aware of. She got good grades in school but couldn't get along with some of the teachers and students. If she didn't like a teacher or a classmate, she'd curse at them. This usually ended up with her being sent home. We had to force her to write several letters apologizing for her behavior. Then, just before the senior prom, she …" Mrs. Westbrook paused and sighed wearily. "She was arrested and expelled for assaulting another student. The girl was voted homecoming queen and asked to the prom by the boy Veronica wanted to go with. She said Veronica pushed her down a flight of stairs. My daughter claimed the other girl bumped into her and lost her balance. There were no witnesses to corroborate either story, so the criminal charges were dropped, and she was readmitted to school. The girl ended up with a broken arm and a concussion. Veronica asked the boy involved to take her to the prom. He stayed home rather than go with my daughter. He told Veronica he was afraid of her."

Crowder knew the poor woman didn't need further prodding. It was like she finally had someone to talk to about what a nightmare it had been raising her daughter.

"We sensed that Veronica was promiscuous. I could see it as early as middle school. The other parents shunned me at school functions. There were rumors about the gym teacher molesting her. She denied it but giggled when she was questioned about it in a meeting my husband and I arranged with the principal."

"Was she ever evaluated?" Crowder asked, sensing the narrative would get increasingly more painful to tell.

"We had her see a psychologist. He tested her. She has a high IQ. She did well on her SATs and even received scholarship offers from several colleges. But her personality was markedly abnormal, according to the psychologist. He told us she lacked feelings of compassion, empathy, and generosity. He found her to be detached, narcissistic, selfish, and amoral. It helped explain why she never told us she loved us. Why she made us feel like she was just a visitor in our home. Why she never had any of the feelings you hope and pray a daughter will have for her parents. I hate to use the word the psychologist used, but he thought she had the character traits of a sociopath."

"What about college? Did she go?"

"Veronica had no interest in college. Her father was devastated. He cried when she ran off with a man we learned had recently been released from prison. After that, she never called or wrote us about how she was doing. Never sent us a birthday or holiday card or asked if we were all right. We only heard from her when she needed money or got into trouble."

"Did she ever want to know about her biological parents?"

"No, but my husband did. He even hired a private investigator to get information about Veronica's birth parents. The report the investigator prepared was so shocking, we almost didn't believe him. But it did put things into perspective for us. It helped us understand better why our daughter might be the way she was."

"Mrs. Westbrook, I know it's asking a lot, but would you be willing to share the investigator's report with me?"

"I can't. My husband burned it in anger."

"What did the private investigator find out about Veronica's biological parents?"

Mrs. Westbrook got up and went to the kitchen counter to get some tissues to stem the flow of tears Crowder knew was coming.

"Veronica's mother was a patient in a mental hospital here in Maryland. She was convicted of murdering her husband and their four-year-old son. She stabbed them repeatedly with a butcher's knife, then removed their heads and placed them on the fireplace mantel. She put their bodies in her bed and slept with them. They were there a week before she was arrested."

Crowder struggled to keep her face impassive. She'd seen a lot of bad shit, but that was extreme in anyone's book. Knowing genetic factors contributed to antisocial behaviors, she probed further. "Do you know anything about Veronica's biological father?"

Mrs. Westbrook took a deep breath and slowly exhaled before responding. "While incarcerated in an asylum, her mother was raped by a male patient who was also psychotic," she replied when she'd calmed down. "Her mother tried to kill him by sticking a fork in his neck. She hid her pregnancy until it was too late for her to have an abortion."

"Why were the girls split up? Isn't that unusual?"

"My husband and I thought so. We asked about adopting both, but Veronica's sister had already been placed with another couple. That seemed strange to us. But Veronica was a healthy, beautiful baby. It was only afterwards that we learned the whole truth."

"What do you mean?"

"According to the investigator, the director of the psychiatric hospital didn't want the infants placed with the same family because there was a history of mental illness. The mother was bipolar and violent; the father was bipolar and self-destructive. He felt that if one of the siblings had the traits of the mother, the other sibling and their adoptive parents could be at risk."

"Did your daughter ever see a psychiatrist?"

"No, only the psychologist. But after we read the investigator's report, we consulted with a psychiatrist about the likelihood of Veronica developing her parents' issues. She explained that there's no one gene that makes someone a sociopath, but numerous inherited genes that make someone at risk of having an anti-social personality disorder. Her opinion was that the chances of someone being a sociopath increase significantly if both parents demonstrated the traits of one."

"Was she ever violent toward you or your husband?"

"No, thank God. Although my husband and I love our daughter, we were relieved when she didn't take us up on our several offers for her to live with us."

Mrs. Westbrook began to weep. Crowder could feel her pain, but didn't know how to console her. How could she find a silver lining in a mother-daughter relationship when the mother was afraid of the daughter?

"Mrs. Westbrook, do you have any recent photos of your daughter?"

"The last one is her senior photo in her high school yearbook," the woman said between sobs. "I can let you see it. It's in her room." Mrs. Westbrook left the kitchen and returned with the yearbook. She opened it to the page where her daughter's photo was posted with a summary of her ambitions in life. Above the name Veronica Lynn Westbrook was a photograph of a beautiful teenage girl with coral-blue eyes and wavy blonde hair. Just below her name was the goals-in-life statement: "To be filthy rich, drive a Porsche, and live in a villa in the Swiss Alps."

Crowder knew she wouldn't be getting further information of importance from Mrs. Westbrook. Her daughter had left no forwarding address, phone number, or email address, and only corresponded when she needed money. She thanked Mrs. Westbrook for her time and left her card to add to others accumulated over the years.

On her way back to the airport, Crowder reflected on Veronica Westbrook's relationship with her parents. She'd grown up a boarder in their home, not a family member. A parentless waif in an orphanage run by people whose names happened to be William and Caroline Westbrook.

It got Crowder thinking about how blessed she was that she'd had parents who were kind and caring and loving. But so did Veronica Westbrook. Yet all the kindness, care, and love in the world couldn't make her into someone capable of feeling that way about her parents, or anyone else.

Almost as though Veronica Lynn Westbrook had been born without a soul.

Chapter 27

February 6, 2018

Westbrook pulled away from St. Alban's School after dropping off Meg on Tuesday and headed northeast out of New Orleans. She had a stop to make on her way to Baton Rouge. The Honey Island Swamp was a forty-five-minute drive and the perfect place to dump a body that would make an early morning brunch for a family of hungry gators.

Booth had wanted a piece of the action for doing no work and assuming no risk. Well, almost no risk. The risk was that the person who did all the work would get pissed off, crush your skull with a hammer, and feed you to alligators. "That's food for thought," Westbrook mumbled to herself as she neared her destination.

The road weaved through wetlands. Signs promised exciting boat tours. A half mile from Carswell's Swamp Tours, she saw a narrow dirt road with a faded, hand-painted sign for "Dock" stuck slantwise in a bouquet of reeds and cattails. She turned down it. Along the way other signs warned, "Beware of Alligators," "Gator Crossing," and "Feed Only the Gators You Want to Feed on You." The road ended at a small landing and beachhead on Talamari Creek. She saw a bridge about a football field away, backed out, drove to it, and marked the spot on the GPS.

The mellow sound of blues singing on the radio made the ninety-minute drive to the state capital pleasant. Once there, she put on her black wig and checked into the Embassy Suites located a couple miles from Ryan Airport for a two-day stay. She registered as Mary Smith, then immediately returned to New Orleans as Ann Livingston for her scheduled visit with Trevor Moore.

It was Tuesday. On Thursday, she'd be back to Baton Rouge as Mary Smith. Then she would fly to New York City to meet her connecting flight out of JFK Airport to Switzerland, arriving in Zurich on Friday morning.

~

"Does anything in my office look familiar to you or remind you of your previous visits?" Moore asked.

"Nothing," Ann answered emphatically, sitting across from him at her scheduled visit. "I wish I could remember being here and the things we talked about, but there's just an emptiness in my mind. It's like my life began when I woke up in the hospital, and a woman I didn't know was holding my hand. When she told me she was my mother, I cried."

"What about now? You've been home more than three weeks. How do you feel when Ben and Meg express themselves to you in affectionate ways?"

"I feel uncomfortable. I hold Meg and kiss her, but it's like she's this nice little girl that I've been asked to look after while her mother's away. I don't know how to be spontaneous or to initiate things with her. I wait until she comes to me, rather than being proactive in her life."

"What about Ben?"

"He's been very considerate, respecting my solitude until I get my memory back and gain some confidence in my roles as his wife and the mother of his child. It breaks my heart to know how much he wants me to love him. But the feelings just aren't there. At least, not yet."

"I know it frightens you, not remembering who you are. That's to be expected. It may be helpful for you to try and do the things that brought you pleasure in your past, like playing the piano or painting. Have you picked up a tennis racket? Trying to do those things may trigger memories."

"I've been afraid to try. My mind is telling me I can't do those things. By looking at photo albums, videos, and my correspondence and emails, I've learned a lot about myself. It's just that I don't feel like the person I see and read about. I know Ben and I are involved in charitable causes and that just before my accident I was about to create and fund a foundation that will help a lot of children. I thought it might help my recovery to go forward with the project. It's such a worthy cause, I feel almost an obligation to go forward with it."

"Does Ben know what you're doing? Someone with an impaired memory shouldn't be handling business matters alone."

"I'm doing the project with a business associate and co-founder. She assured me she can set up our operations in Zurich, where our principal offices will be located. She has dual citizenship with Switzerland. I know Ben needs to be involved, because I'll need his help until I fully recover my memory."

"Yes. He needs to know what you're doing, and the sooner, the better."

"I'll be sure to go over everything with him while we're on our trip to Florida. We leave tomorrow."

"Good. What about how you feel about yourself. Do you see the glass as half full or half empty?"

She had to walk a fine line—be morose enough to maintain the potential for going off the deep end, but not appear so imminently suicidal as to warrant an immediate psychiatric evaluation. "Trevor, sometimes I feel like the glass is empty. Like I'm walking on the edge of a cliff, and that if something else were to happen that hurts me inside, I just might fall off."

"Ann, it's not a sign of weakness to know you may need more help than I can offer," Moore counseled, just as she'd hoped. "It may be the case that you'll benefit greatly from a comprehensive evaluation by a healthcare team that can assess your memory issues."

"Ben has expressed similar concerns to me, and so has my mother. If I don't feel any better by the time we return from Florida,

173

I'll do as you suggest. I'll do anything to get better and not be a burden on my family. It troubles me more than you can know."

She fumbled for the hanky in her purse. Time for more make-believe tears in her make-believe world as Ann Livingston. When the session ended, she scheduled a return visit for the day *after* she was expected to return from the family vacation. Until then, she was to call him day or night if she needed to work through any bad feelings.

One thing was clear to her when the session was over; this was the last visit Ann Livingston would ever make to the office of Dr. Trevor Moore.

~

"Sir, there are only two possibilities," Crowder said. "Either the woman living in the Livingstons' home is Ann Livingston, or she's Veronica Westbrook. If her x-rays make it clear the woman is Westbrook, we can get an arrest warrant right away and bring her in for questioning."

Crowder briefed O'Malley on what they'd learned about Westbrook during her trip to Baltimore: the forged letter, her mother's psychosis, her criminal past, the ovary. Even with the new information, O'Malley had his doubts.

"We have to move cautiously on this," he warned. "Just because this Westbrook woman told her sister she was dead, doesn't mean she kidnapped Ann Livingston. She may have been embarrassed about her criminal past. If she pretends to be dead, that past dies with her. Maybe the ovary's a mistake. Doctors make mistakes every day. X-rays are misread. And, keep in mind, the facts surrounding the collision are consistent with another suicide attempt by a woman with a history of depression."

"But what's the alternative?" Crowder countered. "Do we sit around and wait until Westbrook takes off, and we lose our only connection to Ann Livingston, or until she harms someone else in the Livingston family? She could be intending to play Ann

Livingston for the rest of her life, and that life's a lot easier to live if Ben and Meg Livingston aren't part of it. What more do we need? Ann Livingston's dead body?"

O'Malley punched back. "And what happens if we arrest her and she has a partner who's holding Ann? The partner freaks out and takes off, leaving no evidence behind … like Ann Livingston."

Crowder understood O'Malley's ambivalence and backed off.

O'Malley was finished debating the matter. "We wait until Ben Livingston contacts us and lets us know what his brother-in-law finds out after reviewing the x-rays and the other records. If he believes the woman isn't his wife, we'll get a warrant and bring her in for questioning. After all, who's best able to decide what to do? Us, or the man who lives with the woman and has the most to lose if he's wrong?"

Chapter 28

February 7, 2018

Ann watched from the front door as the Escalade drove away Wednesday morning. The sudden onset of a stomach virus and her insistence that they not disappoint Meg had convinced a reluctant Ben Livingston to proceed with the trip to the Magic Kingdom without her. It was just after nine-thirty. Lucinda wouldn't be there until eleven.

She had plenty of time to steal five million dollars.

She'd sent an email to Jon Knowles the previous day to forewarn him of the transaction he'd be assisting her with when she called him at ten. Smith Reid had recruited Knowles out of the MBA program at Louisiana State University fifteen years earlier. He was punctual, careful, and dependable. Ann was pleased to have such a perfectionist as an unwitting collaborator. He was at his desk when she made her call to his direct line.

"Good morning, Ann. I have the information you requested. The domestic and international Vanguard Premium Funds currently hold sixty percent of the thirty-five million dollars under Smith Reid's management. The other forty percent is in bonds, fixed yield instruments, and cash. The cash in the money market account, as of today, is $6,009,789. So the five million dollars you're requesting can come from the existing cash account, and can be done immediately."

On Monday, Ann had contacted Credit Suisse Bank in Zurich, one of the largest banks in Europe, with assets in the hundreds of billions of dollars. She'd dealt with the Vice President of Corporate Accounts, Heinrich Von Ellison, who'd opened a corporate account in the name of the "There for You Goodwill Foundation LLC." The account could be accessed by Ann Livingston *or* Mary Smith. On Tuesday, she'd had Knowles wire ten thousand dollars from the cash account at Smith Reid to the newly opened account, ostensibly to later pay the foundation's legal expenses. The real reason was so she'd be certain she'd not encounter any problems when transferring the five million dollars.

"I received your wiring instructions yesterday," he continued, "and they match those of the deposit you made on Tuesday to the Credit Suisse account. We're good to go."

"I'll need email verification of the wire transfer," said Ann. "Coordinate your handling of this with Mr. Von Ellison, who knows to confirm when the deposit is made. Thank you for your help, Jon."

It was time to stop by the Livingston ATM for some cash and to pick out some jewelry. When Ben had told her he wasn't sure how much money was in the safe but believed it was "a couple hundred thousand dollars," she'd counted the stash the first chance she got. The fifty thousand she took would not be immediately missed.

When you're worth $125,000,000, you don't readily notice such things.

She put the cash in her suitcase and cherry-picked a few pieces of jewelry from the safe, replacing them with some of the loose, less impressive items from the jewelry case on her dresser.

If you don't know how much cash you have in your safe, you sure as hell won't remember every piece of jewelry your wife owns.

She put her suitcase on the floor under the desk in her office. The only additions would be some clothing items and some documents related to the formation and funding of the foundation.

She was in bed when Lucinda arrived, responding sleepily when she heard her knock softly on the bedroom door. "Just leave the tray on the nightstand," she said when Lucinda opened the door and peeked in. "I'm not ready to get up. I feel pretty weak. It's best I sleep."

Lucinda left a small tray with a biscuit and a cup of tea on Ann's nightstand. "Ana, I check in on you in a couple of hours to see if you need anything. Now, you get some rest."

"Yes, and if I'm asleep, please let me be. I've taken some medicine that's made me drowsy. I'll be down when I wake up."

Ann emerged from the bedroom around one and went to the kitchen, knowing Lucy would be fixing something for lunch. She wanted to engage her in conversation. Say things to her she'd repeat to the police later.

"I don't know what's come over me," she said over a bowl of homemade chicken noodle soup. "I feel real down in the dumps. Ben and Mom wanted to postpone the trip. I wanted no part of it. It would have disappointed Meg too much."

"I know how much the little one was looking forward to the trip," Lucinda said. "And she worry about you. She want you to be the mommy you were to her before you forget who you are. We all do, Ana."

"I feel like such a burden on all of you. I wish I could take a pill, go to sleep, and wake up being the Ann you all remember."

"I stay the night," Lucinda said. "I call my daughter. She bring me what I need. You shouldn't be alone."

"Absolutely not. Ben will be calling me this evening. I know how much you worry about me, and I really appreciate it. But I'll be all right." She managed a slight smile as proof.

She retreated to her room to finish packing and then to her office to work on a letter. Ben called at a quarter after six from their hotel in Tallahassee, the stopover point about halfway to Orlando. "Hello," she said sluggishly.

"Honey, I'm sorry to wake you up, but should you be sleeping so much?" Ann had slept a lot during bouts of depression.

"I'm trying to sleep through whatever it is I've picked up. I'm tired, that's all."

"I still want Lucinda to spend the night. I don't like leaving you alone when you're feeling so out of sorts."

178

"I'm not alone. Buddy's here."

"And I suppose Buddy will call me or Lucinda if you need something. Ann, you know what I mean."

"Okay, I'll have Lucinda spend the night," she lied, knowing full well she'd be sending Lucinda home at seven.

"Good. That's settled. Now I'll have some peace of mind. I'll let you sleep tonight and not bother you with a call until tomorrow morning. Goodnight, dear."

"Goodbye, Ben."

~

Westbrook drove her Lexus from five Owl's Nest Lane on the most direct route to the cabin, arriving a few minutes before eight.

The pickup sat in its usual spot. Only the mice stirred—the large ones affectionately called rats. She pulled around back and parked the pickup alongside her Mercedes with the rear of both vehicles as close to the kitchen door as possible.

The clear, moonlit sky provided enough outdoor light for her to see what she'd be doing. She entered the cabin and turned on the kitchen light. A naked body lay face up on the floor in front of the sink. "Oh! Hi, Sal," she said, stepping around it on her way to the bedroom. The refrigerated coffin still registered thirty-five degrees. She unplugged it and opened the lid. Ann's arms and hands inside burlap no longer rested by her sides. Her elbows were bent and her hands over her face showing through brown-stained slits in the burlap.

Westbrook upended the cooler, and the covered corpse slid out onto the threadbare carpet. The carpet gathered under the body as she dragged it through the living room, jarring a table and knocking over a lamp. Even after an occasional stop to catch her breath, she felt exhausted by the time she reached the kitchen door. A final tug brought the corpse clear of the doorway. It took three rolls of the body to get it to the back of the Lexus less than ten feet away. She strained to lift it vertically, and rested it for a moment on the edge of the rear compartment. The rigid upper body tumbled into the storage area. Stiff legs followed. The rear-hatch door slammed shut.

One body down, one to go.

Westbrook had learned from her internet research that blood inside the body of a corpse thickens and fully coagulates in less than a day, eliminating the potential for bleeding if cut open. She didn't want the place looking all helter-skelter after her chopping and snipping. She put on her garden gloves and, with the pruning clippers in one hand and Booth's hands in the other, snipped off the tips of the body's fingers and thumbs one by one, then placed the morsels in a plastic bag and sealed it shut.

The next task was a bit more gruesome. She'd thought of using a hacksaw, but the blade would pull and rip the flesh rather than cut cleanly through it, and there were no bony structures to saw through, just the cervical vertebrae, brittle by comparison to most other bones in the body. She'd decided that a couple of good whacks with a hatchet would make Sarah Booth join the ranks of Marie Antoinette and that fellow from Sleepy Hollow. She put a bath towel under Booth's head and shoulders and pushed her chin up and back, exposing her neck.

Kneeling beside Booth's corpse, Westbrook gripped the hatchet in both hands and took a practice swing, stopping just short of Booth's skin. She raised it again, higher and well above her head, and with all the force of will and strength of conviction she could muster, chopped through Booth's neck. The blade embedded in the tissue halfway through. Westbrook's next swing went off aim and caught Booth's chin. The jawbone caused the hatchet to slide from her hand.

Sorry, Sal. But the cleft chin suits you.

The third whack severed the vertebrae and went all the way to the kitchen floor.

A piece of cake, once you get the swing of it.

Just some flesh remained attached. Easily snipped with the pruning clippers.

She wrapped the head in the towel, put it in a thirteen-gallon plastic garbage bag, and pulled the drawstring tight, then worked the torso and legs into the second burlap sack she'd bought and fastened it at the feet. She dragged the sack to the Mercedes and placed it, the head, and the fingertips on the floor of the rear seat. The refrigerator chest, she lugged outside and left by the kitchen door.

The kind of person wanting a place like this might have a need for a chest like that.

She'd rented the cabin through February, so she straightened up and left the key on the kitchen table with a printed note: *Had to leave early. Great time here. Saw the sights, fished, and even fed some gators. Thanks a bunch.*

She returned to the Lexus for Ann's trip home. The conversation in the car was decidedly one-sided. "I hope I don't sound callous, Ann. But, in my own small way, I feel like I'm helping you out. You wanted to kill yourself last summer with that overdose. Now, with my help, you'll succeed in what you set out to do. Call it sister-assisted suicide."

She drove carefully. Didn't want to get pulled over for a lane-change violation and have to explain to some nosy cop why she was transporting a dead body that looked just like her. She could almost hear the cop speaking to her, as though it were really happening.

"Ma'am, you didn't signal when you changed lanes back there. Can I see your license and registration?"

"Yes, Officer, of course."

"Ma'am, what do you have in the bag in the back of your car?"

"Oh. That? It's my clone. I just got her out of the refrigerator at the cloning facility that opened up downtown. She's thawing out as we speak. Go ahead. Reach inside the sack. Give her a feel."

When she pulled into the four-car garage, it was almost ten. She parked the Lexus in its usual spot alongside Ben's Jaguar, closed the garage door, got out, and turned on the light. She laid Ann's body on the garage floor and pulled off the burlap sack. "Fuck me," she

181

gasped. Ann's face was unrecognizable. Deep brown grooves marked her cheeks. The surface skin looked as if it'd been peeled off.

An ugly way to die, she thought, but was there any pretty way of dying when murder was involved? "I guess it took a while longer for the end to come. Sorry, sis," she lamented halfheartedly. It didn't matter that Ann's face looked like a teething toy for a pit bull.

Not for what she had planned.

She dressed Ann in the sweatpants, t-shirt, and moccasins she'd worn that day, and returned the wedding band to the finger from which she'd removed it a month earlier. She lifted Ann into the front seat, positioned her feet near the pedals, dropped her cell phone on her lap, and started the engine. The exhaust fumes soon carried their malodorous smell through the garage. The gas tank was three-quarters full. In thirty minutes, gasoline fumes would fully consume the airspace of the garage and become a powder keg ignitable by the slightest spark. Westbrook turned off the light and left through a side door.

She made the house look as though Ann had been in her bedroom most of the day: clothes strewn about, an empty cup of tea on the nightstand, a half-eaten biscuit on a plate beside it, a Bible she found in a drawer of the dresser on the bed, and a colored string dangling from Psalm 23.

Her last act before leaving was to go to Ann's office and turn on her computer.

She'd leave the house, the state, and the country as Mary Smith, dressed in dark gray slacks, a cotton turtleneck, and a leather jacket as black as her wig. She put a pair of two-inch heels in her shoulder bag for her later use and stepped into a pair of Ann's cross-trainers, a necessity for the mile-and-a-quarter trek to the convenience store on the road that led to the interstate. Once there, she'd Uber her way to the downtown train station and take a Lyft back to the cabin.

With the agility of a cat burglar, she climbed out of the house through a pantry window, having previously adjusted the surveillance camera with the pole end of a broom to keep her departure out of view. She moved quickly to the property line about fifty yards from the house and tossed her shoulder bag over the fence. With a boost from a large boulder, she followed. She reached in her bag for the cordless house phone, scrolled down the contacts to Trevor Moore, and tapped.

~

"Trevor here," he answered groggily, the medical journal he was reading when he'd dozed off still open on his lap. He noted that the call came from the Livingston home, and on the other end, he heard Ann's trembling voice.

"Trevor, please help me. I feel so alone. I …"

The phone went dead.

His mind raced with thoughts of Ann doing something harmful to herself that no one could reverse this time. Another overdose? A razor to the wrist? A bullet in the brain? He jumped from his chair, grabbed his jacket and keys, and dashed to his car. On his way, he pressed redial to the Livingstons' house phone. He got voicemail.

Not good.

He left a message, hoping she'd see it, listen to it, and call him right back. "Ann, I'm on my way. If you hear this, please dial 911. Remember that people love you and need you. Think of Ben and your precious Meg. Think of them, and I'll be there very soon."

He next dialed Ann's cell phone. It began to ring, but then suddenly cut off. The phone lay in the lap of a dead woman in a garage where a 383-horsepower engine had been spewing out gasoline fumes for the past half hour. A split second after Moore's call activated the ringtone, a ball of flame blew out the doors of the garage. Second and third explosions blasted through the roof of the garage, forming a bluish haze above a multi-colored geyser of fire.

Chapter 29

Westbrook pressed "Previous Destination" on her navigation system. Up popped the location on the bridge over the Talamari Creek, where Sarah Booth would do some midnight skinny dipping. The woman had been a fly in her ointment, a pebble in her shoe, but was now just another body for her to get rid of. She had Booth where she wanted her: in a sack, in a plastic baggie, and in a towel in a garbage bag.

"Good luck finding enough of her remains to put Miss Humpty Dumpty back together again," she mumbled.

The navigation system did its job. About a mile from Carswell's Swamp Tours, the road came within ten yards of the swamp. She pulled over, reached for the bag of alligator treats, and got out. A few minutes later, Westbrook was back in the car and on her way to the bridge, ten fingertips lighter.

"Your destination is ahead on your right," the GPS forewarned. She drove to the middle of the bridge and turned off the headlights. The creepy, gurgling swamp sounds of the Louisiana bayou broke the still silence. The lazy creek glistened, the moon's reflection off the water providing the only ambient light.

"This place is as dead as you, Sal."

A full minute wait assured her that no vehicles were approaching. Once out of her car, Westbrook had a good view in one direction but a not-so-good view in the other because the road curved a couple hundred yards away. She opened the rear passenger door on the side closest to the creek and reached into the garbage bag for the head. Gripping it by the hair, she dropped it over the guardrail. The head plopped in the water. She caught sight of it just before a sluggish current carried it away.

One headache gone.

Luck is a strange phenomenon. Like the behavior of a precocious child, it can be good or bad and impossible to predict. The child was suddenly misbehaving. "Holy shit! I don't believe it," she groaned. Just as she'd opened the door and pulled the sack with the body halfway out, a vehicle's headlights had appeared at the curve ahead. She tried to muscle the sack back into the car, but it wouldn't budge. Dead weight feels heavier and is harder to move— an unwritten law of physics not found in the high school textbook. But with her experience in pulling, pushing, rolling, dragging, and lifting dead bodies over the past month, she knew it was true.

"Okay. Decision time, Veronica. What are your options?" Pondering options wasn't an option. She ran around the Mercedes, jumped in the front seat, slammed the door shut, and turned on her headlights as she slowly pulled away. Her best bet was to increase her speed gradually and pass by the vehicle as though nothing was out of the ordinary. The half-out body straddling the half-open door was on the passenger side. The driver wouldn't see it as her vehicle passed by.

No such luck.

As soon as she started forward, she heard a thump. When she looked behind her into the rear seat, the burlap sack was gone. The ninety percent of Booth that had remained in the car had dropped out on the bridge.

She watched the other vehicle—a pickup truck—as the distance between them closed. With her left hand raised to cover her face, she peered at the driver through opened fingers like she was looking at him through vertical window blinds. A scruffy-looking man with a puzzled look glared back.

When the pickup got to the bridge, she saw its brake lights come on in her rear-view mirror. "Damn it, he's stopping to take a look," she said, now in full dialogue with herself. "Maybe he'll pull away. How curious are the rednecks who live in the swamps, for Christ's sake? It could be a sack full of garbage for all he knows. Sorry, Sal, no offense intended."

She slowed down as she approached the curve. He was still stopped. "Time to haul ass, Veronica," she instructed herself, gunning it when she got around the curve and saw straight road ahead. The road was narrow and bumpy. No speed limit had been posted for good reason—a chassis rebuild would be required going more than twenty-five. She was doing close to thirty-five. She hadn't deactivated her GPS, so every quarter mile it annoyingly blurted, "Make a legal U-turn and proceed on the same road to your destination."

Her mind raced. "Can't go back, that's for sure." *But what's ahead?* She slowly read the road sign aloud as it gradually came into view. "DEAD ... *fucking* ... END." She was doing almost forty when she slammed on her brakes and fishtailed to a stop within a foot of striking the end-of-road barrier. Suddenly overwhelmed by fatigue, she slumped over the steering wheel.

"I'm screwed. How much time do I have before the redneck calls the police and they find me here trapped?" Speculation overran her brain. It had already been five minutes. More than enough time for him to discover what was in the sack and what was not and call the Sheriff to report he'd found "the dang body of some dang gal with her dang head lopped off." He might even have a CB radio dialed into the police frequency.

He'd be sure to figure that the person in the luxury car driving to a dead end had to be the one who'd dumped the sack. How many people in the area owned luxury cars? The trailers and rundown cabins along the road had a squalid look, likely belonging to owners of rusted-out Ramblers and beat-up, clanking old pickups like the one the redneck was driving. He might even have a shotgun behind the seat and, knowing the road was a dead end, pursue her and try to make a citizen's arrest.

She raised her head from its resting place on the steering wheel. "Wait a minute, are those lights ahead?" she said excitedly. She

186

hurried out of her car and walked around the barrier. Sure enough, there was a road ahead, about a football field away. Headlights flashed by like the turns of a lighthouse beacon, and the night buzzed with the whoosh of vehicles racing along.

It's a highway, maybe even the interstate.

A glimmer of distant light appeared on the road behind her. "The redneck's after me. If I can just get to the road, I can lose the bastard in traffic." She backed up ten feet and squeezed around the guardrail. The Mercedes lumbered forward on the swampy soil until she heard the spin of tires. "No way I'm ending up stuck in mud. Back up slowly," she told herself. "Find solid ground, then move forward slowly, very slowly." She inched back until she found harder earth.

The single beam of light in her rear-view mirror had separated into the two distinct headlamps of the pickup. She had a minute, maybe less, before he got there.

Sweating like an alcoholic with DTs, she thought she might pee her pants. The Mercedes moved slowly through the denser vegetation and brush, where the root systems provided tighter soil. She gradually increased her speed to fifteen, twenty, and then thirty miles an hour. The embankment and highway guardrail came into view. A last look back confirmed the pickup truck was stopped at the dead end.

No time to waste. She turned parallel to the road and drove along the thirty-degree embankment. She could barely maintain control of her car. The vehicles on the road were going twice her speed. She'd be pulling blindly into the path of oncoming traffic. Her raw instincts took over. She floored it as she turned up the embankment and hurdled through an opening in the guardrail. Her front wheels momentarily left the ground. She was airborne, returning to earth with a thud so hard her head hit the ceiling padding.

An eighteen-wheeler barreled down on her as she swerved from lane to lane, trying to gain control of her car. The semi's blaring horn was deafening, and its headlights in the rear-view mirror blinded her so much that she lost all sense of direction. She slammed on her brakes and spun out, coming to a stop in a cloud of dust on the median strip, facing the opposite direction.

Her heart beat so hard and fast she thought it might burst. Bile formed in her throat. She wanted to throw up but dry-heaved instead. She gulped up air and whistled out her exhales until her adrenaline rush passed.

Traffic, though light, moved in both directions. The map on her GPS had her proceeding south, a safer direction to go because the police would think she'd be traveling north, the most direct route to the interstate. By heading south instead, she could exit the highway and weave her way back to the interstate on side roads. The GPS would be her navigator.

About a mile after she'd entered the southbound lanes, she exited the highway and traveled the rural roads until a sign appeared for I-12. The interstate led directly to Baton Rouge and the Embassy Suites, where Mary Smith would quickly shower and then head to the airport for her flight to the Big Apple.

Chapter 30

The sound of Rod Stewart's "Maggie May" was the best his cellphone could offer as a ringtone. He liked the singer and the song, and sang it often with the band, always trying his best to imitate Stewart's gravelly, throaty singing voice. Jenny had the night shift. He was lying diagonally across the bed in his briefs, mostly on Jenny's side, smelling her scent on the sheet and pillow. The early morning call interrupted the dream he was having of her and softened his erection. He reached for his cellphone.

It was Crowder.

"Hey! I just nodded off. You know we have a six o'clock stakeout tomorrow morning ... I mean today." He rubbed the sleep from his eyes as he spoke. "You woke me up in the middle of a dream."

"I know. I saved you from splashing around in it and having to change the sheet when it's over."

"What! Are you outside, looking at me?" He shot a quick glance at the bedroom windows.

"I've got way better things to do, partner."

"What's up?"

"You won't believe this," she said. "A couple of hours ago, there was an explosion in the garage at the Livingston home. It was an inferno when the fire department responded. The blaze is under control and mostly out, but not much is left of the garage."

"And Ann Livingston?"

"Apparently not much is left of her, either."

"What do you mean?"

"No one was in the house when Fire responded. But the remains of a body were found burnt to a crisp in the front seat of Ann Livingston's Lexus. Wasn't enough left to do a visual identification, but it's looking like it was her. Her wedding band was on what was once a finger. Cap wants us to handle the investigation. He's reassigned the stakeout. I'll meet you at the house."

"Damn lucky the rest of the family was away when it happened."

"I know. It could have been worse, a lot worse. She must have waited for them to leave. Must have been planning it around their trip."

"Looks like the third time's a charm," Steele said. "Ann Livingston finally got it right."

~

Captain O'Malley waited for his detectives in the living room of the Livingston home, making small talk with a tall, good-looking man in his early forties. Crowder and Steele arrived shortly after one in the morning. O'Malley waved them over.

"Dr. Moore, this is Lieutenant Crowder. She and her partner, Sergeant Steele, are the detectives heading the investigation." The detectives acknowledged Moore with head nods. O'Malley looked at Crowder. "Dr. Moore is a clinical psychologist and personal friend of the family. He was also Ann Livingston's therapist for many years. I'll let you take over from here."

O'Malley retreated to the privacy of the study for the task of breaking the news to Ben Livingston. Being the bearer of bad news came with the territory of a homicide detective. One thing he'd learned early was that bad news was best delivered the right way, which was right away. He called from the house phone.

"Mr. Livingston. Mr. Ben Livingston?"

"Yes. Who's calling … uh … at two thirty in the morning?" An hour ahead in his time zone.

"This is Captain Francis O'Malley of the New Orleans Police Department. I'm sorry to have to call you at this time of the morning."

190

"Where are you calling from?"

O'Malley heard the question as more of a demand. "I'm at your home in Whispering Pines. There's been a fire, an explosion in your garage."

"Where's Ann? Where's my wife? Is she hurt?" he asked frantically.

"We found two cars in the garage. We believe a woman was in one of them."

"What do you mean ... you believe ... a woman? Why can't you tell for sure, for God's sake?"

"The body was badly burned. We'll know for certain very soon."

"Where was Lucinda? Lucinda Alvarez? She was spending the night. What does she say happened?"

"Sir, no one was in the house when police and fire department personnel arrived here." A period of silence followed. O'Malley wondered whether he'd lost the connection. "Are you there, Mr. Livingston?"

"Yes. I'm here," he said, his voice suddenly flat and emotionless.

"We know you're away on a trip with your daughter and mother-in-law. We'll need to go through your home and look for clues that might help us make sense of all this. Do we have your permission?"

"Yes, of course."

"We'll leave as much as possible undisturbed and provide you with an inventory of anything we've taken as part of our investigation. Do we have your consent to proceed in that manner?"

"Yes. Do whatever is necessary to find out what happened to Ann. I'll catch an early flight back and be home later today."

"Lieutenant Crowder and Sergeant Steele, whom you know, are handling the investigation. They'll contact you when you return and provide you with more information about what happened."

"Yes. I understand. I want to return to my home. Will that be a problem?"

"As soon as the forensic people have been through the house and the debris, you can return. The fire was contained before it could spread to the house. They should be finished today, tomorrow at the latest."

"I'll be staying at my sister's home, which is nearby. I can be reached on my cell at the number you called."

"I know this will be a difficult time for you, Mr. Livingston. We'll do our best to conclude our investigation as soon as possible."

O'Malley didn't hang up right away. He waited to hear if Livingston had anything else to say. What he heard was a click and silence. He held the phone in his hand a moment longer and wondered whether he and Ben Livingston were sharing the same thought.

How do you tell an eight-year-old girl her mother is dead?

~

"So, Dr. Moore, what happened last night?" Crowder asked.

"I received a call from Ann around ten thirty. She was clearly distraught. Before I had a chance to talk to her, the line went dead. I could see the call was made from her home. So I called her back but was connected to voicemail. I left a message. I tried her cell, but that call disconnected."

"And what message did you leave?"

"That I was on my way … that she should think about her husband and daughter, and to dial 911 if she needed help right away."

"What did you do after that?"

"I grabbed my keys, ran to my car, and drove to the house, arriving around eleven. I dialed 911 on the way. By the time I got here, the firemen and police had already arrived."

"And then?

"I went up to a patrolman, gave him my name, and told him what I've just told you."

"And after that?"

"He told me to wait in my car. Captain O'Malley came to my car about an hour later. I accompanied him into the house. He asked me to wait in the living room and not touch anything. We talked briefly, and you showed up."

"Dr. Moore, why would Ann call you?"

"I'm her therapist. We're also close friends."

Crowder shot a glance at Steele. Jaded by their experiences as homicide detectives, she knew they saw the same red flags. Good-looking man *plus* good-looking married woman *plus* therapist *plus* close friends *equals* lovers and reason for suicide.

Maybe.

Maybe not.

"What exactly did Mrs. Livingston say to you on the phone when she called?"

"She said she was feeling alone—they were her exact words—and that she needed to see me."

"Did she sound depressed?"

"Yes, but also desperate, like her world as she knew it was crashing down on her."

"Did she sound like she might commit suicide?"

"Detective Crowder, suicide is primarily a legal term. We, as healthcare professionals, understand suicide to be the *voluntary,* intentional taking of one's own life. Whether the taking of one's life is voluntary depends on the mental health of the individual at the time. Let me explain: A quarter of persons with bipolar disorder will attempt suicide; some studies suggest a much higher percentage. One has to wonder if it's intentional when there's an underlying mental disorder that's responsible for the patient's actions."

"But we know Ann tried to kill herself last summer by overdosing on her antidepressants," Crowder said. The cat was out of the bag on the suicide attempt ever since Livingston had shared Ann's psychiatric evaluation with the detectives. "And that her car crash last month was another attempt to hurt or even kill herself. What happened today is sure looking like more of the same."

"Obviously if someone suffers from depression and has already attempted suicide once," Moore explained, "the person is much more at risk of taking her own life, particularly if she's not being treated for it. Ann, however, was receiving ongoing treatment for her depression."

"Did she sound desperate enough on the phone to take her own life, based on her history of depression and suicide attempts? After all, you were concerned enough to call for help and race over to her home to be with her."

"I certainly don't dispute that Ann was depressed enough to take her own life. But, in her case, you have someone who would be expected to choose living over dying, particularly knowing she's a devout Episcopalian, and that she has a devoted husband and a loving daughter who was the center of her life."

"Her call to you last night. Wasn't she reaching out to you for help, like when she overdosed last summer?"

"Yes. That's the logical conclusion to reach." He bowed his head. "It's just that this time, I didn't act quickly enough to save her."

Crowder sensed how he was feeling. They gave the department's crisis negotiator a hero's salute and a night out on the squad whenever she talked down a jumper, but they left her alone and gave her a two-day furlough whenever the person instead did a belly flop off the top floor.

Crowder had gotten what she needed from Moore for the time being. They exchanged cards with their contact information.

As he left the room, he turned at the doorway and said, with a sagging expression, "I *could* have done more. I *should* have done more."

~

The chimes of the Livingstons' grandfather clock signaled two o'clock.

"It's time for a walkthrough," Crowder announced.

They donned clear latex gloves and, starting from the front door, went room to room looking for clues on tables and chairs. They peered into closets, looked in drawers and under furniture, and inspected the carpet with high-intensity pencil lights. Nothing noteworthy was found.

Steele checked the windows and doors for evidence of forced entry. "Everything's locked up tighter than an untapped beer keg," he said, "except for an unlocked window in the pantry."

"It makes no sense that a depressed woman would leave her house through a window to go to the garage to commit suicide," Crowder said. "Have forensics dust the window and lock for prints."

They proceeded to the second floor and inspected each room. When they got to Meg's room, Steele noticed the sign on the door: *Meg and Buddy's Room*. "Who's Buddy?"

"The Livingstons' dog. A patrolman heard him barking from the room when he did his walkthrough. Moore agreed to take care of it until the family gets back."

Meg's room was neat and clean, with everything in its expected place. Ann and Ben's bedroom required a more in-depth look. They checked the dresser drawers and then the closets.

"Typical guy's closet," Steele quipped when he saw what looked like a miniature Brooks Brothers men's store in one of the walk-in closets.

"Same here," Crowder countered while looking through the other closet. "Her closet's bigger than my bedroom. I don't see a match for the shoe we found in her car. *Geez Louise*! I've never seen so many pairs of shoes in one place."

"Come look at this, Jo. There's a book partially hidden under the sheet."

She walked over, picked it up, and said, "A Bible." Several colored string separators bunched together at the end of the book, serving no particular purpose. A single, red-colored string identified Psalm 23. "Well, partner, I think we have our first clue. She was reading Psalm 23."

"Psalm 23? I must have missed that one in my Bible studies."

"Let me read a part of it. Verse 4, 'Even though I walk through the valley of the shadow of death, I fear no evil, for you are with me.' My daddy made us kids go to Sunday school to study the Bible. This passage is a symbolic description of the inevitability of death. It's been read at the gravesite of every funeral I've ever been to."

"Yeah, I see what you mean."

Crowder put the book in a plastic evidence bag. "We'll want prints from the Bible. Also the tea cup, saucer, and plate on the nightstand. We want to be sure Ann is connected to these items."

They moved into the adjoining room. She immediately knew it was Ann's office from the soft, dainty design of the furniture, the colorful window curtains, and the family photographs that hung on the walls. The screen on the desktop computer drew her attention. It showed a letter in progress. She sat in Ann's chair and scrolled up to where the script began while her partner looked over her shoulder. They read in silence.

My dearest family,

I don't know how to put into words how difficult it is for me to write this to you. I feel so alone. I don't know who I am. All that I know of me is who you tell me I once was. I tried to learn more about myself so that I could be that person. I looked at the photo albums, the videos, and the files in my office. I even followed through on the formation of a foundation I had been working on in the months before my accident stole from me my memory and my life. I felt that if I completed the project with the help of a colleague, it might rekindle in me a purpose in life. Ben, I know you'll step in now and work with her to complete what we started.

I woke up this morning feeling empty inside. I was afraid to tell you how I felt because I know what good people you are, and I wanted to spare you the burdens of taking care of someone like me.

I believe that I must be mentally ill because I've lost the will to live, even though my life has so much to offer me.

I drove around tonight to give myself time to think about whether I could ever be capable of feeling good about myself. God knows that everyone has been so very kind to me. I just don't feel anything inside me that is a connection to you. Even my own mother feels like a total stranger. I just don't think I can take it anymore and put all of you through

The letter ended abruptly, mid-sentence.

Steele arched back to his full height, nodding his head. "That's as close to a suicide note as we'll ever find. Case closed."

Crowder felt a sudden pang of guilt. She'd doubted the woman's memory loss, her honesty, her very identity, and she might have been completely wrong. She looked down again at the letter on the computer screen. "She mentions driving around last night. There's a security surveillance system in the house. There are monitors throughout the home."

"I know, there's one over there," Steele said, pointing to a screen on the wall. "If the system was operating, it could tell us when Ann left and returned to the house last night."

"And if anyone else entered and left the house," Crowder said. "We'll take a look at it on the way out. Make a note to get prints off the computer keyboard to be sure the letter was typed by Ann, and off the desk and phone. Let's see if anyone else was snooping around in her office."

Crowder opened the drawers of Ann's desk and file cabinet and looked inside. She saw folders for the various Livingston foundations, including a folder for the There for You Goodwill Foundation, LLC. She found letters between Ann Livingston and Mary Smith about the foundation and more correspondence between her and Jon Knowles, Jared Hochstein, and Credit Suisse Bank about the foundation's formation and funding.

"She was a busy girl working on forming a foundation. It must be the one she mentions in her letter. This stuff's pretty recent … and look at this." She handed her partner Ann's letter of instructions to Knowles. "How many depressed, suicidal amnesiacs do you think are capable of handling a five-million-dollar business transaction?"

After completing their inspection of Ann's office, the two detectives proceeded to the third floor for an inspection of the rooms there. Nothing appeared out of the ordinary. They huddled up at the front door to commiserate.

"It sure looks like Ann Livingston made good on her third attempt, and did it in a spectacular way," Steele said.

Crowder handed the bagged Bible to a forensics tech who was getting prints off the front door. "Yeah, almost too spectacular," she said uneasily. "Let's see what Ted's found out."

They left the house and tracked down Fire Chief Theodore Moody. Moody had recently been promoted to the top position after twenty years with the New Orleans Fire Department. He'd earned the reputation of a gutsy fireman and a savvy arson investigator. Crowder had previously worked with him on homicides involving arson. "What do you think, Teddy?"

"Well, we haven't gone through all the rubble. We don't know what we'll find when we get some daylight and can see how far the debris was projected from the origin of the explosion. We're also several days away from relating debris to the individual vehicles involved, but it looks like the initial explosion was activated by a spark that ignited a garage full of gasoline exhaust fumes so compressed, the slightest catalyst could blow the place up."

"It sure looks like suicide," Steele said.

"Looks that way," Moody said. "Probably thought it was time to check out. Got in her Lexus, turned on the ignition, and just breathed. She was dead in five to ten minutes."

"Will we learn anything from an autopsy?" Crowder asked.

"There's not much of a body left to work with. Most of the upper body flesh was incinerated. Forget prints. The skull's mostly

198

intact, at least the bony structures, and the teeth. We should eventually be able to get dental records and, if necessary, DNA, and make a positive ID. Assuming there's enough lung left, Bill Sessions might find evidence of carbon monoxide in the tissue." Dr. William Sessions was the chief medical examiner and elected coroner for Orleans Parish. "That'll be your proof of the cause of death and will tell us whether this is a typical suicide by carbon monoxide poisoning."

"Multiple explosions were reportedly heard," Crowder said. "What's the likely sequence of events?"

"Here's how I see it happening. The woman breathes in carbon monoxide and is dead in ten minutes. The gas continues to build. Twenty minutes later, something ignites the gasoline exhaust fumes. There's a fireball. Anything not metal or masonry is like kindling. The heat from the fire explodes the gas tanks of the Lexus and Jaguar. The end result is one overcooked woman, two burned-out vehicles, and a hell of a mess to clean up."

"When do you think you'll have your final report?"

Moody turned and walked toward his vehicle. "A week, maybe earlier," he said over his shoulder. "O'Malley said the Mayor wants it done yesterday."

"Do we need to do anything more tonight?" Steele pouted through a yawn.

"Just the surveillance recordings," Crowder said. "I'll take a look and meet you at your car."

When she returned five minutes later, her partner was leaning against Bugsy with his arms crossed, chin bent to his chest, eyes closed. "Hey, sleepy head," said Crowder, "the security cameras were rolling yesterday, as far as I can tell. We'll take a look at them later. Let's call it a night. We'll brief Cap tomorrow. He'll want our preliminary report before he speaks to the press."

Crowder turned and raised a hand over her head. Steele slapped it, the high five serving as Crowder's way of signaling she was on top of an investigation that would be the subject of intense public scrutiny in the weeks that followed.

The evidence seemed overwhelming. Ann Livingston, suffering from severe depression, found that the finality of death outweighed the uncertainty of life, and chose death.

Or so it seemed.

Chapter 31

"**P**hoto ID, please," the ticketing agent for American Airlines asked the pretty young woman with the jet-black hair. The woman handed the agent her passport. "Ms. Smith, how many bags will you be checking?"

"Just one," she said. The suitcase had been packed with special care in her room at the Embassy Suites. If all went as planned, it would be in Zurich tomorrow morning. The challenging part wasn't getting the suitcase through customs in Zurich, the problem was getting the fifty thousand dollars of pocket money she'd hidden in a garment bag in her suitcase through TSA at JFK and out of the USA. Persons leaving the United States with cash in excess of ten thousand dollars were required to complete a declaration form and prove the cash had a legitimate source.

She lay back in her first-class seat. The combination of a full recliner, fluffed pillow, cool air blowing over her blanket, and two glasses of chardonnay were the prelude to a well-earned night of uninterrupted sleep. While she waited for the curtain to drop, she wondered how the police investigation was going. Crowder and Steele would be assigned to investigate her sister's death. She was sure of that.

What would they find?

She mulled over the hard evidence. An autopsy finding of carbon monoxide in the lungs. The family, Lucinda, and Trevor Moore confirming how depressed she was. A previous suicide attempt. The car crash. The frantic last call for help. A suicide note.

An open and shut case of suicide.

Her last thought before she slowly drifted into a dreamless state was that the trail to her whereabouts was as dead as Ann Livingston.

~

Punctual to a fault, Crowder entered O'Malley's office at precisely eleven thirty Thursday morning for the scheduled briefing. She sat in one of the two chairs in front of O'Malley's desk. Steele stood with his back against the wall next to the door, a cup of coffee in his hand and a stirrer in his mouth.

O'Malley directed his question to no one in particular. "What happened last night?"

"It's looking a lot like Ann Livingston finally got it right," Crowder said as she handed him the detectives' twelve-page report. "You know, when at first you don't succeed."

"How sure are we that the body is the Livingston woman? Not much was left of it, according to Moody."

"The engraving on the inside of the wedding band proves the ring was Ann's. But we'll get her dental records to Sessions for a positive ID."

O'Malley flipped through the pages of the report without stopping to read any of them and tossed it on his desk. He looked up at Crowder. "Short version."

"The circumstantial evidence is pretty compelling. We have a woman with a long history of depression and at least one, perhaps two, suicide attempts, whose last call is to her psychotherapist, who says she sounded depressed and desperate. A woman who prepared a letter saying *sayonara* to her family."

"A handwritten letter?"

"No. She typed it on the desktop in her office. We'll get prints off the keyboard just to be sure."

"How'd she die?"

"Textbook carbon-monoxide poisoning. Just sit in your car and breathe in the fumes, pass out, and it's 'goodbye cruel world' in under ten minutes."

"Sid, anything to add?"

"She'd been reading the Bible in bed. Psalm 23. You know, the one about green pastures, valleys, and quiet waters. It wasn't like the trip she was planning was of the English countryside."

O'Malley let out a deep, gratifying sigh. "Good. Everything points to Ann Livingston committing suicide last night. We can bring the investigation to a close as soon as Sessions confirms she died from carbon monoxide poisoning." He leaned forward and rustled some papers on his desk, a sure sign to Crowder that the briefing was over.

"There's still the wrinkle of the x-ray showing an ovary," she said, her voice a decibel higher than before.

O'Malley leaned back in his chair and folded his arms against his chest. "That's as slim a case as you can have to dispute the obvious conclusion any rational, thinking person would come to. Hospitals, surgeons, and x-ray technicians fuck up all the time. A simple mistake could explain the inconsistency."

Crowder anticipated the scuffle. "But what if the inconsistency can't be explained?" she countered, adopting a challenging tone. "We're back to where we were last week, only the identical twin sister who's dead is Ann Livingston, not Veronica Westbrook."

O'Malley wasn't impressed. "Right now, Ben Livingston believes the dead woman is his wife and that she committed suicide. There's no way he's going to ask his brother-in-law to study her x-rays and prove she's someone else."

"Last night, I was fully prepared to believe it was suicide. But this morning I got up thinking that everything was too perfect and …" She paused to reflect on how best to plead her case.

"And what?" O'Malley said impatiently.

"Ann Livingston transferred five million dollars to a Swiss bank account of a charitable foundation she recently formed with a woman, Mary Smith. She authorized the transaction the day of her suicide. I'm thinking this foundation and Smith are connected in some way with Ann Livingston's death. Money is the root of all evil, and the root might be growing out of that foundation."

"It's your investigation. Find some evidence to back up your suspicions," O'Malley said, his tone less curt. "But I hope your suspicions are wrong. Suicide, while a regretful ending to Ann Livingston's life, is understandable and was probably not preventable. Murder, on the other hand, will embroil this department in a long, complicated criminal investigation into one of the most heinous crimes ever committed in this state."

~

Crowder and Steele showed up at the three o'clock press conference just as it was about to begin and took their places behind O'Malley alongside Moody and the mayor's chief of staff. National broadcasting and cable news stations provided live feeds. A dozen local and national reporters sat in the public section of the city council chambers in downtown New Orleans. The mayor's office was two floors up.

O'Malley read from a prepared text, took a few questions he answered vaguely, then bolted from the podium out a side door with the mayor's aide by his side. Moody took Crowder and Steele aside after they followed them out. "Let's huddle up somewhere private," he said. They found an empty conference room. "I reviewed your preliminary report. Nice work. I saw that Ann Livingston's therapist made several calls in quick succession after the call from her house phone cut off. Something's not right with that."

"What do you mean?" Crowder asked.

"It would've taken at least twenty-five minutes for the gasoline exhaust emissions to reach the concentration level needed for them to ignite. We're talking about a four-car garage with a storage area and workshop on the first floor. That's a lot of open space to fill. But once that concentration level was reached, the slightest spark could ignite the gas, such as the radio frequency discharge from a phone. Ordinarily, the RF energy a cellphone emits is insufficient to ignite ambient carbon monoxide fumes, for example, while pumping gas. It's different when the discharge occurs *inside* the gas tank."

"The therapist says he called the house phone and Ann Livingston's cell after they were disconnected," Steele said. "That was probably the spark that ignited the gas."

Crowder understood Moody's dilemma. "The problem, Sid, is that the explosion occurred a few minutes after Ann's call to Moore disconnected. She didn't answer when Moore called her house phone or cell. The explosion was reported shortly after his 911 call, the very next call he made, and the first responders showed up within ten minutes."

Her partner, now following along, filled in the blanks. "So there wouldn't have been enough time for the gas to have reached the concentration needed for it to explode."

"Right," Moody said.

"Maybe Ann tried to make a call on one of the house phones or her cell phone from the garage after the engine had been running a while," Steele suggested.

Moody let Crowder debunk the theory. "No, because Ann would have been unconscious in five minutes and dead in ten."

"The car's front windows were down and the tailpipe wasn't plugged," Moody explained. "So the gas fumes were dispersed over a broader area, giving her a few minutes longer before she died. Even then, Jo's right, she'd have been incapacitated and unable to use a phone within five minutes."

Crowder's analytical mind raced at full throttle. "Ted, I'm curious about something."

"What?

"Did your people find a cordless house phone in the car, or anywhere else in the garage?"

"I had them go through the debris a second time this morning after I read your report. No phone other than the cell phone was found."

"That explains it," she exclaimed, her eyes widening. "She made the call to Moore from a cordless house phone when Ann was already dead. She knew he'd call her back on her cell."

"Who's *she?*" Moody asked.

Steele looked over at Crowder. Both men's eyes fixed on her when she answered.

"The Lucifer among God's angels."

PART THREE

Beware of false prophets, which come to you in sheep's clothing,
but inwardly they are ravening wolves.
Matthew 7:15

Chapter 32

Lufthansa Flight 833 arrived in Zurich at eight thirty Friday morning. The airport was an eleven-minute train ride to Switzerland's largest city, the banking hub of Europe and the corporate headquarters of Credit Suisse Group. Mary Smith had a three o'clock appointment with its director of corporate accounts, Heinrich Von Ellison.

She looked every bit the no-nonsense businesswoman when she arrived at the bank five minutes early in her navy-blue pinstripe skirt and matching blazer. A pair of Ann's sapphire earrings accented her bright-white, low-neckline silk blouse. Ann's diamond-studded Rolex watch sent a signal that the person wearing it was both punctual and successful. She was asked to take a seat and greeted at precisely a minute before three by Von Ellison's conservatively dressed secretary, a gaunt-looking woman in her mid-fifties with a distinctly French accent. She held a manila folder tight to an underdeveloped chest.

"Mr. Von Ellison will see you now, *madame*. You will come with me." Her words were more of an official demand than a polite request.

Westbrook followed the woman into the office. Von Ellison could have passed as his secretary's fraternal twin. He appeared about her age and, like his secretary, slight of frame with a thin face and pointed nose. They wore matching wire-rimmed eyeglasses. They even dressed alike, wearing conservative-looking, charcoal-colored suits, with Von Ellison's lemon-and-white striped tie nicely complementing his secretary's cream-and-canary polka-dot scarf.

"Good afternoon, *madame*." Von Ellison opened their meeting with the polite stuffiness that comes naturally to someone from a bloodline of snobby bankers. "Before we proceed, I need to see your identification."

She retrieved her passport and U.S. driver's license from her shoulder bag and handed them over. His unblinking eyes moved up and down between the photos on the documents and her face. "I'd smile," she said, "but you might think I'm not the serious-looking woman in the photos." She remembered the police mug shot routine from her arrests. "Don't smile, ma'am," she'd be told. Then, just as the camera clicked, she'd break into a toothy, happy smile to piss off the cop.

Her attempt at humor fell on clogged ears.

"*Madame* Smith, your papers are in order," he said with the emotionless inflection of a bureaucrat of the Third Reich. "What business may I transact for you today?"

"I need a bank check for the full amount of the wire transfers, in Swiss francs, of course. I'll be investing these funds elsewhere and closing the existing account."

The type of check she'd requested, like bearer bonds, did not require a payee be designated. The guarantor was Credit Suisse. Anyone in possession of the check could cash it at any national bank.

That anyone would be someone named Laura Mueller.

"Of course, *madame*. It should take about twenty minutes to prepare the paperwork. May I offer you coffee or tea while you wait?"

"No, I'm fine." She glanced at her watch to suggest he was keeping her from another appointment.

Von Ellison left his office and returned like clockwork twenty minutes later. Since the corporate account had been opened in the names of Ann Livingston *or* Mary Smith, only one signature was necessary to withdraw funds, obtain a bank check, and close the account. He handed Mary Smith a check in the amount of 4,989,000 Swiss francs.

Not bad for a couple months work.

210

She left the bank and stepped into a cool, clear, windless day. On her walk back to the hotel, she stopped at a café on the Paradeplatz, the most famous square in Switzerland, with the bank check safely tucked in her bra. She ordered a Bellini, pulled out her iPhone, and connected to the Wi-Fi. While she sipped her drink, she searched the internet for Porsche dealerships and realtors in Zurich. This weekend, her last as Mary Smith, would be spent shopping for a new wardrobe.

On Monday, she'd wake up Laura Mueller, one of the wealthiest single women in Europe, shopping for her Porsche and dream house.

Chapter 33

Lucinda led the detectives to the study where Livingston sat looking at a photo album on his lap. His eyes fixed on a single photo, one of Ann and Meg smiling at each other at Ann's birthday party the previous summer. He didn't flinch when the officers took their seats across the coffee table from him.

"Mr. Livingston, will you be wanting me to serve the coffee?" Lucinda asked, startling him back to real time.

"Oh, I'm sorry, Lieutenant Crowder … Sergeant Steele. Yes, Lucinda, please bring us coffee."

She left, closing the door to the study.

"Lucinda's been crying most of the morning. I told her to take the week off, or as long as she needs, but she insisted on coming over."

Crowder was speaking when Lucinda returned. "We're sorry we have to speak to you so soon after something like this, but we know you want us to conclude our investigation as soon as possible." She paused while Lucinda put the tray with the coffee and pastries on the table and, with the solemnity of a penitent nun on her way to vespers, left with her head bowed. "We can take our time today," Crowder continued. "If necessary, we can come back tomorrow or the next day if we don't finish."

Steele opened the bag he'd brought and pulled out a handheld recording device. "Mr. Livingston, is it all right if we record your statement?" he asked.

Livingston nodded his assent.

Crowder handled the questioning. "I'd like to start with your interaction with Ann during the weeks before your trip to Florida.

We know she was involved in the car crash last month and had some memory issues. How was she handling all of that?"

"We scheduled a trip to Florida for this week. Ann planned it in December as a birthday present for our daughter, Meg, who recently turned eight. She was looking forward to it as much as Meg. And then she had the accident in January, and everything changed. Her memory loss made it difficult for her to relate to any of us. We were like total strangers."

"Did her memory improve as time went by?"

"She looked at photo albums and videos. All of us talked about her many accomplishments. She seemed ... well, I guess the best way to describe it is disinterested. She met with Trevor Moore, a friend and her therapist, who was helping her cope with her memory issues. But I didn't see much improvement."

"And on Wednesday?"

"She came down with something and didn't feel well enough to make the trip. We wanted to put it off until spring, but she insisted we go and was quite upset with me when I tried to convince her otherwise."

"Did she look well enough to be left alone?"

"She wasn't alone. Lucinda arrived at eleven. The plan was for her to spend the night. My sister was returning from a family vacation today. So I knew she'd be over to see Ann while we were away."

"Did Ann look depressed to you?"

"Not overly so. Otherwise, I would never have left her. Of course, ever since her accident, it's been difficult to gauge how she was feeling. She kept everything bottled up inside her. Her memory issues overwhelmed her. When your captain called me early Thursday morning and told me ..." He paused mid-sentence to catch a breath. "I knew almost immediately that something was terribly wrong and that I'd failed ... failed to protect her from herself."

"When did you last see her?"

213

"Around nine thirty, Wednesday morning. She promised me she'd have Lucinda spend the night. Lucinda and Ann are as close as two unrelated people can be. I felt comfortable leaving Ann with her."

"When was the last time you spoke to her?"

"Late afternoon, around five thirty. We stopped at a hotel about midway to our destination, and I called her."

"How did she sound on the phone?"

"Tired … but I attributed it to the blah feeling you get when you come down with something that drains your energy. I talked to Lucinda twice during the day. She told me Ann was in her room resting for most of the day. She also told me she planned on staying over. Needless to say, I was relieved."

"Why didn't she? No one was here when police and fire personnel arrived."

"She broke down and cried uncontrollably when I spoke to her on the phone this morning. Through her sobbing, she told me that Ann had insisted she go home. Like me, she's feeling she let her down."

"The last person to speak to your wife was Dr. Moore. Ann called him on the house phone. He said she sounded desperate, like her world was collapsing around her."

"I know she was feeling out of sorts, but I didn't think she sounded desperate. Yet, in thinking back, there was something about the way she said goodnight when I called her. She said 'goodbye,' not 'goodnight.' It sounded … well … so final."

Steele interjected. "Was your wife accustomed to reading the Bible at home, Mr. Livingston?"

"Why do you ask?"

"We found a Bible on the bed."

"We kept a Bible in each of the bedrooms. It was a practice my parents, who were devout Episcopalians, started, and we carried forward with it. Ann and I both studied the Bible growing up, but reading it as adults wasn't something we did."

"It was open to Psalm 23," Steele continued. "Are you familiar with it?"

"My sister and I had to learn it well enough to recite it when we were children. It was read at my parents and Ann's father's funeral services"

Livingston suddenly stopped speaking. He rested his chin on his folded hands, his elbows on his knees. To Crowder it seemed as if he was reflecting on his days in Sunday school when he'd been asked to recite a prayer. "The Lord is my shepherd. I lack nothing," he began. "He makes me lie down in green pastures; he leads me beside quiet waters ..." His voice lowered and tapered into a whisper. "Though I walk through the darkest valley ..." He stopped mid-verse, as a child might who can no longer remember the remaining words.

Crowder broke the silence but spoke softly. "Do you want us to come back tomorrow?"

Livingston raised his head from his hands. "No. Let's continue until you feel you have what you need from me."

"We found a partially completed letter on your wife's computer in her office and printed a copy." She handed the letter to him. He read it, let out an audible sigh, and placed it on the table. "Is what's in this letter something you believe Ann would've prepared?" she asked.

"I don't know what you mean," he said. "Of course she prepared this. Ann was depressed ... worried she might be mentally ill. She discussed her concerns with me earlier."

"How much earlier?"

"Last summer, when she took too much of her medicine and had to go to the hospital."

"You mean when she tried to commit suicide?" Crowder felt bad being so blunt, but Livingston was in denial. "In the psychiatric evaluation you shared with us about the incident, her psychiatrist called it a suicide attempt."

"Well ... that was one possibility. Ann was unclear about her thinking when she took the pills. She called Trevor before the pills

215

took effect. He came right over and called for an ambulance. She regretted what she did and told me she had every reason in the world to live. Things got back to normal in a few weeks and then took a nosedive after her accident in January."

"There's mention of a foundation in her letter. Did she ever discuss it with you?"

"No. I'm surprised she didn't tell me about it."

"What about Mary Smith?"

"Never heard of her."

"There was a file in your wife's office with correspondence and notes that suggest there was an ongoing relationship between her and Mary Smith for about six months. That's a long time to keep something like that secret, don't you think?"

"Yes, it's odd she didn't mention her. We have very capable people already involved in the formation and operation of our foundations. Why she partnered up with someone new is something I can't explain."

"A review of the paperwork indicates the foundation was formed last Friday. Five million dollars was transferred from your joint investment account to a bank in Switzerland this Wednesday morning, shortly after you left on your trip to Florida. That's a lot of money to be moving from your account without you knowing about it."

"I know. But I trusted Ann completely." His tone of voice turned defensive. "She was probably going to tell me about it when I returned from our trip."

"But the account she set up gave this Smith woman control over five million dollars. Is that how foundations typically operate?"

"Of course not. There are supposed to be safeguards in effect preventing a single person from having control over that sum of money. Usually, both the CFO *and* Treasurer's signatures are required for transfers and withdrawals of large amounts. I'll be looking into this matter further. You can be certain of that."

"It seemed to us your wife's mental state and behaviors on Wednesday were inconsistent with her being able to handle the kind of business she conducted."

"If I find out this Smith woman took advantage of Ann, she'll live to regret it."

The detectives, eyebrows raised, traded glances. "We'll want to know what you uncover," Crowder said. "We can assist you in taking any … lawful," she let the word linger a moment, "actions against anyone who acted criminally toward your wife." She looked at her partner. "Do you have any questions for Mr. Livingston?"

"A couple. We found an unlocked window on the first floor. Did you know it was unlocked?"

"All of the windows should have been locked. Which one was it?"

"A window in the pantry."

"I have no idea why it wasn't locked."

"One final matter. Do you recall our concern over Ann's x-rays showing an ovary, which is impossible because—"

Livingston interrupted Steele mid-sentence. "Yes. But that's no longer important if it was Ann in the car. And it's my understanding that you'll be able to conclusively determine that."

"Yes," Steele said. "Dental records and, if necessary, her DNA will allow us to make a positive identification."

Crowder had unsettled feelings about Veronica Westbrook's involvement in Ann Livingston's death. As far as she was concerned, Westbrook was the target of the investigation, regardless of how O'Malley and her partner saw it. She didn't raise those concerns with Livingston. She'd wait until Sessions reviewed his autopsy findings with her and he explained the discrepancy in Ann's x-rays.

~

"A finding of suicide is inevitable," Steele said as they drove back to police headquarters. "If Sessions finds evidence of carbon monoxide in the lungs, it won't matter what Ted's calculations show."

Crowder didn't see it that way. If Ann Livingston didn't detonate the fire bomb, Westbrook did. The conundrum she faced was convincing others she was right without any hard evidence proving a direct connection between Westbrook and Ann Livingston.

"He's doing the autopsy over the weekend. I arranged for us to meet with him on Monday at one."

Crowder changed the subject. "Cap left two new assignments on my desk this morning and asked me to pick one for us. He'll give the other to Jack Gardner and Al Jones."

"Cap thinks highly of you to do that. I mean, when has he ever given anyone a choice on which assignment they want? Answer, never. So tell me about them."

"One is a rape case involving the nine-year-old daughter of a local businessman. She was found naked behind a dumpster on River Road. The kid was beaten half to death. The creep hosed her down before he dumped her. Not a whole lot forensics can do. He even douched her, according to the ER doc who treated her. No semen. No witnesses. No motive. And the girl's catatonic. The case has 'cold file' written all over it."

"The other?"

"Double homicide at that townie bar over on Jessup and Patterson. Even Ramsey could solve this one. A woman entered the bar and put a bullet through the brain of her husband and another into the heart of his mistress. She then took the pistol and put one in her mouth. It exited the back of her skull and lodged in the bullseye of a dartboard that hung on a wall. Witnesses galore. One said the woman walked over to the jukebox before she started shooting and very calmly put in two quarters to play "Your Cheatin' Heart.""

"As if I don't know which one you chose. What's our first step in solving the rape case?"

"Already spoke to the rape counselor who'll call us as soon as the girl comes back to earth and can speak to us about what happened."

"Then?"

"Good, old-fashioned, boots-on-the-pavement police work. Parents. Family. Best friends. School teachers. Maybe someone saw the lowlife stalking the girl. I put a hold on the dumpster just in case he threw something in it. We'll check and see if there are other victims raped in a similar fashion. After all, this kind of rapist has a thing about washing his victim. Like he's trying to wipe clean his sin. We'll get a psychological profile."

"Jesus, Jo, as if we don't already have enough to do, like solving the jigsaw puzzle case of Ann Livingston's death."

"But think how much satisfaction we'll have from putting the degenerate in a cage for the rest of his unnatural life."

When the detectives finished the day, it was after six. Jenny had to work the evening shift on Saturday, and Steele had no gigs that weekend, so they agreed to meet at Benny's Sports Bar for dinner on Saturday and then hang out with other cops, watching whatever pro and college games were being aired. Crowder said she'd drive separately. She made a pledge to herself to return to her two-drink limit and be home by eleven.

Crowder's Friday night was already planned. She had a date. The two of them would have dinner together. They'd snuggle up on the sofa and watch a movie. They'd take a late evening stroll, come home, and jump into bed.

On her way home from police headquarters, she thought about how pathetic it was that her Friday nights with Fred had become the rule and not the exception.

Chapter 34

Laura Mueller was on time for her appointment with Charles Rochet, vice president of personal wealth management at CBZ, the Continental Bank of Zurich, Europe's second largest bank, with assets of almost a trillion dollars. A call on Friday afternoon from Laura Mueller was all that was needed for her to get the red-carpet treatment on Monday. It helped that she'd advised Rochet's secretary that the banking transactions would involve nearly five million Swiss francs.

"*Bonjour, madame,*" he said, walking over to greet Mueller as his secretary escorted her into his office. "I was looking forward to meeting you and being of service. Please sit down. Would you like coffee, tea, or perhaps you might join me for a morning sherry?" He shook her hand, the appropriate French greeting whether the business being conducted was with a man or a woman.

Charles Rochet, a handsome man in his early sixties, wore a tailored, royal-blue, pinstripe, double-breasted suit over a white silk shirt anchored by gold cufflinks and decorated with a solid crimson tie. His gray hair, almost sterling silver, lay combed straight back above a slightly receded hairline. His bright-blue eyes, fair complexion, slender-but-athletic build, and impeccable dress and manners gave him the appearance of being a fit, healthy, well-educated, well-bred European aristocrat.

He gave her a warm and friendly smile, and Laura felt an instant physical attraction. She mirrored back his smile. By his lingering handshake and impish grin, she sensed he felt a similar draw. He led her to one of two comfortable leather chairs in a corner of his plush, lavishly decorated office. A rectangular, white-marble table with a beveled, blue-tinted glass top separated the chairs, providing enough

220

separation for maintaining one's private space while allowing for the intimacy of two heads meeting midway for a whispering tête-à-tête.

"A glass of sherry would be lovely," Laura replied, playing to perfection the refined young woman she'd rehearsed. "And please, call me Laura."

"Of course," he said, "but only if you call me Chase, which is the name my family and close friends call me. It's what you Americans call a nickname. My father was an avid huntsman who claimed I was spawned in a flop in the hay with my mother in our stables after a hunt. The name is derived from the French word *chaser*, which means 'to hunt or chase.'" He leaned over and drew his head closer to Laura, who instinctively did the same, and whispered, "I dare say, my father was guilty of both. My mother was the catch of his hunt that day, and the event precipitated an earlier-than-expected marriage proposal and my sooner-than-anticipated appearance on the scene."

"Oh, my!" Laura feigned shock and covered her mouth demurely with her hands. She then giggled to let him know his naughtiness pleased her. Laura's inner self felt ecstatic. She hadn't anticipated this. She'd expected another stuffed shirt like Von Ellison.

She'd googled Rochet over the weekend: oldest child of the late Bertrand Rochet, the wine producer whose family owned the largest vineyard in France; educated, well-bred, and rich; a widower; two daughters who'd married into wealthy families; mansions in Switzerland and France; a villa on the French Riviera. He drove luxury vehicles and played polo, and like his father before him, hunted fox and shot quail. He owned racehorses, one of which ran in the Kentucky Derby and, coming from dead last at the head of the stretch, closed fast, losing by a nose.

Laura was pleasantly surprised to discover that Rochet was charming, brash, confident, and boyishly youthful for his age. Her mind worked in another dimension.

Crystal ball, show me my future.

221

She wondered if a tryst with him was just what the future held. She needed male companionship, not only for the gratification of prurient urges, but also for the loyalty of a faithful ally. What better protection from the outside world than to become part of a closed society that enjoyed private pleasures without worrying about the paparazzi. A safety net of people who would protect her privacy was essential.

She intuitively felt men's stares, and she sensed Chase's watchful eyes studying her. Her unblemished complexion, sky-blue, moon-shaped eyes, dainty nose, and delicate ears were in perfect harmony with slightly arched cheekbones and a long, seamless neck. Her dress showcased a svelte-but-curvy figure and shapely thighs that tapered down to sturdy, thin ankles. When he'd removed her jacket, she'd revealed just enough cleavage to guarantee that what was hidden by the fitted bodice of her dress was God-given.

The sherry arrived just as the two of them resumed upright positions in their chairs. His secretary placed the decanter and two crystal stem glasses on the table, then left, closing the door.

"Laura, how can I be of service to you?"

"I want to open an account with one million francs. I wish for it to carry a reasonable interest rate. I'll use it for my living expenses while I establish myself in Switzerland, where I plan to live. The rest I wish to place in bearer bonds earning a fair return. Can you assist me in these matters of importance?"

"Of course. It will be my privilege."

She opened her purse and pulled out the check. Pressing it with an iron in her room that morning had made it as flat and crisp as the hotel's envelope in which she'd placed it. When she reached over to hand him the envelope, she allowed it to slip from her hand to the floor directly in front of her chair. "Permit me," Chase said, leaning forward to pick it up just as she raised the hemline of her dress and slowly uncrossed her legs.

"My apologies, Chase, I was distracted."

He paused just long enough for a peek into her inner sanctum. "And now, Laura, it is I who is distracted," he said, clearing his throat. "So, Heinrich had the pleasure of your company last Friday," he said cheekily when he saw Von Ellison's signature on the check. "I'm sure he treated you in his usual warm and friendly manner."

She laughed. "Yes, I found myself needing a stiff drink after our meeting."

"Quite understandable after dealing with a man who's stiff in the back and the collar of his shirt."

They tapped their glasses of sherry and took sips. Chase got up from his chair and said, "As painful as it is to leave you, even for a few minutes, I must conscript a colleague to handle the paperwork for us." After delegating the document preparation to a subordinate, he returned to be with his new client and engaged in small talk about what life was like in Switzerland, and where to go to lease a Porsche and mountainside villa.

A half hour later, the papers were delivered.

"Laura, I've established an account for you with one million Swiss francs. It will pay prevailing rate and a half percent, which I reserve for our most valued clients." He handed her a checkbook with a genuine leather cover. He also gave her a credit/debit card. "I placed your credit limit at 100,000 francs. You can never be too solvent these days."

"Thank you, Chase. You seem quite capable of satisfying my every need." Sexual innuendo dripped off every word.

"I have made it a life's goal to do so."

"And your recommendation for the bonds?"

"Yes, my area of expertise. I have put together a portfolio of bearer bonds from three different sources, two multinational European corporations and the country of Kuwait, all clients of CBZ with substantial bank holdings and triple-A ratings. The bearer bonds will be separated into three envelopes, each with roughly a third from each of the issuing entities."

"Where should I keep them? I understand they're the equivalent of cash."

"I recommend three separate safety deposit drawers. There will be no traceable, identifiable name for the cubicles, only a number assigned to each and a passcode for entry into the boxes. I suggest placing equal amounts of your wealth in the boxes. That way, if necessity and expediency require you to access your wealth remotely through an emissary, only a third of your wealth will be lost if your agent proves to be unworthy of your trust."

Laura felt that if she ever needed an emissary, she could place her trust in Chase. She needed to bring someone with the right background into her confidence. Her confidence in him was bolstered when her internet research revealed that CBZ and several of its officers, including Chase, had once been under investigation in the United States for money laundering. CBZ had worked out a civil settlement for hundreds of millions of dollars with the United States government in return for the dismissal of the criminal indictments against the bank and its officers.

"Chase, can I trust you completely, not just with my wealth, but with a matter that involves my personal safety?" Laura spoke haltingly, the tone of her voice as serious as the look on her face. "My intuition tells me you are as honorable in your personal relationships as you are in your business associations."

"Of course, Laura. I value privacy in more ways than you can now know. I am an honorable man, I can assure you of that. I sense we are kindred spirits who have much to share. You can trust my discretion in all matters."

Laura Mueller wanted to seize the opportunity to give her life story. She'd constructed one that would be difficult to pick apart, the perfect tale for someone willing to believe almost anything she said. That someone she now knew was him.

"Chase, what I tell you must stay between us. It will be very dangerous for me if it ever gets out."

"You have my word."

"My real name is unimportant. I was married to an accountant who worked for an organization the FBI believed was linked to organized crime. At first, my husband didn't know the business of the organization was illegal. Later, when a grand jury began its investigation, he was forthcoming about his involvement and was offered immunity to testify about the illegal activities of the people he worked for. The U.S. Attorney put my husband and me in the government's witness protection program. Our names were changed. I dyed my hair. He grew a beard. We were relocated to a small midwestern city. We didn't have children, so the move was accomplished quickly.

"Chase, it was so horrible. While the trial was underway, a United States Marshal picked up my husband to drive him to the city where it was taking place so he could testify. They never made it. They were found dead in a ravine in their vehicle. Both had been shot in the head."

Laura removed a hanky from her purse and dabbed at dry sockets. She took some deep breaths, slowly exhaling, like emotional people do to regain their composure. It was a role she'd played before, and she gave another stellar performance that morning in Chase's office.

"My husband was a brilliant accountant," she continued. "Before he was arrested, he skimmed off five million dollars and moved it to an offshore account. He told me about the money before he left to testify and gave me the information to access the funds if something happened to him. He also gave me the name of someone who could help me with a new identity."

"Your husband must have sensed they were on to him and that the end may very well be in sight," he said, helping her fill in blanks in the narrative.

"He knew there were leaks in the U.S. Attorney's office. I saw how worried he was and tried to convince him to run away with me, but he said the federal authorities were watching him too closely. He thought only of me."

225

It was hanky time again, and time for another doleful sigh.

Chase offered words of support to fill the lull. "He was devoted to you, this husband of yours. I can see how much he loved you, Laura."

"Yes, he loved me and protected me, and it cost him his life. After he was buried in a private ceremony in a different city, I was given another identity and relocated to a small town. But I wasn't about to trust my life with the federal authorities. The syndicate found us the first time, and when they found out my husband made off with their money, they'd surely come for me."

"Yes, I quite agree. Thieves generally want back money they've stolen that's been stolen from them. It seems logical and fair," he said whimsically.

"At first, I wanted nothing to do with the money. I wanted to give it back. But I figured they'd come for me anyway, me being a witness. My husband told me they always cover their tracks."

"Yes, and the best way to do that is for them to do away with the evidence and the witnesses," he offered.

"So I took off one night and met up with the man my husband told me to see. He helped me with my new identity. The end result is the Laura Mueller sitting here in your office, forever in your debt."

She weaved a fairy tale into a kerchief for him. She knew he'd believe what she'd told him because he wanted to believe it. He could now be Lancelot to his Guinevere. There is nothing more irresistible to a man than to be a woman's knight in shining armor.

"I'm so sorry for your misfortune. No one should endure what you've been put through. But now you have the chance for a new life. You can trust me. I work in the secrecy that shrouds the banks of Switzerland. I socialize in a closed community. We, my friends and I, have the power and the wealth to guarantee our privacy. You can be a part of that life, if your wish is to allow me to share it with you."

Laura knew that Chase had every intention of wearing the kerchief she'd woven for him. He'd wear it like a pocket square close to his heart. He wouldn't care if only fragments of her story were true. Based on the fine homes he lived in, the expensive cars he drove, and the stable of horses he owned, she sensed that Chase Rochet needed to possess all things beautiful.

They leaned forward in their chairs, each one's stare fixed on the face of the other, and tapped their glasses for a final toast. He spoke softly, with the confidence of a fortune teller reading tarot cards or a clairvoyant predicting the future. "Birds of a feather are destined to nest together. So it is written. So it shall be."

~

Laura Mueller drove her new 2018 Porsche convertible to Sotheby's on the west end of Zurich. She had a chalet to pick out.

"I have several minimum requirements," she said to the real estate agent. "It must have breathtaking views of the mountains and complete privacy. No neighbors with a view of my home. A security system that warns of intruders. And I want a wine cellar."

"I assume you will want at least two en suite bedrooms, a pool and spa, a garage for your vehicle, balconies, a terrace, and gardens at the front and rear of the property."

"Yes. Of course," she said as though she'd been through the process before.

"I know of three such properties in Lucerne, but the one that is the most enchanting is the one that will guarantee your privacy. It's called *Laurier des Montagnes,* which means Mountain Laurel. Mountain laurel shrubs dominate the region, and the gardens at the chalet have a variety of plantings that are so striking in color as to take your breath away. It's nestled in an inlet off Lake Lucerne. The views are panoramic and include not only Lake Lucerne and our majestic Alps, but also the quaint town of Lucerne.

"It has three bedrooms and all of the amenities you require, including a state-of-the-art security system. Housekeeping, gardening, and maintenance of the pool and spa are included in the rental charges. A private cook and housemaid are optional. Here

227

are some photographs of the property and the views you will have." The agent tapped the keyboard, illuminating her computer screen. A montage of photographs of the chalet came on the screen.

Laura Mueller liked what she saw. "It's perfect. What are the rental terms?"

"A minimum of three months, with options for renewal and purchase. 45,000 Swiss francs, plus a 15,000 franc security deposit."

"Yes. Please prepare the necessary documents."

Twenty minutes later, the agent presented Laura with the lease, keys, and informational brochures about the chalet. "We will require a wire transfer, *madame.*"

"Of course. Here's my associate's business card."

The agent dialed the number listed on the card.

Laura heard a female voice she recognized on the other end. "*Bonjour.* Mr. Rochet's office. Who shall I say is calling?"

Chapter 35

"He's working with a stiff," Joyce Setters said to the detectives. Dr. Sessions' longtime administrative assistant always referred to the cadavers as stiffs. Crowder remembered her rationale. She'd once told her that to refer to them as corpses was too grim, and to refer to them as patients gave false hope that there was still some chance for recovery.

"We had an early arrival this morning," Setters continued. "A female found in a sack on a bridge in St. Tammany Parish. Even I could fill out the death certificate on this one."

"Why so?" Steele asked.

"It's easy to exclude accident, suicide, and natural causes when you find the body on Thursday and the head on Friday."

Crowder appreciated gallows humor. "Does he want to meet in his office?" she asked.

"No. He's slicing and dicing in the meat department. You know the way. Elevator. Press "B" for Bodies. Take a right. Two doors down on the left, just beyond the spa, pool, and cabanas. Enjoy your stay with us. One last thing …"

"What last thing?" Crowder asked.

"The boss said to join him, but only if you haven't eaten lunch. He doesn't want anyone puking on the floor."

The detectives walked to the elevator and pressed "B" for the basement. The doors opened to a narrow, dimly lit hallway reminiscent of a bomb shelter. The cement floor, painted burgundy, had a trail of chips and scuff marks down the center. The grayish color of the cinder-block walls hinted that they'd once, long ago, been painted white.

229

Down the hallway, double swinging doors led to the autopsy room, a cold, metallic place with saws, cutting tools, scales, and steel basins. The detectives went to one of the lockers to get the Vicks VapoRub visitors placed under their nostrils to neutralize the unpleasant smell of body decomposition.

Sessions was busy sectioning the heart of one of two cadavers that lay naked on sheets of clear vinyl on side-by-side metal autopsy tables. One corpse lacked most of the flesh of the torso, arms, hands, head, and face, with barely enough left below the waist to identify the body as female. Close up, it smelled like a forgotten ribeye left to burn on the grill the day before.

The body that had drawn Sessions' attention was that of a young woman of medium height and weight, with two things conspicuously absent—her head, and the tips of her fingers and thumbs. "Crowder, Steele, come over here," he said, his eyes fixed on what he was holding. They walked over just as he pulled out the headless cadaver's heart and handed it to Travis Jones, his autopsy assistant. "Look at the size of it, Travis."

Jones positioned the heart on the scale. "Four hundred and ten grams, Dr. Sessions," he announced as if he'd just weighed the winner at a fishing tournament.

Sessions spoke like he was giving a cardiology lecture to medical students. "Classic case of hypertrophic cardio-myopathy. The heart's much larger than an average man's and twice the size of an average woman's. See how the heart muscle is unusually thick, pale, and scarred? Without an implanted cardioverter-defibrillator, this young woman was a sudden fatal arrhythmia waiting to happen."

Crowder said, "Judging from what's missing, I suppose you've got a Jane Doe who'll be moving into Potter's Field." Potter's Field was what coroners called the public cemetery and crematorium where the remains of unidentified and unclaimed corpses were sent. "When do you think she died?"

"By the degree of rigor mortis and the dryness of the blood, I'd say last Monday, maybe Tuesday. However, we got lucky with this one. The head was found the next day a mile downstream from where the body was found. A local was crabbing and found it in his pot. The crabs had picked away most of the flesh, but the skull is mostly intact. I may still be able to determine the cause of death when I dissect the brain. The way the blood congealed tells me the head was severed after she was dead a day or two. The removal of the fingertips was, of course, to conceal her identity."

"Forensics has a woman, a sculptor, who can reconstruct the face using clay," Crowder said. "So it's possible that an identification can be made by the missing persons team."

"I suppose the state will be doing the investigation," Steele said.

"If there's a connection to New Orleans, we could still get involved," Crowder said. "But that's not why we're here." She nodded in the direction of the charred corpse. "What can you tell us about this one?"

Sessions picked up a clipboard and read from his autopsy notes. "Burned remains of a five-foot-eight-inch female. Most likely blonde, based on the follicles of hair found on pubis. Foot measurement suggests a nine shoe size. Small amount of lung and heart tissue present. Will section and analyze. Brain dissected and sectioned. No evidence of blunt force trauma to the skeletal structures. Fingerprints unobtainable due to inadequacy of tissue. Dental x-rays taken of cadaver positively match the dental x-rays of one Ann Livingston, date of birth June 28, 1985." Sessions looked over at the detectives. "The cause and manner of death, my friends, will have to await analysis of the tissue samples."

"When you determine what caused her death, will you be able to tell us when she died?" Crowder asked.

"Whether the carbon monoxide killed her," he explained, "depends on whether the first explosion was from the exhaust fumes igniting and blowing up the garage. If it happened that way, it's almost certain she died from carbon monoxide poisoning because of the time required for the emissions to reach a high enough concentration inside the garage to ignite."

"That's what Ted Moody told us," Crowder remarked. "He's doing the calculations. How long before death in that case?"

"The victim typically experiences headache, vomiting, convulsions, and then death by asphyxiation. Basically, the person goes into respiratory failure, but if nobody's around to do CPR, she's a goner in five to eight minutes."

"Can you tell from the remains if she had her reproductive organs? According to her medical records, she had them removed eight years ago. But x-rays this year suggested she had an ovary."

Sessions went over to the tray of instruments, picked up two tools with blunt ends, and placed them in the open area that was once the stomach and pelvic area of Ann Livingston. He pulled away the blackened tissue and said, "Take a look inside. Not much left. Even with the extensive tissue loss, I'd expect to see some evidence of the uterus, and there is nothing to suggest the existence of one. The tubes and ovaries could have burned up or melted in the fire."

"You'll have Ann Livingston's medical records to review. They show a suicide attempt last summer, an overdose on her antidepressants. Phoned her psychotherapist just before she passed out. He saved her. Crashed her car into a tree in January, we think on purpose. There's a lot of circumstantial evidence to suggest she was suicidal."

"If you're asking my opinion," he offered, "with that history, ninety-nine point nine percent of the time, something like this will be suicide by carbon monoxide poisoning."

"But there's a twist to the story, Dr. Sessions, and it paints a different picture that's pretty gruesome. We believe Ann Livingston was kidnapped and killed by her identical twin sister, who impersonated her in order to steal from her and then staged her suicide. If you can determine the approximate time of death, it may prove she was dead before she ended up in her car."

"Crowder, you've been involved in enough murder investigations to know that determining the time of death is not an

232

exact science. I mean, if someone is alive one day and found dead in a room the next day from a bullet through the brain that exits the skull and strikes and breaks a wall clock, you can still be off by twelve hours. In the absence of autopsy findings that prove when the death occurred, all that you have is circumstantial evidence."

"Are you saying you can't give a reasonable estimate of the time of death?"

"I'm saying that the explosive fire has invalidated the methods we typically use to determine time of death by autopsy. If we take these two cadavers and compare them, the headless woman's post mortem temperature was ascertainable. When the body was found last Thursday, a rectal temperature was taken at the parish morgue by a coroner's assistant. It was room temperature. That tells us the woman had to be dead for at least thirty hours before the temperature was taken, because the body cools after death about one degree per hour until it reaches room temperature, approximately seventy-two degrees Fahrenheit. In the case of Ann Livingston, the heat from the fire distorts the cooling process. Her body temperature is of no practical use in determining the approximate time of death."

"No other ways to do it?" Steele asked.

"There are. The extent of the *liver mortis,* the discoloration of the skin caused by blood that pools and settles in the lowest portions of the body, is one method. Once again, the extent of *liver mortis* of the headless female clearly indicates she was dead for at least a day or more. The coloration of skin, however, is of no use in determining the time of Ann Livingston's death for obvious reasons. She was a piece of crispy bacon when she was found."

"What about rigor mortis?" Crowder asked.

"True, we commonly use the extent of rigor mortis to determine the time of death, as we did in your last two homicide cases. The rigidity caused by lactic acid fusing with myelin stiffens the muscles. Unfortunately, Ann Livingston didn't have enough undamaged muscle left to reliably determine the extent of rigor mortis."

"You know, Dr. Sessions," Crowder said, "it seems as though Ann Livingston, by dying the way she did—the multiple explosions and incendiary fire—made it impossible for a coroner's autopsy to determine the time of death."

"You're right about that. Now, recently we have been doing a potassium eye test that measures the level of potassium in the fluid to determine time of death. The potassium levels are unaffected by heat."

"Well, why don't you do a potassium test?" Steele asked.

"I would if I could, but her eyes melted in the fire."

Crowder asked, "If there's no evidence of carbon monoxide in the lung tissue, doesn't that mean she had to be dead before she was put in the car?"

"Yes. If she was alive, I'd expect to find evidence in the lung. She would have been breathing in the gas for at least five minutes."

"But how do we know her sister didn't expose her to carbon monoxide and kill her before putting her in the car, then blow the place up, destroying the evidence that would prove when she died?"

"We don't know. That's the one tenth of one percent of the time that death by carbon-monoxide poisoning is *not* suicide."

~

Detective Crowder answered a call from Ben Livingston on her extension. "I want to update you about what I learned from Ann's lawyer and our account manager at Smith Reid," Livingston said. "My lawyer contacted Jared Hochstein, who incorporated the foundation. Ann contacted him two weeks ago in a hurry to form the nonprofit, without my involvement. The final documents were executed at his office the Friday before the fire. He was not involved in the funding of the nonprofit."

"Did he know Mary Smith or have any contact with her?" Crowder asked.

"No. Everything was handled by Ann."

"What about the account manager who transferred the funds?"

234

"She worked with Jon Knowles. We've known Jon for a number of years. Ann called him and was quite emphatic that the five million dollars be transferred to the foundation's account at Credit Suisse in Zurich last Wednesday. She'd had him transfer a small amount of money a day earlier to be sure they'd encounter no problems with the wire transfer Wednesday morning."

"What about Mary Smith?"

"Like Hochstein, he didn't know her or have any contact with her."

"Is the money still in the account at the Swiss bank?"

"I knew the bank wouldn't give me any information about the accounts, Swiss privacy laws being as strict as they are. So I accessed Ann's computer and found an email exchange between her and the bank officer who opened the account. I responded to his last email to Ann as though I was her and asked him to confirm that the funds would be available for my use today. Sure enough, he emailed back."

"And?"

"He said a woman, who identified herself as Mary Smith, withdrew all the funds on Friday and closed the account. She showed proof of her identity and told him she was acting in accordance with Ann's instructions."

"Does that sound like something Ann would do?"

"Of course not. The money that capitalizes a foundation is placed in a secure account. Two officers' authorizations and signatures are required to transfer funds to secondary accounts for day-to-day operations."

"Would you expect Ann to know that?"

"Absolutely. Industry practices and federal and state agencies require independent audits of nonprofits."

"How do you explain what happened?"

"I can't, except that Ann had memory issues and was acting strangely ever since her accident. She wasn't herself."

"Were you able to locate Mary Smith?"

"I looked in Ann's contacts. Mary Smith is there, but the only information is the equivalent of post-office boxes in Charleston, South Carolina, and Zurich, Switzerland. No residential address. A defunct email address. Same for the telephone number."

"The bank officer said that Smith presented proof of her identity. If she used her passport or driver's license, there'll be a residential address and a photo. The address is probably made up, but the photo will be her. Can you try and get copies?" Crowder asked.

"Already did. I waited until I received them before calling you. The photos on the passport and driver's license for Mary Smith are of a woman I've never seen before. The address she gave was in Charleston, South Carolina. I googled it. A man by the name of Harrison Benson lives there. The other persons listed as residents all have the last name Benson."

"If you forward the information to me, Mr. Livingston, we'll investigate Mary Smith and try to determine her whereabouts."

"I'll send it to you, of course. But you know that Mary Smith doesn't exist. The woman who used that name worked her way into Ann's confidence and defrauded her out of five million dollars. Ann was taken advantage of at a time when she was battling depression and trying to come to grips with her own identity."

Crowder sensed from Livingston's tone of voice that his emotions had taken an about face. He'd started the conversation calm and collected, almost businesslike, but when he began discussing Mary Smith, Crowder could almost feel his anger through the airwaves off the cell tower.

"The woman duped Ann, beginning just after her hospitalization last summer when she was most vulnerable. The scheming continued even after her accident, when she couldn't remember things in her past clearly, if at all." His last words before abruptly ending the call were vengeful. "For her sake, she'd better hope our paths never cross."

Crowder hung up, but only after she heard the phone line go dead. A minute later, PDFs of the information Livingston had agreed to send arrived with his email: *Re: Mary Smith ... Find the bitch.*

Steele brought two coffees to Crowder's desk while she was looking at Mary Smith's passport photo on her computer screen. "How did you get it?" he asked.

"Ben Livingston. Just got off the phone with him. That's one angry man. This Smith woman took off with the money almost as soon as it was put in the account. She played Ann like a fine-tuned fiddle. Livingston knows Smith is an alias and that we have zero chance of catching her. He's pissing blood, to put it in technical terms."

"Do you think he'll go private?"

"Good chance. He believes the woman took advantage of his wife. It's not about the money. It's personal. And he has the resources to do it. According to Forbes, he's worth in excess of a hundred mil."

"With that kind of money," Steele said, "he can hire a posse of private contractors who'll catch her scent and track her down."

"And unlike us, the privates can bribe the truth out of people with a fistful of cash and, if necessary, beat it out of them with the butt end of a pistol."

"You bet. The kind of justice you see reported in the newspaper. You know, an unidentified woman found dead at the bottom of a ravine, no leads, no suspects."

"For Ben Livingston, it won't be about the money stolen from them," Crowder said. "It'll be about the wife taken from him." She finished reviewing the documents Livingston had sent and returned to his email. "And right now he thinks his wife took her own life. Can you imagine his rage if it turns out she was murdered, and Westbrook and the Smith woman were responsible?"

Steele read the email over her shoulder. "I see what you mean. There's no telling what he might do. So, what's your take on it?"

237

"Ann Livingston gets conveniently swindled by a business associate out of millions *on the day of her suicide.* It's a stretch. I'm not buying it."

"You're thinking the sister and Smith kidnap Ann, Smith holds her somewhere for a month, the sister stages the car crash to become Ann, then they work together to steal the money, kill Ann, and stage her suicide. I don't know, partner. That's a whole lot more to buy into."

"Not really. Think about it in real time. Sister waits until the family leaves for Florida early Friday morning. She transfers the money before Lucinda arrives at eleven, spends most of the day in her room, sends Lucinda home at seven, leaves the house to retrieve Ann's body, stages the suicide, leaves through the pantry window, and blows up the garage on the way out. Smith's already in Zurich to drain the account."

Steel snorted. "Then the sister flaps her wings and flies all the way to Zurich to join Smith, split the loot, and live happily ever after."

"No, seriously. Think outside the box. Lucinda goes home believing Ann doesn't want her to stay. Alone in the house, Sister plants the Bible and types the suicide note. The explosion and fire destroy any chance of figuring out the actual cause and time of death."

"Maybe you're right. But where are the *bona fides?* There's no way Cap's buying into it, not without proof, and, so far, the evidence points to a desperate woman with longstanding depression, who tried to kill herself twice before, left a suicide note, read the Bible verse for funerals, and killed herself by carbon monoxide poisoning. Oh, I almost forgot to tell you ..."

"What?"

"We got a call from Sessions while you were on the phone with Livingston. The lung tissue showed trace evidence of carbon monoxide. He's prepared to call it a suicide."

238

"Okay. Maybe I'm dead wrong. But we still need to see what the x-ray films tell us and what the surveillance video shows."

"One small problem."

"What small problem?"

"Sessions said the hospital can't find the x-rays films or reports."

"Fuck me."

"Can't. Department regulations."

"Then fuck you."

"We're down to the surveillance video."

"Let's take a look."

Steele slipped the disc into his computer and took the mouse in his hand. Crowder sat in a chair alongside him. "The tape has an hour/minute/second digital clock in military time, beginning at 00:00:00 and ending at 23:59:59," he explained. "The security company's design has six surveillance cameras encircling the house, all recording simultaneously."

The screen illuminated with six separate views, three in each of two rows. The digital clock was rewound to 00:00:00. Crowder said, "Let's begin at nine in the morning and advance the video until a camera shows us something."

At 09:31:22, the garage door opened, and Ben Livingston backed out his Cadillac Escalade and drove it to the front of the house. Martha and Meg came out the front door with their travel bags in hand. Ben loaded the bags while they got in the vehicle. He then went to Ann, who waited in the doorway.

They spoke briefly. Ben kissed Ann, returned to the vehicle, and drove away. Ann entered the house and closed the door at 09:35:39.

At 10:55:56, Lucinda arrived by car. A young Hispanic woman dropped her off. "The driver is probably her daughter," Crowder speculated. Lucinda got out of the car, carrying her handbag and a bag of groceries. She walked to the front door and let herself in using a key. The scene ended at 10:57:21.

At 14:23:15, the postman delivered the mail and rang the doorbell. A minute later, Lucinda came out the front door and collected it.

At 15:38:44 and 18:31:27, Lucinda let the family's dog out a back door, letting him back in after romps of approximately five minutes.

At 19:05:10, the same young woman in the same vehicle came back to pick up Lucinda.

At 19:25:35, a garage door opened and Ann Livingston's Lexus was backed out of the garage and driven away. "Sid, go back and freeze-frame the driver." He did as asked.

"There's no question, that's Ann Livingston driving," she said. "Lucinda goes home at just after seven, and Ann's leaving in her car twenty minutes later."

They saw no further activity on any of the screens until 21:32:55, when the Lexus was driven back into the garage. Steele rewound and freeze-framed the driver. He enlarged the view. It was Ann Livingston.

Crowder said, "She's gone for a little more than two hours. Two hours is a long time to be driving around thinking about killing yourself. Advance the clock to twenty-two-forty. The explosions reportedly occurred about five minutes later. Let's run it in real time."

They sat back in their chairs and watched. About a minute later, Crowder jumped from her seat and reached for the mouse. She reversed the video to 22:41:00 and ran it again for thirty seconds. "Do you see anything?"

"No, I don't see anything."

"I'll run it again. Top row, middle screen. It's a view of the terrace in the back of the house, near the pantry window." As she ran the film again, Steele moved forward in his chair, fixing his stare on that screen alone. It appeared in the stillness of the night, in the lighting that illuminated the terrace, that something moved across the screen. Crowder reversed and advanced again, isolating the

240

footage to a two-second interval. The clock on the screen read 22:41 and the second counter showed 28 and 29. The detectives looked at each other but said nothing. What the security camera revealed over that two-second interval on the night of Ann Livingston's death was a shadow of what was likely a human form moving away from the back of the house.

They let the video run: 22:41 ... 22:42 ... 22:43 ... 22:44. Both moved up in their seats, their stares fixed on a single screen. Two sets of eyes beamed like lasers when, at exactly 22:44:47, the garage exploded into a fireball that blew out the doors. A second and third explosion followed. The camera recorded in color. Red, white, and blue hues spewed from the explosions to form a rainbow cloud. For several seconds, the camera shook from the force of the blasts.

The detectives watched as the fire raged out of control for ten minutes. They stopped the recording when police and fire personnel arrived at the scene. Crowder pulled out the disc and handed it to Steele. "See what forensics can do to enhance the shadow. A better image may tell us more about the person who was walking away from the Livingstons' home a few minutes before Mount Vesuvius blew its top."

Chapter 36

Normally the drive between Zurich and her new home took ninety minutes, but it took less when she was in a Porsche and driving like a race car driver on a Saturday afternoon at the track. Laura Mueller made the drive in sixty-eight minutes. She entered her new home through metal gates that opened inward. A fieldstone wall wrapped around the property like a horseshoe, leaving open the rear property line. A wall was unnecessary there; a cliff that dropped 250 feet to the frigid waters of Lake Lucerne provided sufficient protection from intruders.

Laura established an internet account for her laptop computer and mobile phone while in Zurich. The first person she messaged was Chase Rochet, thanking him for his help. He immediately responded with an invitation to a dinner party. *Laura, my driver, Rolls Royce, will pick you up tomorrow at six. Say no, and I will personally arrange to kidnap you,* he texted playfully.

But who shall Laura Mueller be? I want only you to know my circumstances, she texted back.

Worry not, he replied. *We can work on your life story. Only the two of us will ever know the truth.*

She ended the messaging. *Deal. I knew I could trust you. Eternally grateful, Laura.*

As was the practice of experienced valets and drivers, Royce showed up ten minutes early and waited. The luxury vehicle, a Bentley Flying Spur, had a refrigerator compartment in the rear console that stocked four five-ounce bottles of Rochet chardonnay and two Cumbria Crystal flutes. She opened a bottle and poured herself a glass of wine.

Laura Mueller looked like a million francs in her periwinkle-blue, strapless Givenchy cocktail dress with ruffles and a cut-out bodice. She'd gotten rid of the black wig and returned to her natural look. During their first meeting, she'd explained to Chase that when the witness protection program had given her a new identity, they'd encouraged her to assume a new appearance as well. But now that she was living abroad under a different identity, she felt that part of the deception was no longer necessary. She'd surprise him.

A glass window separated the driver from the passenger in the rear seat. Above it hung a twelve-inch, pull-down, flat-screen television with access to the major news and business networks. She didn't intend, however, to sit mutely and waste her time watching TV. She saw her time with Chase's driver as an opportunity to learn more about Chase and his family.

She opened the window and said, "Chase tells me your name's Rolls Royce. Is that for real?"

"No, *madame*," Royce replied in an English accent that was so polished, it belied his profession. He could easily have passed himself off as a college professor. "It is Roland Russell Royce, but the name has followed me since I was a lad. If only I had the wealth associated with such a valued name. But you can call me Rolls."

"I'm Laura. What's up with the last-minute dinner party?"

"It was put together in a hurry, I must say. Something tells me that a very enchanting young woman had something to do with it."

"Who's invited?" she asked excitedly between sips.

"Very intimate gathering. His daughter and her husband. Two of his closest friends and their wives, and ... and Aunt Rosalind." He cleared his throat.

The guest list was a good sign because members of the immediate family would be there to meet her. She sensed from the hesitation in his voice that he had more to say about the aunt.

"Tell me about Aunt Rosalind. What's she like?"

"Aunt Rosalind is the brains behind the Rochet fortune. I mean no disrespect to Mr. Rochet. I've had the privilege of being in his

243

and his father's service for thirty years. I would do anything for him. But when Mr. Rochet's grandfather passed away, his daughter, Rosalind, took over control of the wineries and grew the business into the third-largest wine producer in Europe. Mr. Rochet's father knew that his sister was shrewd, some might say ruthless, in matters of business. He willingly stepped aside, pursuing more pleasurable activities until his death ten years ago. Mr. Rochet is very much like his father. He's a blue blood, for sure, but never the snob. Most of the others aren't like him."

"Are Chase and his sister involved in the business?"

"Aunt Rosalind is eighty-five, in poor health, and still very much in control. She's a widow. No children. She's groomed her nephew and niece to succeed her. Which one of them will end up with controlling interest is the carrot on the stick."

"Chase is a banker. How does he have the time to run the business?"

"Mr. Rochet handles the financial end of the business. His sister and her husband supervise the daily operations. They all get along surprisingly well. Which one ends up with the carrot is still known only by the one who's holding the stick, and so far she's not telling."

"Why not split everything equally?"

"Aunt Rosalind, who inherited fifty-one percent of the business from her father, knows that equal shares could mean deadlock, which might cripple and ruin the business if there was ever disagreement between them on how the business should be run."

"Chase's friends—what are they like?" She knew better than anyone that you judge people by the people with whom they associate. She'd never found many people very much like herself. Guy? Perhaps. Sal? Maybe. But not anymore.

"Very rich financiers involved in various business dealings with the family. They also hunt fox with Mr. Rochet. One owns a yacht that sleeps twelve. The other is a pilot and a hot air balloonist who's one of only a handful to have made solo transcontinental flights across Europe and Africa."

244

She saved the daughters for last, knowing she'd be compared to them in all ways. "And Chase's daughters?"

"Rochelle, or 'Rocky,' as Mr. Rochet calls her fondly, was an Olympic swimmer for France when she was nineteen, earning two silver medals. She studied art at the Sorbonne and has studios in Paris and Geneva."

"And the other?" she asked, almost not wanting to hear the answer.

"Olivia, his favorite, though he'd never admit it, is an equestrian champion and—"

"Let me see if I can guess, Rolls," she said glibly. "She's climbed Everest and discovered the cure for cancer?"

"Close, but it was Kilimanjaro, not Everest. Five years ago."

"Do I at least get an honorable mention or a participation ribbon?"

Royce controlled his laughter. "Liv," he continued, "is the musician in the family, although Rochelle is also quite accomplished in piano and harp. She studied music, also at the Sorbonne. A concert violinist, she plays an ensemble of instruments and writes compositions. Many are played by orchestras throughout Europe."

"I'll be sure to trade some of my music videos with her," she wisecracked. "I've got a great Amy Winehouse collection."

Their conversation paused. It gave her time to reflect on her claims to fame. How could she compete with daughters with so many accomplishments? Was Royce waiting for her to reel off a list of her own?

Well, Rollsy, old boy, I hold the altitude record. I once had sex with a guy I met on a 747, in the bathroom of the plane, at 37,000 feet … twice!

"Can I share a confidence with you, *madame?*"

"Of course you can, Rolls. I feel like I've known you for years."

"Strangely, I feel the same about you."

"Do you want a glass of wine?" she offered, pouring herself another. "You look like a man who can multitask."

"No. But thank you, Laura." Royce then shared in confidence an observation she'd hoped he might make. "Rochelle and Olivia's God-given talents and their personal accomplishments in life make up for what they lack in natural beauty. I say this with the utmost respect and affection for both."

Royce's comment garnered a thankful smile of appreciation from his passenger. And that's why Laura Mueller knew she'd be welcomed into Chase's life and accepted by his family and inner circle of friends. Because when you look like Grace Kelly, present yourself like the people's princess, and are worth five million dollars, you stand out.

Laura Mueller was a very beautiful woman with a very special skill set. She knew, perhaps better than anyone, that when Chase eventually lay beside her on the satin sheets of her bed, things like medals, music compositions, fancy cars, and mountain summits wouldn't amount to a hill of beans, not when the most beautiful woman he had ever known was fucking his brains out.

Laura Mueller knew that.

Rolls Royce knew that.

And Chase Rochet might soon come to know that.

So it is written. So it shall be.

~

"Sweet Jesus, Rolls. Do they charge to get in?" she asked as the chauffeur drove through the entrance to Château Vallée. The home itself waited a quarter-mile ahead, down a cobblestone road.

"Welcome to Château Vallée. The French Baroque mansion was built in 1752 by a French aristocrat who later lost everything, including his head, in the French Revolution. Its name means 'palace in the valley.' Twenty-five rooms, including ten bedrooms and eight bathrooms."

"It beats a two-bedroom condo by the airport."

"It's been in the family for over a century."

"What's it like inside?"

246

"Typical for a mansion of the French aristocracy. Immense rooms. A grand piano, harpsichord, and harp in the parlor, for the daughters' private concerts. An elegant dining room connected to the kitchen by an enclosed corridor, ensuring the sanctity of their gossip. A formal living room, a study, and a game room for billiards and card playing."

"What, no ping-pong?"

"And, of course, the mainstay of any French palace, a grand ballroom with large, gold-leaf-framed mirrors on the walls and chandeliers hanging from a hand-painted mural that spans the length and width of the ceiling."

"You need someplace to put the karaoke machine."

Royce couldn't suppress a smile. He drove to the front entrance, where magnificent, ten-foot-tall oak doors gave passage into the miniature palace. As he walked around to open Laura's door, he used his cell phone to speed dial her waiting suitor. "She's arrived," he announced.

"Wish me luck, Rolls," she said as she got out of the luxury vehicle.

"Break a leg, as I believe you Americans like to say."

"I just hope it's not my neck."

Chase waited at the entrance to greet her. Her golden locks shimmered in the illumination of a snow moon, and she smiled as if playfully happy, like she couldn't wait to see him.

He bookended her smile. "Laura, if I tell you that you take my breath away, I'm understating how lovely you look this evening."

"I'm just a farm girl from Iowa," she said, already putting her cover story into effect while looking up at the vast entranceway and its domed ceiling. When he'd helped her make up the story, he'd insisted on the wholesomeness of a farm-belt state for where she grew up.

"How do you heat a place like this?" she asked.

247

"You'd be surprised. The bedrooms all have working fireplaces, remnants of the bygone days of heating one's castle. And, of course, we also use more modern ways of heating."

"What, body heat?" she quipped.

"Yes. Imperative you find someone to share a bed with," he said.

Their naughtiness brought on smiles.

"Truth is, we close up sixty percent of the upper floors. Rarely are they in use. The rest is what we Europeans call zone heating and common sense. If you're not in it, don't heat it. You may want to keep your wrap. It's chilly in the Winter Garden; I dare say, it's aptly named."

"What lies beyond, do I dare inquire?" she said with the affectation the moment required.

"I'll explain as we walk." He extended his arm.

She put hers through it, and they strolled through one of the great, privately owned palaces of Europe.

"The mosaic floors, decorative paneling, and moldings are original to the mid-eighteenth century. The fifteen-foot-wide staircases to the second and third floors are all original. But don't worry, they won't collapse if you use them. The first-floor rooms will speak for themselves as we pass by them."

They walked by the rooms Royce had mentioned and several others he hadn't. The doors were open, so she caught a glimpse of the stunning artwork and opulent furnishings inside.

"The rear terraces lead to Rochet Parc, a garden overlooking a valley at the foot of a small mountain. At least, small by Swiss standards. It peaks at just over seven thousand feet, an invigorating hike, if you're up to it."

"So this is what Maria saw when she went to live with the Von Trapp family." The second glass of wine was taking effect, and Laura hoped she wasn't too flippant. It was clear her suitor didn't mind one bit, but she promised herself to be careful around family and friends.

"Laura, my dear, I inherited my wealth," he said, now laughing out loud. "I take no credit for earning the right to live like this.

248

My daughters are dead-set on selling off or gifting away much of what we've enjoyed over the years when they inherit. But I want my grandchildren to get a taste of the history of the place and of a lifestyle that will be bygone a generation from now."

She thought how paradoxical the similarities between Chase Rochet and Ben Livingston were. Both were rich, but Chase enjoyed his wealth, spending it on an extravagant lifestyle—mansions in two countries and a villa on the French Riviera—experiencing life's pleasures like every single day could be his last. The work he did at the bank and his charitable causes were necessary undertakings of an aristocrat, something expected, so the public would see him as a philanthropist rather than a philanderer.

Ben Livingston, on the other hand, worked hard every day, enjoying the simple pleasures of life with his family. For him, the company business was a sacred trust that required his full attention; he had no time for the garish gallivanting of the jet-setting rich and famous. Philanthropy was more than an obligation to him. It was a passion. What would have been a perverse lifestyle for Chase Rochet brought satisfaction and joy to the life of Ben Livingston.

"You've arrived just in time," said Chase. "We have some time to mingle before dinner. You can meet my daughter and my closest friends. Then you'll meet Aunt Rosalind." He cleared his throat, as his driver had done earlier.

"Will she be among the guests in the Winter Garden?"

"No. It's customary for the matriarch of the family to be presented in another room after all the guests have arrived."

"Tell me about her, your Aunt Rosalind."

"Rosalind Rochet Chevalier is a legend. She married a French artist she sponsored and, in her youth, modeled for. Jacques Chevalier was twenty years her senior. At one time he was one of the most commissioned portrait artists in France. The poor man died from cirrhosis of the liver, brought on, I suspect, by a penchant for his in-laws' wines. My aunt was broken-hearted. Never thought about remarrying. Instead, she devoted herself to the family

249

business, tripling the size of the vineyards, doubling the wineries, and marketing Rochet wines internationally. She's considered a titan in the industry, with a reputation for being steely and uncompromising in her negotiations."

"Do I need to be worried about slipping up?"

"In a word, yes. But don't ruminate over it. You will charm her, I'm quite certain. One bit of advice, though: never be alone with her. She's as perceptive as she is intuitive. Not many can go one-on-one and escape unscathed. It's best to outnumber her."

Laura didn't know if he was being honest with her or trying to scare the crap out of her. Probably a little of both. She'd be on her best behavior, keep the verbal jousting to a minimum, and, above all else, never be alone with her.

"Before we go meet our guests, let me introduce you to some members of the family who are dear to my heart."

They walked out a side door near the Winter Garden and onto a cobblestone walkway that led to a large, elegantly styled barn, the stable that housed the family's horses. When he opened the double doors at the entrance, they revealed a groomsman raking fresh hay into an empty stall. "Scotty, come meet Laura."

The Welshman, in his late fifties, put his rake aside and limped over to them.

"Laura Mueller, meet Scotty McPherson," Chase said, "the best man I know on, and off, a horse. He jockeyed his way to his fair share of steeplechase victories in his heyday."

"Wasn't for me bustin' me leg up, I'd still be in the colors. A pleasure, miss." Scotty tipped his tam and bowed slightly at the waist. "Will you be wantin' to ride sometime soon?" he asked. "They love to be ridden, they do. I share me time with 'em. But there's only so many hours in a day. I can only ride 'em one at a time, if ya catchin' me meaning." Scotty looked at Chase as if he had an axe to grind with him.

"Laura, I'm afraid Scotty feels I've been neglecting my good friend Lance," Chase said. "Come meet him."

"Deserves better, if you be asking me humble opinion, is all I'm sayin'," Scotty said while shaking his head.

They walked over to one of the stalls. The nameplate read "Lancelot." A majestic, black-as-tar stallion showed its head. It stomped the ground, shook its head, and neighed as Chase approached. He grabbed an apple from a pail and offered it to Lance with one hand while stroking the horse's long, muscular neck with the other. The animal bit at the fruit until it was gone.

"My good friend. I've missed our rides, the hunts, the matches. No horse I'd rather be on than you, old boy."

Laura was taken by the bond that obviously existed between Chase and his horse. It was like he was cuddling a pet dog he'd raised from a puppy.

"Let's meet the others."

They moved down a stall.

"Meet Thunder. Our champion. Liv's won dozens of competitions on him." The mid-sized, chestnut gelding nodded its head in apparent agreement, then showed its teeth and stuck out its tongue.

Scotty tossed Chase an apple, and the same eating ritual followed.

"Good boy, that's a good boy. I'd ride you, Thunder, but you're way too spirited for me."

"Miss Liv's the only one he wants atop," Scotty said. "Still tries to throw me when me feet are in the stirrups."

"And where's our sweetheart?" Chase moved down and across from Thunder to a stall where an Appaloosa mare waited patiently. The horse had its head turned. Its stare fixed not on the groomsman or its owner, but on the fair-haired beauty who stood about ten feet to the right. Laura and Meadow's gazes met. Laura had the distinct feeling that the horse was studying her, sizing her up.

"Meadow, darling," Chase said as he approached. "You still have the charm you had on the first day we met."

He looked over at Scotty, who remained by the pail of apples. Scotty had begun to reach for one when he saw that Laura already had one in her hand. Chase saw it, too. A hush enveloped the stable as Laura walked slowly over to Meadow, their attention still fixed on each other. She'd never been so close to such a large animal before. She'd stayed back when Chase had fed the other horses, fearful of being bitten. But she felt confident approaching Meadow. She'd never had a pet and couldn't remember ever petting a dog or a cat. Animals typically shied away from her, and she from them. They sensed an inherent incompatibility. But something about the horse made her relax and feel comfortable around it, as if she'd always known Meadow, like they were old friends who'd grown up together.

She reached out with the apple. Meadow sniffed it, the soft warmth of the horse's nostrils touching the back of her hand. She inched closer and closer to the horse, like the pull of a magnet to metal. Before she knew it, she was face to face with Meadow, who nibbled from the apple while Laura gently touched her face, ears, and neck. Laura felt strangely content in the company of the animal.

The two men watched, not saying a word. Beauty and the mare had bonded almost immediately. "My name is Veronica," she said. "Will you be my friend, Meadow?"

She looked at the men just in time to see them exchange a quizzical glance.

"Laura, my dear," Chase said when Meadow had finished the apple, "you've made yet another friend. Let's join the others, shall we? Meadow will understand that we need to share you."

"She likes you, miss," Scotty said as Chase led his guest back into the house.

Whether the others would remained to be seen.

A short while later, they entered the Winter Garden. Laura looked stunning. Her snowflake-white, silk-chiffon evening stole left enough of her shoulders bare to excite the observer, yet created anticipation of what more would be revealed when it was removed.

Chase paused momentarily at the entrance, her arm in his. He leaned towards her and whispered, "Don't worry, we've agreed on Laura Mueller's life story. Let's stay true to the script."

They'd concocted a story to satisfy his family and friends that she was an honorable woman with a scandal-free past. Laura Mueller, three years a widow, had married a man of German descent, whose father immigrated to New York City and wed an American woman who produced a single child, the son Laura had married. Her husband had shunned the family business and entered government service as a field operative for the CIA. He was killed on assignment in the Middle East. "All hush-hush, you know," Chase had told his friends and daughter before the arrival of his guest. The cover story was believable to gullible Americans, but Chase had said that Europeans, particularly the French, were inherently suspicious of foreigners. But it was a tale not easily proved false.

Laura Mueller, the daughter of hard-working Iowa farmers, had attended a small teacher's college in central Indiana and taught second grade in the public school system. A country girl with a strong work ethic, she'd devoted herself to teaching underprivileged children and to volunteerism. She'd inherited her great wealth when her parents died in a boating accident and the farms were sold. Another biography difficult to invalidate.

All eyes fixed on her as they awaited a turn to meet Chase's "enchanting new friend." He began with the three men in the room. "My friends, may I present Laura Mueller. Laura, please meet Nicky Von Steuben, Ax Cavendish, and Reese Eddington. Reese had the good fortune of marrying my daughter Olivia."

The men bowed slightly at the waist, each exchanging a pleasantry with Laura.

The women greeted her warmly with broad smiles.

Chase's daughter spoke first. "My father, like most men, tends to exaggerate his accomplishments. But his description of how fortunate he was to have been of service to you and for you to be so gracious as to accept his dinner invitation shows me that my father is the master of understatement. I'm Olivia. I'm so pleased to meet you, Laura. Please call me Liv."

Laura took this as an opportunity to ingratiate herself with Chase's favorite daughter, someone whose trust she needed if she were to establish a lasting relationship. "My second cousin and dearest friend growing up was named Olivia, and she, like you, wanted me to call her Liv. I see that as a sign we may be connected in some way. I look forward to earning your friendship."

Chase held out his hand, asking Laura if he could take her stole. As she unwrapped it, he leaned forward and whispered in her ear, "Cousin Olivia, really? What a deliciously beautiful liar you are, my dear."

The removal of her stole revealed the full scope of Laura's physical attributes—her long neck, broader-than-average shoulders, and full breasts. She'd purposefully selected a dress with a plunging, cut-out bodice, hoping to evoke lustful thoughts from the men and pangs of envy from the women.

The group dallied over light conversation and gossip. Chase left the room and, after a few minutes, returned to announce that Aunt Rosalind was prepared to receive them. The guests queued up to enter the parlor and pay homage.

She sat between two high-back Queen Anne chairs whose height and configuration exactly matched her wheelchair, the oxygen tank strapped to its back proof that a half century of smoking had caught up with her. Chase had shared with Laura that his aunt had stage four emphysema. The good money had her dying during each of the last three years. But the cantankerous old dame had so far beaten the odds.

Each guest approached separately, and she received them warmly. Chase approached last, with Laura by his side. Liv and Reese stayed nearby to witness the reception. Aunt Rosalind's reserve was as obvious as her forced smile. "And so, Charles," she said, calling her nephew by his formal name, "this is the young lady all the fuss is about. Come closer, my dear, let me see if you are made of porcelain or are truly human." Her comment referred to Laura's heralded, unblemished, unwrinkled complexion, like the face of a porcelain doll.

"I assure you, *madame*," Laura confidently declared, "I will not break, should I fall from the mantel."

"*Touché*, my dear," Chase interjected affectionately.

Laura smiled when she overheard Olivia say to Reese, "Point, Laura."

All had a hearty laugh about the exchange—all but one.

The evening was a huge success for Laura Mueller. She came across as friendly, amusing, and beguiling. She sensed she'd won over the men and all the women but one. Though pleasant and respectful, the family matriarch wasn't about to allow a woman she knew so little about into the family. She'd need to know more, a lot more, about her before she did.

The old woman retired to her bedroom with the assistance of her nurse shortly after dinner. A five-minute fit of coughing preceded the early departure.

The men assembled in the game room to bet on billiards while the ladies sat around a card table and taught Laura to play Écarté, the two-player French card game—each woman awaiting a turn to be paired with their newly made American friend.

After an hour of games and conversation, Reese had to leave the billiards contest, which saw him teamed with Chase against Nicky and Ax. Chase and Laura ogled each other intermittently while the contest progressed, their lustful thoughts passing silently between them like telepathy.

Eventually Chase said, "Laura, Reese has some business to transact that leaves me outnumbered. Do you wish to join me? I can show you how to play as we finish our game."

"Well, if you don't mind teaching someone with two left hands," Laura said playfully. "Ladies, do you mind playing without me while I make a complete fool out of myself?" The women laughed and encouraged her to join the men.

She alone knew she was a better-than-average pool player. She'd learned the game hanging out at pool rooms in her hometown while most girls her age were babysitting. She would challenge boys in games of eight-ball and straight pool after school, earning spending money hustling novices.

She knew how to work a con.

At first, she acted like she was unfamiliar with the game. When Chase showed her how to lean over the table and set her cue stick, she made sure to strike the ball awkwardly, squandering the lead Chase had when Reese left the contest. Later, with the game tied, Laura got her chance to shine. Her shot would clinch the game for them, but success would be difficult because of the alignment of the object balls.

While chalking the tip of her cue stick, she carefully studied the lay of the table. She leaned over the table to position herself for the shot, exposing her cleavage to the watchful eyes of the men, who moved to full-frontal positions while the women gathered behind her. And then, with the confidence and finesse of a seasoned professional, she tapped the ivory-colored cue ball with the tip of her cue stick and watched it bank the side cushions three times and cleanly strike both object balls. Game, Team Rochet.

"*Bravo*, Laura," the three men cheered while the women applauded.

Chase moved closer to Laura and spoke softly in her ear. "Something tells me my friends have just been hustled out of a thousand francs."

She whispered back to him, "If you'd told me we were playing for money, I would've told you to double the bet."

The men gathered their wives and left.

"I've decided to drive Laura home," Chase announced to his daughter as the grandfather clocks in the living room and hallway chimed the eleventh hour in unison.

They completed the fifty-minute drive to Laura's chalet in twenty-eight minutes. Only the motorists whose vehicles the Ferrari

256

overtook heard the engine's roar, and inside the car, the soft sound of orchestral music broke the silence. By the end of their flight, Laura felt relaxed, refreshed, and eager to do what she did best. The gates opened on her command, and Chase, like a jet pilot gliding his plane onto the deck of an aircraft carrier, brought the Ferrari to a sure and certain landing in front of the chalet. She turned her head, smiled, handed him the door key, and said, "We're home, my darling."

They entered the house and stood in the center of the foyer, facing each other. She let her stole slip off her shoulders and stepped out of her high heels. Reaching around with a hand, she unzipped her dress and, with a slight wiggle or two, dropped it slowly to the floor like an escaping feather from a down pillow. The strip tease came naturally to her. She stopped before all was revealed, wanting her suitor's hormones to rage like those of a teenager about to get laid for the first time in his life.

Chase closed the distance between them. Holding her firmly in his arms, he kissed her softly and then more passionately. She could smell the sweet after-scent of sherry on his breath. With a gentle assist from his right palm on her bottom, she arched herself into his groin and felt the firmness of his erection. With every bit of the strength of a man half his age, he picked her up in his arms, and she panted, "Straight ahead, on the right."

In the bedroom, the satin sheets of the king-size bed were folded down and ready to receive them. Instrumental love themes played in the background, and sachets of potpourri scented the air. The room's gentle illumination allowed just enough light for them to see what they were doing and to whom. The atmosphere was perfect for the perfect ending to a perfect evening.

Laura Mueller made sure of that.

Chapter 37

"**M**eg, I have to tell you something that will make you feel sad inside," Ben Livingston said, dreading the coming moment.

It was bedtime. His daughter sat on the edge of her bed at Martha McMillan's home. She looked up at him with a frown.

"There was a terrible accident at home while we were away on our trip. There was an explosion and a fire. Mommy was hurt real bad and ... Meg ... it's so difficult for me to tell you this ... but ... she died in the accident."

He put his arm around his daughter and rested her head on his chest, the natural, fresh scent of her hair a remembrance of Ann. He waited for the tears, the uncontrollable fit of anguish one expects from a child learning for the first time that the mother who'd loved and cared for her every day of her life was dead.

Instead, he heard Meg ask, "Did Mommy start the fire?"

The question implied an awareness of her mother's culpability, and he didn't quite know how to answer her. "Meg, Mommy was hurting inside for a long time. Not physically hurt, like she was after her car accident. The pain she felt was in her mind. She hurt bad inside after Charlotte died, like she was responsible, even though it wasn't her fault. The doctors told us nothing could have been done to save your sister. It was God's will to take her from us."

"Mommy's sister died too," Meg said softly. "She looked just like Mommy, like Charlotte would've looked just like me. She told me it made her sad, but that my sister and her sister were now together in heaven, watching over us. It made me feel good to know that."

He was surprised that an eight-year-old child could have such a positive perspective on such terrible twists of fate. He felt grateful

258

that Ann had been forthcoming with Meg about painful experiences in her life. It boosted his confidence that perhaps someday he could be entirely truthful with Meg about what her mother had done to herself, and why.

"Meg, there's an investigation into what happened to Mommy. You may hear something on television or at school about Mommy and the fire. If you do, and it makes you feel sad, you can come to me or Nana or Lucinda, and we'll comfort you."

Meg held her teddy bear, gently stroking an ear. Although she'd stopped playing with dolls when she was five years old, Martha kept the worn and weathered stuffed animal on Meg's bed. It comforted her when she was away from Ann.

Did Ann tell Meg about her suicide attempt last summer? That would be some serious stuff to ask an eight-year-old to filter. Yet it would fall to him to eventually tell Meg that her mother had succeeded this time. The thought of telling her made him morose. He hung his head in silence.

Meg placed her hand on his arm. "Don't be sad," she whispered. "Mommy's an angel in heaven. She's not alone. She's with Charlotte, who has a Mommy now. We can pray to both of them every night. They will look over us and keep us safe."

Meg's soft, sweet voice felt like a salve soothing the pain burning inside him. How paradoxical that the words of comfort came from a young child. For the first time since Ann's death, there was hope, for Meg, for himself. He suddenly understood why Ann, when she'd descended into the deepest valleys of her darkest moods, had retreated to Meg's room to sleep with her like a sister. Meg's sweet words and gentle embraces had comforted her then, as they comforted him now.

Meg looked at her father, picked up her teddy bear, and handed it to him. "You take Teddy with you tonight," she said. "He'll help you sleep. It'll be like I'm there with you."

She slid under the covers, pressed her hands together, and, with her eyes tightly closed, prayed, "Now I lay me down to sleep, I pray, my lord, my soul to keep. May Mommy and Charlotte watch over us tonight, and wake us with the morning light."

Ben tucked her in and kissed her on the forehead. "Goodnight, sweet Meg." He turned off the table lamp and walked out with Teddy in his hand. As he closed the door, he heard Meg praying again. This time in Spanish. "*Padre nuestro, que estás en el cielo. Santificado sea tu nombre ...*" He'd heard her recite the Lord's Prayer in Spanish many times before, her bilingualism the result of Lucinda's tutelage over the years. A welcomed calm came over him as he stood there listening to her.

Meg would be in good hands with Martha and Lucinda, and he would be in good hands with Meg.

~

Crowder went to Dr. Moore's office to pick his brain—and pick up another puzzle piece. He directed her to a cushioned armchair that would've been familiar to Ann.

"We're trying to get a better understanding of Ann's mental state," she said once seated.

"I intend on being forthcoming about her condition," Moore said.

"Was Ann mentally ill?"

"Losing the baby eight years ago triggered a major depression, made worse by her hysterectomy. With medication and some therapy, you expect a full recovery within six months. But Ann never fully recovered. Her depressive episodes continued. For example, last summer, when she learned of her sister's death and overdosed on her medication."

Crowder leaned forward in her chair. "I'd like your opinion on something, off the record. It may have nothing to do with your diagnosis of Ann's mental health issues, but it could have everything to do with her death."

"I'll do my best."

She outlined the facts the investigation had uncovered: Westbrook's emotional detachment from her parents, her promiscuity and bad acts as a child, her crimes as an adult, her teenage diagnosis of sociopathy, her mother's murders and insanity, and the twins' conception by psychotic parents. She paused a moment, allowing Moore to digest what she'd told him.

Finally, he spoke. "With that history, and knowing Ann for almost eight years, I can tell you that she was not a sociopath. Her mood swings were never characterized by violent behavior toward others. Her sister, on the other hand, likely inherited her mother's bad genes and was a sociopath with great potential for psychopathic behavior."

"I want to share something else with you, again, off the record. Ann's sister is not dead. She forged a letter informing Ann she'd died so Ann wouldn't pursue her. Her plan all along was to impersonate Ann and steal from her."

Moore's face suddenly became a portrait of puzzlement. "You mean to say the woman was actually parading around as Ann? They may look alike, but how do you get away with something like that?"

"You kidnap Ann. You crash her car and fake amnesia afterwards. You appear detached, withdrawn, and depressed. You spend most of the time in your bedroom and office, forming and funding a foundation without Ben Livingston knowing it. Then you stage Ann's suicide and get the hell out of town."

"Please don't take offense, Detective Crowder. But Ben would know his own wife. I'm quite sure of that."

"Humor me, Dr. Moore," she said, pressing the point. "Was there anything in your interaction with the woman you believed was Ann that suggests she wasn't?"

Moore became reflective. "The first visit after the crash was at the house. A couple weeks after her accident. It was brief. I was skeptical of her memory loss. The physical injuries wouldn't have caused it."

"What about the next time you saw her?"

"The Friday before the fire. Here at the office. To my surprise, the memory issues continued. She agreed to a full neurological evaluation. She mentioned a foundation she'd formed, and hadn't yet told Ben about it. I must say, I found it inconsistent for someone with her memory issues to be able to handle a complex business matter."

"And one that had her transferring a substantial sum of money to an account at a Swiss bank on the morning of her supposed suicide," Crowder added.

"But she had the help of a business associate. I remember her mentioning that."

"Yes, a woman who made off with the money the very next day. We believe the woman was working with Ann's sister. The plan was to make it look like Ann got swindled out of the money."

"I suppose the sister could have purposefully raised it at our session to give credence to Ann's business activities," Moore speculated. "Ann had a good business sense. It's hard to believe she would put a business associate in a position to steal money from her."

"I know, but it's easy to believe the sister, pretending to be Ann and working with an accomplice, would."

Crowder returned to police headquarters and found a message from Ted Moody asking her to call him. He was there when she returned his call. "Ted, what do you have for me?"

"The concentration necessary for ignition of the carbon monoxide required the engine to be running for at least twenty-four minutes. The garage light was off. The only other source of ignition was the cell phone found in the Lexus. Ann Livingston could not have ignited the gas, say, with a match or lighter, or by turning on the car sound system, because she would have been unconscious in three to five minutes and dead in eight to ten.

"What I can't determine is whether Ann died from inhaling the fumes, or if she was already dead when she was placed in the car. That's something Sessions will have to tell us, assuming he has enough lung tissue to find evidence of carbon monoxide poisoning."

"He called yesterday. There was trace evidence of carbon monoxide. He's calling it a suicide."

"He's basing his opinion on the one autopsy finding? He may want to reconsider after he sees my report. Still, it's hard to believe she was forcibly restrained in the car until she passed out. Whoever did it would have been in the garage, inhaling the fumes too."

"The person could have been wearing a respirator, or Ann might have been gassed earlier."

"Either way, the murderer's one sick psycho."

"If I'm right about this, Ted, it's true. She is one sick psycho."

When the call ended, she walked over to Steele, who was finishing a diagram in pencil. "What? Forgot your coloring book?" she quipped.

"I'll have to remind myself to spit in your coffee the next time I get it for you."

"Still be a whole lot better than what gets brewed here."

"Piss is a whole lot better than what's brewed here."

"Never really compared the two, but thanks for trying both and telling me."

"Is this when I'm supposed to say fuck off?"

"Consider it said."

"It's a diagram of the radiology department," he explained, turning it around so his partner could see it. "Anyone could easily have gained entry to where the records are kept and walked out with Ann's x-rays and reports. There's only one way in and out. The door's unlocked, and the room's unoccupied. The records department personnel and x-ray machines are across the hall."

"Do films and reports get misplaced a lot?"

"The records clerk said it happens, but usually the films and reports aren't both misfiled. One or the other, but not both."

"Security cameras?"

"Only at the main entrance and in the parking lots. I stopped by hospital security. They'll put a hold on the main-entrance tapes for the past thirty days. We may want to take a look at them."

"We can limit our review to the week before the fire, between eight and twelve in the morning. She started leaving the house that week, and would most likely have gone to the hospital after dropping her daughter off at school. Reviewing the tapes is a tedious job we don't want to do. Let's put a cadet on it. And I have just the cadet for the job."

"Let me guess. Ramsey. I'll get him a photo of Ann Livingston and put him on it over the weekend. I'll tell him you'll give him a rematch if he finds anything."

"What about Mary Smith?"

"I called and spoke to Mrs. Benson. She has a cousin named Mary Smith."

"No kidding. Maybe she does exist."

"Doubtful."

"Why's that?"

"She's never lived there and has been dead for ten years. The Benson woman attended her funeral."

"And the background check?"

"Haven't gotten a report from Interpol or the Swiss police yet, but I got the FBI report. Twenty-two Mary Smiths with photos. The name's so common, there could be others that didn't make it to the registry. Six are dead. Six are doing time. Four are over the age of seventy, living with family or in nursing homes. None of the rest have apparent ties to Louisiana."

More dead ends.

But tomorrow was another day.

Chapter 38

Steele was already at the police station when Crowder arrived with coffees and a couple cinnamon buns.

"Hey, partner. I brought you a new stirrer. I thought you might be finished with that one."

"Thanks, Jo. Did you know there are more than two thousand Mary Smiths nationwide? There are thirty-seven with addresses in South Carolina and thirty-two right here in Louisiana."

"Not surprised. By using the most common woman's name in the country, she made sure many hours would be wasted checking out each one. Let's only contact the ones in South Carolina and Louisiana. By phone. It's a probable dead end, so put Ramsey on that, too."

Steele's phone rang. "She's with me," he said. "We'll be right out."

"Martha McMillan?"

"Yep. I'll get a recorder and meet you in the conference room."

Crowder greeted McMillan in the reception area and led her to the conference room. "Would you like water or a soda? I don't recommend the coffee."

"No, I'm fine."

Steele waited in the room. Crowder led McMillan to a seat opposite him and took the seat at the head of the table. "We're very sorry for your loss, Mrs. McMillan, and want to thank you for coming down to speak to us today," she said. "The medical examiner reviewed Ann's dental records and has positively identified the woman in the car as Ann."

"I suppose you need to be certain in matters like this," McMillan said with the stoicism of someone expecting bad news.

"Well, that's just it, ma'am. The dental records are the best way of being sure." She spared her the real reason. The burned-out shell of a body found in the car had made visual identification by a family member impossible.

Crowder inquired into Ann's depression, past suicide attempt, car crash, and amnesia. She then moved on to matters related to the murder investigation. "Mrs. McMillan, we've learned that Ann's identical twin, whose name is Veronica Westbrook, is alive, and that she forged the letter informing your daughter of her death."

"Why would she do such a thing? Ann reached out to her in good faith."

"We have reason to believe Ann's death was not a suicide." Crowder let the pronouncement hang in silence for a while. "I'm sharing what we've uncovered because you may know things that can help us get to the bottom of what happened last week."

"Why would this woman want to hurt ..." She paused mid-sentence. "... to kill Ann?"

"To become your daughter. We believe she abducted Ann, planned the car crash, and faked amnesia so she'd not be found out while she went about stealing money, a lot of money, from her. I'm being blunt with you because we're running out of time. If what I've said is true, each day that goes by puts her in a better position to conceal her identity and whereabouts. Is there anything you saw, sensed, or suspected about the woman who came home from the hospital last month that suggests she might not have been Ann?"

"I believed it was Ann. Who else could it be? But when I learned Ann's injuries were minor, I questioned her amnesia almost from the beginning. The only thing that made sense at the time was that she was subconsciously suppressing who she was in order to erase her past. I know I sound like an armchair psychiatrist, but she was so different, I thought she had a split personality."

"How was she different?"

"Well, she wasn't interested in Meg. It was instinctive for Ann, regardless of how she felt, no matter how depressed she got, to be attentive to Meg. She remained detached even when she recovered from her physical injuries. Lucinda and I took over the mothering."

"Did the woman ever resume doing any activities only Ann would be capable of doing?"

"Never did, and I thought that was strange. Not once did she try to play the piano or sketch or pick up a tennis racket."

"Anything else?"

"I found a box of tampons and morning-after contraceptives in a bag she came home with after shopping. Ann had a hysterectomy eight years ago and no longer had periods. I asked her if she was having any bleeding. She acted surprised, as though I should have known she was still menstruating."

"What about people she saw? Did you see anyone other than the immediate family and Lucinda?"

"Just Trevor, Trevor Moore." She paused momentarily. "Wait, there was someone else. About two weeks ago, I came to the house to check on Ann. She was showing a woman about her age out of the house. I met them in the foyer. Ann introduced the woman as Sarah, Sarah Booth. She said she was in her high school graduating class and a friend of hers. I didn't recognize her, and I thought I knew all of Ann's high school friends. When curiosity got the best of me, I checked Ann's yearbook and found no Sarahs or Sallys or anyone who looked at all like the woman."

"Do you think you'd recognize the woman if you saw her again?"

"Yes, I'm sure I would."

"Anything else you can tell us about her?"

"One other thing. When the woman left, she was holding one of Ann's designer handbags."

"How do you know it was Ann's?"

"I purchased it. I was told it was one of a kind when I bought it. Ann picked it out herself when we were shopping in New York City. I went back to the store to buy it and gave it to her as a birthday present last summer. She loved that bag."

267

"I guess it could be a coincidence," Steele said.

"I don't think so."

"Why not?"

"Because I checked Ann's closet, and the handbag's gone."

When McMillan had said she'd recognize Sarah Booth if she saw her again, the detectives had exchanged glances. Crowder knew they could be one question away from solving the mystery surrounding the death of Ann Livingston.

Crowder gave a head nod to her partner, who discreetly slipped out of the interrogation room. A few minutes later, he returned and placed two photographs of a woman on the table in front of Crowder.

"Just a few more questions, Mrs. McMillan," said Crowder. "Did the woman you thought was Ann ever mention she was forming a foundation and funding it with five million dollars?"

"No."

"Ever mention a woman by the name of Mary Smith?"

"No."

"But you're sure you could identify Sarah Booth if you saw her again?"

"Yes, I'm quite certain."

She placed the two photos in front of McMillan. The photos were of average quality, as good as the mug shots in police archives, and good enough to make a positive identification of a suspect. She sensed in Steele's wide-eyed glare a plea for her to ask the five-million-dollar question. The answer could prove Veronica Westbrook and the woman in the photo, acting in concert, had just pulled off Louisiana's crime of the century.

"Mrs. McMillan, is the woman in these photos Sarah Booth?"

McMillan studied the photos, picking them up separately, but her facial expression gave no hint of her answer. The detectives leaned forward in their chairs as though doing so would prompt an affirmative response. Instead, what they heard was, "No, that's not the woman. I've never seen that woman before."

Crowder saw Steele slouch back in his chair like the little boy who opened the box of Cracker Jacks and found the toy inside was one he already had. She picked up the two photos of Mary Smith and handed them back to him. She concluded the interview and walked McMillan out.

When she returned, Steele was on his computer. "Already on it," he said.

"We want to know everything there is to know about Sarah Booth," Crowder said. "What we know so far is that she wasn't a friend of Ann Livingston, or one of her high school classmates, and left the Livingston home with a handbag that wasn't hers and probably wasn't empty."

"Your gut telling you something, Jo?"

"You bet. It's telling me there's something's rotten, and it's not in Denmark. It's right here in New Orleans. And it has a lot to do with Sarah Booth."

Crowder opened her desk drawer and pulled out her holstered Smith & Wesson police-issued pistol. "I'm scheduled for the pistol range to re-qualify on my weapon. I should be back around noon. You know where to reach me."

"It's ridiculous the department requires a sharpshooter like you to re-qualify every year," Steele said. "When was the last time you scored less than perfect with your pistol?"

"I missed a few targets on the walkthrough when I was a rookie. I shot a nun in a black habit and a guy delivering the milk. Nuns don't wear black habits anymore, and who in the hell delivers milk these days? So I put slugs in their shoulders, thinking they were bad guys in disguises."

Crowder was referring to the portion of the weapons test that challenges a police officer's ability to discriminate between a perpetrator and an innocent bystander. She was always a perfect shot on pop-ups and moving targets, an expertise she'd acquired from her father, who'd had her hunting with him when she was twelve.

269

Steele chuckled. "If I were a bad guy, I don't know what I'd fear more, fighting you or being shot at by you. Either way, I'm looking at some serious hospital time."

~

Crowder completed the first part of her weapons testing by eleven thirty—another perfect score on the range targets at twenty-five and fifty yards. Next up were the pop-ups and moving targets.

"Crowder, we try making some of the innocent bystanders look more like bad guys, but you still give them a pass. And when we make the bad guys look more like friendly civilians, you pop them anyway." The comments came from Miles Jeffreys, who'd watched her pistol test. "You're spending way too much time at the range. No wonder you've got one fucked-up social life. You need to get out more. You know, a little less shooting and a lot more smooching." Turning only slightly more serious, he asked, "Are you ready to put on your usual show?"

Jeffreys had the class of cadets that included Ramsey with him to do weapons training. Crowder was there to demonstrate her proficiency in using her pistol. The cute, short-haired officer who'd decked Ramsey in the gym didn't disappoint. She shot a perfect score on her walkthrough, hitting only the targets of bad guys and doing so in times unmatched by any officer in the department. The cadets applauded when they posted her perfect scores—even Ramsey, though grudgingly.

Jeffreys walked across to Crowder to speak to her privately while the cadets gathered to review the targets of bad guys she'd shot. The ones carrying knives and handguns got shot in the shoulder, arm, or hand, sustaining what would've been non-lethal injuries. The ones carrying the semi-automatic rifles, sawed-off shotguns, and explosives got a bullet in the head.

Suddenly, Ramsey yelled out, "She missed one, Lieutenant Jeffreys." He was standing next to a target of a perpetrator holding a small child hostage in his arm. There wasn't a mark on the face, head, or torso of the target.

Jeffreys smiled broadly. "Bring the target out in the sun, Cadet Ramsey. Stand next to it and let all of us see it in full view."

Ramsey did as directed, grinning like a jack-o-lantern. As the target came into full view, beams of sunlight shone through two holes about an inch apart in the bad guy's groin. Dead center shots into what would have been his testicles.

Laughter rippled through the class of cadets. The clapping followed.

"It looks to me, Cadet Ramsey, like Lieutenant Crowder was dead-on-balls accurate with her shots, don't you agree?" Jeffreys didn't wait for him to answer. The embarrassed look on Ramsey's face and the heckling he received from his fellow cadets were sufficient rebuke.

Jeffreys took Crowder aside. "I hear you've put Ramsey to work on the Livingston case. Good. It'll keep him out of trouble. Cap's under a lot of pressure from the chief and the mayor to complete the investigation as soon as possible. The big question is whether there's more here than meets the eye. I mean, Ann Livingston committing suicide is one thing, but doing it in such a dramatic fashion is something else. The whole scene looked more like a mob hit. You know, kill the target and then destroy it and the other evidence."

"Did you see the vehicles?"

"I saw them in the yard when Ted's people were going over them. That must've been one hell of an explosion and fire. There wasn't much left to inspect."

"You should have seen what wasn't left of Ann Livingston to inspect."

"Be careful on this one. When there's pressure to conclude an investigation quickly, mistakes are made."

"Miles, Ann Livingston was the victim of a cold-blooded murder. I'm sure of that. I just need some hard evidence to dispute what's likely to be called a suicide."

271

"You know as well as me that murder investigations, particularly those involving families that have the admiration of so many people in the community, cry out to be solved. Anything less than bringing the killers to justice will be seen as incompetence and sloppiness by outsiders, particularly the press."

Crowder's countenance grew grave. "You've always had my back when we were partners, Miles. But you know me. I'm my father's daughter. I won't give up easily. I don't want my name on a cold-case file that will haunt the Livingston family and the community for a long time."

"Duly noted. I'd expect nothing less from you. I'll see you in the gym Thursday night at six. I want to show you a new technique I developed. It can be used to take out a bad guy when you're on the ground and he's standing over you with a weapon in his hand. I need to see if it works in real time."

"I look forward to learning it," she called over her shoulder as she turned and walked away.

Her cell phone pinged. A text from Steele: *Meet me for lunch. You're buying. We hit pay dirt.*

Crowder arrived at the diner around one. Steele was already there. Mimi brought coffee. As usual, no menus. "Hot turkey sandwich is the lunch special," said Mimi. "It comes highly *un*recommended. We need to get rid of the dried-out turkey from the all-you-can-eat dinner special we had two nights ago."

"Ham and Swiss on rye," said Crowder. "Dry. Hold the fries."

"Sid?"

"Double cheeseburger, medium rare, everything on it. Fries. And, Mimi, I'll take Jo's fries."

Once Mimi left, Crowder asked, "What's so important that I'm springing for lunch?"

"We've connected the dots. Sarah Booth's from Virginia; at least, that was her last known address. She's got a rap sheet that makes her look like Westbrook's understudy: prostitution, petty theft, abetting an armed robbery. She did time for the felony."

272

"So she's a bad guy. How are the dots connected?"

"She did her jail time at a women's prison in Maryland."

Crowder's eyes widened. "Let me guess. At the same place Westbrook served her sentence."

"And?"

"They were cellmates."

"Right. Booth's probation officer gave me her sister's address and phone number in Virginia. I called her. She told me Booth was released from prison last month, stayed with her for a week. Then boarded a bus for New Orleans with two hundred bucks in her pocket."

Crowder picked up on the narrative. "Doesn't sound like someone who'd be paying a visit on an old friend, carrying a designer handbag. This changes everything. There's absolutely no chance that the woman from the car crash, who introduced Booth to Ann's mother, was Ann Livingston. Booth must have demanded money from Westbrook, and she put it in one of Ann's handbags. Maybe Westbrook wanted Booth's help. Maybe Booth got wind of the scheme and was blackmailing her. Either way, money's involved. I'm sure of that. When was she released from prison?"

"Middle of January."

"So she couldn't have been in on the kidnapping or car crash."

"Looks like she came here to blackmail Westbrook."

"And it looks more and more like Westbrook went solo on this, or was working only with Smith."

"What do we do now?" Steele asked.

"This is too important to keep from Cap. Booth is the evidence we need to prove Ann's death wasn't a suicide. But we can wait until tomorrow. I want to show Ben Livingston some photos of Booth. Maybe he's seen her. I'll try to meet up with him this afternoon. We'll see Cap tomorrow morning."

"He's not going to like hearing that the case just got a lot more complicated."

"It is what it is, Sid. The dirty little business of kidnapping, grand larceny, and murder has stretched its way from Maryland to Louisiana, and to Switzerland. There are still t's to cross and i's to dot. We have until tomorrow morning to get our penmanship perfect."

~

Livingston and Crowder sat in the same chairs in his office as when the detective had told him his wife's car crash was a suicide attempt. He knew she'd get right to the point.

"Your wife's death was *not* a suicide," Crowder said. "Ann was already dead when she was placed in the car. The suicide was staged. The woman in the car crash was Veronica Westbrook, who impersonated Ann in order to steal five million dollars."

Livingston stared at the detective in disbelief. "I know the money was stolen out of the account in Zurich," he said. "But what makes you think the woman I brought home from the hospital was Ann's sister and that she staged Ann's suicide?"

"A number of things, no one more important than the other, but all pointing to the same conclusion." Crowder summarized several important facts: the intentional car crash, the fake amnesia, Smith's involvement in the theft, the staged suicide, and finally, Sarah Booth.

Livingston was skeptical. "You're saying this Westbrook woman killed Ann, put her in her car, and blew up the garage. How is that even possible?"

"Westbrook left the house and was gone for a couple of hours, more than enough time to bring Ann back and stage her suicide. The call to Dr. Moore just before the explosion couldn't have been made by Ann. Westbrook made it on one of the cordless house phones. She figured Moore would try reaching Ann on her cell phone. The phone was in Ann's car when he called it. When the phone rang, the spark ignited the gas."

"How come Westbrook wasn't killed in the explosion?"

274

"She put the cell phone in the car, waited for the gas to build up, and left the house through the unlocked pantry window. The call to Moore was made from outside the house. We saw a surveillance recording of a shadowy reflection of a person moving away from the rear of the house a couple minutes before the explosion. I believe it was Westbrook."

"But she'd be leaving much to chance," he said, still skeptical. "If Trevor didn't call Ann's cell phone, there wouldn't have been an explosion."

"Not true. Westbrook still had the cordless house phone. She'd have called Ann's cell if he hadn't."

Livingston felt like he'd just been slapped in the face and startled out of a daydream. Strangely, he felt a moment of overwhelming relief. Ann didn't *choose* to leave him and Meg. But a sense of dread soon replaced the feeling. If the detective was right, Ann was murdered, and her sister had killed her. "What's your plan for apprehending Westbrook?" he asked, his voice without inflection.

"I'll be able to tell you more next week when all the reports are in and we've tied up some loose ends."

"Detective Crowder, every day that goes by gives Ann's sister more time to create distance between you and her." Livingston's business-executive side took over, shouting out directives, expecting immediate results. "Have the airports been alerted? Have customs officials here and in Switzerland been notified? Is the FBI involved?"

"We'll be doing all those things. But there are protocols police departments and government agencies must follow." Crowder pulled out a mugshot and a prison photo and showed them to him. "Know this woman?"

He studied the photos. "Don't know her. But leave the photos. Maybe Lucinda's seen her."

"I need to know whether a cordless house phone is missing. We bagged one when we checked the house after the fire. It allowed us to confirm Moore's call to the phone. If another one is missing, it'll

275

prove that Westbrook made the call from a phone she took from the house."

Wasting no time, Livingston called Lucinda, who was at the house. After a brief conversation with her, he hung up and said, "You have your proof. Lucinda says two phones were missing when she came to the house on the Friday after the fire, one from the study and one from a seldom-used spare bedroom on the third floor. She discovered it was missing when she went to the upstairs bedrooms to find a phone to replace the one you took from the study."

Crowder stood to leave. "Any questions, Mr. Livingston?"

"This shadowy figure on the surveillance video, does it look like Westbrook or the woman in the photos?"

"We can't say whether it's a man or a woman. Not yet, at least. We're having forensics enhance the image."

"You'll call me right away if you find out the shadow is a person you can identify?"

"Of course."

"I want to know what's going on in the investigation," he said sharply. "Do I have your word I'll be well informed?"

"You do."

After walking Crowder to the elevator, he passed by his secretary's desk. "Elizabeth, hold all calls. Cancel whatever appointments I have. No interruptions." He didn't wait for a response.

He walked into his office, shut the door, and went to the liquor cabinet to pour himself a bourbon. He sat back in his chair, his mind suddenly bombarded with questions and speculations.

When Ann had been kidnapped, she must have been so frightened. Was she blindfolded, tied up, her mouth covered with duct tape, locked away in some dark, dank basement to rot?

How was she killed? Unless there's an arrest, we'll never find out what happened.

276

Was she smothered, strangled, shot, stabbed, clubbed, poisoned, starved to death? There was so little left of her body that no one could know for sure.

Why didn't someone contact me for ransom money? I'd have paid any amount to get her back, alive and unharmed.

He stared into an empty glass, then returned to the bar and poured another. This time he brought the bottle back with him. His thoughts now followed a different path.

What will the police do to catch Ann's murderer?

They were mostly inept. New Orleans was the violent crime capital of the nation, with one of the highest homicide rates in the country. There were many unsolved killings. Too many. Ann's murder would probably end up being another one. "There are protocols police departments and government agencies must follow," the detective had told him.

Fuck the police. Fuck the FBI. Fuck their fucking protocols.

He had the time, the money, and the motivation to hunt the bitches down like dogs. He'd find them. When he did, he'd want extreme justice, not a sentence of ten to twenty and out in seven for good behavior. No, they'd suffer like Ann had suffered and, like Ann, they wouldn't survive their suffering.

His line of thought rerouted as he re-filled his glass. He'd done his best to love and care for the woman after the car crash. He'd made love to her. Twice. While he was enjoying the best sex he'd ever had, Ann was dying or dead somewhere.

The bitch played me for a sucker.

He felt his grip tighten so much he thought his glass might break. He was suddenly overwhelmed by anger. Or was it hatred? He'd never felt like this before, a malignant desire to harm another person, to cause her excruciating pain and immeasurable suffering, and to have her experience a slow, agonizing death.

He prayed profanely.

Please, dear God in heaven. Holy be Thy name. Give me the chance to be alone with her.

If he could be alone with her just one more time, his thinking now crazed from the bourbon, he'd show her a damn good time. He'd chain her to a bed in some cabin in the woods. He'd degrade her, beat the hell out of her, give her nothing to eat or drink. He'd go back every day to watch her slowly die from starvation, dehydration, and neglect. He'd check on her frequently so he could be there when her last gasp was about to be taken. He'd use toothpicks to keep her eyes wide open, and then he'd put a .38 caliber slug in her forehead at point blank range and blow her fucking brains out.

His rage ebbed, replaced by something far worse. Melancholy consumed him. He'd never experienced sadness like this before. Not when his parents died. Not when Charlotte died. He'd felt he needed to be the strong one then and compartmentalize his grief in the deepest recesses of his mind. But losing the only woman he'd ever loved made his heart numb. The finality of it all. He felt like he might cry, sob like a little boy being punished for something bad he'd done to someone.

His hands shook, his glass now as empty as the bottle. He must have spilled the bourbon on his chin when he'd taken his last sips, because there were drops of liquid running down his chin. Then he realized that the moisture was tears—tears of sorrow, loneliness, and grief.

The glass slipped out of his hand and dropped to the floor.

He rested his elbows on the desk.

He put his head in his hands.

He wept.

Chapter 39

Crowder sat back in bed, working on her report on her laptop. Fred was somewhere between a nap and deep sleep. He growled when he heard the ringtone of her cell phone.

It was Steele.

"What did you find out?" she asked.

"Definitely a human form. Forensics enlarged and enhanced the image. They believe it's a person with a slender build between five-foot-six and five-foot-ten. Most likely a woman."

"What about the message on the house phone?"

"Like you remembered it. It was left at nine thirty the morning after the explosion. Rachel Hathaway telling Ann that her friend, Sarah Booth, was a no-show at work. Didn't make much sense then."

"Does now."

"I contacted Livingston. He had Hathaway go back to the office this evening to scan and send everything in Booth's file to me. It's on its way to you now."

"Have you looked through it?"

"Yep. The application's a bunch of lies. It gave Ann's high school and the University of Maryland as schools attended. Said she was a social worker. Her references were two recent employers for jobs she supposedly had while she was paying her debt to society."

"Were the references checked?"

"Doesn't look like it. She gave Ann Livingston as a reference. She was the only one Hathaway called ... Jo."

"What?"

"Why would Westbrook want Booth working for Ben's company?"

"The more important question is … why didn't she show up for work?"

~

"Outstanding police work, even though you've opened up a can of night crawlers," O'Malley said when he'd finished reading Crowder's report. "We can't keep a lid on this very long. The press has been hounding the chief. Just how much we tell the press and public without a suspect in custody is what I've got to figure out. But I have to admit, it all fits."

"Once we proved the car crash was staged, one thing led to another," Crowder said. "But what made a possible suicide into a probable homicide was the one thing Veronica Westbrook didn't plan on. Sarah Booth."

"That and you insisting something very bad had happened to Ann Livingston," Steele said, nodding at his partner.

"This Booth woman. Why would she want a job at Livingston Industries?" O'Malley asked. "She used her real name. She has priors. She could've been found out."

"Booth knew her credentials and references wouldn't be checked," Crowder said. "When Ann Livingston is one of your references, there's only one reference to check."

"Was Booth in on the plan?"

"No. She wasn't Westbrook's partner; she was her blackmailer." The puzzle pieces were all falling in place for Crowder. "Booth wanted in on the deal and wanted to stay close to her investment. What better way than by working at Livingston Industries until the big payday arrived? Until then, she'd want a down payment to get by on. After all, she only had a couple hundred dollars on her when she arrived in New Orleans, most of which was probably spent by the time she met up with Westbrook."

"So she needed money right away," O'Malley said, now swimming in his detective's stream of consciousness.

"Booth knew Westbrook had access to money, lots of it. She probably had the down payment in the designer handbag Ann's mother saw her take with her from the house."

"Makes sense."

"Westbrook had to make an executive decision. Pay up, or risk exposure. After all, her balloon would pop with a simple phone call from Booth to Ben Livingston."

"So why is Booth a no-show at work? She was supposed to start the Tuesday before the explosion and fire."

"Because you can't show up for work dead."

"You think Westbrook did away with her?"

"She was the fly in the ointment. Westbrook had to get rid of the fly."

"And how did she get rid of the fly?"

"I'm working on that."

O'Malley said, "Westbrook, if not acting with Booth, has pulled off one hell of a crime with the help of maybe one other person, the Smith woman, a crime so twisted and deviant, the State of Louisiana will insist on her being lethally vaccinated against the disease she's contracted." O'Malley gave an audible sigh as he slumped back in his chair. "You know, once we go public on this, we're committed to a manhunt like we've never seen before in Louisiana. The man hours checking out leads will crush us if we post photographs of the three women, especially because we don't know for sure if Booth is dead. Everyone and their Aunt Sadie will be calling with a sighting of one of them. The overtime alone will take us into next year's budget."

"Cap, the public needs to know that contact with Westbrook is dangerous. She's a psychopath, like her mother."

"You know what they say," Steele chimed in. "Like mother, like daughter. Two peas in a pod. A chip off the old block—"

"And the mother," Crowder said, cutting her partner off, "murdered two family members. Killing is second nature to Westbrook, just like it was for her mother."

Her last statement had buzzed around in her head last night in bed. It continued to occupy her thoughts throughout the day. Westbrook was just like her mother, a psychotic killer who'd stabbed her husband and son to death … and then decapitated them. And just like that, Crowder had the answer to the question that had haunted her ever since Booth's involvement became known. How would Westbrook get rid of the fly? The answer was now crystal clear.

"Cap, I need to follow up on something immediately. We'll get the APBs out to all of the usual law enforcement agencies, the FBI, Interpol, and TSA."

As she left, she couldn't help but think that O'Malley looked like someone who'd just learned the lottery ticket he thought was a winner turned out to be one number off. He needed to give the chief and the mayor the bad news. The suicide they thought would bring an end to the investigation was potentially a double homicide.

A shit storm was on its way, and the New Orleans Police Department was directly in its path.

The two detectives huddled up outside O'Malley's office.

"Sid, I need to get over to the medical examiner's office right away. Will you follow up with getting everything going with law enforcement?"

"Consider it done. What's up with the dramatic exit?"

"If I'm right about something, the manhunt just got a lot easier."

~

"Dr. Sessions, I believe I know the identity of the headless corpse," Crowder said. "I need the head found downriver from where the body was dumped on the bridge."

"We still have it," he said, "but like I told you before, there's not enough tissue left to identify its facial features."

"Did you determine the cause of death?"

282

"I opened the skull at the location of a fracture and looked at the brain. Death was by blunt force trauma by an object—a club, a tool, like a poker or hammer, possibly the butt end of a pistol or a rock. Two blows to the anterior fontanelle, the most vulnerable part of the skull. She suffered a massive subdural bleed and was dead within minutes."

"I want to have forensics reconstruct the face. Was there any hair on the head?"

"Yes, a fair amount. It's the last thing eaten by predators and takes a long time to decompose. There's enough to determine the length and color of her hair."

"What about facial tissue and eyes?"

"Not much tissue. The ears and nose are mostly gone. One of the eyes is partially intact. It should provide the color."

"Height and weight?"

"It's in my report. Travis did the measurement and weight with the head back in place."

"Any tattoos or birthmarks that might help identify the person?"

"I didn't note any in my report. So probably not. I'll have Travis check the body again to be sure."

When her meeting with Sessions was over, Crowder called Sylvia St. James, the sculptor the department used to do composites and facial reconstructions. "Sylvia, Jo Crowder here. Do you know about the incident at Ben Livingston's home last week?"

"You'd have to be deaf, dumb, and blind not to. The smart money says it's a suicide."

"Big favor to ask."

"Shoot. No pun intended."

Crowder was familiar with St. James's work. She was involved in the Francis "Fat Franny" Arnoldson case. Fat Franny, a serial killer, had used fluoroantimonic acid, the most corrosive acid in the world, to destroy his murder victims' identity. Not much had been left of the hands and faces of his victims. St. James, using her knowledge of

283

taxidermy and facial sculpting, had reconstructed the heads of two of Fat Franny's victims. They'd turned out to be his parents.

"I need a facial reconstruction by Monday," said Crowder. "The head's at the medical examiner's office, waiting to be picked up."

"What's left of it?"

"Not much. Most of it ended up in someone's crab dip."

~

Crowder and Steele watched O'Malley's press conference from police headquarters. All the national networks and cable news stations broadcast it. O'Malley had told them to stay away and avoid discussing the case with the media.

O'Malley provided very little new information to the press and public, other than to confirm that the dead person was Ann Livingston and that an inquest would be held in two weeks to determine the cause and manner of her death. He made no mention of the opening of a criminal investigation, or that Westbrook was wanted on suspicion of kidnapping, grand larceny, and murder.

"Cap was told to delay telling the public Ann's death was a probable homicide and that her sister is a suspect," Crowder said, grimacing. "He's hoping she'll be picked up before the inquest."

"And if she isn't," Steele said, shrugging his shoulders, "we'll look like fools for not going public right away."

After reading his prepared statement, O'Malley hurried from the podium amid shouts from the gallery of angry reporters.

Crowder understood the reaction of the press. The N.O.P.D. was stonewalling them by not taking questions. "Not good, Sid. The media will have a field day speculating about what happened to Ann Livingston. Suicide. Murder. Some horrible accident. Family members, relatives, friends, business associates, all are possible suspects."

"And no conspiracy theory is off limits."

"Not for two weeks at least."

~

Ben Livingston watched the press conference alone from his home. He'd sent Lucinda home early again. Meg was still at Martha's, where Ben would have dinner later. He just hoped he wouldn't be too drunk to drive over.

He looked at his watch. Almost five o'clock. He nursed two glasses of bourbon, waiting to hear O'Malley's bullshit. The police had their way of doing things. He had his way. He'd known what he needed to do after Crowder told him what she thought had happened to Ann and why.

He picked up his cell phone and scrolled through contacts to Will Goodman. He called the man's cell.

"Goodman," he answered.

"Will, I need your help."

Chapter 40

Three weeks had passed since Laura Mueller met Chase Rochet. Three weeks that had changed both of their lives. The two were inseparable. When he wasn't at Laura's chalet, she was at Château Vallée, or meeting him for lunch or dinner. They exchanged keys to their homes and brought over clothes and toiletries because of their frequent sleepovers.

Laura learned to ride Meadow. Liv trained her. She rode two hours a day, firmly establishing the bond between mistress and mare. When she wasn't riding with Liv or Chase, she explored the countryside alone with her new friend.

Evenings were spent at the opera, watching productions of Georges Bizet's *Carmen* and Charles Gounod's *Romeo and Juliet*. They held hands and whispered to each other scandalous things that made them laugh, their naughtiness annoying those around them. They dined out with Chase's friends, but mostly just the two of them, alone in the intimate settings of the finest restaurants in Zurich and Lucerne.

The days they fell asleep somewhere other than in each other's arms could be counted by fingers on a single hand. Their lovemaking was always passionate; she made sure of that. Tender moments and whispered words of affection followed the cooling of their embers; he made sure of that. What was taking place was a whirlwind romance between two people seemingly head over heels in love.

Laura sensed that Chase accepted her story about her husband being executed by the crime syndicate because he became obsessed with her safety, particularly when she was alone in her chalet. He bought her a handgun, a .45 caliber Glock. She liked shooting the pistol and soon became competent in using it. "There's something about the feel of it in my hand," she told him after emptying a full clip into a target at the firing range, where he'd taken her to learn how to shoot. "I feel empowered, confident, and safe."

"Keep it loaded and accessible," he said, "and always remember to—"

"I know, Chase," she interrupted him. "Aim at the chest, dead center, and keep shooting until the target is down, even if I have to empty the clip."

"Yes, Laura. Sometimes, you only have the one chance."

"I'll keep it in the nightstand by my bed."

"Remind me not to surprise you with an unannounced visit," he quipped.

As the days turned into weeks, she knew she'd never find a man more loyal and trustworthy than Chase. She had feelings for him she'd never felt for any man before. She wondered whether what she felt was love. It was surely different. With him she felt good about who she was as a person. He asked her what she was thinking and how she was feeling as if what she thought and how she felt mattered to him. It made her feel important and respected. For the first time in her life, a man wanted her for more than sex; he wanted her as a friend, companion, confidante, and perhaps as a wife.

A mid-week dinner at their favorite restaurant in Lucerne gave her reason to believe he might soon propose marriage. "Darling, I'm planning a dinner party in Aunt Rosalind's honor on Saturday. She turns eighty-seven," he said.

"A birthday party? How nice."

"I dare say, it could be her last. She's in such poor health. Liv is actually the one planning it."

"If there's anything you want me to do, just ask."

"Yes, one thing: be your charming self and dazzle our guests."

"I'm certain I'll want to stay in the background on her big evening."

287

"Well, that's just it. She'll have to share the limelight with you. I want you to meet my family, all of them, and our inner circle of friends."

"Of course, darling. I'd love to meet them. But I hope they will not be too inquisitive. There's only so much a country girl from Iowa can remember about life on a farm and teaching second grade."

"Don't worry. I'll stick by you. Liv, too. She knows how to guard a straying lamb from a wolf's ambush."

"I saw a hand-quilted shawl in an art studio in Lucerne. It's by a local artist who exhibits her work at the shop. It can be my present for Aunt Rosalind. It's either the shawl, or I yodel 'happy birthday.' Your choice."

Smiling, he said, "The shawl is an excellent idea. Intimately homespun. The perfect gift. I, too, have been shopping for the perfect gift."

"Well, I know it's not yodeling lessons for your aunt. What did you get her?"

"I'm afraid you, like Aunt Rosalind, will have to wait."

Laura sensed something was in the works. Liv was particularly warm and attentive to her during the week, treating her like she was the guest of honor at the party. Liv let slip that her sister, who was flying in from Paris with her husband, was "just dying to meet you and welcome you into the family."

Liv invited twenty-five guests. A nanny would feed and amuse the children elsewhere on the estate, and entertainment in the grand ballroom would follow a formal dinner. An ensemble group from the Lucerne Symphony Orchestra would play a composition of classical and pop music arranged by Liv for the special occasion. Chase told Laura that it had a "distinctly American theme," another sign that his daughter had a different honored guest in mind.

Laura spent the night before the gala at Château Vallée. She already had a bedroom assigned to her—conveniently located down the hall from Chase's bedroom.

By six o'clock on the unseasonably warm February evening, the guests, in their evening gowns and tuxedos, had all gathered in the Winter Garden and on the terrace. Liv and Rochelle greeted the guests, who were abuzz with gossip about Chase and his American princess.

"I'm afraid father is so smitten, a marriage proposal is a foregone conclusion," Liv said to Rochelle.

"What does she have to offer father, other than being young, beautiful, and wealthy?" Rochelle said jokingly to her sister.

"It's strange. I was prepared to dislike her. You know, the rich socialite looking to improve her social ranking by nabbing one of Europe's most eligible widowers. But she's a refreshing change from any woman father has known, including mother, who, like us, had all the advantages of being born into the privileged class. She's very approachable and friendly."

"I hear she's won over Meadow."

"Laura is very much a gift for Meadow. The horse was so morose when mother passed and she wasn't being ridden anymore. She's herself again. I can see it when Laura rides her. She talks to Meadow like mother always did. Strokes her ears and chin the same way, too. She loves feeding her apples, lets her eat them right down to the core and lick her hand. She helped Scotty give her a bath; she was knee deep in suds. He told me she was like us when we got our first horses. It's like she's known the horse her whole life. Must have something to do with growing up on a farm."

"So he's really going to propose tonight?"

"Yes. He's like an excited young suitor. He asked my permission. He knows how much I like her. So he's opened up to me about how much he loves her. I cried; we both cried."

"How does Auntie feel about all this?"

"That's just it. Father knows Laura hasn't won her over yet. Usual reasons. She's too young. She's all looks and no substance. She's not one of us. We know so little about her. But father's his own man. Auntie has no idea he's proposing to her tonight."

289

"How will she feel about being upstaged by Laura?"

"Laura won me over, right from the beginning. Father's friends, and their wives, adore her. The staff thinks she's one of them. She makes everyone laugh. We need laughter in the house again. He's so happy. I don't know what he'd do if she said no. Auntie is going to have to share Father. It's that simple."

"With Auntie, nothing is that simple."

The sisters circulated among the guests, who were more interested in gossip about Chase's enchanting young beauty than in the goings-on of his irascible old aunt.

"Olivia, darling, is it true what they say about her?"

"And what's that, Aunt Edith?" The wrinkled eighty-four-year-old woman was Rosalind's first cousin and closest confidante.

"That your father's American beauty has looks that rival those of Grace and Diana?"

"I suppose you'll soon find out," Liv said, being politely coy, "because there she is."

Chase appeared at the entrance to the Winter Garden with a young woman on his arm.

~

The clock struck seven. They paused momentarily until a hush overcame the chatter. All eyes were on her. She looked stunning in her lavender, silk, one-shouldered, Christian Dior evening gown with rosettes and flowing ruffles. For Laura, the dress showcased enough of her assets to evoke a woman's envy and a man's lustful curiosity. She had her hair styled above her shoulders and wore the updo like a crown. She presented herself as every bit Chase's aristocratic equal. Yet her perfectly chiseled teeth behind an easy smile made her look genuinely friendly and engaging.

She didn't disappoint. Chase spent the next hour mingling among the guests, introducing her to them. He interjected himself and moved to other guests when questioning into Laura's past probed too deeply. She didn't need a repertoire of small talk. The men were content to gawk at her while the ladies, intimidated by her striking good looks, treated her like a member of the royal family.

Laura made sure to make thoughtful comments about Liv or Rochelle whenever alone with one or the other. She regarded both as allies and needed their support to offset the disdain that Rosalind seemed to have for her—the old woman had declined two dinner invitations and a night at the opera for no particular reason. When Laura had raised her concerns with Chase, he'd just laughed and said she'd eventually win her over.

Laura wasn't so sure.

Rosalind made her grand entrance into the parlor with her nephew at her side. He placed her wheelchair strategically to allow the guests to wish her well before they entered the dining room. Family members greeted her first, followed by friends. Laura mustered all her strength of will to walk over to her, a show of respect she did grudgingly.

"Do you want someone to protect your flank?" Liv said, joining her on the way.

"Thanks. Your father cautioned me that there's strength in numbers."

"My dear, how lovely you look," Rosalind said behind an unwilling smile after Laura wished her all the happiness on her birthday. She then inched her wheelchair closer, turned her head, and whispered to Laura, "Let's speak privately this evening, just you and I, in the parlor."

Laura couldn't tell from the old woman's facial features or tone of voice whether the talk would be cordial or confrontational. But she had to appease the old biddy. Once she married Chase, she'd do whatever was necessary to spend as little time with her as possible in the little time she had left. The woman was eighty-seven and in poor health. How much longer could she be expected to live? Or—as Laura mulled over in her mind—when could she be expected to die?

The dinner, by culinary standards, was superb. Chase entertained the guests with humorous anecdotes about his aunt while they dined. All laughed heartily, all but one, whose eighty-seven-year-old eyes remained fixed on the beautiful young woman seated beside her nephew. While the tables were cleared and everyone prepared to take their seats in the ballroom for the evening's entertainment, Chase took Laura aside and led her back into the Winter Garden. They were alone. He held her in his arms and kissed her on the lips. He spoke softly, as though revealing a secret.

"Laura, I do believe I've fallen in love with a thief," he said.

Her ears perked like those of a cat hearing the footsteps of an intruder. For her, the word *thief* always carried a penal meaning.

"You've stolen the heart of a man twice your age," he continued, "and, I dare say, have locked it away in an ivory tower. You've made me feel alive again. You've given me wings. I no longer walk through life; I soar. Will you take my hand and fly away with me? Will you share your life with me, now and forever?"

He pulled out a small, velvet box and opened it. The diamond sparkled even in the dim light of the Winter Garden. She wasn't unaccustomed to men's proclamations of love. More than a few had said they loved her, but they'd uttered the words just before or after they ejaculated, a privilege for which they paid a fee before or after services were rendered. Yet she was moved by Chase's endearing entreaties and responded, "Yes, my darling, you, too, have stolen my heart. We are, in many ways, both thieves, partners in the crime of falling in love."

He slipped the ring on her finger. A tender embrace and gentle kiss followed. As he held her in his arms, she felt an emotion roil up from within. Maybe it was the feeling a daughter has for a father who loves her, or a wife has for a husband who adores her. Whatever it was, it moved her in a way she'd only once before experienced, when she'd looked at a photo in a golden frame—a photo of a little girl who looked just like she had as a child. A child who was smiling.

292

A child who was happy. The feeling she'd had that day looking at the photo was the same feeling she had looking into the face of Chase Rochet.

And for only the second time in her life ...

She cried.

~

The guests were all assembled in the ballroom. The conductor was about to begin the half-hour arrangement Rochelle had prepared for the special occasion. The guests sat in four rows of six, so couples could conveniently be seated together. The front row had an extra space reserved for Rosalind. Her nephew and Laura sat on one side, and her niece, Simone, and her husband, Philippe, sat on the other. The musicians readied their instruments. The conductor took his position before the orchestral group and nodded at Chase.

Chase walked to the conductor's spot and turned to face his guests. "My family and dearest friends, tonight is a glorious night for me, and I hope it is for you, Aunt Rosalind, and for all who are here to honor you on your eighty-seventh year. Aunt Rosalind, you are an inspiration to us all. You've aged like the great wines from the Rochet vineyards, deliciously, gracefully, and enduringly. We look forward to celebrating your eighty-eighth next year. Same time, same place. Do not disappoint us. Your pledge, my dear, that you will attend."

The guests all rose. They applauded. The orchestra played "Auld Lang Syne" while Rosalind smiled, raised her hand, and waved like an English queen in a royal procession. Once the applause subsided and the music ended, Chase addressed his family and friends on the topic Laura knew was in the forefront of his mind.

"With the people I hold dear to me all gathered here, it occurred to me to take this opportunity to share something as joyous as the celebration of the day of my dear aunt's birth. Tonight, those of you who did not know Laura had your chance to meet her. How fortuitous it is that the happy occasion that brings us together

293

this evening is one in which I can share with all of you some very good news. Tonight, I did something presumptuous in the Winter Garden just before we gathered here. I proposed marriage to Laura, presuming to think she might accept. Out of kindness for an old fool who has fallen in love for the last time in his life, I am pleased to say that she's accepted, and that her acceptance has made this fool the happiest man on the face of the earth." He turned and looked at Laura. "My darling, tonight you have proved to me that love is truly a very splendid thing."

The ensemble, on cue from the maestro, began to play an abbreviated version of Handel's "Hallelujah." All who could do so rose and applauded. Laura smiled and, mimicking how Rosalind had acknowledged her special moment, waved her hand just as she had. But when she looked over at Rosalind, she saw a woman with an icy look of disgust on her face and a white-knuckled grip on the upholstered arms of her wheelchair.

The cozy chat she'd requested would not be to welcome Laura into the royal family.

Immediately after the performance, Laura followed Rosalind into the parlor for their face-off.

"Close the door," the old woman barked as soon as Laura entered. She pounced immediately. "It was foolish for Charles to propose marriage without first discussing the matter with me. Now we'll need to unravel what he has done to bring no dishonor to the Rochet name and as little embarrassment as possible to Charles."

Laura was shocked by Rosalind's comments, more so by her tone. "Chase and I are in love," she protested. "Why do you feel such resentment toward me?"

"Because you are a fraud, an imposter, and worse."

"What do you mean?"

"I sent a photograph Charles took of you to the American Consulate and requested a background check. Tonight, I received a call informing me they were unable to identify a Laura Mueller who ever lived in the state of Iowa. But they did find a photograph of someone by the name of Veronica Westbrook posted with Interpol, who bears a remarkable resemblance to you. The person is wanted in the United States in connection with the death of a woman. So far, no one knows about my contact with the consulate. I want to keep it that way, if possible.

"I was going to inform Charles tonight of what I've learned, but I was afraid of how he would react, so I waited. And then he foolishly proposed marriage to you and announced it to our family and most intimate friends before I could stop him. Now a scandal of epic proportions will result unless you retreat from his life. Find a reason to break the engagement and leave Switzerland. It would give me great pleasure to call the authorities, but I want to spare the family and my nephew the humiliation of being duped by you. You have twenty-four hours to come up with a reason to sever your relationship with him. If not, I will tell him what I know, and you, my dear, will be on a plane back to America to face the consequences for whatever you have done."

Laura mentally sifted through what she'd heard. The night had been so beautiful, so perfect, and now the old battle axe was going to screw things up for her. Why couldn't Rosalind leave things alone? Laura had been accepted into Chase's family and inner circle of friends, by all but one. It was Chase's decision, and his wish, to live with the mystery of Laura Mueller's past buried forever. Why couldn't the dying old bitch do that as well?

The excitement of the moment caused Rosalind to cough, and the coughing escalated into gagging. Laura thought the old hag might choke to death right there in front of her. Rosalind reached for her throat with her hand to assuage the spasm, inadvertently dislodging her nasal cannula. She gasped for air. Because she couldn't breathe, she couldn't scream. She was nearly *in extremis.*

Laura's mind screamed, *Die, bitch. Die.*

Rosalind convulsed in her chair, and her wheezing became louder.

Laura heard someone at the door.

295

Think. Do something. Do it now.

"Help! Please, someone help us," she yelled as loud as she dared. The door opened, and Chase appeared from behind it.

"Oh, Chase, please help her. She started choking and pulled off her oxygen line."

He went immediately to his aunt, reconnected her nasal cannula, then held her hand and told her to breathe slowly. "Please, my dear, relax as you breathe. Remember what you were told to do when you have a coughing spasm. That's it, nice and easy." Rosalind's breathing gradually stabilized, but the episode had worn her out, and she slumped in her chair as though she'd dozed off. "It's been a full day for you," Chase said. "Let's get you comfortably in bed."

He took control of the wheelchair and moved her into the foyer, where one of the servants, a nurse, took over. The nurse lived with Rosalind in her home in Zurich and accompanied her whenever she stayed over at Château Vallée. She maneuvered the wheelchair to an elevator adjacent the kitchen that would take Rosalind to her room. There, she'd be readied for bed.

As Rosalind was wheeled away, Laura feigned concern over what had happened. "We were having such a pleasant conversation," she said. "She was giving me her blessing. All of a sudden, she began coughing and choking. It scared me terribly. Thank God you were nearby when I called for help. Does she do this often?"

"I've seen it happen before. More than once these past few months, I'm afraid. Poor Aunt Rosalind. She's losing the good fight. I fear the end for her may very well be in sight."

"If I'd only been told what to expect," Laura said, "I could've been more help to her. I'll know what to do if it happens again."

"Well, at least we know she approves of you and our marriage. I'll go to her tomorrow and thank her for welcoming you into the family. Let's see our guests off and retire to the parlor for a nightcap."

She went to Chase and kissed him on his cheek. "Yes, my love. Let's see them out so we can be alone."

~

The mid-hour chimes of the downstairs clocks broke the pin-drop silence in Château Vallée. It was two thirty in the morning. Laura had forced herself to stay awake after Chase had gone to his room. She'd made sure he would choose sleep over lovemaking by refilling his glass of sherry twice and reminding him of his vow of abstinence whenever Rosalind stayed over. It was etiquette only Chase's aunt would insist on, and it played right into Laura's plan. She needed to solve a problem, and she needed to solve it now.

Rosalind's nurse slept in the servants' quarters on the third floor. A night walker wouldn't be noticed entering Rosalind's bedroom a floor below. As she passed by Chase's bedroom, Laura opened the door just enough to see him sleeping soundly, the uneven sound of his snoring a sure sign of the depth of his alcohol-induced slumber. She closed the door and walked slowly to Rosalind's bedroom. The creaking floorboards followed the steps of her slipper-less feet like shadows.

My good fortune his dogs are hunters and live in the stable.

Laura approached the door cautiously. She didn't want to alarm the old woman if she was awake when she entered. She opened the door slowly, just enough to slip by. The door squeaked as it opened and again when, once inside, she closed it.

Rosalind lay propped up in bed, with two pillows under her head to help keep her airway open. She needed around-the-clock oxygen and was on the highest concentration at night, when she was most at risk of a coughing spasm, something Laura had learned from Chase in the parlor over sherry. Her inquiries also revealed that an alarm bell sounded in the nurse's bedroom if Rosalind's oxygen stopped for any reason or her pulse became low enough to signal an impending heart stoppage.

The old woman was asleep with her mouth wide open. She looked half dead. Laura would ensure the other half died, too. She gently removed the pulse oximeter probe and reattached it to the index finger of her own left hand, the machine now monitoring the vital signs of a healthy woman. The readings on the screen momentarily dropped during the transfer, but not low and long enough to trigger the alarm.

The next step had to be done just right. She removed the nasal cannula from beneath Rosalind's nostrils, cutting off the oxygen needed to inflate her lungs and oxygenate the blood that flowed to her brain. Brain cells were dying. When enough of them died, so would she.

Within seconds, Rosalind woke up, gasping for air in the same way as before. She flailed her arms. Laura reacted by holding them down. The old dame shook so violently that the probe nearly dislodged from Laura's finger. The sound of her gagging became unexpectedly shrill.

I have to stop it, stop it now.

Laura pulled one of the pillows from under Rosalind's head and placed it over the dying old woman's face, pressing down with both hands. Rosalind's chest heaved and, a few long seconds later, deflated like a leaky balloon. Her arms went limp.

All was calm … *dead* calm.

Laura removed the pillow. Rosalind's eyes were wide open, her mouth agape, as though she was about to speak.

The dialogue played out in Laura's mind.

What do you want to say to me, Aunt Rosalind?

Please stop. Don't do this. I want to live, if only for a little while longer. I won't tell on you, Laura. I promise.

Cross your heart?

Cross my heart and hope to …

Die? Yes, dear Aunt Rosalind, it's my hope for you, too.

Laura could ill afford the luxury of a private moment to reflect on what she'd done. There would be time for that later. *Finish up, and get the hell out of here before the bugle sounds.*

She put the pillow back and repositioned the nasal cannula, which now pumped oxygen into the nose of a dead body. A quick scan of the room assured Laura everything was as it was when she'd entered. She returned the probe to the index finger of the dead woman, hastened to the bedroom door, opened it, and turned for one last look. The pulse oximeter monitor had dropped to zero. She closed the door and tiptoed down the hall.

The alarm sounded as she passed by Chase's bedroom. Soon back in her room, she closed the door, her ear pressed tightly against it. The alarm may not have been loud enough to wake Chase, but it was blaring in the bedroom of the nurse who, seconds later, ran to the bedroom of her mistress. "Sorry, Nurse," Laura muttered under her breath as the nurse passed by her door, "a few minutes late, and a few breaths short." Returning to bed, she pulled the covers over her and waited to hear the nurse's cries for help.

"Monsieur Rochet, please come. Please come quickly. It's *madame*. She's not breathing."

The clamor in the hallway signaled to Laura that Chase was accompanying the nurse on the way to Rosalind's room.

Laura got out of bed and put on her robe. She mussed her hair to appear as though she'd been awakened abruptly by the noise, then went to Rosalind's room.

She heard the nurse say, "No pulse. No heartbeat. *Madame* is … dead."

"Oh my God! Chase, what happened?" she exclaimed as she entered and walked to his side. "Is Aunt Rosalind all right?"

"It was her time to leave us," he said in a hushed, respectful tone. A moment later, he walked Laura back to her room. "You go to sleep, my dear. The nurse and I will attend to Aunt Rosalind. It will please my daughters to know that her last conversation with you was a pleasant one in which she accepted you into our family."

She kissed him on the cheek and said, "Yes, my dear. It brought me pleasure, too. I'll always remember her kindness toward me."

Chase returned to the bedroom where an old woman lay dead. Laura returned to her bed, where she lay awake, relieved that she'd dodged a bullet meant for her. Several hours earlier she'd been in the parlor, alone with one of the most powerful women in Europe, a woman with the ability to destroy her.

How badly the night could've gone. She saw it unfolding in her mind. The Zurich *gendarmes* coming to Château Vallée and arresting her. The look on Chase's face as they told him she was wanted for kidnapping and murdering her sister and stealing millions of dollars from her. No man, no matter how much he loved a woman, could live with someone like that. He'd give her up gladly and be thankful he wasn't her next victim.

She suddenly felt anxious. If Rosalind had found out about her, others could, too. A life in Switzerland was no longer an option. Once she married Chase, she'd be more in control of her destiny, and his. They'd live in France. Chase's late father had a beautiful estate there. She'd take up painting, under the private tutelage of Rochelle, who'd offered to instruct her in landscape and still life painting.

One thing was certain. The wedding would be a very private ceremony. It would take place in France, not Switzerland. Switzerland had suddenly become a very dangerous place for Laura Mueller to be living.

Chapter 41

"Sylvia's in the conference room with the head," Steele announced in a ho-hum manner, as though the arrival of heads at police headquarters was an everyday occurrence.

"Mrs. McMillan and Rachel Hathaway are out front," Crowder said. "Let's keep them separated. Since they both saw her, we need both for a positive ID. I'll bring in Ann's mother first."

When Crowder entered the conference room with Mrs. McMillan, Sylvia St. James was busy removing the head from her carrying case. She'd anchored the head to a wooden pedestal and covered it with a white pillow case. A tag affixed to the base read "Jane Doe ℅ Office of the Chief Medical Examiner, No. 4527." Steele and St. James sat around the table. Crowder ushered Mrs. McMillan to a seat. Steele turned on the recorder to preserve the identification in case a criminal prosecution occurred later.

"Mrs. McMillan, before we look at the person's head sculpted by Ms. St. James," Crowder said after they were seated, "I want you to describe the woman you saw at the Livingston home who was introduced to you as Sarah Booth."

"She was in her late twenties or early thirties. Caucasian. Pretty. About two or three inches shorter than Ann. I'd say about five-five or five-six. She had straight, medium-brown hair cut to the middle of her neck, with bangs."

"Eye color?"

"Brown. I'm pretty sure. I'd remember if they were blue or hazel."

Crowder nodded to St. James. "Sylvia, please remove the cover."

St. James did as requested, revealing a head almost exactly fitting the description McMillan had just given of Booth.

"My God, that's her. I'm certain of it. If her hair was parted in the middle and pulled over her forehead more, it's exactly how she looked when I saw her at the house."

St. James opened a small bag she'd brought and removed a comb. She parted the brunette wig and let the bangs fall over the brow.

"That most definitely *is* the woman. How did you know how to model her features so exactly?"

Crowder nodded at Steele, who turned off the recorder. "Mrs. McMillan, can I trust you to keep the information that answers that question confidential while the investigation is ongoing?"

"Of course."

"A dead woman's body was found on a bridge in St. Tammany Parish the week of the fire. It had been decapitated. The head was found the next day, downstream from the bridge. It was unrecognizable. Ms. St. James reconstructed the head from what remained of it. We think there's a connection between Ann's sister and Sarah Booth's death."

"My God! You believe this Westbrook woman killed Ann and ..." Mrs. McMillan didn't need to say her name. She let her eyes do the pointing.

"It's looking that way to us," Crowder said as the meeting concluded.

Rachel Hathaway gave a similar description of Booth and also identified the head as a replica. When she'd left, Crowder took photographs of the sculpture and sent them to Ben Livingston with an explanation of how Booth's head had been reconstructed. Crowder knew that the sordid details of Booth's murder would add gasoline to the fire in Ben Livingston's belly, a fire that wouldn't be extinguished until his wife's murderer was brought to justice.

~

The inquest was not the rubber stamp for death by suicide hoped for by the chief and mayor. The coroner presided over the two-hour

302

hearing in a packed courtroom of reporters and members of the public, most of whom had stood in line for hours as the price of admission. Ann's family did not attend the hearing. Livingston knew the outcome beforehand.

The news conference after the inquest was one-sidedly brief. The mayor and the higher-ups in the department had gambled and lost. Westbrook was not apprehended by TSA security while leaving the country on a flight to Switzerland, nor by customs officers in Switzerland when she arrived. O'Malley gave a statement but entertained no questions.

"Good afternoon. Because the nature of the investigation going forward is a *criminal* investigation, I am unable to provide you with its details. I am able to inform you that Ann Livingston's death, as the coroner found today, was a homicide, and that the New Orleans Police Department and the State of Louisiana have two suspects for whom arrest warrants have been issued: Veronica Westbrook, a thirty-three-year-old Caucasian female, and Mary Smith, a thirty-one-year-old Caucasian female."

O'Malley paused long enough to illuminate the screen of the closed-circuit TV in the city council chambers, where the press conference was taking place. When the photograph of Veronica Westbrook came on the screen, a cacophony of exclamations and shout-outs rose from the people gathered in the room.

"Yes, Veronica Westbrook looks like Ann Livingston, because she is Mrs. Livingston's identical twin sister," O'Malley said.

The din from the crowd abruptly subsided. An eerie hush prevailed as the onlookers stared in seeming disbelief at the photograph of Westbrook—the mirror image of Ann Livingston.

O'Malley used the lull as an opportunity to continue. "Photographs of these individuals have been circulated to state and federal law enforcement agencies and are available to the press and the public on our department's website. We are asking the public to report anyone meeting the descriptions of these individuals by calling the hotline number shown on the screen, which is also posted on the website. I am unable to take questions at this time. Thank you."

Questions bombarded O'Malley as he left the podium and scurried to a side door: "How long have you known these persons were involved in Ann Livingston's death?" "Did you know their identities at the time of the last press conference?" "Why didn't you publish the photographs earlier, so the public could be on the lookout for them?" The unanswered questions, mostly accusatory or rhetorical, followed him out of the room like the honking of a gaggle of goslings.

O'Malley's plan had backfired. "There's still a chance Westbrook will be located and arrested in Louisiana, so going public is a chance worth taking," he'd told Crowder before he left headquarters to deliver his statement.

Crowder wasn't convinced.

She knew that chance was nothing more than wishful thinking.

~

Will Goodman, a tall, muscular, fit, fifty-year-old former Navy seal, had done overseas tours in Iraq, Afghanistan, Syria, and Somalia before retiring at the rank of commander to become director of security for Livingston Industries. His expertise in cybersecurity had landed him the job. Cyber theft was an enormously profitable criminal enterprise. Goodman knew how to detect breaches of secure computer systems. He could hack into the computers of most banking institutions and corporations with only a minimum of insider information. If he couldn't breach the system, he knew the people who could.

"So, what can you tell me that I don't already know?" Livingston asked when Goodman arrived at his office to give his report.

"I was able to access the files of the Maryland agency that handled her adoption. They had the biological mother's healthcare records."

"Normally, paper records that old aren't also electronically stored," Livingston remarked.

"I know. Someone must've made it a passion to electronically archive the agency's paper records."

"What about the mother?"

"Her name is Monica Millings. I know this is difficult to hear, Ben, because Ann and Westbrook shared the same mother. But the mother was a top-shelf psychopath. She killed her husband and four-year-old son. Stabbed them repeatedly. Cut their heads off and put them on the fireplace mantle. Slept with the headless corpses until the rank smell of body decomposition got a neighbor to call the police."

"My God," Livingston gasped. "What became of this"—he shook his head—"woman?"

"Murder convictions for the double homicides, but mentally ill."

"The births? How do they fit in?"

"She was raped by another psychopath while both were incarcerated in an asylum for the criminally insane. She later put a fork into his carotid artery. He almost bled out. Afterwards, she was placed in an isolation cell, where she withered away."

"Dead?"

"Yes, just recently. They thought she was near death. A priest was called to give last rites. She was seventy years old, hadn't eaten by mouth in a month, and weighed less than ninety pounds. The priest was praying at bedside. Everyone thought she was comatose, everyone but her. She grabbed him by the throat. Nearly ripped a hole in it. A guard crushed her skull with his club. Too little, too late. The holy man was a goner."

Livingston looked down, processing what he'd just been told. *There's no way Ann's the offspring of a monster.* Yet he knew from what the detectives had told him that Westbrook was believed to have murdered and decapitated Sarah Booth. His mind was getting the best of him. Meg, his sweet Meg—if her grandmother was Satan's daughter, what of her? The grandmother's blood flowed through Ann's veins and into poor, innocent Meg. Would Meg grow up and be like her? *Will my head one day lie upon a mantle?* He got angry at himself. How could he think such foolish thoughts? There was no way Meg would end up like Nana Monica or Aunt Veronica, not a fucking chance. He'd never let that happen to her.

Livingston returned to present time and the reason for his meeting with Goodman. "What about Booth?"

"Booth was probably murdered by Westbrook, who had some fun with her body afterwards."

Livingston could do without Goodman's embellished commentary. "I know, Will. I know. But what makes you think it was Westbrook?"

"One of our operatives tracked down the guy who saw the person who dumped her body on the bridge. He said the vehicle was a late-model, white Mercedes. A young woman with short, dark hair was driving. He didn't see her face clearly, so he couldn't identify her from the photos we showed him. But he remembered the color of the license plate—lime green. He didn't tell the police when he was interviewed because they only asked him if he got the license *number*."

"What's the significance of the color?"

"Safeway Rent-A-Car uses lime-green plates for their rental cars in Louisiana. I had two guys checking every Safeway location in the state. They identified two Mary Smiths who rented vehicles in Louisiana, but only one rented a white Mercedes SUV."

"Did you check for Westbrook and Booth?"

"Nothing for Westbrook. But a Sarah Booth came up on a Budget rental from downtown New Orleans a month ago. She never returned the car. It was found abandoned in the business district three weeks ago."

"Were you able to locate Smith?"

"Yes and no. We hacked into the Louisiana airport computer system and looked for anyone purchasing a ticket by the name of

Mary Smith. Three women showed up. One was a young woman traveling with her husband. Another was an elderly woman with a service dog. Both were traveling to the West Coast. The last was a woman traveling alone. She was on an American Airlines flight to JFK out of Baton Rouge the Thursday after the fire."

"Where did she go after that?"

"We hacked into Lufthansa, Swiss Air, and several other airlines with direct flights to Switzerland out of JFK. She took a flight on Lufthansa that landed in Zurich Friday morning."

"The police have shared some information with me. But not what you found. Is there a way we can find out what they have?"

"I already had someone on the inside check that out. We know everything they know. They still don't know about the rental cars, but it's just a matter of time before they meet up with the guy we talked to."

"Do you know what this means, Will?"

"Yes, Ben. I know. This means that Veronica Westbrook not only murdered Sarah Booth, she's also Mary Smith."

~

Crowder watched the excerpts from the hospital surveillance security footage that Ramsey had collected. Three women looked like Veronica Westbrook, but nothing was certain enough to make a positive identification.

Steele had the unpleasant task of notifying Booth's sister of her death. He told her the medical examiner's office would be in touch about what to do with her remains.

The manhunt was a waste of time. Many reported sightings. Many wasted hours in patrol vehicles, following up on leads that dead-ended.

Solving the Booth murder was now in the hands of Crowder and Steele. "Easier that way," O'Malley told them. "The Livingston murder is related to the Booth murder. The second doesn't happen, if not for the first."

At her desk, Crowder reviewed the police report from the local St. Tammany Parish Sheriff's Office for the second time. Wes Hitchens reportedly saw a white SUV on the bridge just before he found the body. He offered little else about the vehicle or the driver.

It was time to pay Wes Hitchens a visit.

~

"I seen it was a young woman just before she put her hand up to the side of her face," the young man told Crowder outside Mumford's Garage. Twenty-eight-year-old Wes Hitchens worked as a mechanic at the garage located about three miles from where he'd found Booth's body.

"Did the woman look like either of the two women in these photographs?" She showed him the photographs of Westbrook and Smith.

"Like I says to the other feller, I really didn't see her face. I seen her from the side, just long enough to sees she was a young gal. Short, dark hair. I done chased her after I seen what was in the sack, but she crossed the field out there by the state highway and skedaddled. I called it in after that."

"Can you describe the vehicle to me?"

"Was one of them Mercedes sports utility vehicles. Late model. White."

"I suppose you didn't have time to get a license number."

"Nah, but like I told the other feller, I knows it was a rental vehicle."

"How's that, Mr. Hitchens?"

"Plate was green. Safeway's got'm on all them rentals. I seen enough to know, this here being a tourist area with visitors a wantin' to see the gators and all."

Crowder's curiosity turned to the other feller. "The other person you talked to, was he from the sheriff's office?"

"Nah, some kind of private detective, 'vestigatin' the death fer the dead woman's family."

"When did you speak to him?"

"Last Saturday, here at the garage."

Booth's family wouldn't have hired someone to investigate her death. Crowder's short list had one name on it—Ben Livingston.

~

"I appreciate you seeing me, Mr. Livingston. I wanted to update you on the investigation," Crowder said. This time, Elizabeth had led her to a chair across from Livingston, who sat at his desk. He'd just finished a phone call when she sat down and began to speak. "We've had a lot of calls with sightings of Westbrook," she continued, "but so far nothing to confirm she's still in Louisiana."

"Didn't think you would. She was in Zurich the Friday after the fire, presenting herself to Von Ellison as Mary Smith and picking up a bank check for five million Swiss francs."

Crowder knew Livingston was itching to let the cat out of the bag. "I just came from interviewing Wes Hitchens. Your investigator was given the information about the white Mercedes SUV being a rental last week. I suppose you followed up on that and learned she purchased airline tickets, am I right?"

"Yes, something your office should have done as soon as you figured out the woman in the sack on the bridge was Booth. I put someone on it as soon as Ann's mother told me she had identified Booth. Took my people all of two days to track Westbrook to Zurich after that."

"I know. The deputy sheriff's report made it sound like the witness couldn't provide much information. So his story was put on a back burner until we figured the manhunt was a waste of time."

"Look, I'm perfectly willing to share what we've uncovered so you don't duplicate what we've already done, but my people intend to track down Westbrook and bring her back to Louisiana to face trial, and a death sentence when she's convicted."

"If she's captured in Switzerland, it'll be necessary to extradite her, and the Swiss will require assurances from federal and state authorities that she won't be executed."

Livingston sat back in his chair and paused a moment before responding, "I'm aware of our extradition treaties with the European nations, including Switzerland. I have an extraction team that will apprehend her and bring her back to the States."

"You know what you're proposing to do is illegal under Swiss law, and you and your agents could be prosecuted. Of course, if your operatives find her and turn her over to Swiss authorities, they'll hold her until she can be legally extradited."

Livingston snickered and said, "So we turn her over, and she comes back and gets life sentences for double homicides. She spends time in jail. Where's the justice in that? She'll be a folk hero, like Charles Manson. It wouldn't surprise me if she's paroled or escapes someday, particularly if she continues to control millions of dollars. That buys a lot of corrupt cops, lawyers, judges, prison guards, and independent contractors who can work on getting her out of jail. I can't let that happen."

Crowder understood Livingston. Following the rules would fail to produce a just result. He had the power, influence, contacts, and money to guarantee justice was served. But his way broke the law she'd sworn an oath to uphold, and there was nothing she could do to stop him.

Or was there?

She had to meet with O'Malley. What she needed to do required the approval of the chief and the mayor, and the cooperation of the Swiss police.

Crowder stood to leave but stopped at the door, turned to face him, and said, "Don't underestimate Veronica Westbrook. She's a psychopath. There isn't anything she wouldn't do to avoid being caught. The people you send to track her down better be prepared to cage a wild animal."

~

Livingston sat back in his chair, relieved the detective hadn't come down harder on him for seeking vigilante justice. He knew what he needed to do. And if all went right, it wouldn't be long before Veronica Westbrook was behind bars in a correctional facility in Louisiana, convicted of murder and awaiting an audience with the Grim Reaper.

The ping on Livingston's cell phone awakened him from his reverie. It was a text from Goodman: *Just arrived in Zurich. I'm on it.*

Chapter 42

Chase's family held the funeral service on the Rochet Estate in Saint-Émilion in the heart of the Bordeaux countryside. With its thirteenth-century ramparts and cobblestone streets, the hilltop town presided over the richest wine district in France. The mansions of Rosalind Rochet Chevalier and the late Bertrand Rochet were centrally located on more than a thousand acres of lush countryside, where the vineyards produced the grapes that had made Rochet wines and champagnes popular throughout Europe. Two hundred acres of pastureland separated the two mansions, easily traversable by horse and by vehicle. Fox hunts were held there for the few patrician families who still included the pastime as part of a bygone lifestyle.

Phillippe Defois, Archbishop of Bordeaux and a personal friend of the family, conducted the funeral service in a private ceremony at Rosalind's mansion. The seventy persons who attended included family, relations, and the family's closest friends. Many were elderly aristocrats who, like the Rochets, valued their privacy as much as the vast wealth their families had accumulated.

Little was made of it in the French and Swiss press, but not for want of trying. The paparazzi showed up at the entrance to the vineyards to photograph vehicles and license numbers so they could report the very private list of invited mourners. The security staff made their jobs difficult by giving attendees maps beforehand that identified alternate routes into the estate, leaving a number of disgruntled shutterbugs outside the main gate, photographing vehicles that transported staff, vendors, and caterers.

Laura Mueller felt safe attending the private affair. She remained at Chase's side the entire time, except in the receiving line, where only Chase and his sister accepted condolences on behalf of the family. The casket was placed before a temporary altar in the grand ballroom, which was adorned with glowing candelabra, beautiful flowers, and a crucifix that temporarily hung from the ceiling. Statues of the Blessed Virgin and St. Joan D'Arc, borrowed from the cathedral in Saint-Émilion, flanked the dais from which the archbishop spoke reverently of the dead woman.

Not a tear dropped during the brief ceremony or the homily.

Afterwards, staff served a buffet of hors d'oeuvres and wine, and all the guests left within three hours. Chase's sister and her family, along with his daughters and their children, retreated to the late Bertrand's mansion, leaving Chase and Laura alone with the staff in Rosalind's. They sat in the parlor with glasses of sherry.

"Laura, there's something I need to discuss with you. Just before we left Château Vallée, Max Schulman, director of security for the bank, contacted me. He told me that the bank's personal wealth accounts had been breached. No monies were taken; the hacker just directed searches of all holdings of half million Swiss francs or more." Chase held his cell phone and looked at a text from Schulman while he spoke. "I paid it no mind. We've been hacked before, and each time, our internal security system halted the transfer of funds out of the accounts before our clients could be harmed. In this instance, there were no unauthorized transfers from the accounts."

She listened attentively but felt there was more than what he'd told her so far.

"Max texted me again about an hour ago. It turns out the personal checking and money market accounts were also breached. There was an attempt to transfer funds out of one of the accounts, but it was halted because the amount of money exceeded one hundred thousand francs. My authorization is needed for all such transfers. The transfer failed because the hacker didn't have my protected passcode, which I change weekly. If I hadn't just changed it, the hacker would've made off with the entire amount of the

313

account, almost nine hundred thousand francs. Laura, the account that was breached belonged to you."

Laura let out a sigh of relief. Instinct guided her knee-jerk response. "The syndicate. I was afraid they'd find me," she lied. "They must have found out my husband took the five million dollars and that I fled the witness protection program and left the United States. It's only a matter of time before they find me. I'm frightened, Chase, more than I've ever been in my life."

Chase went to Laura and sat beside her on the sofa. He held her hands in his and gently kissed them. "I would never allow harm to come to you. If I have to lock you away here on the estate in France, so be it."

"And the money and bonds?"

"Your wealth is safe, don't worry. The bearer bonds are held anonymously. You're the only one with the passcodes that allow access to them. You can retrieve them when we return to Château Vallée. I suggest we leave tomorrow."

"Yes, the sooner the better, don't you think?"

"I do. On Monday you can cash out your account and collect the bonds."

"I can't stay in Switzerland."

"Don't worry. You'll be safely back in France by Tuesday."

"But what if they follow me to France?"

"Impossible. I'll get you into France like many refugees. I'll smuggle you in. Ax has a plane and will fly you in. We've used it to avoid customs in France when sojourning to our vineyards. He'll fly you straight to the estate. I'll go commercial."

"And what becomes of Laura Mueller?"

"I'll sprinkle her with fairy dust, and she'll vanish like an apparition. Darling, we'll procure for you a new identity before we marry. America isn't the only country with persons skilled in producing the necessary documents."

"And our marriage?"

"A very intimate ceremony on the estate and, *voila,* you will be Mrs. Charles Rochet forevermore. I'll reinforce with everyone my earnest desire for secrecy. They'll all honor it, I promise. And so the plan is hatched. We'll stay at your chalet when we return tomorrow. Pack your things. Take only the essentials. Leave the rest for the maids. Call Sotheby's and the auto dealer to cancel your contracts, effective at the end of the month. Give a bogus address in the U.S. for the return of any deposits."

"When do I meet you at the bank?"

"I'll go in early in the morning. You meet me precisely at one. I'll have a bank check for the cash. No payee. You can fill it out later with your new identity."

"And the bonds?"

"Bring a suitable bag to put them in. I'll turn you over to an associate, who will assist you in retrieving them. Best we be seen together as little as possible. Make no stops coming or going. Return home, and I'll be there to collect you by five."

She looked into Chase's eyes and squeezed his hand. She had feelings for him she'd never felt before about anyone. He was the trusted friend she'd never had, the tender lover she'd always wanted, and the savior she now needed. She'd be a good wife to him. She'd be loyal to him. She'd never steal from him or harm him in any way.

Would her life's choices have been different if she'd met a man like Chase, or a man like Ben Livingston, earlier in her life? Would she have been able to trust people, make friends, love someone? The terrible things she did to others came so naturally to her. Why was she that way? Could she suddenly change her very nature, what was at her core, what made her tick? She wanted to believe she could. Chase was the one person in the whole wide world who'd given her a reason and the desire to change.

She rested her head on Chase's shoulder. When he put his arm around her and his chin against her forehead, she felt protected, safe, and content. She closed her eyes and saw a reflection of herself in the mirror of her mind. She was smiling, she was happy, and for

315

the first time in her life, Veronica Westbrook was at peace with the person she had been and accepting of the person she could now become.

Chapter 43

Crowder sat in the Zurich Police Department, waiting to see Inspector Nicholas Guttman, her liaison with the Swiss authorities. He'd assist her in the investigation and provide the manpower to arrest Westbrook if they located her. Crowder had planned to find her by taking the same flight from Baton Rouge to JFK Airport that Westbrook had taken as Mary Smith, followed by the same flight to Zurich. She'd then meet with Von Ellison, just as Westbrook had on the day of her arrival. After that, logic, common sense, and what her instincts told her Westbrook might do would guide her actions. First, though, she had to let the local police know what she was doing.

As she waited to meet Guttman, she reflected on the meeting with O'Malley in which he'd decided she should go to Zurich, find Westbrook, and bring her back to Louisiana to face trial for the murders of Ann Livingston and Sarah Booth.

"Livingston is planning his own way of bringing Westbrook to justice, and the department and the State of Louisiana could be made to look foolish if he succeeds," she'd told O'Malley.

"What's he planning? A hit?" he'd asked. "Ben Livingston's a devout Episcopalian. He could never condone assassination. Episcopalians condemn the death penalty."

"It's different when someone murders your wife, the mother of your only child. Suddenly, it's personal."

"What's he likely to do?"

"He's got an extraction team. He knows she's in Switzerland. Told me he's intending to grab her, smuggle her back to the States, and deliver her to us gift-wrapped with a bow in her hair."

"It'll put the death penalty back on the table."

"Precisely. No messy extradition proceedings. Switzerland is a safe haven for fugitives. They may not even extradite her. He can't chance that."

"He exposes himself and those who help him to criminal prosecution. Kidnapping. Assault. Conspiracy. And then there are the federal crimes. The woman hasn't been convicted. She's an American citizen with rights."

"Yeah, with rights, right up until the time the Great State of Louisiana sticks the needle in her."

"What's the department's downside if we do nothing and let him succeed?"

"You mean, in addition to looking incompetent," she'd replied sarcastically. "After all, we let the vilest of murderers slip through our fingers. Livingston cracks open the case by finding her and delivering her to our doorstep. There's no way the State of Louisiana prosecutes him for his brand of vigilante justice. He'll be a superhero. We'll be Inspector Clouseau."

"This Westbrook woman acted alone from day one," O'Malley had said. "I have to admire her resourcefulness, her sheer determination."

"Livingston's resourceful, too. He has the *resources*, the time, and is *full* of determination."

O'Malley had leaned forward in his chair. "He broke the law to find out she was Smith."

"You bet. When you're seeking revenge, the end justifies the means. He'll find her, too. He'll hack into the computers of the rental car companies, airlines, hotels, and banks until he finds her. We have to do it with the cooperation of Interpol and the Swiss police, and a pile of bureaucratic red tape."

"We need a presence in Zurich."

"I can work with the Zurich police," Crowder had offered. "We'll move as quickly as we can to catch up with Livingston's operatives. Our paths may cross. If they do, we can follow their trail to Westbrook and hopefully arrest her before she's taken."

"You're right. Even if we fail, we'll be seen as doing our jobs."

"And if we do make the collar," she'd reflected aloud, "the N.O.P.D. will be credited with capturing the newest member of the FBI's Ten-Most-Wanted List and Louisiana's Public Enemy Number One."

The arrival of the Swiss policeman brought her back to the present. He stood before her, holding out his hand. "Inspector Nicholas Guttman," he said.

"Detective Jo Crowder, but call me Jo," she said, shaking it.

"My friends call me Nick. Please do likewise. Follow me. I have an office for you. It's small, but equipped with a phone and a desktop computer to access our databases."

She followed Guttman into the office. Each took a seat. He ceded the chair behind the desk to her. The detectives were about the same age and of comparable rank. She didn't miss noticing his good looks: tall; glittery, blond hair; deep blue eyes; and the chiseled facial features characteristic of men of Germanic descent. She sensed that he'd be an intimidating presence during arrests and interrogations.

"I reviewed your reports before you arrived. Your fugitive is quite the accomplished criminal. Most impressive resume. Murder's in her blood. That, and her bravado, make her very dangerous. What plan do you have for tracking her?"

"I believe she'd stay a couple days in a downtown hotel. She saw Von Ellison on Friday afternoon. Cashed out the account. Doubtful she had the time to establish another account or invest the funds until Monday. That takes us into the following week. She'd be looking for another bank to do business with, under a new identity, I'm certain."

"A number of banks would be pleased to accommodate her. Five million francs buys a lot of accommodation. The logical next step is to select a bank large enough to get lost in."

"Yes, a bank with international connections."

"Probably CBZ, the Central Bank of Zurich, or perhaps Zurich Cantonal. But CBZ is her best bet. It's been around for a century and has a trillion in assets."

"I thought we'd start with Von Ellison. Then hit the car rental agencies, major downtown hotels, and real estate firms. Will you come with me to see Von Ellison?"

"Of course. But don't expect much from him, or any other bank. Our laws protect the privacy of account holders. Not even their names may be disclosed without complicated judicial proceedings that take weeks. Even then, your request for information is likely to be denied."

"Von Ellison leaked information to someone he thought was the account holder. That's how we know Westbrook, using the Smith identity, cashed out the account."

"What about Mary Smith? Do you want us to check on the whereabouts of persons with that name who fit Westbrook's profile?"

"She's way too smart to use the Smith identity here in Switzerland. The best we can hope for is that she used it to find a hotel or rent a car. And that's a long shot. We need to use the photos of Westbrook and Smith instead and see if anyone remembers seeing her."

"I'll put a couple of our people on it. Check for a single woman registering somewhere during the weekend of her arrival. Same with the car rental agencies."

"I'd like to go to the Porsche dealers and real estate firms. I have a hunch she'd be interested in a Porsche and a villa near the mountains."

"Chalets near the mountains are commonplace. Our beautiful country is sixty percent mountains. I'll put together a list of the top realtors in Zurich. We'll go to them after the Porsche dealerships."

"So we have a plan. Good, old-fashioned, boots-on-the-ground police work. Let's hope it produces fruit."

"Yes, Jo. There's a bad apple out there to find."

Crowder didn't verbalize what she was thinking. *Yes, Nick. And one's that's rotten to the core.*

~

Von Ellison met the detectives with the usual resistance—a banker unwilling to disclose information about clients and their banking transactions. When Crowder told him he'd been duped into leaking information to someone other than the account holder, Guttman seized the opportunity to squeeze Von Ellison for a positive identification.

"Sir, the proper protocol was for you to only communicate with account holders through secure sites with passcodes. You carelessly provided information about an account holder, Mary Smith, to a third party not authorized on the account."

"I was led to believe the communication was from an account holder," he said weakly.

"Misled, you mean. Precisely the reason for assigning a passcode. The person you communicated with was not Ann Livingston. She died two days earlier. What you did is a violation of Swiss banking laws."

"I know, but—"

"But what? Your actions were quite irregular. Let's see if you can right the course of your ship. We need to locate Mary Smith and warn her that information about her account was unlawfully given to a third party."

"What do you want me to do?"

"First, I want you to identify Mary Smith. Is she the woman in any of these photographs?"

Guttman stood up, towering over the diminutive Von Ellison. A half-foot shorter, the banker looked even smaller sitting in his chair. Guttman placed two photos on Von Ellison's desk. "Well?" he barked.

"Yes. These photographs are of the woman," he said, identifying Mary Smith.

321

"Where was she staying when she came to see you?"

"Well, that's confidential, b-but it would be on the receipt she signed w-when she received the check," he stammered.

"Get on with it, then," Guttman demanded. "We don't have all day."

Von Ellison wilted like a three-day-old midsummer rose in a vase with no water. He checked his computer, then said, "Here it is. She was staying at Hotel Schweizerhof."

Crowder couldn't resist a smile. Her Swiss counterpart was an intimidating presence, for sure. When they left the bank, he called the officer assigned to check out the hotels. "Hotel Schweizerhof. Find out how long she stayed and whether anyone remembers her. Did she make any calls, leave a forwarding address, receive any visitors? And get photocopies of her registration information and any messages."

Guttman was clearly a take-charge guy.

They canvassed the Porsche dealerships in and around Zurich using a list Guttman compiled. No sales or rentals of a Porsche to either Mary Smith or Veronica Westbrook. The sales managers agreed to show photos of the women to their sales personnel.

By then, it was after five. The detectives called it a day and agreed to meet at police headquarters at nine. The realtors were next.

On Saturday, they went to five firms that sold and leased upscale properties in and around Zurich. It took them most of the day, and they found no sales or rentals to Westbrook or Smith— another dry well. Again they left photos for the managers to show their agents. They finished their day with a visit to Sotheby's, the last of the firms on their list.

The hotel registration information for Mary Smith confirmed that she'd stayed at the hotel for five nights. No visitors, messages, or long distance calls during her stay. Paid the bill in cash. No forwarding address. Another dead end.

"Unless someone recognizes her from the photos we left, not much else can be done," Guttman said before they parted Saturday afternoon.

"She's driving around in a Porsche," Crowder said confidently. "Westbrook always gets what she wants. The money's burning a great big hole in her designer handbags. She'll pay in cash until she creates a new identity."

"When she starts using her new identity, she'll be almost impossible to locate," Guttman said. "It'll be like trying to find a mountain climber in an avalanche. You need to know where in the snow to dig to have any chance of finding the body."

"You're right. Without a name, she could be anyone, living anywhere."

After the business of the day was concluded and she was back in her hotel room, Crowder prepared a working draft of her report to O'Malley. Not much of importance to report.

She had until Tuesday to come up with a concrete lead. Otherwise, she'd be on a plane back to Louisiana on Wednesday.

Crowder spent Sunday afternoon on a long walk through the heart of Zurich, thinking about the investigation and what Livingston's paid contractors were doing to locate Westbrook. Her cell phone rang. It was Guttman.

"Hey! Would you like to meet for dinner?"

"Sure. Where and when?" she answered, hoping her eagerness didn't make her sound like the infatuated teenager being asked out on her first date. He wasn't wearing a wedding band. Was he asking her out on a date, feeling sorry for her being alone in a foreign country, or just wanting to talk about the case?

Maybe a little of each.

"I'll pick you up at your hotel at seven. The restaurant is my favorite. Nothing fancy. So dress casual."

"You bet. See you at seven."

She had to laugh. Casual was how she'd dressed since making corporal. It was either the police-issued sweats she was wearing on her walk, the same black slacks she'd worn the last two days, or the denim jeans she'd brought in case of an emergency. She had only one blouse left, and it had to get her through the next couple of days.

It looks like it's the jeans and the blouse.

Guttman parked his Saab in front of her hotel at five minutes to seven. She'd been waiting by the door since a quarter till. Other than Sid and Fred, this was the only single male she'd had dinner alone with in over a year. She waited a couple minutes before walking out. "Hey! Nick, good timing. I just came down," she lied as he jumped out of his car to open her door.

He opened my door. This is definitely a date.

They parked in front of a restaurant named Edelweiss, a quaint mom-and-pop-run bistro where the owners greeted the guests with a smile and a friendly chat. Red-and-white checkered tablecloths covered each of the fifteen tables. A wood-paneled bar with a full-length mirror behind it made the floor area appear larger than it was. The lights were dimmed just enough to add intimacy to the cozy environment.

Guttman gently put his hand on the small of Crowder's back. "We arrived just in time," he whispered. "Only one table left. Let's take it before we lose it."

He led her through the crowded bistro to a table in a corner. As they passed by the tables, she noticed a number of the patrons acknowledging Nick's presence with a head nod, a wave of the hand, a wink, or a smile. They knew him well.

He pulled out the chair for her. Another sure sign this was a date.

Memorabilia covered the walls: family portraits; framed news stories; photographs, many of a tall man standing on podiums in ski gear, receiving medals. One bore the caption "2002 Winter Olympics Gold Medalist." The tall man with the flowing blond hair, though sixteen years younger, was Nick Guttman.

The couple managing things in the restaurant came over to their table with the waiter who'd be servicing them. It all fit nicely for Crowder when her date got up from his seat, kissed the woman, and said, "Jo, I'd like you to meet my parents."

Crowder and Guttman soon became comfortable in each other's presence. They talked about their lives growing up, the sports they played, why they became cops, and why marriage was something not likely to work for them.

"I'm married to the job," she said.

"She's a jealous mistress, to be sure," he said.

Crowder took another bite of her grilled kielbasa and cabbage, the house special, and a sip of wine to wash it down. "Do you ever wonder whether it's worth it? I mean, I feel an adrenaline rush when I make a collar or break open a case. There's something about catching a bad guy. But I've given up on what my parents wanted for me: husband, family, a root system."

"I know. My parents were worried they'd be without grandchildren when I divorced some years back. It eased somewhat when my sister married and produced two sons."

"When did you marry?"

"Late twenties. Lasted two years. We had careers. Being also married to our jobs made us both unhappy polygamists. You?"

"Never been. I went to my ten-year high school reunion eight years ago. Most of the girls were married or pregnant, or wanting to be, and spent their time talking about their kids. I had already been a cop for a few years. I spent my time with the guys, talking about hunting, guns, and cars."

"You're young. You may change your mind."

"Not if changing my mind means changing diapers. I don't see me baking in the kitchen or meeting the other mothers at the playground and bragging about our kids' regular bowel movements."

"We have very few women detectives. In fact, I've only known two, and you're one of them."

"And the other?"

325

"She divorced me."

The two detectives eventually directed their conversation to the case. He was concerned about Crowder making contact with Westbrook without backup. "I want you to be careful. The woman is mentally unbalanced. She makes sadism and murder into an art form. It wouldn't surprise me if she's killed others whose deaths remain a mystery."

"I'll be careful."

"What about tomorrow?"

"I want to go back to the real estate companies. I may not know her current identity, but I know what she's interested in. Only upscale villas and chalets. I'll ask them to compile a list of recent rentals. I doubt she'd buy a place. She'd want to be able to pack up and leave on a moment's notice."

"I'll help you, but I must be in court tomorrow to testify in a criminal conspiracy case. I'll be unavailable until two."

"Don't worry. I'll see the realtors and meet you back at the station house. We'll take the properties one by one."

"We'll need a ruse when we contact the people living in the homes. She'd recognize you. So I'll do that."

"Pretend you're interested in renting the house and didn't know it was already rented. If we find her, we'll do a stakeout. Your people can arrest her when she leaves the property."

The conversation turned light when the apple strudel was served. Each shared humorous anecdotes about themselves. The Liebfraumilch loosened their tongues and inhibitions. They filled the occasional pauses with fixed stares into each other's eyes, impish grins, and throaty chuckles.

As they were preparing to leave, Mrs. Guttman took a couple photos of her son and friend as a memento of the evening, perhaps to later find a place on a wall in the restaurant.

Another opened door for her when they got to his car.

The drive back to the hotel passed with an easy, comfortable silence between them while the stereo played pop music. When they arrived, Crowder opened her door before he had a chance to get out. She turned and thanked him for a lovely evening. Their eyes locked. His blue eyes gleamed in the amber glow of the interior dome lighting. She sensed he wanted more to their evening out. So did she.

Without thinking, she blurted out, "Room 420."

His smile broadened.

So did hers.

Crowder had found someone very much like herself, someone she knew she could trust with her life, and just maybe with her heart.

~

"Yes. That's exactly what she'd do," Crowder uttered from a shallow sleep after Guttman had left and she'd spent a half hour in a sudsy bath, thinking about him and their intimate moments together. What now consumed her subconscious mind as she lay there semi-awake was not Nick Guttman but Veronica Westbrook, and how she would establish a new identity. By the time she had her answer, the digital clock in her room read 3:17 a.m.

She reached for her laptop, accessed the internet, and typed "most common first name in Switzerland" into the search engine. Answer? Laura. Next she entered "most common surname in Switzerland." Mueller.

Tomorrow, Detective Jo Crowder would be looking for Laura Mueller. This time she knew where to dig in the snow to find the body.

Chapter 44

"Laura Mueller to see you, Mr. Rochet," the receptionist announced when she called on him, as he'd directed her to do.

Chase came out right away and ushered her into his office, avoiding eye contact with his secretary on the way in. They sat in the same chairs as when they'd first met. This time the meeting was purposefully brief. No flirtatious banter between the two. It was all business.

"Laura, just sign these papers, and the check is yours," he said impatiently. "I know you will be careful with it and with the bonds. I see you brought a suitable bag for them. Good. Do you have your passcodes?"

"Yes," she said. "And I gave notice to Sotheby's and the dealership for my car, just as you told me to do."

"Well, then, let's get you to your safety deposit boxes. Go directly home. I'll come for you by five."

The two left the office together and took an elevator to the third floor. He introduced Laura to the bank officer who managed the safety deposit box accounts. "*Madame*, you are now in the very capable hands of my colleague, Monsieur Gruber. He will assist you. It has been a great pleasure being of service to you. *Au revoir*." Chase bowed slightly as the two exchanged obligatory smiles.

When he returned to his office, his secretary said, "William Goodman is here to see you, Mr. Rochet."

"Does he have an appointment?"

"No, but he said it was important he speak to you. He is director of security for an American company, Livingston Industries. He said it involved one of our account holders."

328

"All right, show him in, but call me in five minutes to tell me I have a meeting to attend. I want a way of getting rid of him."

Chase stood from behind his desk to shake Goodman's hand and pointed to the chairs in front of the desk. Goodman reached into his pocket for a business card and gave it to him before sitting.

"Mr. Goodman, how can I be of service to you today?" Chase asked while studying the business card.

Goodman pulled out two photographs and placed them on the desk. Chase immediately recognized Laura in her disguised and natural appearances. His first thought was that William Goodman was an alias and his business card was phony. He was stereotypical of a modern-day hitman: a tall, fit, clean shaven, military presence with a steely, confident persona. Chase figured he was probably the person who'd hacked into the bank's computers, and he felt suddenly anxious. Laura was one floor up. Goodman might see her in the bank or on the street. His heart pounded in his chest. He felt warm. His mouth became dry. He picked up the photographs. Pretended to study them. Finally, he spoke.

"If I recognized these women, Mr. Goodman, and they were account holders, I could not provide you with any information about them. Swiss law prohibits me from disclosing any information about our clients. And if they were not clients, they may have good reasons for not being discovered by you and, therefore, be entitled to the discretion of a gentleman. So I'm sorry to say I cannot be of service to you."

Chase figured Goodman knew he'd be uncooperative and that Goodman had planned to assess his reaction to the photos. After all, it wasn't every day a beautiful young woman came into the bank and handed over five million francs. The phone on Chase's desk rang, interrupting his pondering. "Yes, I'm aware of the meeting," he said to his secretary. "Mr. Goodman and I have concluded our business." A quick glance at Goodman signaled that the meeting was over.

"I appreciate your time, Mr. Rochet," he said as he stood.

Chase walked to the door, opened it, and waited for him to leave. Goodman offered his hand as he approached the door. Chase shook it as etiquette demanded, hoping the moisture in his palm went unnoticed. During the exchange, Goodman looked him in the eye and said, "If you ever come upon the *woman* in the photographs, I strongly suggest you turn around and go the other way."

Chase returned to his desk, the word "woman" reverberating in his head. He quickly called Laura. The call went to voicemail. He left a simple message: "They found you and are in the bank. Hide from sight and call me right away." He texted her the same message. He couldn't just sit there. She was in too much danger. He bolted for the door and pep-stepped it to the stairwell. There wasn't time to wait for an elevator. The foot race was on.

~

The manager of the Porsche dealership told Crowder that a Laura Mueller had leased a Porsche on February the eleventh. The address on her American driver's license was the Benson residence in South Carolina. Her local address at the time was the Hotel Schweizerhof. With a description of Laura's vehicle and tag number, Crowder had her first good lead.

She looked at her watch—almost eleven. Her next stops were the realtors they'd contacted earlier. The first two had no record of a Laura Mueller buying or renting any properties. Sotheby's was within walking distance. She went there next.

"Yes. Laura Mueller rented a chalet in Lucerne," the manager told the American detective. "Three-month lease. The transaction was handled by an agent who's on holiday and won't be returning until Wednesday, which is why I was unable to show her the photographs you left with me on Saturday."

"I can't wait until Wednesday," Crowder said. "What's the address, and how do I get there by car?"

"This being a police matter, I'll give you its location and a brochure describing it."

With the information in hand, she returned to her car and entered the address in her GPS. Ninety-eight miles. An hour and a half's drive. It was nearly two o'clock. She didn't want to waste time going back to the station house, so she called Guttman. No answer. *Must still be in court.* Her message went to voicemail: "Found her. A chalet in Lucerne called Mountain Laurel. Will text the address. On my way there now. Join me ASAP with backup." After she sent the address, she texted Steele: *Found her. Goes by Laura Mueller. Headed to her chalet now. Swiss police to provide backup.*

She retrieved her travel case from the trunk of her Fiat and placed it on the front seat. In it were her laptop computer, investigation file, handcuffs, .38 caliber police-issued Swiss & Wesson pistol, and two full clips. She figured she'd be there by three thirty. When she got there, she'd find a place to park and wait for Nick Guttman and the Swiss cavalry to arrive.

~

Goodman stopped in the main lobby to text the extraction team with an update. An unoccupied sofa in an area adjacent to the reception desk provided him the privacy needed. He texted his operatives: *Her name is Laura Mueller. Need a stakeout at CBZ. Just a matter of time before she shows up to do some banking.*

He texted Livingston next: *Found her. Goes by Laura Mueller. Has an account at CBZ. Only a matter of ...* Just then, he saw her walking through the main lobby on her way out of the bank. It was surreal. He'd never met Veronica Westbrook, but he'd known Ann Livingston, and he would've bet his life's savings he was looking at her. Livingston had discussed the case with him. So he knew Westbrook had assumed Ann's identity for more than a month as she executed her plan to steal from them. But the photographs of Westbrook didn't capture the full essence of what she looked like in person. She was the mirror image of Ann Livingston.

331

No way would he pass up this stroke of good fortune. He concluded his text: *Gotta go. She's in my sights.* He followed her out. When she entered a parking garage a block away, he ran to his vehicle and drove to the exit, where he waited for her to leave in her car. He'd tail her to wherever she was going and eventually follow her home. He'd call in the extraction team, and they'd take her when she next left her home. Two vehicles would block her path of travel, one in the front of her vehicle and one in the back. She'd be restrained and sedated with an injection of an anesthetic used by the military and CIA for precisely such occasions. A taser was also available to incapacitate her if she put up a struggle. Her car would be driven back to her home and parked in its usual spot. The security surveillance system would be shut off, the recording disc removed and destroyed. The package would be taken to a safe house, then flown the next day by private jet to a landing strip in Mexico once used by the Cortez drug cartel. The package would be smuggled into Texas in the usual manner—by bribing a border patrol officer—and delivered forthwith to the New Orleans Police Department.

While waiting for her to exit, he texted the extraction team: *Got a visual of her. Will tail her home. Be ready when I call.* He put away his cell phone when he saw her leaving the garage. "It figures, a Porsche," he mumbled. His Volkswagen Jetta would win no races with what she was driving. He'd play it safe—stay back behind a couple of cars—and follow her until she got to where she was going.

~

Laura pulled out her cell phone and took it off mute. Notifications showed two calls and a text from Chase. She read the text and called him.

"I'm on my way home," she said when he answered. "I had no problems leaving the bank. I think I'm all right. There's the usual traffic on the highway. Nothing out of the ordinary."

"Laura, a man by the name of Goodman, William Goodman, came to see me while you were at the bank. He said he worked for an American company, Livingston Industries. He showed me photographs of you. Naturally, I didn't say I knew you. I believe he's the one who hacked into your account. Go directly home. I'll have Rolls come for you. He'll take you to Château Vallée. You'll be safe there until I can get you on the plane."

"Of course, my darling. I'll do just as you say."

She hung up, glanced in her rear-view mirror, and picked up speed. The speed limit was 100 km per hour. She increased to 120, then 130. The distance increased between her and the vehicles behind her, as well as the ones she passed. All but one. When she came to her exit, she had only a four-and-a-half-mile drive to her chalet. The narrow, winding road along Lake Lucerne had only a few other upscale homes on it and dead-ended at her chalet. She'd soon know if anyone followed her.

She made a left at the stop sign at the end of the ramp and headed north along the cliffs. And then she saw it. The one car that had kept pace behind her also took the exit and turned left. The car came in and out of sight as she snaked her way through the many curves in the road to her chalet. She opened the gate and the garage and drove in, closing the door behind her. Once inside the house, she made a dash to the second-floor bedroom with the best view of the road, stood at the window, and waited.

~

"Rolls, I want you to pick up Laura at her chalet and bring her to Château Vallée. No stops. Make sure you're not followed."

"Surely, Mr. Rochet," Royce said. "Nothing like a cloak-and-dagger assignment to recharge the old batteries. If tailed, I'll lose them on the main road. When asked, the Bentley soars like an eagle."

"No. I want you to use your vehicle. Remove your license plates so your car can't be traced. If followed, lose them on the side streets of Lucerne before heading back to Château Vallée. Phone me when you get there."

"I will do precisely as you instruct. I know how precious the cargo is."

Chase hung up confident that Laura would soon be safe. He texted the plan to her. She texted back.

We'll need it. I've been followed.

Chapter 45

The GPS guided Crowder to the intersection at the end of the ramp. Proceeding west through the intersection would lead her to the Alpine resort villages. The green arrow had her turning left instead, heading north along the lake to her destination.

The posted speed was fifty kilometers per hour, about thirty miles an hour, on the narrow, winding, two-lane road. Only the foolhardy would travel faster. Her shoulder-less lane ended mountainside. The opposite lane bordered the cliffs that dropped 250 feet into the frigid waters of Lake Lucerne. Not a road she'd want to drive at night if she'd exceeded her two-drink limit, or even if she hadn't. The map on her guidance system had the road ending at her final destination. She slowed to thirty kilometers an hour as she crept closer to the private residence at the end of the road.

A Volkswagen sedan had parked diagonally on the road about a hundred yards from the chalet, out of view from the house behind a curve in the road. She pulled up behind it, shut off the engine, and opened her travel case. She reached for her Swiss & Wesson, loaded a full clip, and put the gun back. It was there if she needed it.

The Volkswagen was unlocked. So was the glove compartment. The temporary registration and rental agreement in it were both in the name of William Goodman, with a New Orleans address.

A member of Ben Livingston's extraction team.

Only the Swiss authorities could lawfully prevent the forcible abduction of Westbrook by Livingston's operatives. It was nearly three thirty. Still no word from Guttman.

Her phone rang. "Jo, where are you?" Guttman asked as soon as she answered.

"Just arrived at her place."

"I was held up in court. My phone was checked with my gun—routine security at the courthouse."

"Been there. Done that."

"Don't go near the house. My first call just before calling you was to my colleagues in Lucerne. They'll have officers there in half an hour. I'm leaving now."

"One small but important problem, Nick."

"What's that?"

"There's a private extraction team getting ready to take her and smuggle her out of Switzerland and back to the U.S. I don't know how far they've gone with this, but one of their vehicles is parked here."

"Go to your car and move it somewhere safe. If they take her, you follow them and report back. We'll catch up with you and stop them. Do not engage them. Do you understand me?"

"Of course. I'll stay back and wait for backup. But I need to get a better look. I'll be careful, partner. Don't worry about me."

"How can I not worry? Please, do nothing rash."

"I'll be back to you after I check things out."

She hung up as Guttman began to speak, probably to warn her again to do nothing. But Crowder needed to know what was going on.

When she walked around the curve, she saw a man watching the house from behind some shrubbery. Not wanting to startle him, she approached slowly and spoke in an easy, conversational tone. "Goodman. William Goodman. You know what you're planning to do is illegal. The Lucerne police will be here shortly. No one wants you to be the one arrested today. If Westbrook's in that house, she'll be apprehended the very next time she leaves it. She'll be detained until she can be extradited back to Louisiana."

Goodman turned around and looked at the detective. He didn't speak until she stopped about twenty feet from him. "Detective Jo Crowder, New Orleans Police Department," he said with a smirk.

Crowder couldn't contain a smile. She'd arrived just in time to thwart the unlawful acts of the extraction team. "Yes, Ben Livingston told me he'd be sending his own people. How did you find her?" Her inquiry had the twofold purpose of buying time for the Lucerne police to show up and satisfying a professional curiosity of knowing how he'd found Westbrook.

"Crowder, you have no authority over me or anyone else on Swiss soil. But thanks for letting me know I must move quickly on Westbrook. My people are waiting for me to bring her to them."

"So how did you find her?" she asked again.

"You first," he said, playing coy.

"I figured she'd establish a new identity and pick the most common names in Switzerland, just as she'd picked Mary and Smith, the most common first and last names for women in the United States. Then I checked with car dealers and realtors about recent sales and rentals by anyone named Laura Mueller. The name came up on rentals of a car and this chalet."

"Good instincts on your part, Crowder."

"I had some help from a high school yearbook. You?"

"I did it the easy way. I hacked into all of the major banks in Zurich, looking for the money. Laura Mueller's name appeared on a CBZ account with almost nine hundred thousand francs in it. The account was opened within three days of Westbrook's arrival in Zurich. I'd have gotten the money back, too, if the bank officer who opened the account hadn't changed his personal security code the day before."

"And how about where she was living?"

"Pure luck. I saw her leave the bank after I paid a visit to the guy who opened her account. I followed her here."

"Let me guess, in her Porsche?"

"Right. So we each found her using different investigative techniques. Goes to show there's more than one way to skin a hellcat."

"Yes, except for one thing."

337

"What's that?"

"Your way broke the law, just as the actions you are planning violate U.S. and Swiss laws."

"Yes, and they also provide a very effective way of expediting the administration of justice. Just as the Israelis did when Mossad kidnapped Adolf Eichmann, who would have continued living the good life in Argentina had they not brought the Nazi murderer back to Israel to be tried for war crimes."

"But that's not how we operate in the U.S. We believe in something called the rule of law."

"Your way, Crowder, isn't justice. Your way, she avoids the death penalty for what she's done. There's no guarantee she won't kill again in prison or, if she were to escape, go on another killing spree. She's bad to the bone. She'll destroy anything and anyone that gets in her way. It ends today. It ends now."

Goodman pulled out his M26C police taser gun from his ankle holster and unlocked the safety. Crowder was familiar with tasers. The department issued them for use in domestic disturbances and riot control. The one Goodman had was standard police issue. Upon firing, the electrical probes would transmit through clothing and result in an instant loss of neuromuscular control and any ability to perform coordinated actions. The targeted person was usually rendered unconscious for several minutes, more than enough time for the person to be cuffed or restrained by other means, like with the duct tape she saw partially jutting out of Goodman's jacket pocket.

"Are you sure you don't want to join me, Crowder? I could use a decoy."

"Not while aiding and abetting is still a crime."

"She's all mine, then," he said without looking back at her. He took off down the road, stopping well short of the gate, where a surveillance camera might warn of his presence. He easily scaled the six-foot-high stone wall. Crowder could do nothing but watch and wait for the Lucerne police.

She had to wrestle her conscience. She was content to have Goodman succeed with his plan. Westbrook's crimes were so horrible, she deserved to die for them. As long as she'd tried to talk Goodman out of what he was doing, Crowder was not abetting his actions. She could go home and wait for him to bring Westbrook into the New Orleans Police Department, like Federal Express delivering a package. It might not be the legal thing to do, but it was the right thing to do.

~

Westbrook packed a few essentials, leaving most of her wardrobe behind. When you're looking to escape danger, and your life's on the line, you travel light. Only the important things. The four million in bearer bonds. The bank check. The jewelry. Any cash lying around. All fit nicely in a Kate Spade shoulder bag. Its zippers and locks went along with a fashionable, sporty look—the perfect travel bag for an upwardly mobile career criminal.

From the second-floor bedroom that faced the street, she'd seen a man standing on the road, staring at the house. She couldn't see his vehicle, but figured he'd parked it around the curve and out of sight. She felt certain he planned to abduct her, maybe even kill her.

Westbrook had other plans.

She was safest in Switzerland, where the extradition of fugitives was difficult to obtain. Even if they caught and extradited her, it would be conditioned on her not being put to death. How ironic, she thought, that capital punishment was only a deterrent for first-time murder; for career criminals, it was an incentive for mass murder and serial killing. After she'd killed Ann, her first experience with murder, the second and third were of no significance. *They can only execute you once.* It didn't matter how many people she killed after the first one. She wasn't a cat with nine lives stored up to be used anytime she needed them.

Would circumstances ever arise requiring her to end Chase's life? What if he found out the truth about her, like Aunt Rosalind?

Could he live with the thought that he could be her next victim? Would he believe her when she told him she was a changed woman, that she'd learned how to love for the first time in her life, and that even someone like her was entitled to a second chance? Would the lovemaking, and the money, be enough to overcome his fear of being euthanized when he got old and sickly?

Her meditations ended abruptly when she saw the man move closer to the front gates, then stop and turn as though someone was behind him. Her mind switched to survival mode. She went to her bedroom and opened the top drawer of her bedside nightstand.

There it was. The gift from Chase—shiny black, with a pearl-white handle, and loaded. She knew how to protect herself if they tried to take her when Rolls came to pick her up. Rolls only needed to drive, and duck when she opened fire.

She put her suitcase and shoulder bag by the front door, disabled the security system, and destroyed the recording disc, leaving no evidence of Chase's presence there. Then she walked into the kitchen and calmly poured herself the last glass of wine from a bottle of Rochet Merlot she and Chase hadn't quite finished the night before.

She glanced at her Rolex—ten minutes to four. Time to go to the front of the house and watch for Rolls. And then she saw him. The man from the road moved across the lawn toward the back of the chalet, his pace swift and deliberate. So was hers in retrieving the Glock from her shoulder bag. She released the safety, held the gun in both hands in an interlocking grip, just as Chase had taught her, and moved stealthily through the house to the kitchen. All doors and windows were locked. Chase had made sure of it. The intruder's most likely way in was through the back door where she waited, pistol against her chest, nozzle up.

A rattling sound came from behind the door, as if someone was using a key or trying to pick the lock—a standard mechanism, easy to pick. But the door also had a deadbolt latch that locked from inside. Even if her intruder could pick the lock, he'd be unable to open the door. He'd have to break through it.

Westbrook's mind worked like a computer analyzing data points. She reached up and put her index finger and thumb very gently on the door latch. She slowly pulled it back, unlocking it.

Better the devil you know.

Chase's admonition came to mind.

You can miss with a shot to the head even at close range. A chest full of slugs beats a single shot that grazes the cheek or scalp every time.

The tinkering with the lock stopped. She backed up several steps and aligned herself slightly to the right of the door. As soon as the door opened and his body came into view, she'd step to her left one full stride and open fire.

The poor bastard wouldn't know what hit him.

~

Crowder waited on the road by her car. She had her doubts about Goodman's plan. He looked military or police, or both, and was probably well trained. But no one should underestimate Veronica Westbrook. He'd only brought a stun gun because he needed to take her alive and shooting her wasn't an option. Westbrook's options weren't limited. She could have a shotgun in the closet, for all he knew. You shouldn't bring a knife, or a taser, to a gunfight.

Crowder heard them. They were loud and in rapid succession, one shot after the other, five, maybe six, shots in all. She couldn't just stand there and do nothing. Her instincts took over, drawing on thirteen years of police work, chasing perpetrators, being shot at, and shooting back. She'd wounded her fair share while apprehending them.

A few, she'd shot dead.

She got in her vehicle, stuffed her pistol in the waistband of her slacks, then started the engine, put it in drive, and floored it. Aiming dead center for the gates at the front entrance, she hit the steel barriers going fifty. The gates cracked open, and the Fiat crashed through. The shrill screeching of her brakes when she slammed them coincided with the reverberating clamor of metal against cement when the gates broke off and struck the pavement. The Fiat fishtailed, coming to a stop seventy-five feet from the entrance. She quickly backed up and parked at an angle, blocking the now-open gate.

With pistol in hand, she got out and duck-walked briskly to the front door. Finding it locked, she proceeded to the back, peering into each window before walking in front of it to be sure Westbrook wasn't on the other side, preparing for target practice. Once there, she saw Goodman sprawled out on his back on the terrace. She went to him. No pulse. The blood that had gushed from the holes in his jacket had puddled on both sides of him. His startled look proved he'd been taken completely by surprise.

The kitchen door was open. She wouldn't repeat Goodman's mistake and try to enter through it. Good police tactics were for her to retreat, block the entrance, and wait for backup. The only problem was that Westbrook was already in her car, the sudden revving of its engine proof of that. Crowder sprinted to the front of the chalet and positioned herself behind the Fiat with her gun pointed over the hood.

The garage door opened.

Like at the start of a drag race, the Porsche's engine revved angrily. A gear shift to reverse shot it rearward into the front panel of the Fiat. Crowder got off three rounds through the rear window of the convertible top before the force of the impact spun the Fiat counterclockwise and knocked her backwards to the ground. The gun flew from her hand.

The back of her head struck the pavement so hard she nearly passed out. Her brain ached like an inflamed nerve in a decayed tooth. She saw double through blurred vision. She heard nothing other than a shrill ringing in her ears, then the sound of a car door opening and footsteps on the pavement. Her eyes made out an unfocused image of a woman standing over her with the barrel of a pistol pointed at her chest.

Westbrook looked down at the detective. "So, we meet again, Detective Crowder. You, more than anyone, should know not to show up uninvited. Your friend learned that the hard way. Anyway, got to go. I'll be saying goodbye now." She readjusted her aim, a sure sign to Crowder that she was ready to shoot.

Crowder slid her foot around Westbrook's ankle, gripped it with her other foot in an interlocking fashion, and rolled over on her side just as she and Miles Jennings had practiced in the gym. And it worked in real time, like he'd said it would. Westbrook's feet came out from under her, and she fell to the ground, landing on her right hip. She screamed in pain. The Glock dropped from her hands.

Crowder felt fatigued and groggy, and the only gun in sight was the Glock lying on the ground beside Westbrook. She mustered her remaining strength and lunged for it, but just as her hand was about to grip the handle, Westbrook kicked the gun away with her outstretched foot and began to crawl toward it. Crowder grabbed her ankle just before Westbrook got the Glock back in her hand.

The sole of a shoe crashed against Crowder's forehead. The next thing she saw was Westbrook pointing the Glock at her face. She heard a gunshot, and then another, and then there was only silence, and darkness.

Chapter 46

Westbrook kicked Crowder's motionless body. The first shot had grazed Crowder's skull, proving Chase was right. The second shot, the last round in her eight-shot clip, had entered Crowder's chest, proving he was right again. Getting away fast was her first priority. There was no way she was waiting for Rolls. She'd call Chase and explain the change of plans when she was on the main highway. But first she had to get the Fiat and the body out of the way.

An adrenaline rush gave her enough strength to drag Crowder's body to the side of the Fiat and manhandle it into the rear seat of the car, where it dropped to the floor. She found the key in a jacket pocket and drove the Fiat to the side yard, pointed it in the direction of the cliff about a hundred yards away, then got out. A shove from behind started the car forward. The downward slope would do the rest.

The urge to see the grand finale gave way to reason; each minute that passed was a minute closer to being caught. Neighbors, though few, may have heard the shots. Crowder would have called for backup. Westbrook returned to her Porsche, picking up Crowder's gun from the ground on the way, and pressed the car's ignition button. Nothing.

"What the fuck are you waiting for? Start, bitch," she cursed. Had the engine been damaged when she'd crashed into the Fiat? And then it hit her. The car was still in reverse. She switched gears to park and pressed again. The engine started, and purred deeply and evenly as she backed out and drove away on her road to freedom.

~

The Fiat moved slowly but deliberately on its one-way, predetermined journey. The car bounced about as it traveled across the lawn and gardens, and awakened the body thought dead. Crowder's eyes opened to a patch of rear-seat carpeting. She was being driven somewhere. With her one good arm, she pulled herself up by clutching the headrest of the driver's seat.

No driver. Not good.

Once she was high enough to see through the windshield, she realized she was in her Fiat, headed directly for the cliff.

The bullet that had entered Crowder's chest had moved quickly through her left side just below the shoulder blade and exited cleanly, the silver lining of being shot up close. She reached for the door handle closest to her one good hand.

Locked.

When she tried the other door handle and found it also locked, she realized that the child safety lock on the driver's door was on. She tried to lift herself into the driver's compartment, but a jolt of shoulder pain and a sudden feeling of heaviness in her upper body caused her to tumble back onto the rear seat.

She struggled to see over the front seats. A quick look showed that she had less than fifty yards to go before the driverless Fiat took its fatal plunge over the edge. A thought passed through her mind that if she braced herself, she might survive the crash, but the reality of doom soon replaced her serendipity.

No damn way I survive. I either die when the car crashes into the rocky shoreline and is demolished, or I drown when it fills with water and sinks to the bottom of the lake.

She lay there supine with only one good arm—but *two* good legs. She repositioned herself and kicked violently at the door, which didn't budge. Then it came to her. *Forget the door. Kick out the goddamn rear window.*

Wrapping her only usable arm around the front passenger seat head rest, she was barely able to lift herself up enough to kick at the rear window with the heel of her police shoe. Three good kicks, and she busted through. Slithering across the rear seat on her belly like an eel, she elbowed her way through the now pane-less window. She pulled herself onto the trunk, her legs still inside the vehicle. Where the vehicle was in relation to the ledge was a matter of speculation, but she knew it was close. Grabbing the back of the trunk with her one good hand, she heaved forward as hard as she could. One leg got out, but her trousers caught on the window frame's metal trim.

The rear of the Fiat rose up, a sure sign the car was tipping forward over the edge. With all of her remaining strength and all of her will to live, she used her free leg to kick hard against the rear edge of the roof. Her pants leg ripped free and released her other leg. The Fiat tipped over like the Titanic before its plunge into the depths of the Atlantic Ocean. The car and Crowder became airborne at the same time—the Fiat on its nosedive into Lake Lucerne and Crowder on her free fall to somewhere.

She landed hard on solid ground, but she couldn't feel her legs. Were they somehow ripped off and still in the Fiat? No, they were dangling over the edge of the cliff.

She heard an explosion—the end result of the Fiat striking the rocky shoreline—and a blast of heat from the fireball shot up from below.

She began to slip backwards. The fingertips of her one good hand scratched at the dirt. In order to pull herself forward, she needed to claw like an animal about to lose hold of a bending tree limb. She clawed hard, and harder, and inched forward, away from the cliff, draining the remaining energy from her depleted batteries.

Badly hurt, she rolled over on her back, sucking in air. Her head throbbed, but it was nothing like the pain she felt in the left side of her chest, where the bullet had blasted a tunnel through her shoulder.

Crowder's mind switched from survival mode to police mode. Westbrook. What would she do? She'd get in her car and drive the hell away.

A car awaited Crowder. It'd been driven there by the man who lay dead behind the chalet and who would now be going home in a body bag in the cargo hold of a 747. She struggled to stand, barely able to maintain her balance, and staggered around the chalet and out the entrance.

A single taillight of a vehicle rounding the curve about a hundred yards away caught her eye. That taillight belonged to only one vehicle. The one being driven by the vilest of women she had ever known, a woman who would do anything and everything to avoid having to own up to her mistakes, answer for her crimes, and atone for her sins.

There was only one way to end the carnage that was the work of a psychopath, a cold-blooded killing machine with no feelings of guilt, remorse, regret, pity, or compassion. An animal too wild, dangerous, and unpredictable to be caged, the kind of animal you don't tranquilize and treat in the hope of curing its illness. The only remedy for an animal whose very nature was to injure, maim, and kill was to put the animal down.

A single thought now occupied her mind: to put an end to the killing, put an end to the killer.

She'd looked for her gun, but upon not finding it, she lumbered up the road to the Volkswagen sedan. Goodman's vehicle would be her weapon. The toes of her shoes scraped the asphalt surface with each step taken. She opened the driver's door and fell in, each leg lifted in with her only good hand. Was the key somewhere in the car or on the body of a dead man?

If the latter, by the time she'd hobbled over to find the key on Goodman and gotten back to his vehicle, Westbrook would be on the main highway and too far away to catch. Crowder struggled to buckle her seatbelt, then pressed the ignition button. The engine cranked and sputtered to life.

Her relief felt bittersweet, because she now knew there was no going back.

347

In one sweeping maneuver, she turned the steering wheel sharply and attempted a U-turn on the narrow road, a considerable challenge for someone with two good hands; she had one. The right rear wheel of the Volkswagen dropped over the edge of the cliff, and the left front wheel tilted up. Two groundless tires spun to no purpose as the car teetered and slowly slid backwards over the cliff.

She floored it. The two tires that still hugged the ground spun wildly and propelled the car forward onto the road, the smell of burnt rubber permeating the air.

Crowder's only chance of stopping Westbrook was to catch up with her before she reached the main highway. She straddled the lanes as she raced forward, not wanting to chance fate while negotiating the curves. Two-and-a-half miles later, the one unbroken taillight of the Porsche came into view. Crowder pulled behind and then alongside it.

But it was Westbrook who drew first blood. She veered suddenly to the left, striking the Volkswagen's mid-section and causing it to crash into the stony wall that bordered the opposite lane. Crowder's head whiplashed sideways, striking the door frame and lacerating her scalp. Blood streamed down the side of her face and into her left eye.

The Porsche pulled away.

Crowder regained control and sped up until she was once again alongside the Porsche. This time shots rang out from Westbrook's vehicle, one blowing out the passenger door window and whizzing by Crowder's face. But Crowder was in full attack mode, and with a single purpose controlling her actions, she slammed into Westbrook, jarring Crowder's gun from Westbrook's outstretched hand and nearly pushing her vehicle off the cliff. Crowder's nemesis reacted by slamming on her brakes and turning back onto the road so sharply that sparks flew when the side of the Porsche sideswiped the granite face of the mountain.

Over the next mile, each traded places with the other, accelerating, decelerating, and crashing into the side of each other's cars. As they neared the highway, only one long curve remained before they'd come to the southbound entrance ramp.

Signs ominously warned "Dangerous Curve Ahead" and "Slow Down."

The vehicles entered the curve, side by side, with Westbrook hugging the mountain and Crowder following the cliff, worse for Crowder because another hit from Westbrook could force her over the edge. But if Crowder could get through the curve, the cliff was no longer a factor; an open field awaited instead.

Midway through the curve, Westbrook veered to the right and smashed into the side of the Volkswagen. What Crowder saw out of her one clear eye was the road tilting out of sight, a sure sign she was airborne and rolling. The hit propelled the Volkswagen into the field near the highway. Through the spinning window she caught a glance of the intersection from the exit ramp, where a tanker truck was carrying its cargo to the alpine villages to the west.

The car overturned and slid through the open field on its roof like a sled on ice. Crowder felt like her insides had been ripped out. She was still in the Volkswagen when it struck a tree and jolted to a stop.

She'd taken Westbrook's best punch and survived the cliffs, but at what price? She'd soon find out, as the light within her brain dimmed to a flicker. Then the flicker was no more.

~

Westbrook had her moment of glory. The last hit thrust the Volkswagen sideways off the road. Crowder was no longer a threat to her path to freedom and new life as the wife of Charles Rochet, a life of privilege and entitlement. She'd be an elegant and graceful *nouveau riche* member of the French aristocracy. The women would envy her. The men would covet her.

Veronica Westbrook would vanish from the face of the earth, taking with her the attributes that made her a monster. The new woman to emerge would have a second chance at life and a first chance to live it with feelings she'd never before experienced. It was all there waiting for her, if she could just get to the highway and to Château Vallée.

Westbrook watched the Volkswagen do a triple axel into the field, the last impediment to her escape gone. A smile came to her face as the Porsche sped forward. The road and her line of vision straightened out of the curve. Only then did she see them, the words *L'ESSENCE* and *inflammable* painted on the side of the tanker truck, growing larger by the millisecond. She didn't need a French-to-English translator to understand the words for *GASOLINE* and *explosive*. Weighed down by a full load, the driver's gear changing only incrementally increased the speed of the tanker truck. It crawled across the intersection.

Her plan had been perfect and had played out to perfection. There'd been obstacles along the way, but one by one, she'd overcome every fly, pebble, and monkey wrench by her firm resolve to do anything and everything to succeed, regardless of the consequences. Yet there it was in front of her, the last and only remaining roadblock to fulfilling her dreams. Slamming on her brakes was a million-to-one shot; she was still going too fast.

With one hand she grabbed the shoulder bag and held the stuff that dreams are made of snugly against her chest while reaching for the door handle with the other. She closed her eyes and took the only action left to her. Only fate was left to determine her destiny.

So it is written. So it shall be.

Epilogue

For dust thou art, and unto dust shalt thou return.
Genesis 3:19

Ann McMillan Livingston's funeral was held at Christ Cathedral Episcopal Church. The public respected the family's request for privacy and stayed away. The national press and cable news stations were less accommodating. Their reporters and photographers stalked the church to capture the essence of the family's moments of public mourning.

A vigil had been held the evening before. The church had overflowed. A garden of flowers and a battalion of candles surrounded photographs of Ann on the altar. Most of those who attended didn't personally know her; knowing of her was sufficient kinship to warrant a woeful prayer and even a tear or two. Ann Livingston had won the hearts of the community by her charitable works, her good example, and what her adoring public saw as a Cinderella-like story they'd had a hand in writing.

Only the tragic ending was not to their liking.

Other players involved in Louisiana's crime of the century were put to rest with much less fanfare. The remains of Sarah Booth weren't claimed by her family. She was cremated at the state's expense. No gravesite prayers. No marker with her name. Just the number 4527 on a metal can in a storage bin at Potter's Field.

The BBC had been the first at the scene to broadcast the aftermath of the fiery explosion that followed the high-speed chase. The truck driver's unrecognizable, charred body lay on the ground. He'd been able to get out of the truck, but only after his body was set afire. He died at the scene.

351

The fire raged a full hour before the last flame was extinguished. By then the Porsche had fused to the underbelly of the tanker truck, and everything in the occupant's compartment not made of metal had incinerated into ash. Not a bone fragment, a tooth, or a gem from a piece of jewelry was located when the wreckage cooled and was inspected. It was like a bullet had struck its intended target dead center and left only a shell casing behind.

Stateside, the Associated Press was the first to report Veronica Westbrook's death. Reconstructions of the crash abounded. One had the windshield and roof sheared off when the Porsche crashed into the tanker's mid-section, slashing away everything in its path, including the head of the Porsche's driver. The cinematic recreation had a mushroom cloud of golden flame rising above the wreckage. All that was missing was a newsman's lament: "The humanity."

Captain Francis O'Malley gave a national press conference describing the heroic efforts of Detective Jo Crowder, who nearly bled to death from her gunshot wound and other injuries. A week-long hospitalization in Zurich was needed before Crowder could fly back to Louisiana to begin her month-long convalescence in a rehab facility in New Orleans. Nick Guttman made a point of visiting her every day in the hospital before her return to the States. He drove her to the airport, used his police powers to guide her wheelchair through security to the gate, and helped her to her seat.

Neither said a word to the other while on the plane. They let their moist eyes do the talking.

The criminal investigations into the deaths of Ann Livingston, Sarah Booth, and Will Goodman were officially concluded with findings that their deaths were homicides committed by Veronica Westbrook. The murder of Rosalind Rochet Chevalier was never uncovered. As for Westbrook, not a single trace of her was ever found. It was as though she'd evaporated into the air like steam from a kettle.

There was no funeral or memorial service.

An obituary by her parents served no real purpose.

Charles Rochet's involvement with Westbrook was never publicly revealed. He retired from his position with the bank, closed Château Vallée, and returned to live on his father's estate in Saint-Émilion, France. Little would ever be revealed about his very private life, proving that within the French aristocracy, skeletons in mansion closets stayed there in perpetuity.

~

On what would have been Ann Livingston's thirty-fourth birthday, Ben and Meg Livingston, Martha McMillan, Emily Simmons and her family, and Lucinda Alvarez attended a private graveside service. The pastor of Christ Cathedral Episcopal Church presided. It was a seasonally warm day with pleasantly cool, late-morning breezes and a radiant sun in a crystal-blue sky.

Ben Livingston had been reclusive for months after his wife was put to rest and her murderer's death was reported. He knew he could never love someone as much as he loved Ann, or hate anyone as much as he hated Veronica Westbrook. But Westbrook's death had brought him no real satisfaction. He'd thought it might when he set out to avenge Ann's murder. He'd learned instead that his revenge came with tragic consequences. Will Goodman had died doing his bidding, leaving another family to mourn the death of a loved one.

Standing at the site of his wife's interment, he thought how cruel twists of fate could be. Sisters, born identical twins, each the mirror image of the other, yet only outwardly were they the same. On the inside, they were polar opposites. They'd shared the same womb. But only one had inherited the bad genes that destined her for a life of amorality and criminality.

His reflections turned to Meg. Ann's blood, like Veronica's, was the blood of the same mother. Meg shared her grandmother's DNA. So had Charlotte. If she'd lived, would she have turned out like Veronica? Perhaps, in hindsight, her death had been divine intervention. And Meg? Would she remain a good daughter? Would she grow up to be a good woman, a good wife, a good mother? What was her destiny? Would fate be cruel or kind to her?

The pastor's biblical quotes made him introspective. Westbrook's demise had proved the vengeance he sought had always been in God's hands. Was it His will the gasoline truck blocked her path to freedom? Certainly, the eye-for-an-eye manner of her reconstructed death—to be decapitated in a firestorm—was more than appropriate. It made him recall the Bible passage:

Vengeance is mine. I will repay; saith the Lord.

Perhaps, like vengeance, how Meg turned out was, and would always be, in God's hands. So he thought as those who were present responded with a collective "amen" to the clergyman's benedictions.

He looked down at Meg, whose hands were pressed together in prayer. He raised his head and turned his eyes skyward as he reflected upon the pastor's words, quoting from Ephesians 26:26-27:

Be ye angry and sin not; let not the sun go down upon your wrath.

Just then, he felt the hand of a little girl reach for his hand. He looked down and saw the eyes of a little girl looking into his eyes. The words she spoke echoed in the canyons of his mind and mellowed the hardened edges of his heart. "Don't worry. Mommy and Charlotte are together in heaven. They're watching over us. We'll be just fine."

Ben Livingston felt the warmth of a noonday sun dry the tears on his cheeks. He no longer felt angry. He knew from that moment on, he would never again let the sun go down upon his wrath.

~

The medal lay on the nightstand by her bed. Twelve hours earlier, in a public ceremony at the state capitol building in Baton Rouge on a Friday afternoon, the governor of Louisiana, after a twenty-minute speech chronicling the life and accomplishments of Detective Jo Crowder, had placed the Medal for Heroism in the Line of Duty over her head and around her neck. It was the highest honor that could be bestowed upon a law enforcement officer in Louisiana.

She'd stood there wearing it like a gold necklace for the photo shoot of Louisiana's favorite daughter, a hero whose bravery would forever live in the annals of the state's crime history and police folklore.

Still, she'd felt anxious. *It's over*, she'd told herself. *Westbrook is dead. Nothing left to bury. Yet, why do feelings of dissatisfaction and uncertainty linger?*

She had a difficult time falling asleep because of the mania she felt from her day-long adrenaline rush. But it finally came at two in the morning, a deep, coma-like sleep too dense for dreams to dwell, brought on by an unyielding fatigue from her nearly fatal injuries and the sheer exhaustion of her rehabilitation. And then, as though a light switch was suddenly turned on in her brain, a flash of thought woke her from the deep, dark depths of her slumber.

She lay there wide-eyed and awake in a cold sweat, her heart racing, and heard herself say, "Oh my God! Is it possible?"

A Note from the Author

Did you enjoy my book?

If so, I would be very grateful if you could write a review and publish it at your point of purchase. Your review, even a brief one, will help other readers to decide whether or not they'll enjoy my work.

Visit my website: richardzappa.com.
Contact me by email: rzappa20@comcast.net.

Would you like to be notified of new releases?

If so, please sign up to the AIA Publishing email list. You'll find the sign-up button on the right-hand side under the photo at www.aiapublishing.com. Your information will never be shared, and the publisher won't inundate you with emails, just let you know of new releases.

Read on for a sneak preview of my next book.

The Easter Murders

Prologue

Friday before Palm Sunday,
St. Stephan's Cathedral,
New Orleans, Louisiana.

Deep sobbing interrupted her speech, causing her to stammer. "Bless me, Father, for I … I have sinned … I'm a-afraid to go home," the young girl said to the priest seated behind the confessional's mesh-covered lattice. The dim lighting of the priest's chamber was barely enough for the girl's tear-filled eyes to see the cleric's hand pressed tightly against his left temple, blocking her view of his face, and his of hers.

An eighth grader at St. Vincent's Parochial School, the thirteen-year-old girl had been the last one to leave her pew and wait in line for the priest to hear her confession and absolve her of an adolescent's sins. She'd walked, heavy footed, to the penitent's crypt-like cell, entering through a windowless oak door which she closed behind her. A low-wattage bulb allowed just enough light for her to see the cushioned kneeler. Before she'd spoken, only the thumping of her heartbeat had broken the stuffy silence.

The priest leaned forward to hear better. "No wrongdoing, my child, should keep you from a mother's comfort or a father's counsel. What makes your fear so great?" he asked.

The girl's sobbing subsided when she heard the mellow tone of the cleric's voice. "I'm going to have a baby, and I don't know what to do," she whimpered, wiping her tears and runny nose on the sleeve of her hoodie.

357

"Are you afraid to tell your parents who the father is?"

"It's my stepdad," she blurted out. "He makes me do things to him and … and he does things to me when my mom's working. She cleans office buildings at night. He comes into my room after she leaves the house."

"To be the victim of another's sin is not a sin in the eyes of the Lord. You need not worry about that. Have you told your mother?"

"My mom can't help me." The girl's tone turned desperate. "He hits her. Makes her cry. She's afraid of him. He … he told me he'd kill my mom and me if … if I tell her what he does to me. … My stepdad wants me to have an abortion. He has someone who'll do it."

"Have you seen a doctor?"

"No."

"Does anyone else know?"

"No."

"How long has he been abusing you?"

"Since last September," she whispered. "It started on the day I turned thirteen, after my mom left for work."

"What your stepfather wants you to do, this abortion, is not only a sin in the eyes of God but unlawful. You did the right thing to confide in me about it. Is there anyone you can go to? A relative? A friend?"

"I have no place to go," she lamented, fighting back another downpour of tears. She took a moment to regain her composure before continuing, "My real dad died when I was six. It's only me and my mom, and an aunt, but she lives in Baton Rouge. I was gonna take a bus there. But I don't have enough money for the bus ticket."

"How much money do you have on you?"

"After I put some clothes and pocket change in my backpack, I took a twenty from my stepdad's wallet while he was sleeping."

"Here's what I want you to do," the priest said firmly. "Take a cab to the convent of the Sisters of St. Mary. It's part of the parish of

St. Joseph's Catholic Church at Jefferson and Thirty-second. There's a taxi stand at the Berkshire Hotel, a block away from St. Stephan's. When you get to the convent ask for Sister Agnes or Sister Anne. They will help you. Can you remember what I'm telling you to do?"

"Yes. The convent's at St. Joseph's parish on Jefferson and ..."

"Thirty-second."

"Yes, Thirty-second. I'm to ask for Sister Agnes or Sister Anne."

"Now go with God's grace, my child. You've committed no sin in the eyes of the Lord."

PART ONE

The Murders

Chapter 1

Palm Sunday

"Sister Theresa, fill the fonts and basins while I turn on the lights in the church and unlock the doors," Father Julian told the nun as he switched on the lights in the sacristy, the room adjacent the main altar where the priest's vestments were kept. It was six-thirty in the morning and still dark outside. He had much to do before the congregants gathered for mass at eight o'clock to celebrate Palm Sunday and begin Easter week.

"Yes, Father," she said obediently. The nun, a rail-thin, diminutive woman twice the priest's age, placed the basket of palm cuttings she carried next to the two baskets she'd brought in the day before.

The priest garments—his alb, cincture stole and chasuble—were laid out on a table alongside a cabinet storing the altar linens and vestments not being used that Sunday. The holy water and sacramental wines used during services were kept in a locked cabinet that the priest had opened with a key from the pocket of his cassock.

The nun reached in and removed a decanter of holy water.

The priest walked to a panel of six light switches and turned them on. Each one illuminated a section of the nave, the heart of the church where the Catholic faithful sat on hardwood pews and knelt on thinly-cushioned kneelers to satisfy their weekly 'holy day of obligation.' A different panel of switches controlled the altar lighting and the peripheral lighting that illuminated the statues of Jesus, Mary, Joseph and six other saints strategically placed to provide a line of vision to congregants who had a favorite one to address in prayer. The priest switched them on.

The nun filled the basins and fonts of the main altar in time to join Father Julian at center aisle. In perfect unison, they genuflected and made the sign of the cross before turning and walking side by side down the aisle to the vestibule at the rear of the church. The holy water the nun carried would be used to fill fonts at each of four ached passageways into the nave and would moisten the fingertips of worshippers who felt the need to cross themselves as the symbolic price of admission.

The priest carried two baskets of palm cuttings that had been interwoven into small crosses for congregants to take with them as mementos of the special occasion. He placed them on a table in the center of the vestibule, then unlatched and opened the front doors —two ten-foot high by five-foot wide solid-oak slabs with religious symbols etched into them. The doors swung inward.

Using a latchkey, the priest then unlocked the remaining exterior, iron-slatted gates that opened outward. In the twilight of dawn, he noticed a shopping cart blocking the gates. It was parked on the half-moon-shaped slab of granite parishioners traversed before entering the cathedral after ascending twelve steps from the sidewalk.

"Someone's put a cart, a shopping cart, directly in front of the gates," the priest groaned, his words within earshot of the nun.

"Something's in the cart, Father," the nun said, joining him at the entrance. "Do you wish for me to go to the front and move it?"

"No, Sister Theresa. I'll open the gates slowly and push it forward until I can slip through and move it out of the way."

The cart, a white sheet covering its contents, straddled both gates. The priest gave the gate on his left a nudge. The cart rolled forward a few inches. Another nudge. It rolled a few inches more. The third time he pushed on the gate, the cart moved forward but didn't stop.

When it no longer blocked the opening of the gates, the priest reached for the shopping cart, but, just as his fingertips touched the handle, the front wheels rolled over the uppermost step. The nun had followed Father Julian out and stood by his side as the cart bounced its way down each step, rocking sideways and jostling about whatever lay beneath the sheet.

Just as the cart reached the sidewalk and upended, the first rays of sunlight beamed across the Mississippi River and erased the dusk-like shadows of morning.

The sheet remained with the cart; its contents did not.

The naked body of a young girl catapulted out of the cart onto the sidewalk. She lay there on her back, arms outstretched, legs together and bent slightly at the knees, head turned down and to the side. Her unblinking eyes and vacant stare fixed on a similarly configured stone body of a dead man nailed to a twelve-foot sculpted crucifix that rose above the cathedral's dome.

The nun's piercing shriek shattered the early morning's tranquility like a clap of thunder. The soft chirping of the meadowlarks and starlings in the trees of the park across the street evaporated into the still quiet of a windless day. Only the sound of the decanter of holy water crashing on granite could be heard above the din of an old woman's wailings.

~

The call came to his cellphone while he was in his bedroom dressing for mass at St. Stephan's Cathedral. "O'Malley," he answered in his usual no-nonsense manner. Frank O'Malley was head of the Violent Crime and Homicide Division of the New Orleans Police Department. The promotion came when he made captain ten years earlier. Since then, he'd had to answer to the police superintendent and the mayor for crimes of violence in New Orleans.

No small or easy task ... in the Big Easy.

Famously heralded for the uniqueness of its French Creole architecture, cuisine and multilingual, multicultural heritage, New Orleans also laid claim to having one of the highest urban murder rates in the country. The massive investment of resources to rehabilitate the metropolitan area in the aftermath of Hurricane

Katrina did little to improve on its ranking as the fourth most dangerous city to live in or visit.

The call came from O'Malley's boss, police superintendent, Russell Sullivan. "Frank, I hate to interrupt you at home on Palm Sunday, but I just got off the phone with Monsignor Rossi. He was calling on behalf of the archbishop."

Irish Roman Catholics, Sullivan and O'Malley were longtime parishioners of St. Stephan's Cathedral.

"What? Someone's been stealing from the collection baskets?" O'Malley quipped.

"If it were only that simple," Sullivan replied soberly.

"So what's so important that it can't wait until after Sunday services? After all, it is Palm Sunday."

"That's just it, Frank. Sunday services have been canceled at St. Stephan's."

"Why?"

"It's hard for parishioners to get around the crime scene tape and naked body of the young girl who's sprawled out on the sidewalk in front of the cathedral."

"What happened?"

"Someone decided to put the body of a dead girl in a shopping cart and park it in front of the gates at the entrance to the cathedral. This morning, while Father Julian was trying to open the gates, the cart rolled down the steps and upended on the sidewalk."

"Who's responded?"

"A couple of black and whites. Forensics. Jones is on his way from the medical examiner's office with a thermometer and a body bag."

Travis Jones was the Medical Examiner's autopsy assistant. He also drove the Meat Wagon, slang for the van that transported dead people from crime scenes to the parish morgue.

"So, let me guess; the archbishop wants the investigation to be resolved quickly and with the upmost discretion."

"According to the monsignor, the archbishop's earnest desire is that we assign our very best detectives to the investigation and ..." Sullivan paused long enough to prompt a query from O'Malley.

"And what?"

"... and that the detectives be Catholic."

"Did you tell the monsignor to inform the archbishop that he can have the best detectives or the best Catholics, but not necessarily both?"

"You want Crowder on the case."

"Right. Crowder and Steele."

"Are they Catholics?"

"Crowder's an agnostic. Steele's a bass guitar player and singer."

"Tell Crowder to keep a low profile on this. You know how she is when she gets her teeth into something."

"She steps on toes. She ruffles feathers. But that's why she's solved eighty percent of her homicide cases. No one in the department comes close."

"Still, I want you to keep a tight leash on her. The press will be all over this one."

"I'll do my best. But it will be like putting a harness and muzzle on a pit bull in heat."

"Use a choke chain, if necessary," Sullivan said, his voice a decibel higher. He paused a moment. O'Malley heard his boss sigh before continuing. "Father Julian has posted a notice for parishioners to attend services at St. Vincent's or St. Mary's. Helen and I are heading over to St. Mary's. See you and Ellen there?"

"St. Mary's it is ... Russ?"

"What, Frank?"

"It's a hell of a way to begin Easter week."

About the Author

Richard Zappa is a trial lawyer turned novelist. A graduate of the Washington College of Law of the American University in Washington, DC, he was an editor of the Law Review and Dean's Fellow to Adjunct Professor of Law and former Associate Justice of the U.S. Supreme Court, Arthur Goldberg. During the course of a distinguished career as a top personal injury and medical malpractice lawyer, he has litigated and tried numerous cases in state and federal courts, many of which resulted in multimillion-dollar recoveries for his clients. He retired in 2018 to write novels full time. A black-belt martial artist and self-taught pianist, he writes from his homes in Wilmington and Rehoboth Beach, Delaware and St. Thomas, Virgin Islands.